The Big Brown Bears

The Big Brown Bears

Robert Elegant

ROBERT HALE · LONDON

First published in Great Britain 1998

ISBN 0 7090 6174 9

Robert Hale Limited
Clerkenwell House
Clerkenwell Green
London EC1R 0HT

2 4 6 8 10 9 7 5 3

For Ling,
who fights the good fight,
with much love

Photoset in North Wales by
Derek Doyle & Associates, Mold, Flintshire.
Printed in Great Britain by
St Edmundsbury Press, Bury St Edmunds, Suffolk.
Bound by WBC Book Manufacturers Limited, Bridgend

PROLOGUE

Picture, if you will, an irregularly shaped tract of some 200 square miles several thousand feet above the Aspet Valley about sixty miles south-west of Toulouse. It is pristine, not despoiled by man, that insatiable predator on other life-forms, plant and animal. That realm is dominated by mammals and great birds, which are tolerant of the harmless snakes and the jewelled lizards. Except where big brown bears follow their ancient trails, no trodden paths cross the natural sanctuary.

The same live oaks, sycamores, and mountain ash have towered over the plateau for centuries, their lives cut short by storms and decay, but never by axes. Golden eagles glide over the sanctuary on six-foot wings, regally ignoring the occasional Egyptian vulture, now as rare elsewhere as the eagle itself. Beneath the canopy of leaves, robins and finches tease bristling porcupines or white-striped skunks, and wild boars sniff out truffles, which they devour with porcine relish.

Snakes swallow frogs and lizards. Hares and squirrels are taken by foxes, which are themselves threatened only by the great eagles. Insects are kept down by the swifts that dart through the spray of cascades to sip on the wing. All life is in perfect balance, an exquisite natural equilibrium, until the shank end of the ninth decade of the twentieth century.

Filth and toxins in adjoining areas were already affecting the animals within the left-over Eden by 1990. The enclave was already being compressed by human expansion with its poison-belching factories and its death-dealing chemicals, its fertilizers and pesticides, its rogue antibiotics and hormones. The big brown bears were suffering. Since each adult required an expanse fourteen miles in diameter, the bear population was falling as the enclave shrank.

The European Community then approved a project put forward jointly by Paris and Madrid. To further develop the depressed region called the High Pyrenees, Brussels allocated $80 million towards a two-lane highway that would link France and Spain through the Aspet Valley. The super-highway would cut straight through the bears' habitat, splitting their territory in half, effectively condemning *Ursus arctos* to extinction. The Community was in violation of its own laws. In order to preserve humanity's most precious asset, the diverse other beings, an assessment of likely environmental damage was required before such a project was sanctioned, much less sponsored.

Jacques Petitjean, the baker, would have roared with laughter over his *fine à l'eau* at the suggestion that the Grand Pyrenean Autoroute was an act of genocide against the big brown bears. Bruno was *meant* to be hunted for his thick pelt, although Petitjean preferred to stalk wild boars, greedy for their succulent ham.

Sipping the powerful acidic wine of the Basques, Pablo Echevirra, who pastured his goats on the Spanish foothills forty miles to the south, would have asked, 'Why sorry about a few mangy bears when the road will open our valleys to trade and make us all rich?'

At first, no one thought about the bears, not even the smugglers, who knew the mountains as they knew their wives' bodies. Noble bruins rescued lost children in the folk-tales their grandmothers had told them. But those were myths – and this was business.

The Aspetois were a practical folk bewitched by the prospect of the highway's bringing truckers and tourists to pour gold into their pockets, while industrialists and Parisians laid out millions to buy presently worthless acres on which to build factories and holiday homes. The Basques on the other side of the mountains were just as hard-headed. A few warned that the new highway would bring in even more Spaniards, further diluting their unique culture. But what good was high Basque culture if most Basques were scratching so hard for a living they were no more than drudges?

The surveyors with their tripods were hailed as the vanguard of new abundance. When the bulldozers and the dump-trucks appeared, the valley people ignored the tumult. They even overlooked the road-gangs' drunken sprees, which destroyed property and outraged decent women. The bourgeois town fathers not only tolerated, but welcomed the shoals of whores who swarmed after the road-gangs.

Wealth was already flowing into the towns along the projected highway. The rambunctious navvies were open handed, while engineers and managers took villas at inflated rents. Outside investors began building commercial and residential premises. Bistros and night-clubs transformed quiet village streets into neon-lit rivers of boisterous gaiety, turning Aspet-sur-Ger in France and Viella in Spain into boom-towns.

Pierre Blanchou, editor of *le Journal des Pyrénées*, and Comte Rougier de Franchoise, the proprietor, had always agreed: 'We stand for free competition and for prosperity'. *Le Journal* was conservative in religion, capitalist in economics, and mildly authoritarian in politics.

The Comte de Franchoise nodded approvingly when he picked up *Le Journal* at the breakfast-table and read the bold headline: *Aspet-sur-Ger: la nouvelle Wild West?*

The antics of the construction crews and their whores were getting out of hand, provoking indignation among the people. Better to check those excesses now and forestall a public outcry, which would be extremely inconvenient.

The *comte* did not want the electronics giant Millénaire 2000 frightened off. Although a Franchoise *never* sold land unless his life was at stake, he and Mille-Deux-Mille were discussing a long lease of fifty-five of his ancestral acres. A strong warning should persuade the construction firms to rein in their workmen.

The *comte* popped a croissant into his mouth and began to read. Twenty seconds later, he choked and coughed. The *comtesse* looked up from her *Elle* magazine and asked, 'Rougier, my dear, what's wrong?'

'That old fool Blanchou's gone mad,' he spluttered. 'Just listen to this: *The carousing and the destructiveness of the road-gangs is turning our lovely valley into a new Wild West. Aspet-sur-Ger is becoming as dangerous as boom-towns like Dry Gulch or Fargo.*

'Showing off his erudition,' the *comte* muttered. 'The worst is yet to come: *We must think again about our enthusiastic support for the transmontane super-highway. Perhaps, being human, we erred. If the behaviour of the navvies and their camp-followers does not immediately improve, strong measures must be taken . . . . It is not too late to halt this pernicious project. Though we originally derided the few protests against destroying the sanctuary of our giant bears, perhaps, in truth, the big brown bears are more important to our children's future than tarmacadam and concrete.*'

The *comte* gulped his *café au lait* and exclaimed, 'Sophie, the old fool could ruin us. *Out he goes*!'

'Pierre's been with us for twenty years,' the *comtesse* protested. 'Now, just for one slip, you'd ...'

'Be quiet, Sophie! What woman understands business?' Rougier de Franchoise growled. 'Out Blanchou goes! The sooner the better.'

His hand was on the white telephone on the sideboard when it shrilled.

'*Oui, c'est moi. Vite!* Make it quick!' he directed. '*Monsieur qui? Oh, pardon, Monsieur Brinks* .... To you, I have, of course, leisure to speak at any time. Naturally.'

Frowning at his caller's stilted French, the *comte* protested, 'But, Monsieur Brinks, he will ruin us. Blanchou is an old fool who opposes progress. Past time he retired.'

After another pause the *comte* made the limp rejoinder, 'Oh, you support him .... Be assured, Monsieur Brinks, I shall review the entire matter. Perhaps I was mistaken .... No, *monsieur*, it is I who must thank you .... Tonight at half-past six, then.'

Replacing the handset, the *comte* declared, 'Amadeus Brinks is dead set against the super-highway. Blanchou's inspiration came from this egregious Anglo-American.'

Raising her eyebrows, the *comtesse* asked, 'And old Pierre?'

'Oh, he'll stay. Brinks "apologetically requested" that I not punish Blanchou. Then this busybody "humbly begged" me to reconsider the entire question of the highway. I'm going to him for drinks this evening.'

'And what of the Mille-Deux-Mille deal?' She raised one eyebrow still higher. 'Rougier, must you see this interfering nonentity?'

'I have *no* choice.' The *comte* shrugged ruefully. 'Whatever else, Amadeus Brinks is *not* a nonentity. Anything but! No matter what the Mille-Deux-Mille deal is worth .... If he insists, I must reverse my position on the highway. Brinks could ruin us with a snap of his fingers.'

'Ruin us, Rougier? My dear, you surely exaggerate.'

'Sophie, what do you know about Amadeus Brinks?'

'I remember we were presented to Prince Richard at Brinks's enormous villa on the river bluff. The cousin of the English Prince Regent, a charming young man. The parkland is more than a thousand acres. This Brinks creature must be very rich. But ruin *us*?'

'Sophie, that enormous villa is only one of Brinks's eight residences. Eight that I know of. The Basques call him *il Billionario*. Still, his immediate personal fortune is only three or four hundred million.'

'Then this Brinks is just another reasonably rich man. Why so worried, Rougier?'

'Sophie, you've heard of Brightman/Schreiner Industries?'

'Of course. I'm not a fool, Rougier. The biggest conglomerate in the world. All run by a woman, Theodora Brightman. Rougier, does not *our* company have some dealings with Brightman/Schreiner?'

'True! You could also say Brightman/Schreiner possesses Franchois et Fils. They control two-thirds of our markets and hold a third of our shares.'

'So? What's that to do with Amadeus Brinks?'

'They are brother and sister; twins. Amadeus Brinks and Theodora Brightman.'

Sophie de Franchoise observed inconsequentially, 'Their names both mean God-lover, hers Greek and his Latin. Some parents are very odd.'

'Do you recall further that Theodora Brinks married old Henry Brightman, the shipping and communications magnate?' the *comte* asked. 'Her *dot* was the massive Schreiner interests in steel, oil, and electronics inherited from her mother. When Henry Brightman died, Theodora took over the combined corporations and made Brightman/Schreiner the colossus it is today.'

'This Amadeus?' the *comtesse* asked. 'He is an idler, a ne'er-do-well? Why does he not involve himself with the affairs of the colossus?'

'He's no idler, Sophie, but a passionate environmentalist ... a gargantuan crusader for butterflies and whales and rain-forests. And now for bears.' Rougier de Franchoise was heavily ironic. 'Sister Theodora happily runs Brightman/Schreiner on her own. Perhaps she thinks his do-gooding compensates for her profit-grabbing. But his actual holdings amount to at least a quarter of the six hundred billion-dollar corporation.'

'Which holds a third of Franchoise et Fils! I see now, Rougier. This Brinks is so powerful it would be foolish to ...'

'Precisely, Sophie! It would be insane to oppose him on such a small matter. Let Brinks try to stop the highway if he pleases. Let him see if he can.'

Le Journal des Pyrénées published a second front-page editorial attacking the highway. Inspired again by Amadeus Brinks, Pierre Blanchou declared:

> *Some things are more than gold. Our big brown bears are beloved by all Aspetois because of their role in the dreams of our childhood. Thirteen bears, we are assured, is not too few to permit*

the colony to survive and to expand, since it includes eight nubile females . . . . The transmontane highway must not *go forward!*

Pierre Blanchou marshalled his two young reporters. Both were staunch environmentalists and convinced Socialists, and they were delighted by their assignment.

Marie-Jeanne Erlanger hammered home to the baker, Jacques Petitjean, the harm the highway would do him personally. With irrefutable logic she pointed out that not only the bears were threatened, but the wild boars he loved to hunt would also be exterminated.

The baker, a fervent convert, then declared for *le Journal*: 'Shopkeepers, artisans, and farmers will be ruined if the highway goes forward. The quality of our lives will be irreparably damaged, as will be the quality of our food. How could I continue to produce my bread, my croissants, and my fantastic gateaux? Who could compete with the shoddy goods of the *hypermarché*?'

Le Journal's Hector Poirefitte crossed the Pyrenees to speak with the goatherd Pablo Echevirra, who was now aggrieved at the highway. Abolition of tariffs within the European Community had already ended smuggling between France and Spain, depriving him of much of his income.

'So called progress,' Echevirra declared, 'is a monster that will devour us all. We Basques may not have political independence, but we do have moral and cultural autonomy. How long would that last once the highway was complete? We would all be glued to the TV. Mickey Mouse and Arnold Schwarzenegger would be our heroes.'

The final argument of *Euzkadi ta Askatasuna* the movement called Freedom for the Basques, was always violence. ETA blew up the dam eight months after construction of the highway had begun. It was only a little dam, but the consequences were huge. Communities already riven by dissension were shaken by open strife.

Those who expected to be enriched by the highway sneered at those who warned of the havoc it would wreak. Epithets flew: *Philistine, snob ... Fascist, hypocrite ... plutocrat, Bolshevik ... exploiter ... Anarchist*. Bricks and stones also flew.

The highway was inching towards the mountain range like two giant tapeworms, the French segment from the north and the Spanish segment from the south. Hatred flared among the men and women who were, willingly or unwillingly, playing host to those parasites. Stringent self-control kept the antagonists from hurling themselves at each other's throats. In the concealing night, however, some hurled Molotov cocktails, petrol-filled bottles with burning wicks.

Then ETA dynamited the small dam built to divert a small river so that the super-highway could lunge unswerving into the mountains. The torrents that swept away the dam also swept away the restraint of the people of the valleys.

It was, however, not ETA that blew up the bakery of outspoken Jacques Petitjean at three one morning just as he arrived to start work. It was, it appeared, navvies from the road-gangs. Constantly blasting to clear the way for the road, the navvies were as much at home with gelignite and detonators as Jacques Petitjean was with flour, yeast, and eggs.

Nor could it be known with certainty who set off the blast that two days later killed two steel workers and toppled the syndicate's uncompleted bridge across the River Ger. But the foremen on the road swore vengeance. Seventy-two hours later, Jacques Petitjean's house burned down at four in the morning, and his sleeping wife was suffocated.

That same night the outspoken goatherd Pablo Echiverra was beaten with iron rods. He was saved from death only because some late night drunks stumbled over his broken body and called an ambulance.

The next morning, shotguns and hunting rifles were reverently cleaned and oiled. Military weapons emerged from their hiding places: Garands left over from World War II and Mausers left over from World War I.

Cordiers' Hardware ran out of all ammunition within two hours – and was flooded with orders for heavy steel sheeting. To repair the roofs of old barns, the farmers said with tight smiles. The hundreds of jute sacks they bought were required, they added, to store a bonanza crop of sunflower seeds.

Yet everyone knew that barn roofs were patched with corrugated aluminium, not with heavy steel sheets. And it was plain to even an idiot that sunflower seeds dried on the stalk before they were pressed for their oil.

The men opposed to the highway were preparing for war. A tractor armoured with steel sheets might not be as formidable as a true tank, but neither side possessed anti-tank missiles. Sandbags were, of course, sandbags. They made improvised strongpoints, if not invulnerable, at least resistant to small arms fire and even mortar bombs.

Accustomed to defiance from the Basques, the Spanish Government sent armoured regiments to the valleys. The tanks strengthened infantrymen trained in riot suppression, who, it was confidently assumed, would not need to open fire.

North of the Pyrenees the syndicate brought in hundreds of strong-arm men in the navy-blue uniform of private security guards 'to protect property' – and to intimidate the Aspetois. The goons were overbearing, and the locals were enraged.

Since both sides bristled with guns, shots were soon exchanged, wounding a number, some severely. The foes shortly met in fire fights that lasted for several hours and inflicted heavy casualties: Aspetois – eight dead and thirty-three wounded; security guards – ten dead left on the field, the number of wounded unknown, since all were immediately helicoptered out of the region.

The President of the French Republic was perturbed by disorder *le Journal des Pyrénées* called ... *far worse than the Wild West ... more like the civil wars in Yugoslavia and Central Asia.* Bypassing her reluctant premier, the president ordered the riot police to re-establish order with lead-loaded capes and submachine-guns, and thus make the Aspet Valley safe for road-building.

For three weeks the outgunned Aspetois sullenly watched the road lunge forward again. During the fourth week, detachments of security guards in brown uniforms began to arrive. Although, it was rumoured, they were armed with heavy machine-guns, even trench-mortars, the brown guards did not attack the road-builders. Ostentatiously orderly, they offered no provocation, but set up guard posts and mobile patrols to protect the Aspetois from the syndicate's goons. Emboldened, the foes of the road renewed their hit-and-run raids. Once again, the syndicate suspended new construction in order to repair the bridges, tunnels, and dams blasted by the resistance.

The people believed the brown-clad guards were paid by Comte Rougier de Franchoise to keep his people from being browbeaten, manhandled, and shot by the syndicate's blue-clad goons. The *comte* himself believed the brown guards were paid by Amadeus Brinks from his clifftop villa. For himself, Brinks spoke to few aside from his lawyers, who were pressing suits against the road in French, Spanish, and international courts.

Only massive intervention could get the super-highway moving forward again – and safeguard the great sums already invested in the Aspet Valley. The President of France ordered the army to impose civil order by expelling both brown and blue guards. The commanding general declared he would stand between the opposing factions – and would not hesitate to shoot.

With order restored, the highway surged forward again. Most Aspetois resigned themselves to the new way of life imposed by the bureaucrats and the politicians of Brussels, Paris, and Madrid. Anyway, there was money to be made.

Skirmishing continued, but the fire had gone out of the resistance. Seven automobiles were blown up; twelve men and two women were beaten up; and several families decided to leave the valley. Still, thirteen months after the surveyors appeared in the Aspet Valley, the road was moving steadily forward. The syndicate offered generous bonuses, and the pace of building doubled. After thirteen and a half months, the highways to the north and the south of the Pyrenees were approaching overhanging cliffs that were already half-pierced by long tunnels.

On the sixteenth day of the fourteenth month, all construction ceased. The international court had handed down a judgement in favour of Amadeus Brinks.

> *The regulations of the European Community* [the court declared] *require that a comprehensive survey of likely ecological damage be conducted before any major project is undertaken. No such survey has been conducted. The Community is, therefore, in blatant violation of its own laws in providing funding. All funding must cease immediately. It is further recommended that the functionaries responsible for the violation be charged with criminal negligence.*

Normally the bureaucrats would have ignored the verdict while leisurely preparing an appeal. Yet, just for receiving a few favours for expediting a doubtful undertaking, they were now facing dismissal, perhaps also prison for corruption. The verdict was delivered at eleven on the morning of the sixteenth day of the fourteenth month after construction began. All European Community funds had been withdrawn from the Trans-Pyrenees Super-Highway by five that evening. By early morning on the seventeenth day of the fourteenth month the chain of private financing had snapped.

The President of the Republic smiled ruefully when she read the news at the breakfast-table and instructed her military secretary: 'Tell the general no further work is to be done on the highway. Not a millilitre of concrete is to be poured, not a single nail driven!'

By evening of the seventeenth day of the fourteenth month, the road had stopped dead. On both sides of the Pyrenees, four shining lanes of concrete led up to sheer cliffs – and halted.

A road-gang foreman shrugged and swore, 'It's a fantasy! The road to nowhere! All our work ruined for the sake of a few mangy bears!'

*

Thus ended the prelude to the drama the big brown bears, unaware, launched on the world of men. Having performed their allotted roles, most of the players would appear no more. Only the reporter Marie-Jeanne Erlanger was to play a continuing role as were the two men who stood on a bluff high above the river early that spring evening.

Amadeus Brinks smiled, his full lips curving benignly beneath his sweeping white cavalry moustaches while he watched soldiers keep the navvies from mounting the mechanical dinosaurs that were the true road-builders. Yet he was not triumphant, but pensive when he looked down from the marble terrace of his thirty-eight-bedroom villa on the lights blazing across the valley in celebration.

'Don't believe it!' He gestured with his flute of champagne. 'It's only temporary. I've learned that much in fifty-two years. Our great victory cannot last!'

Prince Richard of Greece and Denmark asked, 'Why not enjoy the moment? Why cloud it with foreboding? We've won outright – and I'm for celebrating.'

Prince Richard, younger by twenty-two years, no longer called him Mr Brinks. No more did Amadeus call the prince, Your Royal Highness. They were far too close for such formality. Richard had come into Brinks's circle only three years earlier when he was twenty-seven. But they had already done great things together.

Like the adept politician he was, Richard could say almost anything and wholly believe what he said at the time. His palpable sincerity invariably convinced his audiences.

He won the hearts of women with the aquiline good looks and the golden-blond hair inherited from his grandfather, Prince Peter of Greece and Denmark, the younger brother of King George of Greece. More slender than his burly grandfather, Richard uncannily resembled his cousin King George V of Great Britain. He, too, wore a pointed goatee, and he, too, was a sailor, having attended Dartmouth, Britain's naval academy.

'All right, Richard,' Amadeus Brinks conceded, 'I'll drink to our victory.'

'Amadeus, you *must* be happy, despite your fears.'

'I keep thinking of the poor old giant panda,' Brinks persisted. 'The poor beast's too cuddly for its own good. The Chinese first turned him into a clown riding bicycles in circuses. Then they made him an instrument of foreign policy and a dollar-earner, selling pandas at three million dollars a clip. Finally, the Chinese built a road into panda territory ... a dirt road, mind you, not a super-highway ... and the influx of settlers is killing off the last few dozen.'

Despite his bulk, Amadeus Brink walked with an elastic gait, seeming to bounce on his toes. His domed head, which was quite hairless aside from a few wisps around his ears, shone ruddy in the light from the French windows. Still taut-muscled beneath the plumpness of self-indulgence, he was two inches short of Richard's own five foot eleven. Erudite and tough minded, Brinks convinced not so much by charm as by intellectual vigour.

His slate-grey eyes were oddly flat, lacking lustre or depth. Like camera shutters, his irises took in images and snapped shut. The pupils at their centres were opaque pinpoints.

'You know, Richard, my lad,' Brinks said, 'we've won here. But new funds will be found. The highway will blast through the plateau where the big brown bears live. The bears will perish, bringing the human race a little closer to its own *Götterdämmerung*.'

'What's to do, then?'

'We must move now on a broad front. We must be swift and daring, also ruthless. Otherwise humanity will destroy itself by destroying its environment.'

'Are you talking violence?' the prince asked. 'Coercion ... forcing humanity to reform?'

'If need be.' Amadeus Brinks smiled starkly. 'Imagine this: a woman faces grim alternatives – a radical mastectomy or certain death. Her self-indulgent husband will inevitably drift away when she has lost her physical perfection.

'Paradoxical or not, she has no choice, regardless of the odds against the operation's succeeding ... against his staying with her if it does. She *must* face the surgery and pray – if only for hope!

'So it is with our Mother Earth!'

I

Three small twin-engined jetliners pounded down the central runway of Haneda Airport in a tight V, the needle noses of the rear pair almost nuzzling the leader's sweptback wings. Their afterburners cut in at the same instant and hurled the aircraft off the oil-stained concrete at a sixty-degree angle. The flames belching from their tailpipes left six greasy trails against the ashen sky.

The swashbuckling military take-off was, oddly enough, intended for concealment. Rather, since concealment was impossible, it was intended to make the aircraft's sensitive missions appear routine. So was using Haneda, the old suburban airport that was now close to the city centre, engorged by Tokyo's ceaseless growth.

With access to twenty-two other airfields in the Japanese isles, what prudent commander would despatch anything but routine flights from Haneda? The old airport was a goldfish bowl to the agents of some twenty governments and to the camsenders of the world's five dominant satellite cable networks. Yet *no* airfield was now remote in Japan, which was a single urban knot 1,400 miles long from the tip of Hokkaido, the northern island, to the farthest point of Kyushu, the southern island.

A rift opened in the overcast, and a dusty shaft of sunlight broke through. The V formation flashed bright in the blue-and-white livery of the United Nations Air Service. Each aircraft was a gleaming arrowhead, a flying wing with a vestigial tail. The three arrowheads hurtled into the clouds, boring through the feathery grey mass like children carving tunnels in a snowdrift.

Their movements uncannily synchronized, the right hands of three co-pilots flipped the switches that activated their electronic countermeasures. The supersonic Concordia Execujets were, of course, stealth-configured, and their exhausts were damped to delude heat-seeking missiles. Their electronic defences soaked up radar impulses like sponges, wiped the characteristic signatures of their complex metal alloys and carbon compounds, and turned heat sensors back on themselves. Any missile launched against them would boomerang to destroy its own launcher. At the moment, *no* missile could be launched against the three. They were invisible to ground observation, and even the eternally vigilant spy-in-the-sky satellites above could not see them through the cloud cover.

Hidden in the clouds, the three blue-and-white aircraft veered onto new courses. The leader flew south-west at 1,150 miles an hour. The second flew due west and the third due east.

The westbound craft, its call sign UN Hawk, was to set down in Alaska after a very slow six-hour passage. The pilot, who wore the uniform of lieutenant colonel in the German Luftwaffe, had descended to 15,000 feet, shut down his electronic countermeasures to mimic a major malfunction, and cut his speed by half. His co-pilot had fired two synthesized 'fellow travellers', which kept pace with the Hawk for an hour, suggesting the passage of three aircraft.

The invisible tentacles of several hundred radar, ultra-heat, and carbon-metal sensors had reached out thousands of miles across the Pacific Basin to trap UN Hawk in an immense spider-web. Twelve spy satellites had caught the plane in the cloudless sky over the mid-Pacific, and their on-board inforobots had reported its location, its course and its speed to their ground stations.

But UN Hawk was a decoy. Its apparent electronics failure and its sharply reduced speed were intended to attract attention, just as a bird feigns a broken wing to draw danger away from its nestlings. The Hawk's two sister ships had, however, vanished, evading surveillance with ease.

Group Captain Kelvin Sykes of Britain's Royal Air Force, commanding UN Dove, had not spoken while his co-pilot, Lieutenant Commander Salisbury Smith, US Navy, set his autopilot, which was rather archly still called George. They were flying west at an altitude of 75,000 feet.

After two hours the Dove would have flown in a great circle to approach its objective from the west. It would then descend below a thousand feet, kept from ploughing into the ground by an array of sensors and computers that operated feather-response controls directly. The Concordia would rely on its spectacular top speed of 2,200 miles an hour to thwart the obsolescent electronic sentries guarding its objective.

The Independent Principality of Mongolia was poor but virtuous. It was ruled with benevolent ferocity by Archprince Hutuktu Gaishen, who claimed direct descent from the Great Genghis, the Supreme Khan of All Khans. Above all, the principality was stable.

The Mongols looked with contempt on the inability of their neighbours to govern themselves. Religious and ethnic warfare simmered in the cauldron of Central Asia long after the collapse of the Soviet Union, which had, at least, kept its subject peoples from tearing out each other's throats. The Independent Principality was, however, a haven of tolerance and peace. Population-poor, it accepted with only slight restraints the refugees from the conflicts that tortured its neighbours, accepted even refugees from its traditional enemy, the splintered People's Republic of China.

Laudably enlightened, Mongolia was deplorably impoverished. Only by allowing the rump Chinese regime in Beijing to test nuclear weapons on the steppes could Mongolia earn enough foreign exchange to survive. So, at least, three intelligence agencies had reported.

Lieutenant General Aichi Tsugiyama of the Active Measures Self-Defence Corps of Japan was aboard the Dove as the UN's senior observer. He had been directed to determine whether the regimes in Karakorum, the Black Tents of the Mongols, and in Beijing, the northern capital of the Chinese, were indeed conspiring. Were they truly in violation of the General Agreement on Banning Nuclear Weapons?

The Concordia would not land, since its hypersensors would without fail locate any trace left by nuclear testing. It was, however, essential to avoid identification, as well as any clash with the Mongolian armed forces. Given the level of competence of the Royal Mongolian Air Force, the Dove's commander did not expect that to be difficult.

The high plateau of Mongolia appeared like a cliff before the watery-blue eyes of Group Captain Kelvin Sykes, and he gasped involuntarily. Lieutenant Commander Salisbury Smith glanced with scorn at his commanding officer and braced himself in his wraparound safety seat.

The American momentarily stepped out of the personality that had won him the affectionate, if obvious, nickname Berry. His golden-brown eyes were for once cold, and his normally casual manner was steely.

The needle-nose of the Concordia pointed straight up, and the aircraft climbed vertically, hardly losing speed. The pilots' stomachs plunged, and their eyes bulged from their sockets under the pressure of five times the normal force of gravity. Their seats had already wrapped around them rubberized tentacles whose pressure kept their blood from puddling in their shanks. When the Concordia flipped back to the horizontal, these tentacles withdrew.

This spring morning, the high plateau was not only green with long grass, but ablaze with red and yellow wild flowers. Flying at a hundred feet, the plane pitched and bucked as its computers hurled it up, down, and across the sky to avoid obstructions. No civilian aircraft could tolerate such violent manoeuvres, but the Concordia was a military aircraft in flimsy disguise.

The joint manufacturers in Britain, Switzerland, and Malaysia had concentrated their vast technical skills to make a superb aircraft. They called it an Execujet, though they had not sold a single airplane for private use. However, the world's richer air forces loved the supersonic craft for its speed and its adaptability. It could operate superlatively as a fighter-bomber, a heavy bomber, a quick-reaction transport, or a reconnaissance platform so swift and so elusive it need carry no protective armament.

The Concordia called UN Dove had been fitted out as a personal aircraft for senior officers. Lieutenant General Tsugiyama revelled in its pigskin-and-walnut burl comfort, despite the sheepish half-smile on his square face. The three women and two men of his staff were, however, ill at ease amid ostentatious luxury totally at odds with the ostentatious austerity on which their general normally insisted.

Himself no puritan, Aichi Tsugiyama was conscientiously enforcing official policy. The Active Measures Self-Defence Force had expanded its geographic range enormously since ultra-nationalist Shinto extremists began to gain control of Japan – and to impose stringent self-denial on the nation.

The purser, Chief Petty Officer Betty Yang of the US Navy, was strapped down at the rear of the passenger cabin. She was petite and dark beside the rawboned Slavic blondness of her assistant, Flight Sergeant Adam Livonsky of the British Royal Air Force. They did not speak, although Livonsky paled as the Dove gyrated. When the aircraft settled again into reasonably stable flight at 200 feet, Betty Yang glanced at Adam Livonsky and jerked her chin peremptorily.

They slipped behind the curtain that concealed the small galley. He drew boiling water from a spigot into two Japanese teapots and placed them on a tray with six handleless cups. She poured steaming black fluid from the ever-simmering coffee pot into two large mugs, adding cream and sugar to one.

Before opening the curtain, Betty Yang stooped to twirl the combination lock on the drawer under the counter. UN Air Service regulations required all personal weapons to be locked up during flight – except on combat missions, which the UN Air Service did not fly, not officially.

Betty Yang handed a small machine-pistol to Adam Livonsky, who slipped it into the back of his waistband where it was concealed by his starched white jacket. He watched appreciatively as she raised her blue skirt to tuck her pistol into the waistband of her tights, where it would be readily accessible through the skirt's slit pocket. She winked at him and smiled as she smoothed the blue wool over her hips.

He lifted the tea tray and whispered, 'For the restoration!' She echoed the pledge as she slipped the coffee mugs onto a tray.

Betty Yang sidled past when Adam Livonsky stooped before the coffee table at which General Tsugiyama was seated with his staff. She slipped into the flight deck and closed the door behind her. Group Captain Sykes and Lieutenant Commander Smith nodded their thanks for the coffee.

Betty Yang spoke softly, and Commander Smith turned halfway round in his seat. His hazel eyes widened when he saw the machine-pistol in her hand, and he demanded, 'What's this nonsense, Chief? You know the regulation: no weapons out in flight. Put that thing away before somebody gets hurt.'

'Only you, sir,' she replied. 'If you don't turn immediately to course two seven three and climb to fifty thousand feet.'

'Young woman . . . .' Group Captain Sykes turned to expostulate.

'Now, Commander! Do it now!'

Betty Yang glared at the RAF officer and clicked off the safety catch of the machine-pistol.

'Better do what she says,' Salisbury Smith advised. 'She's hell on wheels once she gets started. I wouldn't put it past her to blast . . . .'

Flight Sergeant Adam Livonsky's voice was half-muffled by the door. 'All secured here. They're all tied up.'

Reaching behind her, Betty Yang opened the door, and Livonsky entered. The lanky, slow-moving flight sergeant had been transformed into a lean visionary whose ice-blue eyes glared at the pilots.

'They givin' you aggro?' he demanded. 'Old man Sykes not doin' what he's told?'

The RAF flight sergeant slammed his pistol down on the grey-thatched cranium of the RAF group captain. Kelvin Sykes collapsed against the control column, which immediately overrode the computer and the Concordia dipped towards the ground less than a thousand feet below. Salisbury Smith hauled back on his control column and pushed the throttles forward for full emergency power.

The Concordia soared all but vertically, and the hijackers gripped the emergency handholds above them. But they kept their machine-pistols trained on the co-pilot.

Salisbury Smith instructed the computer to fly a course of 273 degrees at 50,000 feet and drawled, 'I think you've both gone nuts.'

'Anything, but, Commander,' Betty Yang said in the excessively cheerful accent of Santa Barbara. 'We're doing it for our ancestors – and for the future. You'll see when we land at Lopnor.'

'Betty, Lopnor's the dead heart of Chinese Turkestan. Blasted by that runaway nuke experiment a couple of years ago ... when Beijing goofed. What the hell for are you ...?'

'Not completely blasted. You'll see.' She stabbed a vermilion-nailed forefinger at the expanded aerial chart on the central view-screen. 'You'll land right there.'

She paused and then spoke again, appearing incongruously to plead for understanding and forgiveness.

'We're both good citizens, Commander. Adam's a loyal Brit, and I'm a patriotic Yank.'

'Then why the hell ...?'

'We can't forget what's happened to our first countries. China all split up, rich in some places, but very poor in others and practically disarmed. Also ...'

'The heroic Soviet Union destroyed,' Adam Livonsky cut in. 'All the work of all them great commissars wiped out. It's gotta be set right. And we're gonna do it. Get back to the glory days.'

Convinced that he was held captive by two fanatics, Salisbury Smith nodded non-committally. God alone knew what he would see when they arrived at their destination, a point in the Takla Makan Desert 150 miles south-west of blasted Lopnor.

As he let down through the heavy cloud cover, Salisbury Smith felt sweat soak his shirt. To ensure that the Concordia would respond instantly, he flipped off all computer functions except the infinitesimal adjustments of control surfaces and retrojets, a hundred a second, that kept the plane from stalling and dropping out of the sky.

Emerging from the cloud cover at 2,000 feet, Smith gasped. A temporary runway of aluminium and plastic plates stretched 12,000 feet in the shadows of immense sand dunes. Beside the strip stood emergency and utility vehicles, flanked by a red Cadillac and a silver Rolls Royce Phaeton.

'Good afternoon, Commander Smith,' a cream-smooth Englishwoman's voice said through the flight-deck speaker. 'Please come north to heading 0-one-0 and follow my instructions.'

While Lieutenant Commander Salisbury Smith was glumly slotting UN Dove into the landing pattern directed by that seductive voice, Colonel Samuel Marchington Rodgers, US Air Force, was watching the island of Bintan south of Singapore grow in size and detail on the full-colour ground-imaging screen projected just in front of the windshield of the third Concordia, whose call sign was UN Swallow. Though he would begin flying a box search pattern within five minutes, there was no need to bring the Swallow below its present altitude of 35,000 feet. The ground-imager would still give him a three-dimensional projection of the sea and the islands through its hypersensors, which combined radar, magnetic, visual, heat-sensitive, auditory, and movement-activated functions.

The consortium of Nippon Electric Company, Bogor Indonesian Electronics, and Slough Knowledge Systems that produced the complex system boasted that the image was 'better than being on the scene'. True, the ground-imager could not allow you to smell or touch what you saw close up. But no observer on the ground could simultaneously see such detail and the overall picture. The image could range from the label on the undershorts of a pirate captain, if he wore undershorts, to a view of twenty square miles of sea and land.

Such projections were touted as 'better than reality'. The satellite cable networks bragged that their processed sights, sounds, smells, and touch-sensations were *more* real than being on the scene.

On scene, you couldn't put your fingers into the blood spilling from a soldier's wound, not without getting shot by either his enemy or his buddies. But you could do just that in your own easy chair, courtesy of total infotechnology.

Virtual reality was worst of all, Sam Rodgers reflected, not for the first time. Virtual reality was disgusting – aesthetically loathsome and morally deceitful. Above all, it was blasphemous, the ultimate sacrilege committed by a sacrilegious age. God did not wish His works to be reprocessed and distorted by the hands of man, much less by man's electronic tentacles.

Sam Rodgers grimaced in revulsion, his forehead corrugating. His face was blue-black, so dark it was almost purple. When he was growing up in Connecticut, the old Sicilian who ran the kids' favourite soda-fountain used to call him *melanzane*, egg-plant. Neither contempt nor dislike had tinged that nickname. In fact, the old man's wry affection often gave the black boy an extra scoop of ice-cream.

There was nothing affectionate in the vile names others had called Samuel Marchington Rodgers or in the vicious hazing he had endured as he climbed from the single chevron of an airman first class to the silver eagles of a full colonel that now glittered on the collar of his powder-blue shirt. The air force, like the United States itself, believed it had legislated prejudice and discrimination out of existence. The truth was more simple – and more stark: the only way to drive racism out of the rednecks, who were a majority among USA military officers, was to kill them.

Sam Rodgers turned and smiled at his co-pilot, Commandant Claude Sestiere of France's Armée de l'Aire, whose rank was the equivalent of major. No more than five foot seven, Claude was stocky and powerful. Swarthy himself, he had said many of his fellow Corsicans were dark because of Arab blood or black blood. And what was wrong with that?

Claude was a good man and a good buddy, the right man to have beside you in the air or on the ground, in a dog fight or at the bar of the officers' club, where trouble could still erupt. Few bigots dared tangle with a bird colonel. When they did, Sam Rodgers took his rank off with his shirt – and beat the hell out of them. He was thin for his six foot two, but his muscles were wire cables and his slow anger, once aroused, was implacable. Claude, who had fought beside him twice, had said in awe, 'My friend, when you start, the only way to stop you is to kill you. And I am not certain even killing will stop you.'

A pity about Claude, but there was no help for it. It had to be done.

Sam Rodgers was not particularly concerned about Major General Tun Thant of the Buddhist Theocratic Republic of Myanmar, which had once been called Burma. Tun Thant had brought his own staff, even to the stewardesses, slinky in their glossy silk lungyis. Sam Rodgers did not know the Burmese, and he could not allow himself to care about them.

A pity, too, that the first anti-piracy patrol would be a bust. It had taken more than a year to get the ponderous United Nations' machinery to set up a liaison and command centre for the campaign against the pirates of the South China Sea and the Indian Ocean.

Of course, not all the governments of the region were whole-heartedly committed to the struggle to suppress the pirates, who had grown ever more numerous, more daring, more vicious, and more sophisticated technologically as the region's economies bounded forward.

Many of the pirates were in league with officials – from customs, naval, air force, and police officers who believed themselves scandalously underpaid to presidents and prime ministers who took their cut as a matter of course. Corruption had become almost universal in East Asia, the powerhouse of world commerce, finance, industry, and technology.

'Claude, why don't you go back and see how the general's doing?' Sam Rodgers suggested. 'He's a swine, but we'd better be nice to him. Take your time. When I've got the search pattern set up, you'll have to come back as observer.'

'OK, Sam. He's not only a swine, he drinks nothing but tea.'

When the squat swarthy Frenchman had closed the door of the flight deck behind him, the tall black American locked it electronically. Tightening the safety straps that bound him to his seat, he assured himself that all anti-electronic counter-measures were functioning. Then he advised through the cabin speakers: 'Descending to twenty-five thousand feet for better visibility. Please fasten safety-belts. Box search will begin in ten minutes.'

Sam Rodgers pushed the control column forward, overriding the computers, and the Concordia streaked downward at 2,200 miles an hour. The air pressure rose inside the air-tight cockpit, and his ears popped. He did not ease back the control column when alarms drummed, shrilled, and shrieked.

'*Allah akbar*!' Sam Rodgers almost regretted his apostacy from the hardshell Baptism of his ancestors. '*La illaha, il 'llah, Mohammed rasula l'Allah! Ya Saddam Hussein!*'

The tall, black American colonel repeated the Arabic prayer in English. 'Allah is omnipotent! There is no God but Allah – and Mohammed is his prophet! Hail Saddam Hussein!'

The order had been explicit: UN Swallow was to disappear without a trace. There had been no explanation, only the order that could not be questioned. Sam Rodgers' faith was perfect, although he was not absolutely certain that sinuous houris awaited him in Paradise. Well, he would soon see.

He did not move when the needle nose drilled into the blue-green sea. Driven by its enormous momentum, the Concordia plunged in seconds to sixty fathoms, where the pressure of thousands of tons of water crushed its flimsy fuselage like a hazelnut. Its crew and its passengers were already dead of shock.

II

'In Mombasa, an Airbus Six-forty crashed on landing, catching fire and killing all but fourteen of the five hundred and fifty-two passengers. The crew of twenty-eight escaped with minor injuries.' The synthesized voice of the information robot that monitored and edited inward transmissions was wholly without emotional tone. 'Early reports say oxen ploughing the strip between runways were frightened by the aircraft's approach and bolted across the runway. Attempting to avoid the oxen, the Airbus swerved out of control and crushed the oxen.'

The sexless voice paused and then advised, 'Action footage available. Taken on the ground by an amateur. Quality unknown. Aerial and satellite footage also available. Professional, but aftermath only. Request immediate order for . . . .'

The inforobot broke off and interjected, '*Urgent update*: five stewardesses, sorry, professional in-flight attendants, were killed when passengers stampeded. Troops restored order by firing into the rushing passengers. Further updates to be winnowed as receive . . . .'

The droning voice halted in mid-syllable when Mitchell Goldsworthy stabbed a peremptory forefinger at the six-inch screen that glowed green, red and violet in the miniaturized control panel before him.

'Chris' sake!' In his irritation, Goldsworthy's native New York hissed consonants overcame the place-class-and-education neutral accent he had acquired for broadcasting. 'Just because we're doing a big global act, the inforobots want to dump all this Fourth World shit into our laps . . . . Mombasa, for Chris' sake! An Airbus Six-forty! Are they still making those cheap crates out of plastic and super-glue?'

'Only in Hungary and the Czech Republic,' Janet Seager, seated beside him, replied. 'It was heavily overloaded. Capacity is no more than four hundred and ninety-five passengers. Probably an old Six-forty, the one with the paranoid computer. Look, Mike, nearly six hundred human beings're dead. That's surely worth noting! How's the inforobot to distinguish what you want if you don't tell her?'

Automatically chiding him, Janet sounded prissy even to herself. She knew she sounded aggressive to the studio crew, assertive and nagging. She hated to appear a know-it-all, but she had recently completed a mini-series on the world's airlines.

She would have to be careful. Even now, even in this enlightened era, a woman could not indulge her moods like a man. The crew would say she was a shrew – or worse.

Off the air or on the air, Mike Goldsworthy got under her skin, especially when he talked with great authority right off the top of his head. Details of their stormy on-air clashes were relished throughout Satellite Cable Network Alpha One, indeed throughout the sprawling comdustry: the communications industry that dominated human affairs. Their bruising off-air quarrels were reported with glee by the scurrilous 'In Your Eye' column of *Big Screen Guide*, which had a certified readership of 1.9 billion in fifty-three languages, four times the audience of the most popular regular show. She could hardly object to the column invading her privacy. After all, she lived by publicity and privacy was for her a quaint outdated notion.

Her verbal brawls with Mike were also well publicized by Satcabnet Alpha's flacks. These brawls were the unique *hook*, as the comdustry put it, that had lifted them both to stardom. Not yet stars of the first water, not yet in the $40 million-a-year class, they were rapidly getting there.

The tension flickering between them made them prime entertainment. As a team, they were unmatched. Catherine Loomis, president and chief programmer of Satcabnet Alpha One, acknowledged happily that together they were far better than any other performers in her news and documentary units. Far better, she declared flatly, than the gilded, pampered anchors of regularly scheduled infotainment.

Catherine Loomis, who never called Janet by name, but usually 'lassie' or 'my girl', had told her, 'You and Mike're a great double act, young woman. Apart, both of you're more lucid ... more informative. Especially you, my girl, and that's *not* good. Great reporting, who needs it?'

When Janet began to object, Catherine Loomis overrode her. 'Alone, my girl, you're flat. No fizz, no sparkle. Individually, you're each piss-poor theatre. Together, though, you're dynamite! The tube-boobs even think they understand you!'

It was, Janet reflected, odd that Mike had come up through the print media, which were now virtually extinct. That route to stardom was so unusual he was considered a freak by the semi-literate electronic generation. The strictly sound-and-picture boys and girls also rendered him curious respect, as if having worked on a 'serious tabloid' like the *Inside Mirror* had made him not only an intellectual but an original thinker.

Nonetheless, half her own disagreements with Mike sprang from his invariably opting for the whiz-bam comic-strip approach. Although herself wholly a product of the electronic media with their twenty-second span of attention, she could see a show whole, view it as a whole entity. Mike, on the other hand, would always go for the most melodramatic action and the most horrifying pictures, even when the total impact of a show was lessened by such a diversion.

Glancing at his profile in the subdued light of the studio, Janet remembered telling him sarcastically that he shouldn't even pretend to report actual reality, but should be making virtudramas, which titivated audiences with the synthetic sensations of virtual reality. He could, she had said, play a leading role in those hodgepodges: the sophisticated older man who made the heroine go weak in the knees. Not that thirty-six was so old, but that he had the essential world-weary manner and the rough chiselled looks.

His sandy hair curled like copper wires above his broad forehead, which was creased as if with deep thought. His straight nose thrust assertively above a wide mouth that could curl sardonically. His deep-brown eyes, which appeared to have seen everything, nonetheless could still glint with indignation and glow with desire.

Shortly after meeting Mike, when she was still attracted to him physically, Janet had made her former college roommate laugh by observing that she was interested in his mind.

'With those bedroom eyes, you're interested in his mind!' Maggie Shea had snorted. 'My dear girl, he's a sex object if I ever saw one. Why don't you give it a whirl?'

Janet had given it a whirl, but not until two years later, and then disastrously. She closed off that memory, jarred back to the present by the inforobot's delayed response to Mike's grousing about its selections. The tinny voice asked, 'Precisely what do you wish, Mr Goldsworthy? Please be specific.'

'Is she really tuned to me?' Mike asked. 'Can I stay on voice, not go to keyboard?'

'Obviously, or she wouldn't call you by name,' Janet answered, as the producer said, 'Sure, Mike baby. Just tell her what you want.'

'Why it's a she, I'll never figure . . . .' Mike Goldsworthy had been working with inforobots for three years, but still hated to sweet talk a cranky computer. 'Anyway, my legless friend, you should know we're doing a super-documentary, not straight news infotainment. Yeah, we're news people all right. But from now on I want only earth-shattering items. Do you understand?'

'Of course, Mr Goldsworthy. No problem here!'

Was there a shadow of resentment in the unearthly voice? Unlikely, in fact technologically impossible. Though an inforobot could be programmed to recognize irritation in a human voice and respond in kind, for obvious reasons none was ever so programmed.

'No more shitty little crashes from Africa,' Mike Goldsworthy directed. 'Please stick to our theme: *Report at Mid-Term: The Next Thousand Years*. We're going to be working together for a long time – unless somebody screws up. So no more plane crashes unless they're absolutely earth-shattering. Not that there'll be any more. We've had our quota for the day.'

'The theme is very large,' the computer objected. 'Too comprehensive ... very difficult to select for. I have made a marginal note: needs explication.'

'I haven't got time to wet-nurse you, baby. Just do your best, such as it is.'

The inforobot flashed an affirmative green on the control-screen, but said no more.

Janet Seager shook her head. She was puzzled by his irritability and annoyed at his bullying the robot. Mike was normally the suavest man alive: Joe Cool in an $8,000 suit, hard ambition behind a warm smile. He was normally so amiable to everyone except himself that she sometimes called him 'the saccharine kid'. Urbane as ever, he was charming to the crew today, but appeared bent on tangling with the hapless inforobot.

Did they, Janet mused idly, really have feelings? But of course they couldn't! Reactions, even *apparent* sorrow or joy, could be programmed into their chips, but not *felt* emotions. Yet some inforobots displayed almost feminine sensitivity to slights. That was why the human crews called most of them she and gave them women's names. Wondering if she would ever come up against a namesake, Janet glanced at her control-screen and saw that Inez was in attendance today.

Janet by no means understood all the electronic intricacies of the super-studio the satcabnet had built from scratch for the portentous new series, *The Next Thousand Years*. The super-studio was so nimble it required a crew of no more than three: a producer, whose function was unclear; an editor, who was essential; and a gofer, since no one had bothered to programme inforobots to make coffee.

But who did fully understand the super-studio? The satcabnet's vice-president for technical matters had ruefully told her that even he did not. Who could comprehend the precise function of every inch of 113,000 miles of fibreoptic channels or every circuit in the 8,000 dynamic chips, each of whose individual memory was 50 million times larger than the entire memory of the early personal computers.

Janet knew the studio had cost Alpha One more than $1.5 billion. That was no trade secret. Hardly anyone among the 6 billion inhabitants of the earth did *not* know that figure.

Not only splashy advertising, but a thunderous publicity campaign had told the entire world Alpha One was not counting the cost of this flagship series for a new era called *The Next Thousand Years*. Cost, the flacks said, was a remote consideration, a distant second to the sheer quality of the dramatic inquiry that would redefine the human condition. But the flacks invariably let slip the fact that the expenditure, the *initial* expenditure for the most advanced technology in the world had been more than 1.5 billion dollars – not counting additional costs for talent, personnel, and production that would total another half-billion.

Janet herself often hesitated before touching the AFFIRM dot on the screen of her personal mini-comsat-communicator to pay $60 for a loaf of bread or a bottle of milk. Fortunately, the stratospheric prices of clothes, music or video disks, and those books that still appeared, seemed cheap in comparison with the cost of such foodstuffs. Otherwise, she might have bought hardly anything that seemed, however wrongly, to be a luxury. Yet her salary, her bonuses, and her allowances for clothing, housing and entertaining, which totalled some $35 million, were awesome by any standard.

The super-expensive studio was uncluttered. No booms with dangling microphones: no clumsy cameras being waltzed around the floor; no intrusive self-view screens; no banks of receivers, monitors, relays, and jacks for in-and-out satellite or cable feeds; no glaring arc lights. Above all, no control room wallpapered with dials, switches, levers, recorders and meters constantly tweaked by engineers labouring like cave-bound gnomes behind a thick glass partition.

Awed technicians said that every piece of equipment behind the sky-blue acoustic drapes was self-reactive, inter-reactive, touch-reactive, voice-reactive, all but thought-reactive. The view-control screens and the inforobots operated all the hidden equipment, performing every function previously discharged by so many different modules – and performing them better. All data – visual, auditory, and conceptual – went directly onto the 150,000 gigabyte disks of the mainframe compubrain, which processed every syllable, every pixel, and every thought for the final disking.

The compubrain and its inforobots were constantly developing a more complex and more efficient relationship with each other, a unique way of working together employed by no other compubrain complex in the entire world. That constant evolution enabled the studio not only to identify individual voices, human or synthesized, but also to discern the characteristic work-patterns of different individuals, whether flesh and blood or silicon and plastic.

'Just don't let them get the upper hand!' Alpha One's vice-president for technical matters had smiled deprecatingly when he warned her, but Janet knew that he was deadly serious. 'Not that they're actually thinking or consciously pulling your strings. Not that they have a will of their own, much less free will. Far from it! They can't create a single thought that hasn't been anticipated by a human. All potential for reaction has to be input into their circuits.'

The vice-president's smile had faded for an instant; a shadow had passed over his bright contact lenses; and he had warned, 'But bear this in mind. To a certain extent you are yourself being reshaped by the machines, by the way they work with you.'

Janet had laughed, but she had not quite forgotten the warning. Still, neither she nor Mike Goldsworthy, who was particularly obnoxious this morning, was made of fibreoptic cables and silicon chips inside a plastic integument.

Janet glanced up from the small view screen in the console before her. Mike was intent on the image unrolling on his view-screen. He would take the lead on this first day of their renewed collaboration. He was good at breaking a trail, cutting through the underbrush of false starts, but she would lead when it came to fine points. She touched her screen to summon the image on his and saw three bottle-nosed dolphins sporting around a naked boy in a sea whose intense blue could only be the Aegean. An odd sequence to be considering for the very beginning. But, then, why not?

The twenty-foot-square master-screen hanging directly opposite her could split into a hundred separate screens (or any lesser number) to display as many feeds (or different perspectives of one feed) as were ever likely to be required simultaneously. When even a dozen of those smaller screens were lit, sound was a problem. Unlike the eye, the ear could not discriminate and select. But the studio was now eerily hushed, silent as a church when the bell chimes for the Eucharist. And nothing moved on the master-screen.

The matt black surface that promised almost infinite depths was littered with captions and stylized logos, as if a giant hand had been doodling on an enormous sketch-pad. The logos ranged from miniature globes to gangs of gladiators and pairs of lovers.

The Story of Mankind, one caption had read before *Mankind* was crossed out and replaced by *Humanity. From Dinosaurs to Stellar Ships* was almost obliterated by a single bold stroke. Written three times in different script, *Where Have We Been? And Where Are We Going?* had obviously been a strong contender.

Janet thought that proposed title was mock-naïve for a series that aspired to the commanding heights of significance. She also reflexively opposed that title because Mike had been enthusiastic about it. Let him seize the initiative, and there would be no holding him. She could find herself playing a purely decorative role if she did not fight for her fair share of both dramatic shots and analytical passages.

Their working title was now: *Report at Mid-Term: The Next Thousand Years*. That compromise had been adopted because neither he nor she was particularly enamoured of it. No one in the hierarchy really liked it, but no one disliked it strongly.

The title was, inevitably, misleading. They would be dealing primarily with the *past* thousand years with particular emphasis on the past hundred years. But that was a small matter beside the major distortions that could crop up in the final cut if Satnet's executives on the 123rd floor got their hands on the disks.

Not that the 123rd floor wasn't entitled to its say. You either accepted the rule that entertainment was Satnet's overriding purpose or you didn't work there. Show biz paid the rent and bought the caviar yielded by the few sturgeons left in the depleted waterways of the Caspian and Amur regions. The simpler the show, the more obvious it was, the better.

Yet the 123rd floor wanted even more piffle. The cold-blooded salesmen and accountants were hell bent on registering not just a constantly rising profit, but a rising rate of *increase* of profit every quarter. The executive suite wanted news to be entertainment *first* and mostly, if not entirely. Their approach could sabotage the lofty sixteen-part series, and, ironically, reduce the prestige, as well as the consequent profit, Alpha One hoped to draw from it.

In this case, Janet subscribed to the conventional wisdom of the comdustry, which she normally deplored: *It doesn't matter what anything really is: it only matters what it appears to be.*

The Apocalypse series, as the crew called it, had to appear not only worthy and well meaning, but also pioneering and penetrating and, above all, deeply serious. If it were turned into tinsel entertainment, it would appear schlocky and might as well not be made.

But Mike and she, united on that issue if on few others, could hold off the vandals. Above all, Catherine Loomis was solidly on their side – so far, at least.

'Feeds ready and waiting now total seventeen. Live in real time from Atlanta, Cape Town, Colombo, Frankfurt/Oder, Indianapolis, London, Los Angeles, Paris . . . .'

Inez's flat voice droned out the cities where correspondents, commentators, politicians, and experts waited to listen to a briefing from the co-presenters and then offer their own suggestions for the series. The master-screen flashed the cities' names in big red letters, listing beside each the names and qualifications of its participants.

Janet picked up her scrawled notes. Mike had agreed that she would lead off and he would come in later. At this stage, when the only audience was potential participants, she could trust him not to upstage her. In fact, he would probably play it straight until the final disking – unless he sensed an irresistible opportunity to make himself look great at her expense.

'I'm sure you all know why we're doing this show,' she began softly. 'But, for the record, I'll explain.

'As we get closer to the year 2000, there's a *fin de siècle* feeling in the air, the end of an era. Nobody's predicting the end of the world, not like in AD 1000. But some high-powered people are very gloomy.

'We do not share their gloom. Quite the contrary! Times've never been better for the comdustry. Most people possess more and better material things than they ever did before. Yet philosophers and theologians are worried ...'

'Because they can't adjust.' Mike interjected, and Janet nodded. 'There's not enough for them to worry about. No big spiritual or intellectual ills – and the big brains're out of work.'

Inez, the inforobot, emitted a mechanical whirring like a human clearing his throat. Janet paused for a moment to listen, but heard no more.

'Also, in fairness,' she added, 'because there's so much new to adjust to. Until we got voice-guidance, I felt every new machine was breaking me in – instead of the other way round.'

'*Bulletin*!' Inez broke in. 'Two further aircraft incidents: A Boeing 747-900 *en route* Vladivostok to Tia Juana crashed into the sea off Nome, Alaska, owing to multiple engine failure. Pilot had an hour after malfunctions began to declare an emergency. All hundred ninety-four passengers and crew were rescued.

'Second incident: A Boeing 777-100C was tossed around by gale-force thermal currents coming from the active volcano, Mount St Helens. The airplane lost twelve feet of wing, but landed safely at Seattle.

'Inforobot Inez speaks on authority of direction from Mr Goldsworthy that further crashes would be extraordinary, therefore meriting notification.'

Mike glanced at Janet, who was smiling stealthily. He had been ambushed by his prediction that there would be no more aircraft crashes today. Mike grinned, touched the blackout spot on his control-screen to ensure that they would be neither seen nor heard, and leaned over to whisper, 'All right, toots, you've got me fair and square.'

'Happens to the best of us, Mike,' Janet rejoined. 'You and I still haven't got the knack of dealing with the new generation of inforobots. Anyway, the 777-100C is a very tricky airplane. It carries the biggest ever payload: thirteen hundred passengers plus tremendous cargo. A Taiwan design, which should make it very reliable, but still . . . .'

Surprised by her mild reaction, Mike looked hard at Janet, who had resumed her introductory remarks. 'But none of those ingenious techniques can see into our hearts or our brains,' she said. 'They can probe everything except the most important things: moral and intellectual values. That's why we're here: to lay out the gross facts and draw some hard conclusions.'

She was getting a little heavy, Mike Goldsworthy reflected, a shade portentous. He gazed at her intently, admiring in spite of himself. Also puzzled. He would love to pierce the enigma she presented – both as a colleague and as a woman.

Her throat, rising petal-white from her lime-green blouse, was set off by her jet-black, page-boy hair-do. She was leaning forward intently, her deep-blue eyes now indigo. Against the sky-blue drapes, her profile was virtually classic, redeemed from insipid perfection by high cheekbones and the arch of a nose that was slightly rounded at the tip.

Her intertwined fingers revealed that she was marginally ill at ease.

There was no microphone for her to address, no focal point for her attention. Janet loved the microphone too much. Once, furious after she had upstaged him three times running, he had accused her of making love to the microphone like a porn star miming fellatio.

Sex was still a raw point between them. Just once, after a long day covering a massacre of Muslims in Kashmir, they had turned to each other – as much for mutual comfort as in passion. But she was exhausted, and he was half-drunk.

No! He would not think of that débâcle again. It was bad enough that it had happened. Why relive it in his memory?

A pity that neither of them could be as successful independently. Alone, neither he nor she could make the audience's adrenalin flow. So they stayed together, outwardly getting along despite occasional flare-ups, but never in true harmony. And inwardly? But why pull apart and analyse something that worked, indeed worked fine, except when they were tired or overwrought?

They needed each other, even if mutual wariness had been turned into mutual distrust by their single sexual encounter. Their fights were not like lovers' spats, but, rather, like bitter quarrels between brother and sister who detest each other because they know each other too well. Yet their interests were inextricably bound together – and they dared not break the tie.

'*Flash! Flash! Flash!*' The inforobot's flat tone did not alter. 'Two more aircraft incidents. Make that three, three in all at this time of reporting. A total of six within the past eight hours!

'A Japan Airlines Mitsubishi Super-Clipper 100 went out of control and dropped into the sea on take-off from Kobe-Osaka West Japan International Airport. No details available yet. However, all five hundred sixty-six aboard are feared lost.

'A Lufthansa trimotor Messerschmitt 320 flying boat is down over the Sargasso Sea. Wreckage and several inflated liferafts were reported by satellite eight minutes ago.

'Third: a XAW-32 airliner made by Xian Aircraft Works ran into a hill while landing at White Cloud Airport in Gwangzhou. No further details available yet. Informatively, this aircraft, called a Deng Xiaoping in China, was originally produced in conjunction with McDonnell-Douglas as an MD-130. It is known outside China as a Marco Polo. Informatively, Gwangzhou is the city in South China also known as Canton.

'Further details will be relayed as received. News value rating: *extraordinary*!'

Was there, Mike wondered, a hint of triumph in the flat mechanical voice? But there could not be.

'Is somebody trying to prove something?' He did not bother to touch the blackout spot that would cut off his hidden microphone. 'What the hell's going on, Jan? You're the aviation expert'.

'Not on this one, Mike. I'm not taking this one on. Funny, though, that they're so many different types of planes. Maybe somebody *is* making a point.'

'What somebody? God? Let's not be silly, Jan. It's a bad day. That's all!'

'I'd love to dig a little,' she replied. 'But better leave it to the regular news staff – and dig into our own production.'

He nodded agreement just before Inez spoke again. '*Bulletin*: reported overdue over the Indian Ocean a supersonic Concordia Execujet with ten aboard in flight from Tokyo in Japan to Colombo in Sri Lanka via Perth, Western Australia. Noted because of number of aircraft incidents this day, Mr Goldsworthy. Informatively, the Concordia is a joint product of Switzerland, Britain and Malaysia. No Concordia has previously been involved in any incident, none ever reported overdue. And no accident ever.'

III

The entire outsize bedroom quivered as the helicopter approached, and the red-leafed maples on the terrace outside danced in the rotor's down draught. Yet neither the engines' growl nor the rotors' clatter was heard in the hushed bedroom, only the soft sighing of the air-conditioning. The sheet-glass windows, sixteen feet from floor to ceiling, were triple-glazed against sound, 125 storeys above the noisy streets of mid-town Manhattan.

Mounted on the wall between the windows was an old-fashioned pineapple microphone that bore the logo of satcabnet – a Greek alpha superimposed on the numeral 1. A silver plaque hanging from the microphone on a silver chain read: *We want our viewers to be good citizens and moral persons, but it's our job to see they have a good time!*

The banally opulent living-room behind the double doors was so vast it could easily swallow a cocktail party for 500. The dominant colours, dove grey and old rose, somehow failed to create the intimate effect they sought. The room was just too big and too ostentatious. The cold crystal grandeur of its six great chandeliers had once hung in the throne room of Sanssouci, Frederick the Great's palace in Potsdam. They had been traded to Alpha One for a satellite station by the Russians, whose troops had looted Sanssouci in 1945.

Gaudy in dayglo pink and chartreuse, the 60-passenger helicopter swooped down on the heliport twenty-five storeys below. A third of a mile above Park Avenue and 42nd Street, the helicopter landed below the needlelike tower that bore an array of satellite dishes and housed satnet's executive suites and the penthouse.

'Do you have much trouble,' Mike Goldsworthy asked, 'with low-flying clouds?'

He smiled lazily at Catherine Loomis, president and chief programmer of Satellite Cable Network Alpha One, who lay white, gold and pink against the black satin sheets of the empress-size bed. Glowing after their strenuous coupling, she was, for the moment, not obsessed with satcabnet and her triumphant career. She was, however briefly, detached from the Byzantine intrigue and the unremitting vigilance of her normal existence.

'Trouble with clouds?' The slurred lilt of her native Liverpool underlay the painstakingly acquired upper-middle-class accent. 'Not really. But I often can't see the ground.'

'Who needs to look at reality?'

'Don't start that again, Mitchell. Reality is as reality does.'

'Ah's sorry, massa.' His execrable parody of a black slave amused her; after fifteen years, she was still soaking up Americana. 'Don' sell me down de river.'

'Whatever else, I'm not your master.'

She glanced down complacently at her breasts, which were pearly white and, as she put it, tip-tilted. Not bad, in fact damned good, since she admitted to being 'fortyish'. She was, however, closer to the end of that decade than its beginning. Although she was childless, her proud bosom had assuredly benefited from the plastic surgeon's art. But, nowadays, whose hadn't?

'Mistress, then!' he laughed. 'If you don't feel that's demeaning.'

'Demeaning? Hell no! I *like* being a sex object.'

'What about low-flying planes?' He enjoyed baiting her – up to a carefully chosen limit. 'You'd think the Federal Aviation Authority or the Air Force would make you drape the tower with red lights like a Christmas tree.'

'How vulgar, my darling! That *would* be unsightly!'

'The tower is damned well a hazard to aerial navigation,' he insisted. 'How do you get away with it?'

'Get away with it? No need to! Screw all regulations!'

Catherine Loomis sat up, her eyes narrowed, and the pitch of her voice dropped dramatically. Quite a performance, Mike Goldsworthy reflected, for a slightly fleshy, wholly naked woman undeniably past the flush of youth. Plain to see she had begun her spectacular ascent as an actress.

'Who'd dare quarrel with *me*?' she asked. 'The FAA or the Air Force don't mess Alpha One about. They know better!'

'Know better?' he echoed her outrageous remark. 'Know better than basic air safety? Who do you think you are? More to the point, who do *they* think you are?'

'I'll tell you!' Totally unselfconscious of her nudity, she knelt and declared: 'We, you and I, are the rulers. There's no place on earth we don't reach – from the cabins of supersonic airliners to giant submerged cargo submarines. No tropical jungle ... what's left of it ... no Arctic waste can keep us out. We are universal: omnipresent, omniscient, and omnipotent.'

'That's a good working definition of God!' Mike smiled at her extravagance. 'Do you really think you're God?'

'Shut up and listen. You asked, and you'll bloody well hear me out.'

She was no longer bantering, Mike realized, and prudently closed his mouth. Catherine's intensity, the sheer force of her character, transcended the potential farce of a naked woman's kneeling on black satin sheets to declaim her personal creed.

'It's a babbling world, this so-called information age. And we control the babble. We decide what's going to happen. We dictate the decisive events of this age of mass taste and mass emotion. We set off conflicts with horrific pictures. We end them with even more horrific pictures. We define morals and manners. We enrich, and we impoverish. We elevate by our praise, and we destroy by our condemnation. We tell kings, presidents, and prime ministers, generals, scientists, and poets, billionaires, judges, and so-called lawmakers, even soccer, baseball and tennis stars, where to be at what time and what to say.'

She paused, consciously dramatic, before concluding, 'Putting it baldly, we rule absolutely ... as long as we don't overreach ourselves.'

'As long as we avoid *all* subtlety – eschew any thought, feeling, or topic with any depth,' Mike muttered. 'Our output's like a fish's scales: brilliant, sparkling, brittle – and no more than a millimetre deep. God knows what ...'

'Do you really believe in God, Mitchell?' She was genuinely curious. 'How quaint!'

Mike did not answer. His generation could discuss almost anything without embarrassment, anything from the techniques of abortion or torture to psychopathic murderers, public bestiality, and mass extermination. But his generation could not without shame even refer to the transcendent power of a god in which a few of them sometimes trusted. To avow religious faith was not only a social gaffe, but could seriously interfere with one's career in a freethinking satcabnet.

'Sorry, Mitchell, that's meant to be your business, not mine,' Catherine uncharacteristically apologized.

Mike had almost confessed that he thought he believed in God – in good part to show Catherine she could not bully him. If he let her dominate him, she would soon despise him – and it would all be over, whatever was between them. His career, too, might be over, although she was capable of large-minded generosity, as well as petty malice.

'You were talking about your ... our ... power,' he said. 'The domination of our pictures and our words.'

'Not so much words. They're largely a distraction. Maybe I should bring back silent movies.'

'Few could read the captions,' he interjected. 'Fewer every day.'

'That's almost true. Anyway, it would sabotage our social mission.'

'But we have *no* social mission,' he said. 'We divert, we amuse, and we titillate, but we do *not* preach.'

'Above all, Mike, never forget that our unremitting entertainment diverts the masses. And they forget there's nothing useful, nothing worthwhile, for them to do with their lives. Governments see that they've enough to eat, also clothing and housing. And they, the great idle poor, let robots and refugees do the work they're too lazy, too squeamish or too stupid to do.

'To keep the clods from yearning we give them wraparound-screen, eighty-two-speaker, three-dimensional, super-colour feelies. We keep the idle poor from revolting against authority now that technology's made a third of the working-age population unemployable. We keep the leisured masses, the idle poor, from raising Cain ... from turning the streets into battlegrounds just to give themselves something to do. Like Roman emperors staging gladiators' battles, we feed their bloodlust, alleviate their boredom – and thus ensure their docility.'

Mike Goldsworthy never played the courtier by flattering her or lying to her. But he could this time agree sincerely.

'It doesn't always work, but think what it'd be like otherwise!' he mused aloud. 'There'd be bloody anarchy in the streets, instead of violence and lust on the screen. We go for the jugular! We arouse elemental emotions or we're no use. We're a mass medium, attracting audiences of billions or we're nothing. You're right, Kate.'

'For God's sake, don't call me Kate. And don't tell anyone I'm capable of abstract thought. It'd ruin me.'

'Everybody calls you Kate,' he protested. 'Kate the Great! Chris' sake it's flattering: Catherine the Great, Empress of All the Russias! For your power and your grasp and ...'

'And my sex life, no doubt.'

'Yeah,' he grinned. 'Though I've got that under control – for now.'

'You know, Mike, I'm not that foolish. I don't really think I'm omnipotent. Like the centurion in the Bible, I'm a woman *under* authority, the authority of the mass taste. But I'm also a woman *of* authority. I say to this man "Go!" and he goeth. I say to this man "Come!" and he cometh.'

Catherine Loomis chuckled. The woman who controlled 56,000 employees directly and 2 billion viewers indirectly chuckled and pulled Mike Goldsworthy down to her.

After a time, they disentangled themselves and lay quiet. Her head was pillowed on his arm, and his fingers played with her gamine blonde hair. Her blue-shadowed eyelids fluttered, and she looked up at him fondly.

Despite her somnolence and her vulnerability, her eyes were somehow still terrible. Mike was no longer frightened by her unblinking gaze, but he was, nonetheless, a little chilled. Normally pallid, almost beige, the colour of her eyes varied with her moods to pale amber or blanched yellow, like the unearthly eyes of a Weimaraner hound. When shuttered to keep her thoughts within, her eyes were shallow and lustreless. Often luminous with enthusiasm, they were from time to time distant and uncommunicative, as if gazing into space.

Only at the height of passion did Catherine's eyes open wide. Only he, Mike reflected complacently, knew her when all her defences were down. Only he and, perhaps, some of her past lovers.

Mike grinned in self-mockery. He was jealous of Catherine Loomis's affection – and that was simply ridiculous.

She was called Catherine the Great for her power, her vision, her ruthlessness, and, of course, her vigorous love life. Like the Empress Catherine, she had taken many men into her bed.

Unlike the great empress, she was no nymphomaniac. She was simply a lusty woman, her strong desires magnified by the hormone replacement therapy every woman of means took nowadays. Unlike the empress, she chose one lover at a time and kept him as long as she could.

It was not, Mike believed, that Catherine *wanted* to change her partners, but that she grew bored despite herself. Or, worse, that she learned that her current lover was profiting from his liaison with one of the two most powerful women in the world. The other, of course, was Theodora Brinks Brightman, president and chief executive officer of the colossal Schreiner/Brightman conglomerate. Unlike the empress's bed-fellows, Catherine Loomis's did not influence her rule of her empire, Satcabnet Alpha One. Any attempt to impinge on Alpha One meant a lover's instant dismissal. Kate the Great would sacrifice anything, even her own happiness, for the satnet.

She was, Mike reflected, still stunning. Her small straight nose was conventionally pretty. Her lips, now showing only traces of bright vermilion lipstick, were wide and full and firm, at once sensual and decisive. Her lifelong battle against excessive flesh was, despite liposuction, revealed by the minute fullness along her jawline, as well as the slight plumpness of her hands, her knees and her elbows, which were almost dimpled. The swell of her nearly circular hips from her narrow waist recalled an odalisque in a Victorian painting.

Mike realized that his gaze was fixed on her thighs – and he coloured. Quite unembarrassed, Catherine observed, 'No dark roots down there. I'm not a suicide blonde, dyed by my own hand. I'm a natural blonde, top and bottom. Nowadays, though, I have it touched up – for your pleasure. Hell, for my pleasure, too!'

Mike could only murmur, '*My* pleasure, Catherine!'

'It doesn't taste, the rinse, does it?' she asked. 'The hairdresser swore it wouldn't. Anyway, all the perfumes of Araby sweeten that little patch.'

Mike Goldsworthy was always a little uncomfortable when she fell into that raunchy mood and assessed him with a detached eye. He hated being inspected like a prize bull, though he looked over every woman he met – and he had just looked Catherine over again.

'Do you like what you see?' he blurted defensively. 'All in order?'

'All present and correct,' Catherine laughed, enjoying his discomfiture. 'Nice, soft, big brown eyes. Lovely long smooth biceps and big bony wrists. None of that bodybuilding over-development. I do like your long narrow feet and your bobbly toes. They're a real turn on. All in all, a satisfactory specimen. Very male!'

'And who better a connoisseur of males than you?'

He challenged her in the same bantering manner. They fought a constant undeclared battle, each striving for momentary ascendancy. If he gave in, he would despise himself. Worse, she would despise him, and their affair would be over.

'Beyond all that,' Mike added impulsively, 'I'm rather fond of you. You know ...'

'For God's sake, *don't* say you love me,' she broke in. 'A little honest affection never comes amiss. But I *know* you don't love me and I don't want you to.'

'I wasn't going to say I loved you. Just that I'm very fond of you ... and growing fonder.'

'I know they say you're screwing your way to stardom,' she said. 'I can practically hear them now: "She's slipping. Kate the Great's slipping at last. Mike's got the job because he's in and out of her bed ...

also in and out of her regular as the Staten Island Ferry's in and out of its slip." But that isn't so.'

She leaned over to offer an intimate caress with tongue and hand. But she pushed Mike away when he responded.

'Even if you weren't so good in bed, my lad, you'd still be doing *The Next Thousand Years*. You'd still have the job.'

'Why?' he asked, risking a rebuff. 'Why me?'

'Because you're the acceptable semi-egghead face of Alpha One, my pet. The earnest sincere face. A lot of prigs and elitists out there don't trust the market ... think they know better what the public should get . . . . Even though political power isn't what it used to be, we've still got to keep them sweet. That's why you're doing the big series ... to prove we're a public service satnet. *The* public service satnet, ahead in public service as in everything else. So make it good!'

'The lip service vice pays to virtue, Kate?'

'Exactly, my darling!'

She was clearly amused by his studied effrontery. He was playing with her volatile temper like a lion-tamer taunting a big cat. But, hell, he was a man, not a teddy bear.

Nonetheless, women held ultimate power in his world. More ruthless than men because they were more logical and because their vision ignored all but essentials, women were an overwhelming majority among the audience and a decisive majority among the decision-makers of the comdustry.

'So *The Next Thousand Years* is just window-dressing?' Mike asked. 'It's hard to ...'

'Shit no! That's not the only purpose, not even the main purpose. I know what they think of me. They reckon my brains're between my thighs and my big mouth's always flapping. Just like our average viewer.'

'Don't run yourself down, Kate,' he broke in. '*Nobody* thinks that.'

'Thanks, Mike. Anyway, I want you to give this your best shot. You know I'm concerned with a lot of things that don't come anywhere near my crotch, my share options, or our audience figures. I really want to see what you and that girl ...'

'Janet,' Mike supplied automatically. 'Janet Seager.'

Kate the Great could never recall the name of her best female reporter, who was also her lover's screen partner. If she had, as Mike suspected, begun by faking that lapse, pretence had now become reality.

'Janet, of course. Funny, I always forget. Anyway, I want to see what you and ... and ... Janet come up with. Hell, I live in the real world, too. I'm not a comic-book character, whatever some people may think. So, Mike, shoot straight – right down the line. Don't pull any punches. I want this series to be absolutely honest!'

Mike Goldsworthy held his tongue. He expressed neither his scepticism regarding her injunction to be totally honest nor his queasiness at being used to win Alpha One the respectability Catherine Loomis had once scorned. Instead of speaking, he let his hand stray to her golden delta.

'Just a minute, Mitchell.' She took his hand in both of her own and placed it firmly on his own thigh. 'Time for fun and games later. Right now there're a few points to clear up. Rules of engagement, you might say.'

Mike sighed ostentatiously. Last-minute briefings with sweeping, sometimes contradictory, instructions were Kate the Great's trade mark. So was her deafness to words she did not wish to hear.

'I don't want you to find that abortion or contraception are good for the future of humanity,' she forged ahead. 'Just go with the conventional wisdom.

'I don't want you to step on the toes of do-gooders, not even the flat-earthers. Don't rough up the ecologists. But don't give them a pulpit either. No soapbox to stand on and blather. I know some're daft, but you've got enough on your plate without getting into their fond belief that nature can be forced to conform to human will.'

Mike grunted. When it came to specific instructions from Catherine, it was best to be noncommittal.

'I'm not saying no criticism at all,' she emphasized. 'That would be self-defeating. But do tread very carefully with environmentalists. No wholesale indictment, but definitely no endorsement. You're not Richard the Lionheart – and this is no crusade.'

Mike decided that he would ignore those last-minute instructions. With a little luck she would herself forget them, diverted by her other concerns. Ruling a satcabnet that ran forty-two channels and had a finger in another 150, she had many projects far more important in dollars and cents terms than *The Next Thousand Years*. As issues surfaced, he would deal with them one by one. He would not shackle himself by agreeing beforehand on what to censor or to include. Neither would he provoke her by protesting now.

Mike Goldsworthy knew well how badly he needed to make *The Next Thousand Years* – and to make it superlative. A powerful series would crown his career. Searing analysis and gripping drama would triumphantly vindicate nearly two decades spent in a calling that did not always walk on the sunny side of the street. If *The Next Thousand Years* turned out bad, it would not simply be a botched series: it would be a botched life – *his* life.

Clearly, Kate the Great did not want him to botch it. But the principle of editorial independence, still sacred for the remaining print media, had never guided the electronic media. Accustomed to laying down the law, Kate did not realize she could be tying his hands. Well, he would just have to see how tough she really was when it came down to images and words on disk.

In the pocket of his jacket, which lay crumpled on the deep-piled silver rug, Mike's minisat communicator squealed.

'Inforobot Inez on duty,' a tinny voice said. 'In the seventh repeat seventh such incident today, an aircraft of Independent Taiwan Airways has crashed into a mountain south of the national capital, Taipei City. No indication yet of the number of passengers or casualties. Preliminary reports point to a radar and/or a ground control approach malfunction – a technical failure, rather than a human error.

'The aircraft is an MD-132, produced in conjunction with McDonnell-Douglas of Long Beach, California, by Taiwan Aerospace. Engines are made by the Emperor Chien Lung Electronic Works in Harbin in Manchuria.'

'That's goddamned odd!' Mike was happy to change the subject. 'Seven in one day. The previous record was five – and that was mass terrorism.'

'Of course it's terrorism. Some cranks'll say they did it ... all in due time.' Catherine frowned. 'Now can we get back to business? As a matter of fact, just skip ecological issues .... Getting into the environment's simply not worth the *tsouris*.'

Mike hardly noticed the alien word meaning trouble, annoyance, aggro. Kate the Great seasoned her speech with Yiddish, Italian and Spanish words that had virtually passed into the American language. So did all New Yorkers, even the denizens of that last WASP stronghold, the New York Real Tennis Club, even the violent Saddamites, who were virulently anti-Semitic and militantly Islamic.

'Also, no heavy criticism of the media,' she decreed. 'You can just skim over that thin ice, but no fancy figure-skating.'

When Mike frowned, she conceded, 'All right. You can take a swipe at the prints ... just to show we don't pull our punches. But I don't want them to piss all over *The Next Thousand Years*. I definitely do *not* want to read a lot of shit about the nets: our bad taste ... our total amorality. Nor that nonsense about our running the world.'

Mike was no longer listening. Kate had begun by instructing him to make an incisive, honest series, an objective examination of the past and the future of mankind and the likely fate of the earth. The constraints she was now imposing could make it impossible to make a decent series at all.

How could he tell Janet about those constraints? Although she had started on fashion programmes, she was obsessively dedicated to abstract truth, whatever that might be. How could he persuade her to go along?

He could not dump Janet, even if he wanted to. Kate the Great had made it grimly clear that she wanted the two of them as a team or not at all. Even if they survived as individual performers, neither would remain at their present exalted level.

Janet could be a major problem. Hell, he might be a problem himself.

For the time being, he would not mention the constraints to Janet, lest she go up in smoke. They would just go ahead. Kate might for a time not get wind of anything she would not like. But she would surely know before the final editing.

Would *The Next Thousand Years*, Mike wondered, ever get made? Would it ever get on disk, much less be aired?

IV

'His Eminence and His Excellency *must* come up together,' Janet Seager commanded. 'I need them to strike sparks off each other. If they'll only come up alone, one at a time, we'll have to do without either. I think they're both wonderful: great men with great ideas. Also great charm. But to the viewing public today, separately, they'd just be two pretentious old farts.'

Samapati Namboodripad's outraged expression dominated the master-screen, and his outraged gasp sighed through the super-studio. Alpha One's powerful general manager for Asia enjoyed coming on air for a major take-out like *The Next Thousand Years*. At seventy-six, he was well seasoned, but hardly ancient in a world where more than a third of the population would soon be over sixty. By satcabnet standards, however, he was older than Methuselah, antediluvian. Every class of Alpha One cadets joked that Sammy had sailed as first mate to Captain Noah.

Janet winced. Sammy Namboodripad had always been very kind to her, though his Edwardian gallantry was rather quaint nowadays. A shrivelled little man who looked like Mahatma Gandhi, only darker, he was extremely susceptible to feminine charm.

Sammy was obviously disturbed by her profanity, which defiled his image of her as a well-born and well-brought-up young lady. But she had to swear a little to prove that she was a tough no-nonsense professional.

Besides, it had evidently taken him hours of cajoling to persuade two such distinguished and difficult personages as the cardinal archbishop and the premier to appear at all.

Both were notoriously cantankerous, surprisingly unimpressed by the might of the media. Yet no public figure could wholly disregard the satcabnets.

Premier Chalkorn Premsarit of Thailand was this year also President of the East Asian Federation of Nations, the world's greatest concentration of economic power, as well as military power. Cardinal Archbishop Alois Muhlenberger, papal nuncio to the Federation, was the star of the brilliant Vatican Diplomatic Service. He was also the prelate most likely to be elected pope after the death of the aged incumbent. At the very least, he would become the Vatican's secretary of state – and thus exercise even greater day-to-day influence on world affairs than did the pope himself.

Janet Seager's mind flipped automatically through those salient facts as she waited for the general manager's prolonged silence to end.

'There's also the timing, Jan,' Sammy finally said. 'You want them at five in the afternoon your time. That's five in the morning here.'

'I'm sorry, Sammy. Mike's got an appointment he can't break.'

'An appointment with you-know-who, I presume?'

'I guess so.'

'Even so, Jan,' Sammy Namboodripad argued, 'Cardinal Muhlenberger has scheduled an early mass for Labour Day. It's meant to mark a grand reconciliation between labour and management. It's very ecumenical. There'll be many worthies from other religions, maybe the Daoist pope himself. Probably the Dalai Lama, too. Definitely Premier Chalkorn and the Grand Abbot of Beijing's Patriotic Buddhist League.'

'Tell the cardinal he won't miss his mass, Sammy. We'll get through it as fast as we can.'

'But, Jan, how can I say to ...'

'Look, Sammy, that's the way it is.' Janet hated being so hard-nosed, but she had to establish her authority. 'Tell His Eminence to say his mass the night before ... or afterwards.'

'Jan, I'll do what I can. But it's not easy.'

'I'm sorry, Sammy.' Janet was truly contrite. 'But, you know, that's the satnet business. If we tried to meet the demands of everyone we're talking to, we'd never get this show made. If *you* can't talk them into it, no one can.'

'Oh, they'll turn up. In the end, everyone's hypnotized by the big glass eye .... And I've got a bonus for you, Jan.' The general manager for Asia, who dealt with vast sums and with the fate of nations, was delighted to play reporter again. 'Prince Richard ... Richard of Greece and Denmark. I know you've been trying to pin him down. I can get him on the same transmission.'

'That's great, Sammy. We really need him for the series. But please make him understand we want his historical input first. Then he can do his green world act . . . .'

'He's eager to talk about logging and dams in Asia.'

'Fine, only later. *The Next Thousand Years*, it's like a kaleidoscope. We're all over the place: earth and space, past and present, oceans and mountains, humans and beasts. Here, there, and everywhere.'

'A great opportunity, Jan. It makes me proud to be associated, however humbly, with ...'

'And, Sammy, this mass, I've been thinking . . . .'

Mike Goldsworthy had been wandering in and out of the studio carrying a blue-and-white Wedgwood pot of coffee, while Janet arranged interviews. He poured a cup and set it before her with a flourish.

'Sammy, you've never been humble in your life,' Mike interjected. 'Only mock humble. But who has a better right? Jan and I're delighted to have you aboard as our guru for Asia. By the way, I ...'

Janet Seager winced, and in Bangkok Samapati Namboodripad drew in his breath. When Mike Goldsworthy used a throw-away line like 'by the way', it was time to be on guard.

'Yes, Mike,' the plummy voice from Bangkok said. 'What can I do for you?'

'I was just thinking. This grand reconciliation mass for May Day ... Labour Day. Can we get, say, twenty cameras on it? Also a chopper overhead? I'd like to make a big production of it ... play it as a new renaissance, a spiritual rebirth for humanity, the great coming together of nations and creeds: East and West, Buddhist and Christian, Daoist and Confucian!'

'I don't see why not, Mike. But a chopper's noisy. Why not a mini-blimp?'

'Let's do it. We'll do it in depth for *The Next Thousand Years*, and shallow for regular news programmes. Sammy, please, very humbly ask the cardinal and the premier if we may talk to them just before the mass. Together of course. We could maybe fit in Prince Richard while they're setting up.'

'Perfect, Mike. I'll be the hero of the hour.'

Janet did not join in the mutual congratulations. Somehow, Mike always managed to grab the initiative and the glory. She had been on the point of giving the same instructions when he broke in to pre-empt her ideas. Although Mike and she were formally equals, it usually worked out that way. That's what came of not being aggressive enough, whatever the men said about tough hard-nosed bitches in the comdustry.

*

'Anything on those planes, Jan?' Mike Goldsworthy called through the open door between their adjoining offices, blithely unaware that she was still irritated after an hour. 'What's the verdict?'

'What planes, Mike?' she stalled. 'What've you got in mind?'

'For Chris' sake, Jan!' he barked. 'You know goddamned well: yesterday's airplanes. How often do eight planes fall out of the sky in twenty-four hours? And two still unreported, their disappearance inexplicable – like the *Marie Celeste*. For Chris' sake!'

'Oh, *those* planes ...! Mike, you know I've asked you not to blaspheme.'

'You do pretty well yourself, don't you Ms Prim? Swear a blue streak.'

'I'd hardly say that. Anyway, who taught me to swear?'

Janet knew she sounded like a prig. She also knew they were moving towards a clash. Still simmering, she would be glad of a chance to let off steam.

'The *planes*, Jan!' His voice creaked with ostentatious forbearance. 'What've you heard about the mystery? You're the aviation expert!'

'Let me think.' She knew nothing annoyed him quite as much as her pretence of feminine vagueness. 'I know there was something, but I can't quite . . . .'

Is he treating me like a secretary, Janet wondered, or is he really appealing to me as an expert on aviation? Either way, of course, he's using me. When we get down to the nitty-gritty, he needs me as much as I need him, maybe more.

Why, she asked herself, is Catherine Loomis, our very own and very horny Kate the Great, keeping Mike and me together? Why is she all but pushing us together?

Of course, they *were* very good together, a sparkling team, Seager and Goldsworthy. But what else did Kate have at the back of her mind? Why did she insist on linking her lover with a younger and, just possibly, more attractive woman?

'Aw, come on, Jan,' Mike insisted. 'Cut the bullshit and give.'

'All right, loudmouth.' She automatically fell into his style of abuse. 'No formal verdict's in ... won't be for months. You know how cautious investigating agencies are, even ... particularly ... in such a weird case. There is a buzz, not that it'll help us much.'

Mike strolled into her office uninvited, carrying two cups of the Philippine-Java coffee blend his male secretary brewed afresh several times a day. A bribe or a peace offering? Did it really matter?

'What's the buzz, toots? Be a good girl and tell Daddy.'

He was again talking to her as if she were a slightly backward six-year-old in a pinafore and pigtails. That was his revenge for her pretending not to understand his question. But she grinned at him and spoke crisply.

'Someone always comes along and claims credit for an act of terrorism. Most of them nuts and publicity seekers. But this time there's nothing. Zilch! Nobody claims credit for the worst day in aviation history: eight planes down, two of them vanished without a trace.'

'So?'

'The pundits are agonizing,' she said. 'Can it be entropy?'

'For Chris' sake, entropy! I have to look that word up every time. It's so vague ... so shapeless! What a theory: everything finally gets so complicated it comes apart of its own accord. Everything from the smallest atom to the solar system ... every human product from razor blades and roller blades to space ships. Entropy finally gets to everything.'

'Got it in one, Einstein. Entropy also means that human society, all civilizations, finally break down because of their own complexity.'

'That's pushing it, isn't it, Jan?'

She liked him better when he stopped hectoring her. He was speaking with her as an equal; in this particular case she was better informed than he.

'Mike, there *is* one simple answer, though maybe it's not really an answer,' she replied. 'I saw an article in the *Neue Züricher Zeitung*, the paper they call the daily encyclopaedia. By a Swiss authority on chaos theory, fuzzy logic and emulative intelligence.'

'Nobody talks about artificial intelligence any more, do they? Now it's emulative intelligence,' he commented. 'If the answer's that complicated, it's *no* answer. Like some girl giving six reasons why she can't keep a date. Just too many excuses to be true.'

'Maybe!' She smiled. 'Anyway the Swiss professor says six crashes and two disappearances in twenty-four hours are *not* remarkable, but should've happened long ago.'

'How come?'

'Because of the inevitability of random events. You know the old chestnut: *Give a hundred chimpanzees a hundred typewriters and enough time, and they'll write all the works of Shakespeare and the* Bible *to boot.* Enough planes in the air, and you're sure to have an eight-crash day.'

'Who woulda thought it?' Mike whistled in mock awe. 'Of course, that theory's got a high horseshit content.'

'Could be, Mike. But only one other explanation makes sense. It's teleological . . . .'

'Which means somebody did it.' As always, he simplified the complex and made it more understandable. 'And that somebody could be a human. Somebody could also be a superhuman agency.'

'God, in short!' she said tartly. 'Even if you don't believe He exists.'

'I never said that, so let's not get theological as well as teleological. But why should God want to knock eight planes out of the sky? It doesn't make sense.'

'Not to anyone who's *not* God. But why should any human want to knock out eight aircraft at random – and then neither claim credit nor acknowledge blame?'

'Beats the hell out of me, ma'am.'

'Mike, why can you be so nice sometimes?' Janet asked impulsively. 'And such a creep at others?'

'Just natural talent.' He grinned. 'What've you got in mind?'

'You knew I was going to zero in on the cardinal's reconciliation mass, didn't you? But you had to butt in first.'

'Maybe I did know,' he conceded. 'It's a tough business, baby. If you don't like it, you can always go in for cocktail hostessing or propagating the human race.'

'You're impossible.' Janet rose and faced him, her eyes indigo in anger. 'A synthetic redneck, a hick from Brooklyn with a perpetual erection.'

'How would you know, babe?'

'You're right. It wasn't perpetual that night, was it? Rather pathetic ... a shrivelled, limp little cocktail sausage.'

'Why you miserable tight-assed excuse for a good lay . . . .'

Mike Goldsworthy flung down his cup and saucer on her desk so hard the bone-china cracked. He stalked out, slamming the door so that the flimsy partition wall swayed.

Janet almost threw her own cup at his back. No provocation was worth the sickening fury he had once again aroused in her. Tautly controlled, she set down her cup and saucer on the horseshoe-shaped desk. Glancing down, she saw that coffee had spilled on her crêpe de chine blouse. Dabbing the spots with a small linen handkerchief only made them worse.

'What am I doing here?' Janet Seager asked herself ruefully. 'Why am I in this disgusting industry?'

*

Kate the Great had stopped at the newsdesk to read the incoming wire-service copy during her daily tour of the studios. She glanced up at the commotion. The doors of Mike and Jan's adjoining offices were open to the newsroom, for the comdustry prided itself on its democratic ways. Catherine Loomis heard the door slam and watched her lover snap a metal ruler with his bare hands. Janet Seager – the name came easily – was sitting stiffly behind her showy desk, hooked fingers shredding a handkerchief.

Kate the Great smiled discreetly. It would not do to be seen gloating. She naturally assumed that the noisy antagonism between the two arose from mutual attraction, although neither knew it. But just as long as they kept fighting, they would not start billing and cooing. Best of all, the electric current of hostility that flowed between them would keep attracting viewers.

Kate knew *exactly* why she was in the comdustry. She had really had little choice. She had grown up in a particularly noxious part of Liverpool, with a work-shy father and an alcoholic mother. The '60s were meant to be glorious: swinging London, the Beatles, flower power, free speech, damn all inhibitions. But not for her.

She had seen clearly that she could either make her own way or she could fall into marriage – *after* she got pregnant – to a local lout. With no education and no contacts, she would be a slave to the washing machine, the sink, and a brood of screaming children.

She had to make her *own* way! She could either get some training somehow or go on the game, become a prostitute.

She did both. A sympathetic woman teacher, who saw the quick mind behind the pinched features and the virtually unintelligible accent, had helped her cram for the examinations to the Liverpool Polytechnic. Weekends, she had stalked the streets where toffs and wide boys looked for a lively girl in a miniskirt that skimmed her bum and showed off her black suspender belt and sheer black stockings.

Stubbornly, she had stayed on the game for four years, until she was nineteen and had finished college, which the Americans called high school. Then, through one of her regulars, had come the chance at a typist's job in a cinema.

Her looks, her efficiency, and her careful choice of whom she now slept with had carried her to the Paramount offices in Wardour Street in London. Afterwards, she had worked very hard, first behind the typewriter, then before the camera and on the casting couch. Small parts leading to bigger parts, she moved into television – where the future lay – first as an actress, then as a producer.

So here she stood today. The cameras had given her everything: respectability and wealth, fame and power.

Mike Goldsworthy and Janet Seager were different! Kate had read their personnel files very carefully and she was puzzled.

Neither Mike nor Jan had been driven to the golden trough by need. Anything but! Both had enjoyed security, privilege, and parental love while growing up. Both their fathers had been highly successful in conventional, old-fashioned occupations. Both their fathers had said they employed others to use computers – and had not deigned to touch a keyboard themselves. Both their mothers had held television in contempt. Why, then, had both gone into this rackety, hi-tech, insecure, ulcer-breeding calling?

Boredom, perhaps? Perhaps also an inborn need for excitement?

Mike Goldsworthy's father had made women's clothing. Nothing spectacular, nothing to excite *W* or *Harper's & Queen*, but attractive, durable bread-and-butter stuff that sold widely. Much garment manufacturing was returning to the United States after migrating abroad in search of cheap labour. American productivity, which was again high, and American wages, which were now competitive, made it attractive to produce for the US market at home.

Yet Mike felt that business was ignoble, somehow contaminating. He had only lately learned to speak with pride of his immigrant father, who had come from Hungary in the 1950s. And Mike had married a super-WASP from Old Virginia.

Lizbeth had given him two daughters in rapid succession and then twins, a girl and a boy. Nevertheless, Lizbeth and Mike had in time coolly decided they could not live together. Perhaps not so much that they could not, but that they saw no particular reason to live together.

Although paying large sums to maintain children he rarely saw, Mike was, nonetheless, happier than he had been with Lizbeth. The energy he had put into wooing her and later to placating her was now devoted to his work. No wonder he was so tightly focused on his career.

And Janet Seager? The same story superficially, but quite different in reality.

Both her mother and her father came of solid old banking families in Cleveland, Ohio. The money was still there – copiously. But after graduating from Princeton, Janet had refused to take any more from her family. Too much of their wealth, she had declared, came from exploiting Africans and Latin Americans, the last peoples on earth left to exploit. She had, further, told her father angrily that the spread of prosperity throughout the so-called Third World, fuelled by First World banks like his, was ruining the world environment.

Janet's father was patient, but not infinitely so. When she picketed his bank under the aegis of the Future Green Society, he had been deeply wounded. Although they disapproved of Satcabnet Alpha One as 'vulgar', both her father and her mother were proud of her celebrity. They would happily have welcomed her back. But she would not return, not even for a visit, not yet anyway.

After an affair with a naval officer that began gloriously but ended searingly, Janet had bricked herself off from normal affection behind the walls of her career. (As, Kate reflected, in a sense she herself had done.) Now thirty-two, Janet was hearing her biological clock ticking ever louder as it counted down the days left for her to conceive.

Kate still had no definite answer to the question: *Why had both chosen to go into satnets?*

Yet nothing else could compare. Politics? The old road that led through government to power, fame, and wealth was now discredited. Moreover, politicians had been largely deprived of real power. Business? Both Janet and Mike were repelled by trade, which was fundamentally dull and was even more than the satnets at the mercy of the whims of a fickle public. The satnets were the cutting edge of the new society. However diffused their power, it was *real* power.

Janet rose, straightened her raw-silk skirt, and strode purposefully through the connecting door into Mike's office. Kate discreetly left the newsroom. With a little luck, another acrimonious quarrel would begin – and widen the moat of misunderstanding that separated them. Sadly, Catherine Loomis would not be there to enjoy it. She could not allow herself to be caught openly spying on her subordinates.

'I'm sorry, Mike.' Janet noted idly that his red braces glowed bright against his Oxford-blue shirt. 'I shouldn't have said that about . . . .'

'Neither should I.' He swung his cordovan loafers off the desktop. 'It was just one of those things . . . .'

She smiled and completed the thought: '...that didn't quite work out.'

She could smile now at the memory of their fumbling in the dark under the rain-drummed canvas of a field-tent in the Vale of Kashmir, where Hindus were massacring Muslims. Alternately, of course, Muslims would slaughter Hindus. The two groups were equal in beastliness.

Her encounter with Mike had not been on equal terms. He was much experienced, while she was, though not virginal, relatively inexperienced. Besides, he had already drunk too much, and she was very nervous. Jan winced again as she remembered pushing him off her, turning away on the canvas cot, and weeping bitterly. She could now smile at the memory – just.

'You know,' she said, 'we've never got down on paper exactly what topics the series'll cover.'

'Let's play it by ear. It'll practically decide itself.'

'Mike, we've only got six months till final disking. We need a tentative list, at least. For starters, I'd like two sections on the environment: one the past, the other the future.'

'No present?'

'The present is contained in the past and the future.'

'You're not going to make a great series by quoting T.S. Eliot,' he evaded. 'We've got to deal with the nuts and bolts. The *big* problem is the structure. Do we make it strictly chronological or do we divide it by topics?'

'Both! That's the only way. Take the environment. With two full sections, we'll give an overview of the basic problem. Also the alternating concern and disregard for ecology. Also an unusual ... maybe unique ... insight into the past seen through an ecological lens.'

'Sorry, babe, no can do. Got to play down ecology, soft pedal it.'

'Why, in Heaven's name?'

'It's old hat ... overdone ... the same old clichés. Same goes for Prince Richard. We'll let him talk about the history of the Danube Valley – he's hot as a pistol on the history – but a few bland words on the environment'll be more than enough.'

'Mike, don't beat about the bush. We *need* an objective, deep examination of an issue that's obscured by the exaggeration and the lies of both its champions and its enemies. That approach'll make *The Next Thousand Years* great.'

Mike reached across to the sidetable to pour fresh coffee. He handed the cup to Jan, who was standing over him.

'Sure, babe, you're right ... *except* for one thing: we *can't* be objective.'

'And why not?' she flared. 'Who's stopping us?'

'Nobody. Only the nature of television. If it's objective it's boring. We need controversy.'

'I know that. But we can offer opposing views.'

'Sure we can. But I've never seen a good show that didn't come down hard on one side or the other!'

'You'll see, Mike. It can be done. And it will be done. Otherwise, we're just wasting our time; we could be doing sitcoms and making a pot of money without all this *tsouris*.'

'We'll see, sure. Anyway, Jan, do me a favour: forget the environment for a while. Don't make it an issue.'

'Mike,' she retorted, 'I feel so strongly about this I'll go to Kate myself. I'll fight you tooth and nail on this one.'

'Don't bother. Kate won't back you.'

Janet sat down hard in the chair facing his desk. She put her cup down gently and said tautly, 'Of course! I should've known. You fixed it up between you, didn't you? But why?'

'No, we didn't.' Mike Goldsworthy never lied if he could help it, but prevarication was another matter. 'I swear we never fixed that up.'

'Then why, Mike, why? How can we work together if you don't come clean with me?'

'Jan, we won't be working at all if we don't work together. Just don't kick up a fuss with Kate, and I'll work it out. You'll get your environment, though maybe not two whole sections. Just trust me.'

She smiled at that threadbare plea, and replied gently, 'But, Mike, I *don't* trust you. Why should I?'

'What other choice've you got? We're bound together. Professionally, we're Siamese twins.'

'For the moment, perhaps, Mike. But not for ever!'

V

'I'm getting studio fever.' Janet's laugh was strained. 'Not even a week into it. But it feels like months we've been locked up here.'

'It's going to be a long haul,' Mike replied. 'But we'll be out in the field, too.'

'At least we'll see some action on old Cyclops' eye today.' She pointed with her rounded chin at the twenty-foot-square screen opposite the control console. 'But it still makes a long day.'

'We both want to get the dawn mass on disk. Seven on a Bangkok morning is ...'

'The evening before in New York. I know.'

'Nobody's making us work an eighteen-hour day, Jan. We could've let the crew disk it without us.'

'Could you *really*?'

Jan felt an incongruous thrill of wry affection for the man to whom she was so closely tied professionally. Knowing him so well, she laughed at the notion of his leaving the first big set scene of *The Next Thousand Years* to be captured by the studio crew with neither of them present. Much of the footage they shot for the series would never make the screen, but this dawn mass was a sure thing. The celebration of reconciliation – between East and West, between labour and management, and between rival religions – promised to be not only symbolic, but a gorgeous spectacle. The dawn would be bright with the many coloured robes of Daoists, Confucians, Shintoists, and a dozen Buddhist sects, as well as the gilded vestments of the Roman Catholic and Greek Orthodox priests.

'I guess I couldn't,' Mike acknowledged. 'We have to be here.'

He grinned thinly and brushed his coppery hair off his forehead. That sheepish gesture further touched Janet, who was weary of the brittle politeness that kept them from clashing openly. Mike and she also needed reconciling, for the quarrel that had boiled over two days earlier still simmered. They had to go on working as a team – which was much easier if they were not at daggers drawn. She turned to face him, and her eyes glowed deep blue as she smiled.

'Let's get Sammy on screen,' she said. 'Now, please.'

A tinny voice replied, 'Inforobot Jason reports slight transmission difficulty from Bangkok. Please stand by.'

An instant later the big master screen glowed, and Samapati Namboodripad appeared. The three-dimensional effect was so real that Janet almost reached out to hug him. Sammy loved hugging. Today he was clearly uncomfortable in grey morning coat, wing collar and striped trousers that had replaced his customary safari jacket and slacks. This was a different Sammy: dignified, almost aloof; his broad nose and his big aviator's glasses somehow regal above a pearl-grey cravat with a star-sapphire stickpin.

'Good morning, Janet,' he said formally. 'Good morning, Mitchell.'

'Good evening, Sammy,' Mike replied. 'Thanks to you, I've cancelled my date. What else can I do for you?'

'Prince Richard is standing by in the mobile studio.' Sammy ignored the mild sarcasm. 'Better quality picture there. I'm on a roving camera outside. I thought I'd first thumbnail him for you.'

'You want to get on air, you old ham, don't you?' Mike laughed. 'And why not?'

'Please be careful as to how you use his interview. The prince is a prime source. Also a truly good man.'

'Sammy, you can view it before final disking. We don't often let the peons in the field do that. But for you . . . .'

'I am profoundly grateful.'

Was there, Janet wondered, irony in that formal expression of thanks? Sammy was always elaborately courteous. But he did not enjoy being patronized by his juniors.

'His Royal Highness Prince Richard of Greece and Denmark is a unique figure in the modern world,' Sammy declared in a resonant baritone. 'Scion of four dynasties, including the Hapsburgs and the Windsors, he is dedicated to many diverse causes. All seek the happiness of mankind and the purity of nature. He believes profoundly that human happiness is impossible if pristine nature is not conserved, *actively* conserved: nature in *all* her forms, whether animal or plant. Even the shape of the land.'

That introduction, Mike Goldsworthy sensed, was Sammy's *quid pro quo* for Richard's consenting to talk about the Danube Valley. The prince would never dismount from his green hobbyhorse.

'We won't cut him off when he gets on his soapbox, Jan,' Mike whispered. 'Let him spout! We can cut out the green garbage later.'

'Why so edgy, Mike?' she asked. 'He's preaching better management of the earth, not anarchy.'

Just nine words summed up Mike's reason for worrying about serious ecological coverage: Catherine Loomis, President and Chief Programmer, Satcabnet Alpha One. Why, he wondered, was she dead set against the environmentalists? If it omitted the ecological issue, *The Next Thousand Years* would be lopsided.

But she'd change her tune by the time they'd spent a couple of hundred million on the series. Rather than junk that much expensive footage, she'd likely say: 'If you must, you must. But for God's sake be careful!'

Samapati Namboodripad continued, 'His Royal Highness will first talk about the history of the Danube Valley, today, as always, an arena of conflict. The Danube was long dominated by the Hapsburgs, who are among the prince's ancestors.'

'Not so formal, so stiff, Sammy, please!' Janet cut in. 'That cutaway's making you stuffy. You sound like a commercial for royalty. Relax!'

'All right, Jan.' Visibly relaxing, Samapati Namboodripad continued more lightly, 'Anyway, he's got a dollop of Hapsburg blood, and he studied at Charles University in Prague and at Cracow University, as well as Cambridge and Columbia. He believes his own hereditary privileges carry obligations; above all, the obligation to strive for the good of humanity.

'His dedication is reinforced by his wife, Alexandra, of the Thyssen steel clan. His mother picked Alexandra to bolster their own dwindling fortune from Richard's great-grandmother Marie Bonaparte . . . .'

'Let's wrap it up,' Mike directed. 'That's all we need. Doesn't the mass start very soon?'

'Richard speaks seven languages. But, somehow, he can't reason rigorously on his own. He needs a leader, a guru,' Sammy finished in a rush. 'He is virtually a disciple of Amadeus Brinks, who, by the way, we really must get into the series.'

'That's great, Sammy. Thanks loads.' Janet soothed the general manager's irritation at being cut short. 'Now can you get the prince for us? And what about the premier and the cardinal? Aren't you cutting it very fine?'

'They said they'd talk to you *after* the mass.'

'Who said June 21st was the longest day of the year?' Mike

muttered. 'It's really May 1st, today. We'll be here all night at the rate we're going.'

A head taller than Samapati Namboodripad, Prince Richard of Greece and Denmark appeared on the big screen in white trousers and a light-blue jacket with a stand-up collar.

'A Nehru jacket,' Mike observed. 'As worn by Pandit Jawaharlal Nehru, founding prime minister of the Republic of India.'

'Good morning, Ms Seager, Mr Goldsworthy.' The prince spoke in a pleasant tenor, his accent cultivated mid-Atlantic. 'I'm delighted to be with you. Since I am obviously a stop-gap, I shall speak first about the environment. Then I'll talk about the Danube Valley.'

'Tough cookie, this one,' Mike muttered, forgetting to cut off his unseen sound sensor. Prince Richard's delighted grimace showed that, half the world away, he had heard the remark.

'We face a major crisis today,' the prince continued. 'Not the final crisis of humankind, but harrowing nonetheless. If present trends are not reversed, there will soon be so many ageing humans living on this globe that the human race is driven into mass schizophrenia. We already see an excruciating incidence of severe mental illness among the dispossessed, the hundreds of millions driven from their native places by political, racial, and religious prejudice … by hatred and persecution. Driven also by economic pressures, by need and by greed.'

'Sir,' Janet interrupted, 'I don't see the connection between mass migration and mental ailments.'

'Ms Seager, totally new environments mean totally new pressures. Many people are not strong enough … their mental fibre's not tough enough … to stand up to those alien pressures. So they retreat into dissociation and madness.

'Overpopulation, too, destroys mental balance. Perhaps the earth can just feed the six billion humans alive today. But we must not forget the rats.'

'You mean,' Mike interjected, 'rats eat up food stores?'

'What happens when a colony of rats gets too big? Regardless of adequate, even abundant food supplies, the rats turn and rend each other when their number per square metre goes over a certain limit.'

'This could be a different approach.' Janet turned off her sound sensor and whispered to Mike. 'A way to get into the environment sideways.'

'Yeah, let's hear more,' he replied. 'It's a little airy fairy, the way this royal bozo puts it. But the potential's there. With good pictures of harrowing cases we might just have something.'

Prince Richard was in full cry. 'We must use every possible means to impress upon humanity the gravity of its position ... the acute danger of its self-destruction because it is pressing so hard on the environment. Even violence if nec—'

Glowing yellow, emerald, and scarlet, two enormous paper kites displaced the prince's image on the big screen. His melodious voice gave way to the rumble of crowds amid a cacophony of car horns, drums and gongs. There was no perceptible transition. The prince simply vanished in mid-syllable, and the soaring kites appeared.

Inforobot Jason belatedly explained: 'As instructed, coverage has been shifted to the cardinal's arrival at Lumbini Park. The shift was ordered regardless of whatever was programmed at that moment.'

'Shall we get Richard and Sammy back?' Janet suggested. 'Be a while before the mass really starts.'

'We can pick them up later,' Mike said. 'Just look at that! I've never seen kites from above before. The mini-blimp's worth every cent we're ...'

'Jason, please come in closer to the kites,' Janet directed. 'We'd like a better view.'

The literal-minded inforobot that was guiding the small unmanned airship 11,000 miles away brought the cameras so close to the kites that the big screen showed only a single scarlet flank.

'Jason, back away,' Mike directed. 'Give us an overall.'

Swirls of brilliant light wheeled for a few seconds, and then the screen filled with dozens of many-coloured kites, all soaring, swooping and diving. A tawny tiger and a jet-black cobra circled each other warily. An enormous white elephant with wing-like ears crossed strings with an elongated emerald and purple dragon. The elephant dipped and rose, dipped and rose repeatedly – then the dragon suddenly soared untethered above the struggle.

'Powdered glass on the kite-strings,' Mike muttered. 'Once cut free, the kite's lost. They cost more than a hundred thousand bucks.'

'Jason,' Janet directed, 'let's see the ground. How many cameras've you got working?'

'Fifteen, Ms Seager. Four in the air, the rest on the ground.'

Images danced across the master-screen, which was now divided into ten smaller screens. Slender palms spread their tattered fronds above banyan trees whose twisted boughs and trunks writhed as the cameras moved. Scarlet double hibiscuses thrust their phallic pollen-stalks at the lens. Orchids hung from trees in fragile abundance: violet and tangerine, pale yellow and dark blue.

The enormous crowds moved amid festoons of red-white-and-blue bunting. Blue jeans rubbed against haunches in gaudy saris, sarongs, and skirts cut tight to show off buttocks. Starched and sparkling white shirts were pallid beside dress uniforms gleaming with gold braid and clanking with medals. Thousands of Buddhist monks were sunbursts in saffron and orange robes that left one shoulder bare.

A multitude of food stalls offered satay, curries, fruit and ices. Families picnicked beside muddy water-courses; chubby babies sleeping happily amid the din to aged great-grandmothers whose cropped hair bristled like white brushes.

'The police estimate a million and a half here,' Samapati Namboodripad's voice boomed through the studio before the compubrain adjusted the volume. 'The abbot of every Buddhist *wat* in Thailand, *and* the king and queen. Nowhere is the monarchy more revered, more central to the existence of the nation, than here in Thailand . . . .'

'Sammy, not now,' Janet said. 'We can get the background later. And pick up Prince Richard, of course. For now, though, let's stay with the picture. Tell us what's happening.'

'Something funny's going on,' Sammy said tentatively. 'You see those placards ... the green ones in the midst of the crowd on the right?'

The camera obediently shifted from the kites to the green placards, and Sammy continued, 'The closest reads in Thai: *Heaven will punish the wreckers of the world!* And another: *Buddha himself weeps in anger when he sees only raw earth where only a decade ago our splendid forests stood!*'

'What's it all about, Sammy?' Jan asked. 'I thought the Thais were so happy being rich they didn't give a damn about their raped forests and rivers.'

'There has been protest,' Sammy replied. 'Also loss of wild life ... sacred elephants. And more timber smuggled out of Cambodia. Now the Thais are logging in Central America, stripping bare new forests. But there's been nothing as strong as this before. Why, two of the placards promise: RUTHLESS PUNISHMENT FOR RUTHLESS CRIMES! DEATH STANDS BEFORE THE CRIMINALS WHO DESPOIL THE LORD'S EARTH! EVEN THE BUDDHA IS VENGEFUL!'

'Let's see what develops,' Mike suggested. 'Maybe you'll get your environmental angle easier than you think, Jan . . . . Now, Sammy, why do they call it Lumbini Park?'

'Under a banyan tree in Lumbini in north-east India, the Gautama Buddha attained enlightenment,' Sammy obliged. 'This Lumbini is also sacred: it is the cremation ground of the kings and queens of Thailand, who are ...'

'Thanks, Sammy,' Mike cut in. 'What's happening now? I can see a big, black, open car flying a yellow and white flag. The cardinal?'

'The cardinal archbishop is arriving with Premier Premsarit. They'll make their obeisances to the king and queen before the cardinal mounts to the altar.'

Surrounded by dozens of shaven-headed monks in saffron robes, a young monk sat cross-legged under a banyan tree, his stubbled head bowed in prayer. The cameras closed in, and the three-dimensional figure filled the 400-foot-square screen, except for the black touring car in the upper left-hand corner flying the yellow and white papal flag with the crossed keys of St Peter. The two images became one when the car slowed before the banyan, and the young monk raised a face of anguish to the morning sun.

'Look, Jan.' Mike saw it first. 'Underneath him.'

The monk, who, close up, looked no more than fifteen, was seated on a heap of logs. Janet saw tongues of yellow flame and realized that the logs were faggots heaped for a bonfire. The flames licked greedily at the youth's bare feet.

Massive in his scarlet vestments, Alois, Cardinal Muhlenberger, opened the car door and strode towards the youth on the pyre. Six burly monks planted themselves in the cardinal's path. He pushed one aside, but the remaining five grasped his arms, careful neither to harm him nor to impair his dignity.

From the touring car Premier Chalkorn Premsarit, slight and short, called out anxiously, 'Come back, Eminence. There's nothing you can do.'

The cardinal tossed off his assailants and made again for the flaming pyre. Eight monks now held him fast. He fought them no longer, but stood unmoving, his big lined face set in grief beneath his scarlet skull-cap. His fierce black eyes, unblinking, watched the fire leap high.

The young monk's shrill scream of despair floated over the silent throng. He screamed again as the fire advanced and again as he felt its full heat. An unbroken wailing welled from his throat when the flames reached his legs and leaped towards his face. He struggled to rise, but he could not move.

'They've manacled him.' Sammy Namboodripad explained sombrely. 'They promised he could escape if he changed his mind ... the chains would break under a slight pull. They always promise, but . . . .'

'Why, Sammy, why?' Mike's voice shook. 'What's this all about?'

'The monks're shouting,' Sammy Namboodripad explained. 'It's a protest against Buddhists' joining in the mass, even symbolically. Remember Vietnam in the '60s, the same protests? Cremation alive? Somebody called them "Buddhist barbecues". The abbots always say the sacrifice is voluntary, an offering to the Buddha. But they always make sure the victim can't escape.'

A banner unfurled behind the pyre to declare in English: THE BUDDHA WARNS: CEASE DESPOILING THE EARTH FOR PROFIT AND PLEASURE – OR PERISH!.

The black car moved on at a funeral pace. The cardinal and the premier sat upright on its red-leather seat, silent and unmoving. Tears trickled down the cardinal's seamed cheeks, and the premier looked away.

Greasy smoke rose from the pyre, and the smell of roasting meat blew through the holiday throng, which, otherwise, exuded the scents of jasmine, garlic, incense and sugary cakes.

The altar had been raised green, gold and violet on a manmade hillock at the junction of the twin lakes of Lumbini Park. On the right, the king and the queen were enthroned on a dais only a little lower than the altar itself. They were surrounded by the glowing Thai-silk gowns of court ladies and the hardly less gorgeous uniforms of noblemen. In orange, saffron, and yellow robes, the senior Buddhist clergy formed a fiery fringe around the court.

To the left of the altar, dignitaries and diplomats in morning coats set off their formally attired ladies. The robes of the Dalai Lama and his entourage were a sombre maroon beside the black academic gowns of Protestant clergy.

A stream of scarlet and purple flowed through the throng. Behind a great gilt cross borne aloft by black-cassocked Jesuits, Alois, Cardinal Muhlenberger was followed by the five Asian archbishops who were also cardinals. Behind them came forty-two bishops from every quarter of Asia. Their faces were variously pallid white, old ivory, cinnamon brown, cordovan, and blue-black, but their demeanour was identical. Eyes cast down, the Roman Catholic prelates of the most populous and now richest continent renewed their pledges to the Almighty – and to their flocks.

Behind priests in the robes of the missionary orders that had brought Christianity to Asia, marched scores of nuns of a score of different orders, heads held high, eyes turned proudly upward. Some wore short-sleeved blouses and knee-length skirts of light tropical fabrics. A few wore wimples with anachronistic, almost archaic, medieval habits.

Behind bold heraldic shields and gilded icons lifted high on silver poles strode the metropolitans of Beirut, Moscow, Alexandria and Kiev. Bearing long, golden shepherd's crooks, the metropolitans glittered golden in their Byzantine splendour.

A triumvirate led the Anglicans and Episcopalians;: the Archbishop of Canterbury, lean and grey in vermilion vestments trimmed with ermine; the Archbishop of New York, ruddy and brisk, as confidence-inspiring as an investment adviser; and the Archbishop of Cape Town, whose sable skin was set off by a purple gown that hung loosely on her six-foot-two frame, draping her ample bosom.

As he came over the brow of the hillock, Alois, Cardinal Muhlenberger saw behind the altar twenty Hasidim in long black coats, Homburg hats pulled over their side-curls. Their forward-looking rabbi had given them permission to attend. The Hasidim now stroked their long beards in embarrassment beside Central Asian shamans in bearskins, Native American Indian medicine men wearing eagle feathers, Dahomey witch doctors carrying human skulls, and animist seers from the Himalayan fringe.

Japan had sent twenty Buddhist abbots in stiff vestments modelled on Chinese robes of the ninth century. Five others wore leather armour, horned helmets with fierce masks, and long swords like Japan's medieval fighting Buddhist abbots. Japan had also sent priests of the Shinto cult, which was enjoying a spectacular revival. The Japanese people were nostalgic for Japan, pure and isolated, as it had been before Commodore Matthew Perry forced open its gates. The Shinto priests were splendid in tall hats, broad *hakama* trousers, and sweeping robes, in austere brown, green and black.

On the edge of the park, where the tides of traffic on the urban expressways lapped at green Lumbini Park, the crowds were craning their necks to gaze into the ethereal blue vault of the sky. Some stood motionless as if in awe, while others looked wildly about, as if searching for an escape route through the impenetrable throng.

An angular helicopter swooped low with a menacing whop-whop-whop of rotors. Men and women ducked their heads, though the ungainly machine was still 200 feet above them.

The cardinal looked up when he heard the rattle of automatic weapons and lifted his hands in a prayer of despair. He sorrowed for those under the muzzles of the helicopter's turbo-guns, and he grieved for the mass of reconciliation.

With enormous relief, the cardinal saw a rain of red-paper fragments falling on the crowd. The sustained explosions came not from guns, but from the twenty-foot-long swatches of fire crackers East Asians set off to celebrate.

His relief was soon shattered. The helicopter descended to less than a hundred feet, careless of the danger to the crowd. Behind its yellow fuselage trailed banners with slogans in the curly Thai alphabet and in the universal language, English: DISPERSE IMMEDIATELY! LEAVE THIS IMPIOUS COUNTERFEIT CEREMONY!

Through the helicopter's loudspeakers a hectoring voice spoke from the sky, warning in Thai and then English: 'The satanic cardinal will suffer death! Do not take part in these sacrilegious rites! Else nirvana will elude you through eternity!'

A scarlet explosion flared against the ethereal blue sky, then a second and a third. The cardinal, who had seen many armed conflicts, recognized the explosions as air-bursts, which looked like ripe tomatoes hurled at a window. The hail of jagged steel fragments spewed by those air-bursts would scythe the crowds.

The voice from the sky spoke again: 'Go home immediately! *Next time* the shots and the bombs will be *real*! Go home and destroy all your sacrilegious modern gadgets!'

Shaken by the macabre incident, the cardinal was even more determined to say mass. He ascended to the altar, passing a group that glimmered like fresh fallen snow in the morning sunlight. The monks and nuns in white robes were devotees of Daoism, China's oldest religion, which had recently revived. Beside them, the Neo-Confucianists wore the court robes of the Manchu Dynasty, red and yellow silks with wave-like borders representing the ocean.

Their unwilling neighbours left a distance around thirty-two Hindu sadhus. The sadhus wore nothing but a coating of ashes, which turned their dark skin sickly grey. Beyond shame, if not beyond desire, they eyed the strangers around them truculently and threw fierce glances at abashed women.

An old Malay wearing a white cap to show that he had made the pilgrimage to Mecca glared in disgust at the sadhus. His wrinkled wife covered her eyes with her long white scarf. A few green turbans declared the presence of a handful of hadji from Pakistan, as did white fezzes from Indonesia. But the Muslim world was painfully under-represented. Fewer delegates from the world's second largest religion attended the mass of reconciliation than even the most pessimistic forecast had expected.

The cardinal raised his hands above his head in greeting and walked around the altar, always facing outward to the throngs. He greeted different groups in their own languages. The message was always the same. In Chinese: *Huanying Hoping*! In German: *Willkommen Friede*! In Italian: *Bienvenuto Pace*! And in English: Welcome Peace!

Facing again the west from which he had come, the cardinal spoke the same message in Latin: *Ave Pax*! His arms remained extended over the silent crowd until the last echoes of his words died. He turned to face the altar – and vanished in an eruption of scarlet flame.

Hundreds of thousands held their breath, awed by the theatrical conclusion of the cardinal's welcome. A few seconds later, the shock wave of an explosion rolled across Lumbini Park. On the high altar billows of smoke were skewered by lances of fire.

A second explosion threw the holy altar high into the air, and its fragments rained down on unprotected heads. The shock wave and the debris raked the crowd, but struck hardest at the priests and nuns who had marched behind the cardinal a few minutes earlier.

A third explosion thundered, and the crowds scrambled for their lives. Children and old people were trampled by panic-stricken men. Women shrieked in despair when their infants were torn from their arms. Burly monks and slight schoolgirls were equally powerless in the grip of the mob.

The king had thrown himself on the queen to shield her with his body. When the explosions ceased, he rose and looked across Bangkok and saw that five pillars of smoke were rising from explosions across the city. The Emerald Buddha in its temple near the river had been targeted, as had the Democracy Monument, and the royal palaces. Parts of Bangkok were aflame.

'So sudden,' Sammy Namboodripad gasped into the microphone he still clutched while the cameras passionlessly recorded the devastation. 'So sudden ... so senseless. Who could have ...?'

VI

The metropolis in the north-west of China perversely spelled Xian is pronounced *Seeon* – not solely to bedevil foreigners. Xian had grown like a great pearl during the past few decades, throwing layer after layer of buildings around the town that had been the capital of the Chinese Empire a millennium earlier. The new growth displayed none of the beauty of a pearl. It was utilitarian and ugly.

Xian owed its glory as a tourist mecca to the discovery of thousands of life-size terracotta soldiers created to guard China's First Emperor in the otherworld after his death in the late third century BC. The first reaction of those who found the terracotta army had been incredulity. Profound awe followed. The Chinese draw their immense self-confidence from the immense age of their culture and here was solid proof of ancient grandeur.

Cupidity had soon succeeded awe. How gratifying to prove how deep were the roots of China's greatness by inviting the world to look upon the terracotta soldiers of the First Emperor – and charging for the privilege!

The sheer size of Xian now proved the logic of that reasoning. All the diversions of restless modern life had sprung up to serve those visitors: hotels, restaurants, and cabarets; museums, theatres and galleries; tourist agencies and research institutes; bordellos, pimps, whores and casinos. The city, once poor and enmired in history, was now almost as wealthy as the industrial and commercial cities of the China coast.

A potholed road led some fifteen miles north to the tumulus over the tomb of the First Emperor. Roadside stalls sold the half-cured fur of wolves and foxes, while farmers hawked long cabbages, white radishes heavy as bludgeons, and bubble-gum-pink chunks of pork. Their wives offered waistcoats, dolls, and soft toys sewn of cotton fabrics in bright primary colours.

Not far from the tumulus of the First Emperor stood a stone arch whose upswept beams had been set on square granite pillars in the nineteenth century to commemorate the virtue of Madame Wang Entai. Widowed at sixteen, she had remained chaste until her death at eighty-six. Local folklore related that the virtuous Madame Wang had scandalously indulged her appetites with lusty farmboys. Newcomers were warned that her malevolent spirit would hurl into fiery torment anyone who desecrated her memorial.

A Manchu Dynasty magistrate's *yamen* had almost as miraculously survived largely untouched a hundred yards from the arch. A district magistrate was the lowest official appointed by the emperor, the interface between a remote government and the local people. He lived in a broad compound, which enclosed buildings housing his family, his offices, his subordinates, his courtroom, and his prison cells.

The old *yamen* was an ideal forward base for Amadeus Brinks, offering both space and seclusion, both easy access and effective secrecy. Xian was a major airline centre, and torrents of tourists poured along the road to the tumulus of the First Emperor. Amadeus Brinks's callers were, therefore, inconspicuous, regardless of their nationality or their race. He had bought the *yamen* through a Chinese subsidiary of the great conglomerate, Brightman/Schreiner Industries, which his sister Theodora controlled. The Everbright Corporation was engaged in legitimate technological research and sales.

The communications and computer facilities Brinks had installed were inferior only to the massive array at his chief base. That camouflaged camp near Lopnor, surrounded by blasted desert, was remote. He trained his shock units in the area where the former People's Republic had developed its nuclear arsenal. Yet even a new pantry boy was conspicuous in the desert, which was populated chiefly by nomads and itinerant traders. Since no gathering of any size could be convened at the Lopnor base in secrecy, the *yamen* at Xian sheltered the periodic meetings of Amadeus Brinks's chief lieutenants, which he called the working group.

Lieutenant Commander Salisbury Smith, listed as *Missing* by the US Navy, piloted the Concordia Execujet that carried Amadeus Brinks from Lopnor to Xian in early May. Berry Smith deviated widely from the direct route of some 800 miles in order to appear to conform to a flight plan that began at Sarawak in Borneo, where Brightman/Schreiner had extensive interests and corresponding influence. Berry Smith was already an old hand at deception. Shortly after being forced to land the Execujet codenamed UN Dove at Brinks's

Lopnor base, he had embraced the fiction that he no longer existed – at first under duress, but soon with relief.

Ceasing to exist would thwart both his wife, a domineering neurosurgeon, who was determined to divorce him ignominiously, and also his mistress, a second-rank actress noted for her nude roles, who was determined to marry him with maximum publicity. Even in the enlightened first decade of the twenty-first century, a messy divorce followed by an even messier marriage was not the best route to promotion – or even to survival in grade – for an officer of the US Navy. Why not then just disappear?

The Muslim fundamentalist, Colonel Samuel Rodgers, USAF, had dived his Execujet into the sea on the day of the eight aircraft disasters. Berry Smith had been spared by Amadeus Brinks's wish to possess an unregistered Concordia – and by the strong disinclination of Purser Betty Yang and Steward Adam Livonsky to commit suicide. During his first week in Lopnor, the pragmatic Berry Smith realized that he was very lucky to be given a choice. He could, like his stubborn flight commander, Group Captain Kelvin Sykes, and the Japanese officers they had carried, subsist in stringent captivity that must end sooner or later in death. Or he could join the crusade Amadeus Brinks was mounting. Through lengthy conversations with his captor, who seemed to have all the time in the world to chat, the pilot had become an enthusiastic convert to the ecological cause.

Despite the light of belief that now glowed in Berry Smith's eyes when they talked, Amadeus Brinks had not revealed his ultimate purpose. Perhaps, the pilot conjectured, there was *no* ultimate purpose. Perhaps Brinks was, in good pragmatic American fashion, feeling his way towards a better world for all living things, for plants as well as animals, but, above all, for mankind.

Berry Smith had arrived at that judgement quickly and facilely – as he arrived at all his judgements. He was given neither to strenuous soul-searching nor to strenuous effort.

After a few years of gentlemanly loafing and carousing at the University of Virginia, he had volunteered for the navy's flight cadet programme on a dare. All through the demanding training, he had remained so detached, so laid back that, unlike his classmates, he never worried about washing out. Since he truly did not care, he was never handicapped by nervous tension. Since he exerted himself as little as possible, he just squeezed by to graduate in the bottom tenth of his class and just claim his golden wings.

Charm, good looks and good luck had thereafter protected him from the backlash of his audacity and his sloth. Charm, good looks, good luck, and the pleas of three senior officers' wives whose beds he briefly enlivened had made him a lieutenant commander at the age of thirty-two, despite some unenthusiastic efficiency reports.

He appealed to all women. There was about him a wistful air they were eager to assuage. But he appealed particularly to older women. They saw a chance to rekindle their youth with a younger man who looked, even in uniform, as if he had just dropped in from a college campus.

His voice was deep, slow and soft, just tinged with a southern drawl. His five-foot-eleven-inch body, which was wiry and lithe, aroused great expectations in his women. His casual manner and his mocking smile challenged them, and his detachment intrigued them. His dark hair fell over his forehead when he was animated. He was never agitated. His golden-brown eyes were warm and sympathetic, seeming to sense the feelings of others, especially women's feelings, before they were expressed.

Salisbury Smith was, in short, a charmer, the masculine equivalent of the professional beauty who lives on her looks, her hauteur and her nerves. He was also a natural pilot who had finally learned to take sufficient pains before taking the controls.

The old magistrate's *yamen* intrigued Berry Smith. The high, grey-stone walls enclosed an acre and a half of yellow soil, which was divided into a series of courtyards surrounded by single-storey buildings with high-peaked roofs and eaves. The rows of semi-circular grey tiles that covered those roofs were, Smith reflected, like the corn-row hairstyles once so popular among black women.

Amadeus Brinks and his entourage now occupied the capacious family quarters around the last courtyard, which in May bloomed with purple lilac, golden laburnum, and pink hawthorn. Some twenty guests were now accommodated in the retainers' quarters, still leaving ample room for the computers that were the nerve-centre of the *yamen*. All the rooms smelled not unpleasantly of mould, drying plaster, and ozone generated by the electronic devices, as well as their ancient ingrained scents: chicken feathers, sweet incense, rancid cooking oil and a trace of human excrement.

Knowing he would not be flying for two days, Salisbury Smith was lying on a scarlet-canopied four-poster in the air crew quarters. He was alone except for the fourteen-year-old Thai girl who prepared tiny black pellets for his opium pipe over a minute wick. He had smoked opium for years at widely separated intervals, and the ivory-barrelled pipe with the minuscule bowl was for the moment all the company he needed.

He was startled by voices heard across the courtyard. Normally velvet smooth, Amadeus Brinks's voice was vibrant, either in anger or in enthusiasm. Berry Smith was lapped in the drowsy yet clear-sighted contentment induced by opium, which Brinks surprisingly commended as a 'natural narcotic, more gentle and more consistent than alcohol'.

But the clamour startled him. Berry had never seen his patron angry – and he did not wish to do so.

Amadeus Brinks was elaborately polite, his courtesy as archaic as his sweeping white mustachios. But his slate-grey eyes were never less than intimidating. Even when they glowed with zeal, something of himself was always held back. Of his sincerity and his honesty there could be no doubt, but he was not always wholly candid. His eyes, flat and lustreless, were not windows into his mind but one-way mirrors. He looked out guardedly, but no one would ever look in.

Berry Smith felt that his patron was always weighing him. Amadeus Brinks's vigilance was never off duty, even when they shared a pheasant and a bottle of red-velvet Rioja. Berry knew from his experience of admirals that such reserve was a component of power. Brinks looked like an amiable, self-indulgent pleasure-lover: plump with good living, flushed pink, and ruddy bald. But no one trifled with him, not ever.

Though Berry Smith could not make out the words, he heard Amadeus Brinks and Prince Richard in heated discussion. Normally, Brinks spoke and Richard listened, occasionally dropping a pertinent comment. Not remarkable for intellectual depth, His Royal Highness was more closely attuned to the concerns of men and women who worked for their living than was the billionaire.

'Let me show you Hunts Point Avenue in the Bronx.' Brinks attempted to ease the tension by throwing an avuncular arm around Richard's shoulders. 'It looks as if it had been nuked. Yet not so many years ago, a half century or so, Hunts Point was a pleasant lower middle-class ...'

'Amadeus, I asked you about the bombings last week, not about the Bronx half a century ago,' the prince rebuffed his mentor's charm. 'Not hypothetical nukes in New York, but a real high explosive bomb in Bangkok! Amadeus, were *we* behind it? What possible justification can there be for ...?'

'Yes, Richard, we were,' Brinks conceded. 'We, you and I, are ...'

'How is that possible?' Richard exploded. 'Our goals are noble ...'

'Essential to human survival!' Brinks interjected.

'But the things we do!' Richard continued. 'Abominable! And you talk to me of some place called Hunts Point! Amadeus, I'm beginning to wonder how long I can continue to ...'

'Richard, it *had* to be. I mourn Alois Muhlenberger deeply! He was my friend, a true friend of the heart. We shared many ideals ... had many dreams in common. He was not meant to die. That mistake has already been punished severely. But it was necessary, absolutely essential, that his activities be halted.'

The prince extended his hands, palms up. That Mediterranean gesture was neither farcical nor undignified in the tall blond man with the pale-blue eyes. When Richard of Greece and Denmark threw out his hands, one thought of the spellbinding orators of the ancient world. Demosthenes and Cicero came to mind, not Athenian fruit-sellers or Neapolitan fishmongers.

'Sometimes, Amadeus, I simply don't understand you,' Richard protested. 'Why, in the name of God, destroy .... Why even thwart that man of God? He was bringing the peoples of the world together. He was on our side, the side of humanity, tolerance, and peace.'

'True enough, Richard. But you overlook one factor. You see ...'

'And the king himself! How could you take the risk? If he hadn't thrown himself on the queen to protect her, he might not have taken the bomb fragment in his side: he might also have been killed outright. Not to speak of that little Indian chap, Sammy Namboodripad. Why did *he* have to die? You know, you almost got me at the same time.'

'I warned you not to get too close to the altar, Richard.'

'So you did. But I never thought ... and others were killed because I never suspected .... But the *king*! Do you know what would've happened to Thailand ... to the East Asian Federation ... if he had died?'

'Partial disintegration. An unravelling at the very least. That's another reason why ....'

Brinks clamped his full lips together under his white moustache. He had not yet decided how far he could trust his associates, not even Richard, who was, at once, a major asset and a grave danger. Better for the moment to let Richard vent his indignation at peril to a fellow member of the trade union of royals.

'Forty-three dead, Brinks!' Richard spoke with regal indignation. 'Mostly priests, as you know. Also a sprinkling of diplomats. Not to speak of seventy-eight injured, many seriously. The police of ten nations are after the terrorists. How *could* you, Brinks?'

Chilled by that peremptory use of his last name, the billionaire wondered if it was time to lift a corner of the veil. Otherwise, revulsion could alienate those among his followers who were genuine idealists, those few who were animated neither by self-interest, by hatred, or by thirst for revenge. In any event, the revelation could not be long delayed now that the militant phase of his plan had begun. Perhaps today he should come clean – reveal much, though not all of his total strategy, and separate the wheat of loyal disciples from the chaff of sentimentalists and opportunists.

'Richard, I shall be utterly frank,' Amadeus Brinks said. 'Alois Muhlenberger was a good man. He was *too* good. Therefore he had to go.'

'Yes!'

'The movement towards unity Alois led was the greatest single threat to the future of mankind. He might well have brought together the opposites: East and West; management and labour; women and men; Buddhists and Christians. That reconciliation could *not* be tolerated. I had to ...'

'In the name of God, why?'

'The reactionary tendencies Alois sponsored would have caused untold suffering. Just think what he *really* stood for. He would have reinforced the grip of the most exploitive region of the world, East Asia, with its rampant materialism. He would have given new vigour to the present order of mankind.'

'I begin to see ... our talk about the bears in Aspet. But this was so ... so extreme. I cannot accept ...'

'Desperate measures we talked about that night; the woman with breast cancer considering her future ... choosing radical action. *If* the evils of the present system are allowed to destroy nature unchecked, *if* the human habitat is ravaged, *if* the streams are poisoned and the forests denuded, *then* the Apocalypse will become reality. *Then* humanity will have destroyed itself by destroying the world God gave us.'

Amadeus Brinks paused, shaken by his own emotion, then added, 'All those *ifs* are the realities of today. Worse than the Europeans ever were, the greedy Asians are recklessly, ruthlessly, destroying the earth that has given them sustenance.'

'But Amadeus,' Richard protested feebly, 'what you're doing ...'

'Is necessary, absolutely essential. The surgeon's knife must cut deep.' The crusader's tone was no longer hectoring, but almost pleading. 'Remember the bears, Richard, the big brown bears! They are now increasing. Two more cubs were born last month. There are now sixteen big brown bears in the Pyrenees.'

'A clear success,' Richard replied. 'A clear success by legal, non-violent means. All the more reason to ...'

'Yet throughout Europe, other bears are being tortured every day. Not only forced to learn to "dance" by being placed on hot coals and whipped unmercifully. Being starved ... tormented in so many ways.'

The billionaire wiped his face with a red bandanna extracted from a pocket of his immaculate white linen suit.

'In Asia it's worse ... far worse. Tens of thousands of bears are being bred like cattle. The old Beijing regime officially – openly, unabashed, and unashamed – set up the first farms. Thousands of bears are now immobilized with drains in their gall-bladders. Bear's gall is a fabulous aphrodisiac. When the poor beasts finally perish in agony, their internal organs are dried and sold as medicines.'

'Terrible, Amadeus, but does it really justify slaughtering ...'

'Our abominable cruelty injures ourselves almost as severely as the poor beasts.' Brinks was no longer impassioned, but didactic and reasonable. 'We destroy our own humanity and behave even more viciously towards each other. All this must cease – if mankind is to survive as human beings.'

'What,' Richard asked, 'do bears in China have to do with Hunts Point in the Bronx, Amadeus?'

'Everything, Richard.' Brinks strove to recapture his most prominent disciple. 'Both are about dehumanization, the self-destruction of humanity: the maiming of the natural order.

'Take Hunts Point. Seventy years ago it was an unpretentious neighbourhood where clerks, foremen, salesmen, even the occasional lawyer or doctor, lived in pleasant propinquity.

'But the decades following World War II reduced the neighbourhood to a festering slum. The clerks, foremen and salesmen moved out – and the impoverished moved in. They made Hunts Point a battlefield for black and Hispanic gangs, a no man's land of gaping doorways and shattered windows.

'Fifteen years ago, City Hall decided to rehabilitate the neighbourhood ... poured in hundreds of millions of dollars. For a while, it improved: less crime, less filth, fewer racial clashes, even a drop in drug trafficking. Then it all came apart again.'

'Amadeus, I still don't see the connection.'

'The connection? Simply this: all the power of the existing order was concentrated on that rehabilitation and it all came to nothing!

Drugs are again rampant: super-crack, paradise powder, and the latest designer synthetics. Even the street whores shun Hunts Point, not only in fear but because there's not a cent to be picked up there.'

Deeply moved by the stark picture he was painting, Brinks continued, 'Street gangs fight for turf with machine-guns, hand-grenades, and rocket-launchers. What's next? Heavy artillery?

'Crackheads with yellow and grey faces scream at each other over the roar of the satcabnet outdoor screens. Scores of women, as well as men, wander around orating to the air: their suffering, their grievances, the injustice they've endured. Hundreds, thousands, shrieking and weeping and howling day and night.'

'The point, Amadeus,' Prince Richard broke in, 'the point!'

'This nightmare, Richard, this purgatory on earth, is the final fruit of our modern hi-tech civilization. All in the foremost city in the most advanced country in the world. At the very least, it shows that something is radically wrong with the way the human race goes about its business of living today.'

VII

The nun stooped to finger the giant purple blossom on the rose bush. Her movements slow, her manner demure, she laid her prayer-book down and buried her face in the velvet petals.

The afternoon sunlight was languorous. The garden of the convent sparkled with a rainbow of colour. The tinkle of a distant fountain at once soothed and stirred her. This, too, was the glory of God, not only dusty incense, endlessly repeated prayers, and the cold stone floors of the Tuscan-yellow convent on the hill.

Just visible between the flower and her stiff-starched wimple, her big brown eyes glanced sideways shyly. She reached out tremulously, but snatched her hand back.

A distended male organ filled her vision, its head purple and shiny, its stalk a fiery scarlet. The nun saw nothing else in the world. Tentatively, then boldly, she reached out and stroked the stalk.

'For God's sake!' Janet Seager swung around in her chair and exploded. 'This is supposed to be the main channel, not the porn channel. What *is* all this rubbish?'

'It *is* the main channel, Jan.' Mike Goldsworthy turned to face her in the half-gloom of the studio. 'The image is great, isn't it? You'd swear it was happening right here in this room. Three-dimensional television's worth every penny it cost.'

'What's this crap doing on the main channel, Mike?'

'It's a classic. "The Nuns' Gardener and How He Ploughed" from Boccacio's *Decameron.*'

'And that justifies ...'

On the master-screen the encounter was playing itself out in glowing colour in the round. Scores of millions in the worldwide audience felt they could reach out and touch what they pleased, whether the hairy testicles the nun now clutched or the white globes of her buttocks revealed by her hiked-up habit.

'Come on, Jan. Alpha One's got to keep its viewers. If you don't like it, let's go to the feelies. There's a great show at the Roxy, a virtudrama.'

Janet shook her head, but nonetheless smiled at his ribbing. She disliked the virtual reality dramas popularly called feelies. Somehow, it seemed immoral to enjoy all the physical sensations of galloping on a horse or schussing downhill on skis while seated comfortably and safely in a sensationful theatre seat.

Besides, she disliked anything even remotely risqué when she was with Mike. Despite the fiasco of their only night together, she sensed that he still had lecherous thoughts about her. She did not want to encourage him, although he might deceive himself that it was also deep affection. It was really just his constant itch, the same itch that drove him into the arms of Catherine Loomis.

Anyway, he was only teasing about going to the feelies at the Roxy. He and she could not appear together in public without attracting a mob of many adoring fans and a few jeering critics.

'Did you know,' Mike asked, 'Alpha One's working on putting virtudramas on air?'

'It's too complicated. How could they ever?'

'Yes, it's still too expensive to put the equipment in every home. Not to speak of maintaining it. Masks, gloves, and robes. Not to mention the unmentionables: electronic bras, panties, undershorts, that kind of thing.'

Janet winced. He was trying to embarrass her, and he had all but succeeded. More adventurous friends had told her that the feelies could now reproduce every sensation imaginable, 'just like the real thing, sometimes better', with their newest sensationful seats.

'Now you've had your fun,' she said, 'let's get back to work.'

Mike asked instead, 'Don't you see this junk is also a public service?'

'How do you figure that?'

'What else would you do for the tribespeople?' he asked. 'A third of the world's population who can't work ... won't work.'

'Can't is more like it,' she said. 'Too slow mentally for skilled jobs in the information age.'

'And too proud to do menial jobs,' he riposted. 'Ours is the first society where the upper classes work hard and the underclass doesn't work at all.'

'Mike, you can't blame the tribes for the pickle they're in. That's why they're called tribes ... from the German *Ausgetriebene*: those driven out. Society's got no place for them.'

'So the satcabnets fill an essential function. Unemployment is now hereditary for one out of every three human beings. But we keep the tribes reasonably happy ... keep them from rioting in the streets.'

'Mike, we have to make them better, not just keep them in a stupor.'

'Such idealism! Have you ever seen a tribes riot? Close up? Not just on screen?'

'Not really. But the clips are pretty frightening.'

'You can smell their dumb rage: inchoate and bloodthirsty. Rage makes them very dangerous. So demagogues and gangsters can threaten to bring the tribes on to the streets and make even presidents tremble.'

'Why should the president of the US or France be brave?' she asked. 'They have so little power they're as impotent as palace eunuchs.'

'I meant presidents of satcabnets. The presidents with *real* power like Kate the Great.'

'So the satnets stun the tribes with psychedelic spectacles, with game shows, with three-dimensional violence, and with porn. So what's next?'

'We win time and space and tranquillize for others to make scientific discoveries, to paint great pictures, and to write wonderful novels.'

'And, meanwhile, we, the satnets, debase everything worthwhile. We drive out good music, good art and good literature. We make a mockery of selfless devotion, a travesty of aspiration and reverence.'

'If you and I take the high road,' he retorted, 'we'll be for the high jump.'

'But we *can* do our best with *The Next Thousand Years*. After all, we're free!' She looked at him hard. 'Or are we?'

'I love it when you go all idealistic.' He did not answer her question. 'You're really something. Dynamite!'

Impulsively, Mike leaned over and kissed Janet's lips. Involuntarily, her arms tightened around his neck. The next instant she pushed him away, angry at him and angry at herself. Abashed, they subsided into their swivel chairs.

'Definitely *not* what the doctor ordered!' Mike laughed shakily. 'I'm sorry, Jan. My fault entirely.'

'No! Just as much my fault.' She smiled feebly. 'Mike, let's forget it. It didn't work in the past. It doesn't work now. And it won't work in the future.'

'I guess so, but, Jan, you know I . . . .'

A blast from the wraparound speakers diverted Mitchell Goldsworthy from whatever declaration he might have made. The sound feed, a few seconds in advance of the picture, was a high-pitched male voice gabbling in heavily accented English over the crackle of turbo-rifle fire. The master-screen showed a slender, white-marble column rising from clouds of smoke.

The flat voice of Inforobot Inez declared, 'Feed from Jakarta, Indonesia, shows series of explosions during past hour. Subsequent images will be real time. Informatively, no Alpha One bureau or stringer is kept in prosperity-fat Jakarta owing to extremely high costs. Pictures as usual by taxi-drivers equipped with mini-disk camcorders and hand-held satellite transmitters. Anonymous phone calls alerted them to be on scene. Small arms fire in background is troops suppressing demonstrators.'

The white-marble column began to crumple on the master-screen, and the sullen roar of prolonged explosions rumbled from the wrap-around speakers. The column folded gracefully from the base up as if kneeling in prayer. Almost leisurely, the mid-section struck the ground and flew into fragments. Finally, an enormous golden sunburst glowing in the sunlight settled upright amid the debris.

'National Monument of Indonesia.' Inez was drawing on library disks for background information. 'Some five hundred feet high, built for the despot Sukarno in 1961. Because of its phallic shape and because the lecherous despot was overthrown in 1965, it is popularly known as "Sukarno's last erection". The sunburst is covered with thirty-five pounds of thick gold-leaf.'

'And the people,' Janet observed, 'are helping themselves.'

Men in checked sarongs swarmed across the debris and clambered onto the sunburst. Hacking with short-bladed knives, they peeled off the gold-leaf. Nine soldiers in mottled jungle green, raised stubby turbo-rifles to their shoulders and fired. Two men toppled – and the remaining thirty-odd scuttled away, sarongs held high so they could run faster.

A wave of more than a thousand demonstrators swept around the ruins to engulf the nine-man squad. Many waved unintelligible banners or placards. A moment later, a wedge of troops, 300 strong, hammered into the crowd, clearing its way with swinging rifle-butts.

Remembering Indonesia, Mike Goldsworthy could almost feel the brazen tropical sun and the sweat dripping down his back. He could all but smell the crowd. Heavy with the stench of hate, reeking of mould and sweat, though most Jakartans bathed three times a day, and redolent of over-ripe tropical fruit, sweet frangipani flowers, and the tang of curries.

'Inez,' Janet asked, 'any word on who's responsible?'

'The taxi-drivers know nothing, Janet,' the inforobot replied. 'One muttered about an Arab accent on the telephone. Nothing further. The AP-Reuter wire gives five possible explanations.'

'Which mean *no* explanation,' Mike said. 'Only wild guesses.'

'Search continues, Mr Goldsworthy,' Inez responded.

Janet glanced at Mike. His brown eyes were hurt, and his lips were deliberately clamped shut. He was clearly annoyed by the inforobot's calling her Janet, but him Mr Goldsworthy. How desperately he needed to believe that everyone loved him, even emotionless inforobots.

The image on the master-screen was shifting, and the wraparound loudspeakers were filling the studio with the wail of sirens. The big screen split in half to display two different images simultaneously. On one side, the narrow Jakarta Catholic Church with its high-peaked roof and red-brick walls; on the other, the Harmonie Club, looking like an enormous white igloo.

'Feed now in real time,' Inez announced. 'Left-hand screen shows Catholic Church. Right-hand screen shows the Harmonie Club.' The inforobot added pedantically, 'Harmonic Club was the hub of social life and the informal centre of power under the Dutch colonial overlords.'

Crowds surrounded both buildings, surging against cordons of soldiers in camouflage uniforms. The clamour half-drowned the shriek of police sirens and the rattle of distant small arms from the riot at the National Monument. Abruptly, the crowd broke through the cordon around the church, torches sprouting in its hands.

Just as the throng reached its walls, the church's peaked roof rose entire as if lifted by a gigantic invisible hand. For perhaps five seconds, the roof hung in the air. Then it settled heavily back on the collapsing walls and broke up. Fire spouted from the wreckage and the mob fell back.

The igloo-like Harmonie Club went three minutes later. The explosions blew great holes in the white walls, though the ponderous structure did not collapse. Flames shot from those openings and the mob's anger flared higher.

Young men wearing the black fez-like *songkok* of ultranationalists hurled themselves at the troops, who had evidently been ordered not to fire. Around the ultranationalists surged several thousand men and youths wearing the white turban of Islamic fundamentalists. Behind the white turbans advanced additional thousands with bare heads, the ever-restless rabble of Jakarta.

'Running amok,' Mike said, and Inez volunteered, 'The expression "amok" comes from the Indonesian language. It means to go berserk.'

'From the Norse bearsark, meaning to fight all-comers armoured only by your shirt.'

'That's not fair, Mike,' Janet whispered. 'You know she's not programmed to understand irony.'

Programmed or unprogrammed, a low hum that could have been anger rose from the loudspeakers. But Inez spoke in her normal flat tone. 'According to AP-Reuter, handbills distributed throughout Jakarta within the past half-hour read in part as follows:

'*Nahdatul Ulama, the Society of Imams, declares today a holy war, a moral* jihad *against the pervasive influence of the decadent infidel West in our holy islands. We have today wiped from the face of the earth two temples of unrighteousness, exploitation, concupiscence, and sin.*

'*The Christian churches are agents of unrepentant Western imperialism. The evil they do is manifest. They lure our people aside from the true religion.*

'*The Harmonie Club was not only a shameful monument to harsh and greedy Dutch rule, but a shameless brothel where Indonesian men, many of them high officials, went to drink alcohol and to lie with whores.*

'*Both defile Allah's good earth by their greed. Both destroy the fabric of the earth.*

'*We have this day struck a blow for true independence from the moral and material horrors of decadent Judaeo-Christian Western civilization. We must return to the clean, clear truths of Islam in our thoughts, our hearts, our souls and our daily lives.*'

'Whew!' Mike whistled. 'Cultural cleansing with a vengeance.'

'And we thought the Indonesians were so happy, so content in their prosperity they'd never run amok again.'

'Be careful,' Mike smiled wryly. 'Madame Inez will be correcting you in a second.'

As if on cue, the metallic voice resumed. 'More from Jakarta. The Nahdatul Ulama declares it will *next purify Singapore, which is an island of unrighteousness in a sea of Islam*. The statement says Bangkok and Jakarta *were spared more than token destruction. Singapore, with its alien Chinese population and its wholesale Western influence, will cease to function. We are attacking in East Asia*, the statement adds, *because it is the most materialistic region of the world, the most destructive of God's environments. Even the sins of*

Europeans and Americans recede before the sins of bloated East Asians.'

'Well,' Mike said heavily, 'finally a villain for this melodrama.'

'Looks like it. But these Islamic extremists may only be piggy-backing.'

'Whatever, it looks very big. Enormous. We've got to rethink the segment on terrorism in the series. It looks like anything but a spent force. Jan, I think . . . .'

'Mike,' she interrupted, 'I want to go to Singapore.'

'Are you sure you can handle . . . .' He caught himself and added amiably, 'Why not? The budget'll cover it easily. I don't see why Kate should object. But, Jan, be very careful.'

VIII

The main courtyard of the walled *yamen* on the edge of Xian was capacious to accommodate the throngs who had once come to petition for justice or to hear criminals tried. Early on a mid-May afternoon, a century after the last sitting of the Imperial Court, five rows of benches stood before the magistrate's dais. They were occupied by thirty-three highly diverse men and women who were Amadeus Brinks's working group.

Some were greybeards, and some were pink-cheeked youths. Some were grandmothers, and some were apparently schoolgirls. Some were Africans; some were Arabs; and some were Caucasian Europeans or Americans. Among the Asians were squat yellow Mongols, lithe brown Malays, and chubby South Indians, as well as Chinese and Japanese. Some wore minute earphones for translation, but most attended directly to the English of the bald man with the sweeping white moustache who sat in an armchair on the dais.

Amadeus Brinks, who wore a short-sleeved safari jacket and trousers of lustrous tan cotton, was flanked by two figures on the dais. The elderly Singapore Chinese woman who was the director for East Asia of the Future Green Society wore a sack-like blue cotton dress. The tall man with the blond beard who was Prince Richard of Greece and Denmark wore a powder-blue Nehru jacket.

Brinks effortlessly commanded the respect of the diverse group. He was not only their paymaster, but their mentor. The fanatics among them looked at him with the glittering eyes of falcons eager to be thrown against their prey. His eyes singled out those who, he already knew, would play major roles in the campaign he called Operation Survival.

The light-skinned Arab, with the flattened nose and the brilliantined black hair, Brinks called Comrade Sheik Semtex. He was a virtuoso with high explosives, who was zealous to avenge his people's humiliation by the West, as well as a great scholar of the Sacred Koran.

Although Islamic fundamentalism acknowledged no single leader, Comrade Sheik Semtex was its focal point. His command had sent Colonel Samuel Rodgers USAF plunging into the South China Sea at the controls of a Concordia Execujet. His interpretation of three obscure passages in the Koran had emboldened the Ulamas of Indonesia to strike at the wicked metropolis of Jakarta.

Beside Comrade Sheik Semtex sat the man Brinks called His Black Eminence, although he was blond and his complexion was ruddy. He was known to the world as the Reverend Father Luigi Bernando, Society of Jesus, a physician, zoologist, biochemist, and sculptor. A renaissance man in the twenty-first century, Luigi Bernando was prey to an obsession. He believed that mankind's so-called *progress* was an illusion – worse than an illusion, a long trek towards damnation for its destruction of the works of God.

The Jesuit drew authority from his stand from Pope John Paul II's 1987 Encyclical Letter *The Social Concern of the Church*, which declared: *... one cannot use with impunity the different categories of beings, whether living or inanimate – animals, plants, or the natural elements – simply as one wishes, according to one's economic needs.*

But Monsignor Luigi Bernando preached that *all* development was inherently evil, the road to self-destruction. Fiercely derided by established interests, he nonetheless attracted devoted followers. One of the most zealous was seated behind him, the fervour in her pale-blue eyes behind square, gold-rimmed glasses lighting her spare features.

Marie-Jeanne Erlanger, sometime reporter for *le Journal des Pyrénées*, had been fired by the victorious struggle to save the big brown bears. She had become an itinerant propagandist for the struggle to preserve the human race by preserving its global habitat. That vocation required her to be on intimate terms with the satcabnets, who were the ringmasters of popular enthusiasms.

Yet Marie-Jeanne loathed those electronic spiders, whose invisible webs spanned the world. She despised the satcabnets for their slovenly ways, above all, their total lack of rigorous Gallic logic. She hated them for slowly annihilating newspapers, which she loved. *Le Journal des Pyrénées*, where she had been happy for the first time in her twenty-six years, had already perished. When readers could select from a vast electronic storehouse those stories they wished to see, few would put up with a physical newspaper of limited capacity and fixed content.

Programming by choice had, however, failed to charm the vast audience for drama, sport, exhibitionism and porn. Aside from the satcabnets' constant availability everywhere on the globe, their greatest attraction was their immutability. A channel, once selected, offered no further choice. As your parents had, when you were a coddled child, the satcabnet decided what you were to see and when you were to see it.

A number of magazines, however, survived. Even the most rapacious satcabnets did not covet the limited audiences of niche publications that attracted targeted advertising by their snob appeal and their specific audiences. Like insects whose gaudy colours proclaim them to be poisonous or, at least, unpalatable, specialized paper-mags survived in cracks in the mass comdustry.

Despite her contempt for the satcabnets, Marie-Jeanne needed them. As a hard-headed Frenchwoman, she would not waste her life railing against the electronic parasites that had destroyed what she loved best. Instead, she used them. Her vehement English made charming by her French accent, she was a favourite guest on self-consciously thoughtful programmes. She presented one side of the issue, and she twisted fact to make her points. But her passionate advocacy made her irresistible to producers who needed the drama of conflict above all else.

Beside Marie-Jeanne, sat Temujin II, a Tantric Buddhist Mongol who believed himself to be the reincarnation of Ghengis Khan, the Scourge of God. And behind her, a radical-orthodox Shinto priest in black robes and tall black hat, who was too extreme even for the Shinto extremists who ruled Japan behind a gossamer curtain of parliamentary government.

An unreconstructed Maoist sat a little apart, conscious of her unique virtue. Tse Hu, the Vixen, would not wear her tailored Mao suit in public anywhere in what had once been the highly regimented People's Republic of China: she would be lynched. Brinks marvelled at the serene beauty of the Vixen's oval face, so like a gilded statue of Kuan Yin, the Goddess of Mercy. He marvelled even more when he remembered her coarse description of her orgasmic delight in slaughtering the enemies of the Chinese People's Secret Service with a cook's cleaver. She was coldly determined to restore the turbulent golden age of Chairman Mao Zedong.

Three former KGB stalwarts were equally determined to revenge themselves on history for spurning the golden age of Joseph Stalin. Beside them sat two men called Smith and Jones, who had been among the last operatives of the dirty tricks department of the US Central Intelligence Agency.

The CIA itself still existed, indeed thrived. But it was now essentially a public relations agency that from time to time undertook a little espionage. Among its clients it still counted the President of the United States, though no longer exclusively. Satcabnets eager to get the jump on their competitors contributed a large part of the CIA's revenue, commercial firms another large part, and the US Government the remainder.

Smith was five foot nine and wiry. His dark hair was crew cut, and his rimless glasses were shiny. He wore a white shirt with a subdued tie and a pin-striped three-piece suit. Jones was a few inches taller and enormously corpulent. A beer belly bulged like a watermelon under the hula dancers on his gaudy Hawaiian shirt, and his blue eyes were bloodshot.

If Smith looked like that former model of excellence, a reverent, clean-cut, FBI special agent, Jones looked like a hard-drinking truck driver. Naturally, they hated each other. But they hated everyone else even more.

'Ladies and gentlemen of the working group,' Brinks began. 'This may appear just another plenary session. Of course, none of our meetings over the past two years has been routine, but today we are passing from theory to practice ... from talk to action.

'We must assure the survival of the human race. We must remove the man-made afflictions that threaten mankind's very existence.

'First, illusion everywhere supplants reality. We see what is not, and we do not see what actually exists. We believe the real to be false and the false real. Extreme illusion is called virtual reality.'

Brinks grimaced ruefully at the latter-day Islamic prophet Comrade Sheik Semtex. To that fundamentalist, the making of any image of God's creation – whether human, animal, plant, or inanimate – was an abomination.

'Men and women now feel the exultation of danger overcome or great tasks arduously accomplished,' Brinks added, 'but they endure neither danger nor toil. They need only loll back and let diabolical devices manipulate them. They need only give control of their senses and their minds over to electronic robots. That is inhuman! An insult to the Creator.'

Scattered handclaps rose to a thunderous crescendo. Temujin II clapped loudest. Round face shining, he windmilled his arms over his head.

He had given up his exalted position as abbot of the wealthiest

Buddhist lamasery in Mongolia, when an itinerant lama revealed to him that he was the reincarnation of Genghis, Khan of Khans, who had scourged the world with divine fire. Temujin *knew* it was his destiny to scourge the world again – and to drive out the devils who had taken possession of the human race.

'The second affliction is excess,' Brinks resumed as the applause died away. 'Our society is *too* centralized, *too* technologized, *too* fast moving, *too* intense, above all, *too* big. Error and evil – dysfunction, in a word – are inevitable. Why? Because the cast of mind, the articles of daily use, even the dreams of the peasant up to his knees in water in a paddyfield in distant Java, as well as his wife's dreams, are all determined by slick, ignorant, greedy satcabnetniks in New York, London, Tel Aviv, Tokyo and Bangkok.'

Brinks rapped on the broad wooden arm of his chair to still the applause and declared, 'The third affliction poses the greatest, the most immediate danger to human survival. It is our despoiling of nature. Since our grasp of reality is so feeble, we know not what we do when we loot and rape the Creator's bounty. Most are unaware that humankind is destroying not only other creatures, but, above all, ourselves.

'If that devastation is *not* halted immediately, mankind will not long endure on this ravaged planet! As the dinosaurs perished, so shall we perish. Not, however, because the environment has become hostile due to natural events, but because we ourselves have *made* the environment hostile to our own species.'

The applause was hesitant. He had moved them deeply with his denunciation of mankind for flouting the will of the Creator, but the gross ecological imbalance, even the eventual extinction of the human race through its destruction of Nature's environment, that theme was too abstract. It did not pluck the heartstrings of the idealists, the revenge-seekers, and the fanatics who were the captains of his striking force.

'Look about you!' he urged. 'Look at the works of our so-called civilization. Here in Xian cancerous economic growth that deals death to the human spirit as it grows. Elsewhere we see the aftermath: torn-up roads, burnt-out or crumbled buildings, the land poisoned and abandoned. Human beings living in the ruins like scavenging rats.'

Looking directly at the Vixen, that ardent Maoist, he said, 'Yet some areas thrive precisely because they are *not* productive. Financial markets have become places of entertainment, gambling casinos. They create the illusion of wealth by shuffling futures, options, shares and derivatives. Some of our brightest waste their talents manipulating paper non-values, rather than producing goods, services, or concepts of real value.

'Humanity is withering intellectually and morally, even materially. That perverse evil we must alter radically by radical deeds.'

A ripple of applause swelled to a thunderclap, and Brinks knew that he had them once more. Already committed to fighting for the environment, they could not be moved by further ecological warnings. To a call to action, they would, however, respond.

'We are imprisoned from infancy in an enormous bubble of illusion. The satcabnets spread everywhere the illusions that are destroying us. They are the absolute rulers of the entire world.

'Yet they are totally devoid of any reverence for any higher power or any eternal truth. Blind to moral values or ethical principles, they have no regard for history or for tradition. They do honour education, but only as a ladder to material rewards and to social prestige for themselves and their children. So-called education, really training, also produces the computer-drones whose labours make them wealthy.

'These Philistines bow down to "art" in the shape of rotting calves' heads, junkyard gears brazed together and paint-splattered canvases.'

The audience was stirring. Brinks knew he must now come to his fiery peroration.

He glared at Marie-Jeanne Erlanger, who was waving her hand above her head. He would finish his peroration without interruption.

'The satnets pull the strings of their marionettes, the so-called sovereign governments.' He thundered, 'Their allies are the enormous corporations that dictate the material life of the planet and hold the livelihood of every human being in their greedy hands.

'All work together for a single purpose: *Profit! Profit! Profit!*

'There is your enemy! The enemy must be destroyed!'

As the applause finally dwindled, Brinks nodded to Marie-Jeanne Erlanger.

'Amadeus, you stress too much the human element,' she exploded. 'Also you both understate and overstate the ... how shall I say it? ... the ecological element.'

'And how is that, my dear Marie-Jeanne?'

His voice was cold. She was attractive to him and he disliked such emotional dependence almost as much as he loathed her contradicting him.

'You understate,' she replied, 'by placing too much emphasis upon human manipulation of humans and too little emphasis upon human ravaging of the natural world. You also overstate. You cry too much about the destruction of other species.'

Brinks lifted an incredulous eyebrow at Marie-Jeanne's decrying the chief tenet of her secular creed and said, 'Clearly the survivability of mankind is inextricably linked to the fate of other species, plant and animal, as well as to the state of the land and the oceans.'

'I have been rethinking environmentalist positions.' Marie-Jeanne slipped off her gold-rimmed glasses to polish their lenses with her silk scarf, and her pale-blue eyes were naked and vulnerable. 'Species die in nature. Not only the dinosaur and the dodo, but millions of other animal and plant species have died since the Creation. Like individuals, species die to make way for the new.

'Conservation of biodiversity may already have gone too far. It is one thing to attempt to limit the damage done the environment by humans, it is another thing to attempt totally to prevent the natural death of species.

'Ultimately, we cannot alter the fundamental differentiations laid down by Nature, differences such as gender and physical or mental capability. No more can we force Nature to commute the sentence of death she passes on entire species – in the end, of course, on our own as well.'

A puzzled silence settled on the group. Some were silent because they could not understand what she had said. Others were silent because they could not believe that Marie-Jeanne Erlanger, the doyenne of environmental propagandists, had uttered those words.

'Well said, Marie-Jeanne!' Brinks all but purred; she had unintentionally given him the opening he needed. 'But sadly irrelevant. You are right in principle, but *not* at a time of acute crisis. Not when we are destroying other species at a constantly accelerating rate. Not when the human sub-species is itself gravely threatened.

'It may well be that the human race will in time become extinct by natural process. I only seek to postpone the moment when the human race perishes and to ensure that it does not perish by its own hand.

'To that end we must preserve the natural world. We cannot live otherwise.'

'What are you *doing*, Brinks?' the Vixen interjected harsh-voiced. 'What've you done besides bleat at us? What've we done except kowtow to you? Where are we going, if anywhere?'

Amadeus Brinks smiled thinly. She was not his favourite human being, certainly not his favourite woman. The Vixen tore to the heart of the matter far too quickly and far too crudely.

'About time I stopped blathering, you mean? All right, comrade, I shall,' he responded coolly. 'You all know that we arranged the crash or disappearance of eight aircraft in one day. But you may ask: *why*?

'Simply to heighten the insecurity that now stalks the earth amid great prosperity. Even the non-working tribespeople are far better off materially than they were twenty years ago. But they, too, are apprehensive – or would be if they knew the word.'

Waiting for the bitter laughter to subside, he resumed, 'The spectre of futility haunts the human race: a foreboding of imminent doom. We are now feeding that fear. Hence the explosions in Thailand and Indonesia. The resulting panic is gratifying ... will in time convince the masses of the necessity to save ourselves by saving our world.

'But do not congratulate yourselves prematurely, my friends. All this is just preliminary skirmishing. The big battles are yet to be fought.'

The Shinto priest in the tall black hat called out, 'What big battles are to be? Please, master, be specific!'

Flushing at the rebuke, Brinks replied, 'What battles? You will be told as you are needed to fight them. And only those needed will be told!'

'Get to the kernel!' the Vixen demanded. 'What is your objective? Men! Always palavering, never doing!'

'Madame, I shall be specific. We are in a state of siege, we who hold to fundamental values. We must strike before we are overwhelmed by the new Vandals.

'Take New York City. Civilization, as we know civilization, now exists only south of 92nd Street in Manhattan. All else is virtually lost to chaos.

'Moreover, nuclear igloos now stud the entire world, built over disused nuclear power generators. But concrete igloos cannot fully contain the lethal contents. Leaks are commonplace. Further, radioactive waste from hundreds of generating stations still operating is poisoning the land and the sea.

'Are we suicidal to tolerate such poisons? Just look at the genetic flaws and the direct injuries inflicted by radiation, by rogue hormones and antibiotics, by pesticides and fertilizers! Look at the Devil's work of deliberately altering the genetic code of every species from protozoa to man!

'Dams, highways, and tunnels are destroying the contours of the land and making normal existence virtually impossible. The Aswan High Dam has ravaged the Nile Valley. No more yearly deposit of silt and no more yearly renewal of the extraordinary fertility of the soil. Hence famine!

'The Three Gorges Dam, built against all informed advice – and the mass protests of the Chinese people – will soon devastate the Yangtze Valley. The land is already leached with salt, flooded in places, suffering drought in others. Tens of millions have been displaced.

'The greatest malefactor has been the so-called development banks, the World Bank chief among them. Charged to relieve human misery, they have intensified misery; they have been *creating* poverty by development.'

'Comrade, enough!' A voice among the ex-KGB operatives demanded in melodious Russian. 'What is to be done?'

'The system is rotten clear through,' Brinks replied. '*Nothing* can be done with it. The system must be altered root and branch if humanity is to survive. I ask ... no, demand that all of you here join me in the struggle for human survival!'

Applause and shouts swelled high, rising to a new crescendo just when it seemed it must end. Seated on Amadeus Brinks's left, Prince Richard marvelled that so few could make so much noise. He marvelled even more to see terrorists cheering like schoolchildren alongside the prophets of extreme fundamentalist cults. But they had just been given licence for unrestrained violence in the name of survival.

When the cheering finally murmured away, Richard spoke. 'I should like to express the thanks of all here present for this lucid and moving analysis. One personal note: I was wavering because I was appalled by the casualties in Bangkok and Jakarta. But I am now convinced that Amadeus Brinks has shown us the only road to human survival. He has also assured me that loss of life will be kept to an irreducible minimum.'

A barrage of practical questions was aimed at Brinks. Who, one asked, would be the vanguard? Where would they strike next? Was kidnapping or assassinating leaders not the best way to destroy the existing system?

A dozen further questions followed each answer. Some Brinks answered, even more he declined to answer. He could not answer substantively and specifically, as this audience deserved, without imperilling future operations.

No one, however, asked what was to replace the old order they now all agreed must pass.

IX

'*En principe*, I've no objection to your going when the time comes, my dear girl.' Catherine Loomis reached across the glass slab of the coffee-table and patted Janet Seager's hand. 'It'll be good for Alpha One: our very own Girl Guide, intrepid into danger.'

Janet's smile hid the revulsion she felt at that soft touch. Like the brush of ancient cobwebs in the dark, it sent a cold ripple down her spine. Still, she would happily pay a much higher price to cover the Islamic fundamentalists' coming assault upon the inordinately wealthy city-state of Singapore. She consciously repressed her contempt for Kate the Great's relentless commercialism and shameless promiscuity.

'Of course, there's no question of Mike going with ...'

'Chris' sake, Catherine,' Mike Goldsworthy broke in. 'I never thought of going. Jan doesn't want ...'

'I was about to say, Mike, we need you here to mind the store.' Catherine ignored his outburst. 'If you both went haring off after every rumour like the rumour of an attack on Singapore, the series'd never get off the ground. Besides, she ... ah, Janet ... can work better without you. No danger of her being recognized and mobbed if she's alone.'

The woman who was one of the ten most powerful individuals in the world was fleetingly transformed. Catherine Loomis was no longer the all-knowing, all-powerful, ruthless chief executive who was concerned only for the imperial enterprise she ruled. She was for a moment an insecure, jealous older woman who was afraid that her lover had found a new playmate. Her husky voice was almost shrill when she tossed out that last barbed remark, which implied that Janet was so little known no one would recognize her if she did not have Mike in tow. And that in Singapore, where an Alpha One presenter was not merely a star, but virtually a demigoddess!

Janet knew she would have a hard time avoiding recognition when she got to bored and therefore entertainment-mad Singapore. Every household owned at least three television sets, to which government-controlled Lion City Cable piped twenty-four hours a day of 'wholesome and uplifting' programmes, attempting in vain to pre-empt satcabnet 'pollution' raining from the sky. Janet had already decided to use a pseudonym, perhaps change her hairdo and clap on large sunglasses. Otherwise, she would be swamped by fans.

This late afternoon meeting in the penthouse on the 125th floor of the Alpha One Tower appeared to be a routine conference of the presenters with the chief programmer. But Kate's concern was more than routine. She had committed her personal prestige to *The Next Thousand Years*, defying widespread prophecy of doom if she deviated from the proven model. Ceaseless titillation and superficial reporting had made Alpha One the biggest satcabnet in the world. Yet she was tinkering with the formula.

Mike grinned self-deprecatingly, but asserted, 'I know you're scheming to keep me here desk-bound, and tamed, like a court eunuch.'

'How could I possibly?' Catherine murmured. 'You a eunuch!'

'All right,' Mike said. 'I'll hold down the desk when Jan goes. But I'm going to do some field reporting later.'

'I just can't spare you right now,' Catherine said. 'Later you can go where you please ... take a moon-rocket if necessary. Only try to stay somewhere near the budget. Now can we get back to work?'

Janet realized that she had been allowed a glimpse of the inner working of a complex relationship. Mike Goldsworthy was normally charming to almost everyone, though often abrasive towards herself. He now challenged Catherine Loomis, as if to prove to her – and to himself – that he was not a kept man. Obviously, Catherine would sometimes give in, as if to prove that she was a sympathetic female after all. Then came the crack of the whip to show she was the boss.

'Catherine, what's your agenda today?' Janet asked casually.

If Mike wanted to provoke Kate the Great, let him. But Janet had to keep on her good side. She had no intention of falling with Mike if he misjudged Catherine's threshold of tolerance – and stumbled on it.

'Jan.' Catherine remembered her name, which was itself memorable. 'I'm wondering about the string of disasters this past fortnight. Eight aeroplanes down in one day. Violence in Bangkok and Jakarta. Threats to Singapore. Are they all parts of a single pattern? Or is it just chance they happened so close together?'

'You ask some tough questions, don't you?' Mike said. 'Easy to ask, but a bitch to answer.'

'Mike dear, that's what I'm paid for.' Catherine's smile was saccharine sweet, but her light-brown eyes were lit by petty malice. 'I'm paid to ask tough questions. And you're paid ... very well paid ... for coming up with answers. Division of labour, they call it.'

'I hear you loud and clear!' Mike smiled defensively. 'But we have to go out to get the answers. We can't sit in the Alpha Tower and expect them to come to us. That's why Jan's dying to go to Singapore.'

'I want an answer now, Mike!' Catherine demanded. 'A professional would've been thinking about the question. And Alpha One's got no place for amateurs.'

'Let's start with the planes then.' He ignored her brutality. 'Lots of lurid speculations but no facts. Jan's our aviation expert, but she can't give you a definitive answer. Nobody can, except the mastermind behind this show. *If* there is a mastermind ... *if* it is one single show. But Jan can cast some light on the darkness – if anyone can.'

'Thanks loads, Mike.' Janet now smiled too sweetly. 'Thanks for the hot potato. I'll try, but ...'

'Go ahead, Jan,' Catherine directed. 'Don't let him rattle you.'

Janet wondered whether that expression of female solidarity made her feel more secure or more apprehensive. The last thing she needed was to become a shuttlecock hit back and forth between Catherine and Mike. Shuttlecocks got battered, lost their feathers, and were thrown out.

'We can only establish negatives,' she ventured. 'We have no evidence that one agency took out eight airplanes in a day. And no one's claimed credit. Normally, hundreds of cranks would've deluged us with calls, faxes, E-mail, and satbites. So . . . .'

'You're saying we've got no facts. Zilch!' Catherine cut to the core of the issue. 'So logic is useless.'

'When do we ever have all the facts?' Janet rose to the challenge. 'When we're on deadline, we go with what we've got.'

'Granted!' Catherine was again magisterial, above the fray. 'Proceed!'

'Thanks so much!' Janet hoped her irony was not too blatant. 'If you toss a coin a million times, it'll come up roughly half-a-million heads and half-a-million tails. But that doesn't mean every head will be followed by a tail. And you can toss the coin a hundred, even a thousand times, and heads and tails won't necessarily come up equal. Too few tosses to establish a pattern.'

'Come on, Jan!' Mike prodded. 'I send in my pinch-hitter, and she doesn't even swing at the ball.'

'Mike, I . . . .' Janet quashed her anger at his needling. 'Anyway, probability's what it's all about. There's no reason why eight aircraft can't come to grief in a single day, rather than over weeks, months or years. So, it's never happened before. All the more likely it's now happened by chance.'

Jan paused, absently flicked the cracked scarlet polish on her left thumbnail, and summed up, 'That's the logical answer. But I *don't* believe it for a second.'

'Why not?' Catherine demanded.

'*Because* it's never happened before. So why should it happen now *without* human agency? Considering their maintenance and crew training, it's possible ... probable, the Chinese and African planes just ran into grief. But *not* all eight, certainly *not* airplanes maintained by Japanese and Malaysians.'

'Where,' Mike prodded, 'do we go from here?'

'My hunch is someone clawed those planes out of the sky,' Jan replied. 'Some megalomaniac. I'll bet we get a message when he decides to show his hand.'

'Brilliant reasoning, Jan dear, though a a little complicated for the tube.' Catherine Loomis smiled at her new ally. 'What about Bangkok and Jakarta? Also directed by a single person?'

'Catherine, really ...' Janet stalled. 'I think Mike ought to tackle that one.'

'You must have an opinion, Janet,' Catherine pressed. 'That's what we pay you for.'

'Well, meanwhile . . . .' Janet was, somehow, relieved that Catherine had dropped her pretence of female solidarity. 'I think the tentative answer has to be *yes*.'

'Yes *what*?' Mike heckled. 'You've lost me.'

'Yes, a single human agency. If all the planes were destroyed by the same force, then the outrages in Bangkok and Jakarta, they're most likely due to the same group. Otherwise, it's stretching coincidence way too far.'

'So you think a band of nuts wants to blow up the world!' Mike needled. 'The Islamic fundamentalists say they set the Jakarta bombs. So they also knocked down all those planes? How? Do they have a direct line to Allah? Do they duck into the nearest mosque to change into their Superman duds? How about it, Jan old kid?'

'You really think the fundamentalists were behind both the Jakarta and the Bangkok bombings?' Jan retorted. 'Only them? I'm not so sure.'

Catherine had managed to set Mike and Jan at each other's throats. They were competing for her approval while she alternately goaded them and praised them.

Was Catherine's manoeuvring automatic, Janet wondered, simply the way she handled everyone? Divide and dictate? Or was she deliberately undermining a relationship that did *not* exist?

Janet wished she could say flatly: 'Look, lady, there's no danger to you. I don't want Mike, and he doesn't want me.'

Mitchell Goldsworthy was undeniably attractive, very attractive, not only physically, but intellectually and emotionally. In many ways she and he were akin. Nonetheless, Jan reminded herself, any serious inclination she might once have felt towards Mike had been quashed by his behaviour towards her since that tragicomic night in Kashmir. If she had ever truly wanted him, she certainly did not want him now.

Yet, Jan acknowledged to herself forthrightly, she wanted, *needed*, a man. Even on the verge of her biggest opportunity, an earthshaking story, the hectic excitement and the preening self-importance of satnet life were not enough for her. She wanted another human being who shared her emotions and her values, wanted him badly. Despite the scars left by her one searing passion, she was ready to try again.

But not with Mitchell Goldsworthy, she told herself again, surveying the enormous reception room of the penthouse to keep her thoughts from showing on her face.

Two plaques now hung from the oversize chrome microphone on the strip of wall between the windows. One bore the motto often attributed to that conquering Caesar amid media moguls, Rupert Murdoch: *We want our viewers to be good citizens and moral persons, but it's our job to see that they have a good time!*

The second was still strictly in house while Alpha One experimented with the feelies, virtual reality: *After you've tried virtually everything else is plumb unreal!*

That, Janet mused, was the ultimate slogan. Alpha One's billions of viewers would soon be totally detached from the disorderly world previous generations had believed to be reality. Contrived images, counterfeit emotions, and induced sensations were more pleasant and more *real* for this generation than the frustration, pain, and occasional unforced joy of the chaotic material world.

All the senses would soon be deceived by electronic transmissions, and all wishes would be fulfilled! No need then for the myth of

Heaven! All that Heaven could offer would be available to almost every one of 6 billion humans right here on earth.

Why, Janet wondered, was Catherine Loomis, Empress of All the Realms of Unreality, working against her own interests? Alpha One's continuing growth was assured by continuing to project illusions. Yet Kate was encouraging her best team to explore the gritty reality lying outside the electronic circus tents scattered over the entire earth.

But how much leeway would she allow them? Some of their material was bound to be distasteful, perhaps even harmful to the Satcabnet. How far would she let them go?

Catherine Loomis lit a long cigarette tipped with a lipstick-red filter. Despite the vehement anti-tobacco propaganda of this tense era, she flaunted her smoking, as she did her tumultuous sex life. Yet she hardly ate at all, at least in public. Despite such conspicuous abstinence, despite her heavy smoking, she was always a little too plump. Today she was wearing a tight teal-blue skirt; to show off her excellent legs it barely came down to her knees. Her long overblouse of neutral beige was slashed on the sides to show off her tiny waist, while camouflaging her broad hips and her overblown bosom.

Sipping bourbon on the rocks, Catherine demanded, 'Mike, do you really believe Islamic fundamentalists're behind it all? Those nutters, religious maniacs running around in bedsheets and tea towels!'

'My money's on entropy,' he replied. 'The fundamentalists are just another symptom of entropy. When everything gets too complicated, systems break down and people go ape ... want to blow the whole world back to the ninth century.'

'You're just playing with words,' Catherine admonished. 'Don't be so bloody silly!'

'Sorry!'

Mike Goldsworthy smiled lazily, but tension knotted his forehead. To Janet's knowing eye, he was clearly enraged by that brusque put-down, Kate the Great at her most imperious.

Catherine Loomis might sleep with whom she pleased – and parade her sexual freebooting – but would, however, treat her favourites with no particular kindness in public, even with particular harshness.

'So we need to look for first causes.' Mike's rough-hewn features were set in a masklike grimace. 'Not being bloody silly, I'm pretty sure it's entropy. A symptom and a cause in itself. Take Ireland ...'

'Where's the entropy?' Catherine demanded.

'I see it.' Janet made up for earlier needling Mike by supporting him now. 'For all anyone can do, conflicts go on.'

'Head of the class, Jan!' Mike beamed, careless of irritating Catherine further. 'You want more entropy? The tired old European Union stumbles along, not splitting, just getting bigger and bigger – and vaguer and vaguer. It's broken down, but it goes on spinning.'

'What's all this,' Catherine demanded, 'got to do with terrorists in Bangkok and Jakarta?'

'It just shows again events don't occur logically and systems break up on their own, especially political systems. Do a couple of hundred million Muslims in Central Asia join the economic surge of East Asia or do they go for Islamic fundamentalism, that prime symptom of entropy? Meanwhile, they keep sniping at each other. They're sitting on fabulous mineral deposits, but they're too busy killing each other to use their natural wealth.'

'Where's all this going, Mike?' Catherine was impatient. 'Let's get back to *The Next Thousand Years*.'

'*No future without the past!*' Jan interjected. 'Our motto for the series. Also: *No past without the future!*'

'Thanks,' Catherine said shortly. 'Now let's get down to brass tacks. What're you planning to do with the mountain of raw data you're accumulating?'

'We want to look at the big trends,' Janet answered. 'Put them into historical perspective and project them into the future.'

'But they're so negative,' Catherine protested. 'I can't offer my audience unrelieved gloom.'

'Maybe projecting into the future, we'll find reasons for optimism.' Janet forgot Mike's warning to avoid environmentalism; it was the perfect answer – and Catherine was receptive. 'Meanwhile, there's one great big reason for hope.'

'And what may that be?'

'One group of good guys is getting stronger every day. They're working hard to preserve civilization ... to conserve all that's good in humanity and in the natural world.'

'Yes?'

'The environmentalists. They're fighting entropy in nature and in human society. And they're terrific on camera. Two great women performers: a Frenchwoman named Marie-Jeanne Erlanger and a Chinese woman called Vixen. Plus two top men: Prince Richard of Greece and Denmark and also Amadeus Brinks, who owns half of Brightman/Schreiner, but devotes his energy and his fortune to ecology. Amadeus Brinks is a great performer ... a wonderful man.'

'I wouldn't be so sure of that, my girl.' Catherine's voice was devoid of emotion. 'Amadeus isn't exactly what he appears.'

'You sound like you know him well, Catherine.' Mike tried to avert a confrontation.

'Yes, I know him. I know Amadeus Brinks very well ... too damned well.'

'But, Catherine, we can't ignore a major movement just because you don't like its leader!' Janet protested. 'Environmentalism is too vital to ignore. We've got to ...'

'Oh, can't we, young lady?' Catherine's colour was high, and her eyes were obsidian. 'Just watch me!'

X

The stream tugged at the green baseball cap pulled over the ears of the still figure in the mottled camouflage suit. The stream chortled as it tumbled along the ravine between two sparsely grassed dunes.

The stream had been born only two hours earlier, when a cloud-burst loosed a flash flood on the wrinkled face of the Takla Makan Desert 120 miles south-east of Lopnor, where the Beijing regime had once tested its nuclear missiles. After another two hours the stream would have ceased to exist.

The frail figure lay face down, swaying slightly under the buffeting of the torrent. Tugging insistently, the fast-flowing water tore the cap from the still head and carried it triumphantly away.

A long braid of red-tinged black hair uncoiled slowly. The young woman had hidden her braid under her grimy cap for her own comfort and to avoid reminding the men who were her fellow peace-warriors that she was different from them. Yet the concealed braid had been clasped with a gimcrack diamante clip mounted on a velvet bow whose cheap scarlet dye was now tingeing the glass-clear water.

That pathetic vanity brought tears to Marie-Jeanne Erlanger's pale-blue eyes. She blinked the traitorous moisture away, as ever determined to prove herself as tough as any man and more ruthless than most. But her throat tightened with pity for the slight young woman who had drowned in the shallow stream, which was already slackening as the earth drank in the floodwater.

Marie-Jeanne shivered in the morning cold and knelt. She gently turned the frail figure over. The sodden hair twined around her fingers as she lifted the head onto the sand beside the stream.

She and the young woman called Fatima had often laughed together at the idiocies of their male comrades. A passionate spirit had once looked out from the light-brown eyes with the dark irises that now stared at her utterly vacant, finally beyond both tears and laughter.

The slender Frenchwoman gently thumbed the bruised eyelids closed, sketched a cross in the air, and began to say an *Ave Maria*. Her sudden piety astonished herself. Marie-Jeanne had not been inside a church for eleven years and then only for a requiem mass for her mother.

Fatima herself had been a militant non-believer in any deity, an angry foe of all religion, whether organized or spontaneous. Above all, she hated and despised Islam, to which she had been born.

Rather a slave than a woman! Even her father, who loved her above her four brothers, had often reiterated that maxim to his sons to remind them of their own good fortune. That banal saying was to Fatima the quintessence of Islam, which humbled and oppressed women.

Nonetheless, Fatima loved her father. Unlike his friends' daughters, she had been given all the time he could steal from his work as a camel and horse trader.

She delighted in being his favourite, and she basked in her elder brothers' affection. But she realized as she approached fifteen, when she would be ripe for marriage, that she had to escape their harsh religion – and the narrow realm it created.

If she remained, she could expect to marry a clansman and enter a lifetime of subjugation. The abject subordination of women was as fundamental to Islam in practice as was in theory the immediate ascension of the warrior slain in battle to Heaven, where he would be attended by seven insatiable *houris*.

Fatima hated the Islamic fundamentalists. She despised Allah and denied Allah. But she feared His manifest wrath.

Her nomadic clan never approached closer to Semipalatinsk than sixty miles. They should have been safe from the pestilences that ravaged that city: spontaneous abortion; deformed new-borns, lacking arms or legs, ears or mouths, some with two heads; widespread blindness; blood pouring in cataracts from mouths, noses, ears; and, among other curses, sensible men and women suddenly babbling like demented children. But they were not safe.

Semipalatinsk was a centre of scientific research, which meddled with the world Allah had created. His anger was audible in thunderous earthquakes that shook buildings and shattered underground pipes, pouring sewage into the streets. His anger was visible in the clouds of debris-laden smoke that opened into great mushroom canopies several thousand feet high – and cast darkness over the land at midday.

One afternoon when she was almost fifteen, Fatima had been watching a pick-up game of polo played with a sheep's bladder stuffed with wool. Though no one touched him, nineteen-year-old Abu Bakar tumbled from his horse, shrieking in pain. His left leg was bent sharply, almost doubled over, and his foot had slipped out of the stirrup. Yet he had been riding easily an instant before he fell.

Her father was talking of her marrying Abu Bakar, the son of a wealthy sheep owner. Although she had sworn that she would run away rather than marry into a life of slavery, Fatima was fond of the young man. When he became an invalid trundled on others' backs, her father consoled her clumsily. It was a curse of Allah, he said, and Abu Bakar would soon be dead.

When she stole away from the clan encampment one cloudy night, the young man was already a haggard cripple who did not want to live. His face was splotched with great pustules, which drained continually and he refused to see anyone except those who looked after him. His father had sent for a shaman to drive out the demons, but the magician was too late.

Fatima had later learned that Semipalatinsk was afflicted not by evil demons, but by massive radioactivity. The region in Central Asia had been set aside by the Politburo in distant Moscow to develop and test nuclear weapons. It was administered by the KGB, the world's largest, most intrusive, and most ruthless secret police force. Above all, the Politburo did not want its own people or the world to know that it was testing sophisticated nuclear weapons under primitive conditions.

Doctors could, therefore, offer any diagnosis they wished, except the correct diagnosis: *poisoning by nuclear radiation*. Doctors might try any cure they wished, as long as the true complaint was not revealed. Twentieth-century physicians experimented like medieval alchemists with rigorous and painful cures for a complaint they knew, but could not name.

Between those who died and those who fled, the human population declined sharply. Even the fish died as the lakes were drained through fissures opened by nuclear explosions. Semipalatinsk was damned – a Martian landscape that poisoned souls as well as bodies.

The enormity of both Islamic fundamentalism and those man-made horrors heavy on her mind, Fatima had been an eager listener when the outriders of the ecological movement came to the clan's encampment. Outwardly good Muslims, they preached the conservation of the good earth which Allah had bestowed on man and beast. They declared that all men and all women were responsible for protecting the earth and all its denizens. Those scouts of the environmental movement would not alienate the clan elders by attacking female subjugation frontally, but their essentially secular message assumed the equality of women and men.

An enthusiastic recruit, Fatima had fled to the movement and had been swept up by it. To her extreme surprise, she had after several years' apprenticeship found herself studying biology at Cornell University on a Brightman/Schreiner scholarship. She had, however, volunteered for training as a peace-warrior in the assault battalions Amadeus Brinks was mobilizing as the shock troops of the ecological revolution.

'At some point,' he had told the trainees, 'it may become necessary to use force to assure the preservation of the earth. I mean, of course, minimum force applied discreetly to the worst malefactors. I pray to God that you will never be used. But if you are needed, you will be ready. You are my peace-warriors.'

Fatima had not been surprised to find herself training beside rabid Islamic fundamentalists. Grown wiser in the West, she recognized that the cause could be served in different ways by different human beings – as Christians said of the Lord of Heaven.

Looking down at Fatima's wan features, Marie-Jeanne barely kept herself from weeping. Fatima had died by the hand of Amadeus Brinks. He had killed her as surely as if he had shot her with a pistol.

'You must not pause for those who fall,' Brinks had instructed his platoon leaders. 'If a weakling falls, let him lie. Equally let *her* lie. Those who are basically fit will rally, recover, and reach camp by themselves. Those who are too weak to save themselves are not worth preserving. We must winnow the weak from our ranks.'

Fatima had been overcome by exhaustion during a night-long march staged to test the peace-warriors' mettle. Having disdained to claim the privilege of weakness at the onset of her painful monthly period, she had marched until she fell.

Fatima had then been abandoned by her fellow peace-warriors in obedience to Amadeus Brinks's orders. Left to struggle or perish, she might have recovered and made her own way back to camp. Or Marie-Jeanne might have found her and helped her homeward, having set out into the desert in defiance of Brinks's orders when the unit returned without Fatima. But the flash flood had found Fatima first and she had drowned.

Why, Marie-Jeanne wondered again, is Amadeus Brinks so ruthless? Why so brutal?

He truly felt profound compassion for humanity, indeed for all living beings – from whales to toadstools. She had seen his eyes tear when he had heard that the gorgeous green-and-gold paradise birdwing butterfly of New Guinea was verging on extinction. Wondering how he would react if it were the common brown clothes'-moth, she asked herself again; why did the man to whom they gave total allegiance test his devoted followers to destruction?

He would surely reply: *Our enemies will never cease their rapine and pillage of Mother Earth. We must be hard in mind and body, strong as titanium steel, if we are to overcome them.*

Amadeus had, however, just lost a valuable servant by his ruthlessness. Fatima could have given him greater access to the downtrodden women of Asia. She could have helped transform their inchoate longing for freedom and dignity into a force for the preservation of the living world.

But Amadeus had not really lost Fatima; he had thrown her away. She should, of course, never have been permitted to join the peace-warriors. Tough as her nomadic life had made her, she was too frail to march alongside those zealots.

Fatima was irreplaceable. Yet, Marie-Jeanne wondered, how many more Fatimas – and Abduls as well – would be sacrificed to Amadeus's vision of an irresistible élite force? Was he blinded by his own dedication?

That thought was ridiculous. Amadeus Brinks was the clearest in thought, the most acute in vision, and the most judicious in judgement of all the men and women she had ever known. He had already done so much. And he would do even more for the world when his forces attained the peak to which he was driving them.

Look at what he had wrought in the Aspet Valley. Bulldozers now rusted beside the unfinished Trans-Pyrenees Highway, and the big brown bears lived in peace in their sanctuary. A great victory for the forces of virtue.

And yet! And yet!

The Aspet Valley was now sunk in economic depression. The aborted promise of prosperity had blighted the valley dwellers' enthusiasm for new endeavours and had further deprived them of both customers and capital. No one would now invest in the Aspetoise who had so disappointed such great expectations. Entrepreneurs were withdrawing from the valley, as were all the young who could get away.

Patches of the forest made accessible by the partially completed highway were now invaded by licensed hunters. The big brown bears were forbidden game. Yet men wearing broad-brimmed hats and cartridge-heavy bandoleers trekked through the forest on the edge of the enclave to hunt wild boar, deer, and pheasants.

How long, Marie-Jeanne wondered, before a bear cub was shot 'inadvertently'? How long before the pristine environment was destroyed? What had their victorious struggle truly gained for the long run?

And yet! And yet!

The big brown bears *were* alive, and they were thriving. Two cubs had been born last autumn.

Amadeus was now engaged in even greater struggles. It would be a fatal mistake for him to become entangled in detail, tending to what the Americans called the nuts and bolts. Others could do that. And the big brown bears must, for the moment at least, be considered no more than nuts and bolts.

Above all, no excess of Amadeus's could damage the cause more severely than his followers' losing faith in him. Marie-Jeanne knew she *had* to believe. What else was there?

XI

'The biggest, the most artful, the most dangerous enemy of our cause is the satcabnets,' Amadeus Brinks told the smaller working group who were effectively his war cabinet, the stalwarts who had accompanied him from Xian to the secret training base south-west of Lopnor. 'They appeal to the lowest instincts of human beings, who are, after all, just relatively less hairy and marginally more intelligent monkeys.

'If monkey can do, monkey will do. That is why men went to the moon – only because it was possible, regardless of any true purpose or benefit to humanity. The latest technology will *always* be used, regardless of whether its effects are benign or malevolent.

'The hi-tech hucksters of the communications industry are like monkeys with machine-guns. Advanced digital techniques and fibre-optics have made it feasible to use thousands of TV channels. Six hundred are already in operation.

'What can we expect when six hundred gangs of hucksters are fighting over the vast but still finite audience? Naturally, broadcasters are hurtling downmarket. Since anything goes in the battle for audience, distortion is universal.

'Hucksters and audience are both subliminally altered. They will soon possess no moral standard whatsoever, no notion of a concept called morality.'

Brinks paused for translation into Japanese and Arabic for the Shinto high priest and Comrade Sheikh Semtex. No translation was necessary for the Vixen, for Marie-Jeanne Erlanger, or, naturally, for the former CIA agents known as Smith and Jones.

Brinks resumed: 'Viewers are inculcated with: Obscenity! Violence! Rudeness! Self-seeking! Hostility! Superficiality! All compressed into thirty-second takes. Dramas and so-called news shift constantly from scene to unrelated scene, even to unrelated plots. Some scenes last hardly twenty seconds.'

'Very interesting, but what's this to do with our mission?' the Shinto high priest intervened brusquely. 'The satcabnets are an irrelevance.'

'Hardly that, my good Matsumura.' Amadeus Brinks was unruffled. 'The satcabnets are *most* relevant to our mission. We shall have to fight them to get our message out. As you know, they control *all* communications. No one anywhere – not even in the dark fastnesses of Africa, Latin America or Siberia – can speak to anyone else at any distance without the satnets. Without the nets no one can order goods, whether shoes or helicopters. No one can earn a living or write a money-draft if he doesn't pay tribute to one of the six nets.

'Controlling all communications, they control the lives of all. If they wished, they could bring all human activity to a halt.

'They can punish fearfully any individual, corporation, or government that dares defy them. And they will undoubtedly attempt to sabotage our crusade!'

'You are entirely right, Comrade Amadeus.' The Vixen tossed her short black hair. 'I know a little about mass persuasion . . . .' The neo-Maoist activist paused for a titter at her sardonic wit.

'People today are far more malleable than they were under the old proletarian dictatorships,' the Vixen resumed. 'They used coercion to control their people: spies, threats and brutality. Men, women, and highly susceptible children are now moulded by the satnets with no need for coercion.'

'The people of today are the new lemmings,' Sheikh Semtex interjected. 'They throw themselves off cliffs into the warm seas of ignorance and self-indulgence.'

'Thank you, comrade.' Amadeus Brinks smiled. 'We take your point. Now shall we see the training?'

The working group was crowded into a sandbagged bunker to peer at the battlefield through narrow slits. The bunker was neither heated nor air-conditioned, and they sat on up-ended green boxes marked: *Ammunition, Tracer, .60 calibre*.

Barbed-wire entanglements were strung before the shallow trenches in front of the bunker. A shattered village stood a little way off, a few intact houses still capped by russet roof-tiles accentuating the surrounding desolation.

The sun was just beginning its retreat at four in the afternoon, and it was still very hot. It would be very cold after three hours.

The slim, former dirty tricks *honcho* of the Central Intelligence

Agency who called himself Smith stood behind a lectern in the dimly lit bunker. He twirled a swagger stick in his left hand and clutched a small microphone in his right.

'Ms Erlanger, Ms Tse Hu, and gentlemen,' he began. 'First thing you need to know is we don't fool around. You're gonna see an exercise the same in every respect as our daily training. The peace-warriors will come under fire with live ammo. They'll be dodging real grenades and real landmines.

'Also, just in case it ever happens, they'll run into a few puffs of nerve gas. It's not real ... too deadly to play games with. And the stuff's coloured purple to give them a break.

'Also, they see a coupla bacterial warfare training films showing what happens to rabbits, rats, and dogs that get hit by a new designer virus. But it's too gaddamned risky fooling around with real killer bugs.'

He flicked the name tag at his chest and added, 'My ... ah ... associate, Mr Jones, is out with the troops ... with the peace-warriors, that is. So is the head Mongol ... the fellow Mr Brinks calls Genghis Khan Number Two.'

In the gutted village 2,000 yards away, clearly visible through binoculars, floated a filmy substance. Alternately glinting pale violet in the afternoon sun and all but vanishing, the apparition drifted amid the charred beams that marked the main street.

'Nerve gas!' Smith observed.

A file of peace-warriors in mottled camouflage suits entered the street at the far end. They carried stubby turbo-rifles, and green-canvas pistol holsters hung from their webbing-belts. Trotting, almost running, the figures were clearly visible, but their faces were hidden by black masks with snoutlike protuberances.

Smith said: ' ... Forty-four, forty-five, forty-six. All present and accounted for.'

The sinister, faceless figures trotted awkwardly towards the trenches that scarred the earth before the bunker. Abruptly the first rank stopped.

A big apricot poodle was gambolling before them, and the trainees in front halted to avoid the unwary dog. The rest stumbled over their comrades and the entire unit halted as if on command.

Two figures in mottled combat suits strode to the fore of the unit. Although their faces were hidden by snouted masks, the short, stocky figure was surely the Mongol Temujin II. The tall, heavyset man beside him was as clearly the ex-CIA agent called Jones.

The Mongol snatched off his gas-mask to reveal a round face flushed with exertion and with rage. He bellowed, and the unit began to move again. Bunched into a compact mass, the trainees advanced at a trot.

In the bunker, Tse Hu, the Vixen, once Deputy Security Minister of the People's Republic of China, laughed harshly and translated the Mongol's command into precisely enunciated English: 'Nobody ordered a halt. Move your asses, your pricks and cunts. I don't care if it's the Devil himself. Run it down if it won't get out of the way!'

The apricot poodle darted back and forth before the unit, which was now advancing at a hard trot. The poodle made a playful feint at the foremost trainees. When none responded, it lay down on its back. Rolling to and fro, the poodle barked loudly, inviting caresses.

The vanguard paused for an instant, recoiling minutely. Glancing fearfully at the Mongol, the trainees picked up an even faster pace. None recoiled when they ran the poodle down.

The group in the bunker saw the dog vanish among the peace-warriors. They did not see the dog trampled underfoot, but they heard a scream uncannily like an infant's wail abruptly cut off.

Almost upon the barbed wire protecting the trenches, the unit halted on command. Three figures in the first rank were bloody-legged, their camouflage trousers stained with bits of fur and tissue.

One pulled off his gas mask to reveal a sallow pockmarked face above a black beard. He shrieked in fury at the Mongol.

'Filthy Buddhist idolater,' the Vixen translated. 'Contaminating a good Muslim with dog's blood! What's next? Filthy pork?'

The Mongol laughed and pushed the trainee away. He gestured, unmistakably commanding the enraged Muslim to return to the ranks. Instead, the Muslim snatched his pistol from the holster on his webbing-belt.

The hog-fat ex-CIA agent called Jones stepped behind the enraged Muslim and pressed his pistol against the man's neck. With the muted report, the Muslim crumpled. He twitched violently then lay still.

'I told you so!' Smith exulted in the bunker. 'I told you we don't fool around!'

XII

'More and more, more people are flying more – and enjoying it less and less!'

Mike Goldsworthy offered the virtually obligatory parody of the slogan of Universal Global Airways, which controlled ninety-two per cent of all international flights – scheduled or charter. *More and more*, that slogan asserted, *more people are flying more – and enjoying it more and more!*

'Every flight's an ordeal,' he added. 'You're lucky to get a super-class seat.'

'Who're you kidding, Mike?' The prospect of flying always made Janet irritable. 'Remarkable if I hadn't. D'you really think Global's going to spit in the eye of Alpha One?'

They were waiting for her much delayed non-stop flight to Singapore while sipping papaya juice and rum in the bamboo and Thai-silk VIP lounge of the New York Jetport.

The runway had been built into the Bay for protection against marauders, who, nonetheless, mounted occasional hit-and-run raids by speedboat. The barbed wire and sandbagged land entrance was patrolled by rangers wearing kylar-titanium body armour. Marauders had made it perilous to use La Guardia and Kennedy Airports on Long Island.

'Sorry I snapped at you just now.' Janet raised her glass in a concil-iatory toast. 'Airports always make me edgy. And the thought of being catapulted in a Super-797 Concord ... a fragile two hundred-ton aircraft shot like a stone from a slingshot!'

'Anyway, you're on your way,' Mike comforted her. 'I know you're praying they wait till you get to Singapore to blow the place up.'

Although automatically tense before the flight, Jan was more relaxed with the new amity that had prevailed between herself and Mike since they tacitly agreed that in the series *The Next Thousand*

Years their interests were virtually identical. It might prove only a brief ceasefire before hostilities were resumed, but it was very pleasant to be able to speak to him easily and candidly.

'You know, Mike, for a while I thought I'd never make it. Kate the Great was really furious with me, wasn't she?'

'So she was. But, by her lights, she's fair. What'll help Alpha One, she's for; anything that could hurt Alpha One in any way, she's against. Thinks it's evil.'

'What a convenient moral code!'

'Nobody said she was *Saint* Catherine. Just be glad she believes your Singapore assignment is good for Alpha One. And that she stays convinced that we ... you and I ... make a great team.'

'But she's glad to see the back of me for a while? Why's she *so* angry.'

'On the environmental business, you mean?'

'What else?'

'Jan, I promise we'll give the environmentalists as much coverage as they deserve. We'll praise or condemn just as they deserve. Just leave it to me.'

'The last time you asked me to trust you . . . .'

'That was another time and another Goldsworthy, the bad old Goldsworthy. The reformed new Goldsworthy is a hundred and ten per cent trustworthy.'

Janet stifled the automatic jibe with which she would have responded only a week ago and asked, 'It's not just a reporting issue with Catherine, is it?'

'It's not the cause she hates, though the tree-huggers and the snake-cuddlers really get under her skin when they get going on mental pollution by the satcabnets.'

'Then it's Amadeus Brinks himself?'

'She loathes Brinks. She'd happily see him boiled in oil, preferably *after* he was publicly castrated.'

'Why, Mike?'

'The usual reason. He picked her out when she was nothing, a lousy little stenographer in Liverpool. He picked her out and trained her ... remade her.'

'Was she his mistress?'

'I can't believe she wasn't, though she's unusually coy on the subject. Normally she likes to shock ... to keep me in line by talking about her scandalous past. But she dries up after cursing Mr Brinks. I'd guess he tossed her out in a particularly humiliating way.'

'You know, Mike,' Janet said impulsively, 'you're not such a bad old stick when you let yourself go.'

'Thanks, Jan,' he grinned. 'You're a pretty good old broad yourself when you stop hassling everybody, specially me.'

'Mike, why do we act that way? Why're we all elbows and brass-knuckles ... nasty cracks and dirty tricks?'

'It's the business, Jan. We can't let up for more than an instant – or somebody'll walk all over us. Catherine can't let up for even an instant.'

'I can see that in her case, Mike. She's got to be in perpetual motion or she'll topple over. Because of her anxieties ... her sad background. If she lost the satnet, she'd be nothing, absolutely nothing. A nonentity after being an empress. Very hard to take ... excruciating. Practically cause for suicide.'

'Don't worry about Kate the Great. She's not the type that commits suicide. She makes others commit suicide.'

'But we, Mike, you and me, we don't come from that kind of background. We don't define ourselves ... base our entire identity ... on our jobs. Somehow, though, we fall into typical satnet behaviour. We run as fast as we can in the beginning and then can't stop ourselves, no matter who we jostle, knock over and trample.'

'That's about it, Jan. Though with you and me it's different. I really don't understand why you make me so goddamned angry sometimes. But you do.'

'But we'll be all right on *TNTY*, won't we? It's too important for us to squabble.'

'Totally important, Jan. If we make this a good one, it'll make up for everything else I'm ... we're ... not so proud of: the ass-kissing, the hyped stories, the fake stories, and the absurd oversimplifications. I'll even feel good about myself. For a while, at least.'

At a moment like this, virtually unique in their relationship, Mike had to remind himself of his basic rule: he would never, *not ever*, get seriously involved with a satnet woman. They were all too tough, too competition-centred, too integral a part of a world he had to forget from time to time if he were to remain sane.

What if it hadn't worked with Lizbeth? There had to be someone out there, far from Alpha One, with whom he could make a go of it.

The red-jacketed steward rose from the reception desk and approached them. Nothing as crass as a loudspeaker for the VIP lounge. He bowed slightly and said, 'Ms Seager, your flight is ready for boarding.'

*

America, Jan reflected, had produced the most successful commercial aircraft the world would ever know in the Boeing 700 series. American aircraft companies had subsequently transferred much technology to their East Asian partners, albeit grudgingly. The Super-797 Concord was the finest fruit of that collaboration. A little longer than a 747-400 and just as wide, it could carry a full commercial payload, as the needle-thin original Concorde could not. Nor did its top speed of 950 m.p.h. make the same demands on metallurgy, avionics, or pilots as had the 1,400 m.p.h. Concorde.

The Super-Concord was also gloriously opulent. Every possible entertainment was available, even virtudramas, as was instantaneous communication to any part of the world. Super-class passengers, VIPs all, were coddled with luxurious beds, as well as with bountiful dinners and splendid wines.

The vibrant colours of the cabin, reassuring to apprehensive passengers on this early evening departure, would be muted and restful after takeoff. Before the landing at Singapore, the entire cabin would glow crimson and violet to match the sunrise. Thus subliminally cheered, super-class passengers would face the new day with renewed confidence – and would presumably make a mental note to fly Super-Concord again.

The lower class, super coach, was not enlivened by such psychological magic, for the Super-Concord had to pay its way. Universal Global Airways could not charge enough for super-class seats to reclaim its costs; besides, most super-class passengers flew on complimentary tickets.

If super class were a foretaste of an exclusive heaven, super coach was purgatory. Haunch to haunch, legs bent double, cramped around their own luggage, super-coach passengers suffered to pay for the Super-Concord's flights. Advanced technology was expensive.

Yet all airline passengers were like medieval travellers with caravans through the forests of Northern Europe or across the deserts of Central Asia. Medieval travellers had feared attack by brigands or marauding barons whenever they were outside the sanctuary of a fortified monastery, a walled city, or an oasis. Twenty-first-century air passengers hurtled from one haven to another across wildernesses where civilization was giving way to hi-tech savagery. A forced landing could plunge them instantly into a new purgatory. The lucky would be traded for ransom by local despots; the unlucky would disappear, their misfortune having been to survive the crash.

A half-dozen small conflicts were always in progress across the globe as warlords contended for land, for treasure, and for power. They were not mere clashes, but wars that killed thousands and maimed tens of thousands.

Most warlords possessed nuclear weapons. Some they bought from criminal syndicates like the Union Corse, the Yamaguchi Gumi, and South China's 24K Triad Society, as well as from Balkan and Caucasian gangs with unpronounceable names. Those enterprising merchants of death stole the doomsday weapons by bribing officers of the guard.

But conventional weapons were always available in great quantity from legal dealers. Prince Richard charged that the high civilization, the hi-tech purveyors of death, encouraged conflict and thus preyed on the impoverished of the earth.

Janet came to the bleak terminus of that train of thought after dinner while sipping Viparo, the bitter black liqueur from the hills of Umbria. Having decided that she would not attempt to catch up on the constant reading her work demanded, she was free to muse. Smiling away the steward who flourished the big bottle invitingly, she closed the door of her stateroom.

Despite the soothing soft lighting, despite the muted strains of old Admiral Rimsky-Korsakov's *In a Persian Garden*, despite the fragrance of night-blooming stock wafted through the stateroom, her expression was strained as she undressed. She looked wary and defensive, though hardly defenceless.

'This story is make or break,' she lectured herself as she creamed her face. 'I've never smelled gunpowder ... never seen the carnage of a battlefield. Here's the chance to make up for it!'

Slipping into bed, she smiled ruefully, and told herself, 'Nobody ever said satnet reporting was easy, not if you want to stay honest. Especially not for a woman! There *are* other things, but I'm not ready yet for baby buggies and nappies. Besides, a baby needs a father, if only to get it started. But there's not a potential father in sight.'

When the aircraft swooped on the skyscrapers of Singapore, Janet felt she might almost be returning to New York, so high and so steplike was the skyline. The German who was Universal Global Airways' vice president for Asia came aboard to greet her and apologize. The bristling independent little city-state would *not* waive Customs and Immigration formalities for Universal's sake – or for Janet Seager's.

But the swift check by courteous officials was hardly an ordeal. Besides, the atmosphere was more like an efficient cathedral than a busy terminal. She had known much worse receptions in the US, but none better.

Janet deftly turned aside the vice president's invitation to the dinner his wife was giving the next evening, explaining that she had to work. Normally, she would have been delighted to accept; the ready-made introductions of a dinner party would open doors for her. But she declined, afraid of the news of her arrival spreading.

'You've had instructions from New York, haven't you?' she asked. 'No publicity at all ... no mention of my arrival.'

'Yes, of course,' he replied. 'But I thought just a small dinner. We've asked a few interesting people to meet you.'

'Normally, I'd be delighted. But I'm afraid not. You know Singaporeans go mad over Alpha One personalities. I can't work if I'm being mobbed.'

'They're all very discreet, my guests . . . .'

'Well, I'll see. Anyway, I'm grateful.'

The vice president gave her his visiting card after handing her into the Jaguar-Daimler sent by the Mandarin Oriental Hotel. Snug in the lightly air-conditioned, faintly jasmine-scented limousine, Janet peered out through the one-way glass and was disappointed.

The roads were broad and uncluttered; the buildings were sleek and hyper-modern; the pedestrians were orderly and purposeful. No sign of the romantic white-pillared mansions or the open-fronted shop-houses the name Singapore evoked. No trace of the colourful and tumultuous streets she had expected. If almost all the pedestrians had not been Chinese, Indians or Malays, she could have been on the East Side of Manhattan or in Beverly Hills. Except, of course, the people on the streets of Manhattan or Beverly Hills were neither as well dressed nor as well behaved as the Singaporeans.

Janet slipped out her purse-mirror and scrubbed off her raspberry lipstick. Creaming off mascara and eyeliner, she added a few lines with her eyebrow pencil, and applied a pale face powder. Like the stage, the satnets taught you quick make-up tricks. When she looked into the mirror again, she was pallid and drawn.

Now she only had to slip on a pair of oversize sun-glasses and a big straw hat. Her glossy black hair and her matte-white skin were her trademark. No one would associate the washed-out creature she saw in her mirror with the glamorous Janet Seager they saw on their screens.

A portly man in a cutaway and striped trousers stepped forward to greet her when the Jaguar halted, and Janet felt guilty. Not only was the Oriental's general manager, who was Mike Goldsworthy's good friend, to be disappointed by her drab appearance, he was to be balked of the publicity he must expect to garner from her visit.

'Miss Seager, delighted!' He opened the car door and extended a hand to help her step out into humid warmth that reeked deliciously of strange fruits and strong spices. 'Mike rang me. We're delighted to have you with us.'

'Ms Thompson,' she corrected him. 'While I'm here, I'm Ms Juliet Thompson of *Eve* magazine.'

'I see,' he said. 'Actually, I don't really see. You *are* Janet Seager, aren't you?'

She acknowledged her identity and explained why she was incognito and in disguise.

Installed in a three-room suite on the fourteenth floor, with two amahs in white tunics unpacking her suitcases, Janet chuckled at the manager's confusion. Among the messages awaiting her was a note from Alpha One News's local correspondent, Diminity Oei, who declared that she was at Ms Seager's disposal night and day. Janet swept into the waste-paper basket twenty-six invitations to dinner and requests for interviews from station owners, directors and reporters. She must simply disappear, since she could not appear in public in her own identity.

Janet yawned. On second thought, she decided muzzily, she would accept the invitation of the Universal Airways vice president. What was his name? She fished in her capacious travel handbag and found under a lipstick, missing its cap, the small pasteboard card bearing his name. There it was, the UGA logo in scarlet and green and beneath it: Johannes Graf von Erbschlichter.

The man himself was urbane, quite undisturbed at being telephoned at one in the morning.

No, he said, it was no imposition at all. He was used to untimely telephone calls. Besides it could never be an imposition, but a pleasure to be of the slightest assistance to the beautiful and famous Ms Janet Seager.

He was delighted that she could come. And, yes, he would introduce her as Ms Juliet Thompson. Of course, he added, they would all know who she was, but they would be very discreet.

Besides, he and his wife, Ingeborg, would enjoy the transparent impersonation, which was like something out of a Renaissance *commedia dell'arte*. Shedding his continental suavity for an instant,

Johannes Erbschlichter actually said he and Ingeborg would get a big kick out of the masquerade.

XIII

Spending an entire day with Diminity Oei, pronounced *Wee*, was exhausting. The granddaughter of the second president of Singapore, she was short, dark, volatile and tireless. Delighted to conspire to keep Janet's identity secret, she managed to charm, cajole or bamboozle both officials and tycoons into giving the unknown Ms Juliet Thompson the same attention, facilities, and information they would have given the famous Janet Seager. Of course, most of them recognized her as Janet Seager anyway.

By four in the afternoon of her first full day in Singapore, Jan felt she had done a good day's work. She had spoken to Mike Goldsworthy on the view circuit, and he had assured her that all was well at his end. What's more, she had film for a feature on Singapore's crocodile and ostrich farms, which she had yet to see. She had also gained a general impression of the hard-working, spick-and-span city that lay under threat of a mass terrorist attack.

The city-state of 3½ million people, most of them materialistic and agnostic Chinese, was a multiracial, multicultural, and multirelgious island in an Islamic sea. Quasi-theocratic Malaysia lay to the north and spottily fanatical Indonesia to the south. Singapore was, therefore, always on the alert, like Israel among the Muslims of the Middle East. From what she had learned that day regarding military and civil defence preparations, Janet wondered how any terrorist could hope to penetrate Singapore's bamboo-and-steel screen.

She was now well prepared to cover any outrage that might occur. The salient facts and the all-important atmospherics of Singapore and its role in East Asia were embedded in her mind, so that she could ad lib authoritatively. Now she need only deploy the twenty-three researchers, camera crew, sat-communications specialists, computer wizards, and producers of her team.

Smiling at such self-indulgence at four in the afternoon, Janet lay down to nap under the imperial-yellow tribute silk canopy of the seven-foot-square bed in the master bedroom. Tomorrow, she would edit, voice, and transmit her feature on the crocodile and ostrich farms to keep her face on screen. She might even find time to have a quick look at those breeding centres. Meanwhile, a nap before the dinner at Johannes and Ingeborg Erbschlichter's.

'Everybody calls me Johnnie,' Janet's host greeted her at the door of his eighty-sixth floor penthouse in Universal Global House just off Orchard Road. 'You, too, I hope.'

Having taken little notice of him at the airport, Janet looked again at Johannes Erbschlichter. He was truly more of an old shoe Johnnie than an imposing Johannes: round, short, and grey-haired with soft blue eyes set in chubby cheeks.

Ingeborg Erbschlichter was half a head taller than her husband, lean and slightly faded, her skin crêpy with fine lines. She offered Janet a crystal flute of champagne from the silver salver proffered by a diminutive Filipino butler in a white jacket.

'Roederer Cristal, Miss Seager?' Johnnie asked. 'It's 1977, the best vintage since the fifties. or would you prefer the 1983 Dom Perignon?'

'Ms Thompson,' Janet corrected. 'Ms Juliet Thompson of *Eve* magazine, temporarily on assignment for Alpha One. Please remember, Johnnie. And do call me Julie.'

'Fine, Julie. My beloved Inge will introduce you to the others. I have to see to the wine.'

Janet wondered why on earth her host had to see to the wine. Besides the butler, she had seen a Filipina in a black dress and a white apron carrying another salver laden with champagne, presumably the less-favoured Dom Perignon. She had also seen two young Caucasian women in the same garb. Australians, she assumed.

Filipino servants were now hard to find, Diminity Oei had told her. The Erbschlichters, she said, paid their Filipino couple twice the going wage and kept them on largely for swank. Australians were not only harder workers, but gladly accepted lower wages, eager to send money home to their distressed families.

In the drawing-room, Louis XV armchairs were grouped with Regency settees under the gaze of late Victorian portraits. Just touching her elbow, Ingeborg Erbschlichter guided her. All the men she met wore crisp white dinner jackets. The women had brought out their most-elaborate finery, and cascades of jewels flashed in the light of crystal chandeliers. All were obviously well-to-do; most were Chinese, though there was a sprinkling of Indians and Caucasians; and most were smugly self-important.

Janet shook forty hands and murmured gratitude for their adulatory remarks. All the guests obviously knew that she was Janet Seager, not the mythical Ms Juliet Thompson, despite her dowdy brown dress.

She could have worn her gold-and-crimson Pucci-Matsumura, Janet reflected, the one she had thrown in at the last moment in case she had to attend a state function. The stiff fabric embroidered with firebirds and stylized clouds in metallic thread had been woven for a Japanese wedding kimono, the kind that could cost as much as $250,000 nowadays. God knew what Pucci-Matsumura would have charged anyone else. She had paid $35,000 and had given a vague promise to wear it in public, especially in Asia, where the best customers lived.

Janet remembered Samapathi Namboodripad and mourned in silence for the ebullient Alpha One General Manager for Asia, who had died in the Bangkok bombing. She missed his Edwardian gallantry and his sly humour. Above all, she missed his shrewd guidance. If Sammy were at her side, he would have told her the name, the pedigree, and the bank balance of everyone present.

'Mr Fellows ... George Fellows,' Ingeborg Erbschlichter murmured. 'May I present you to a compatriot of yours, Miss Sea—ah, Thompson.'

'Ms!' Janet snapped, staying in character. 'Miss is for young women in the marriage ... the slave ... market, selling their bodies for luxuries. I'm self-supporting ... an independent woman. Call me Ms.'

Abashed by her own tirade, Janet glanced up at the man called George Fellows. He was smiling broadly, apparently amused by her outburst. The smile did not reach his expressionless, dark-green eyes.

'Charmed, *Ms* Thompson . . . .' The heavily stressed Ms was clearly ironic. 'I haven't heard such feminist eloquence for years. You take me back to my misspent youth.'

'Which was not so long ago,' Janet replied. 'We've met before, haven't we?'

'Regrettably, no!' Fellows replied. 'I could never forget anyone so striking, Ms ... ah ... Thompson.'

'You're sure?' Janet uncharacteristically persisted. 'There's something about you that's so familiar. I wonder . . . .'

Somehow she felt that George Fellows was no more what he appeared to be than she was what she appeared to be. Something about him was pleasurably reminiscent, particularly his nonchalant manner and his off-hand attentiveness.

'Of course, I know you, Ms Thompson.' He chuckled. 'You're the famous Ms Juliet Thompson of Satcabnet Alpha One, aren't you? Always on the air.'

'Guilty,' she conceded. 'For God's sake, call me Janet. I'm dropping this Juliet Thompson act for tonight. It's only I can't work in public if everyone knows ... I get mobbed and . . . .'

'I understand. No need to explain, Janet.'

Something about the way he said *Janet* piqued her, the slight prolongation of the first vowel, the hint of a Virginia drawl. She *knew* she had met him somewhere, sometime, however briefly.

That half-recollection was annoying, for he was interesting. His beautifully cut white dinner jacket set off his light tan. He was not too tall, almost six feet, just tall enough. He moved as lithely as an athlete, yet he was almost assertively relaxed. A thought, a name, fluttered at the back of her mind. Something about that ultra-casualness and that air of total self-confidence, as if he'd just stepped off an Ivy League campus.

'Mr Fellows is doing some hush-hush work with Johnnie,' Ingeborg Erbschlichter explained. 'He's executive vice president of Everbright Software and Avionics.'

'Bright for Brightman/Schreiner,' Fellows volunteered. 'We're a B & S company.'

Janet was silent in amazement. It could not be! Yet it had to be! The connection with aviation had opened the lock on her memory.

It had to be the same man. True, his eyes had been golden-brown and lively, not the flat, dark-green disks that now looked out from his mobile features. And his hair had been dark, falling over his forehead. His brush cut was now blond streaked with grey, almost silver-gilt.

But contact lenses easily change eye colour, and any good barber could have transformed his hair in half an hour. Unless he had a twin brother, it could only be Lieutenant Salisbury Smith, Berry Smith, the navy pilot.

Mildly embarrassed, Janet remembered details. They'd had a torrid affair about five years ago. He had been very attentive until summoned by a telephone call from a senior admiral's young second wife. They had parted without regrets, without recriminations, and without illusions. Explaining candidly, almost gracefully despite his essential crassness, that all his hope of promotion rode with the admiral's wife, he had said a hasty goodbye and left within a half-hour.

At the last moment of their brief parting, she had, however, told him briskly, 'Berry, it's been fun. But never come back!'

Nonetheless, Janet felt a certain pleasure at meeting him again. Berry Smith was a man who instinctively pleased women. But that would be all now. Nothing else! He was too much the butterfly, swooping from flower to flower. He was also far too self-centred.

Why, Jan wondered, this masquerade? Hadn't she heard that he had vanished in a plane crash? Certainly she had. She remembered clearly now. He had vanished on that black Tuesday when eight airplanes went down.

Yet here he was, undoubtedly alive, though sailing under false colours. Well, she would not call his bluff as he had called hers. She would let him think he was undetected. He was sure to give himself away in time.

XIV

'Don't be so blamed impatient, Jan. Give it a little more time.'

His back to Janet Seager, the man who called himself George Fellows watched the oncoming dusk from the balcony of his seventeenth-storey duplex in Brightman/Schreiner House overlooking the American Club and the Goodwood Park Hotel. Having all his life played one role or another, though rarely himself, he was at ease within the fraudulent skin of the green-eyed, silver-haired aeronautical engineer. Nonetheless, Lieutenant Commander Salisbury Smith, posted *missing* by the US Navy, hardly troubled to dissemble with Janet.

Although she did not confront him, she was now certain that he was not George Fellows, but Salisbury Smith. And he knew it was too late for him to protest credibly that he knew nothing about the Berry Smith she thought he resembled. It was too late to put her off the scent.

Perhaps, he told himself, he was too casual about the risk of her telling the world that George Fellows was not what he said he was. He had always been too casual. That was the bane of his life. Still, he suffered from neither ulcers nor high blood pressure, unlike so many of his more zealous contemporaries.

Of course, he should have vigorously maintained his false identity when he met her again at Johnnie Erbschlichter's party. He should then have left on some pretext and thereafter taken great care never to run into Janet Seager again.

But how could he? How could he spurn the provocative smile that made her eyes glow sapphire? How could he reject the sensual promise of her full lower lip and her subtly rounded body?

His brother officers, his *former* brother officers, had leered, only half joking, that he was a cad who preyed on women. In truth, women preyed on him. He was the victim, for he simply could not resist an attractive woman who responded to his charm.

Janet, he saw, responded strongly. Evidently seeing through his deception, she was presumably waiting for him to reveal himself – and to justify himself.

In truth, Janet had coolly decided to play a waiting game. After all, she had broken off the affair though she sometimes wondered whether he had not stage-managed his dismissal at her hands. Was it only that he was monumentally selfish and fearful of making any commitment? Might it not have been gallant to let her believe the decision was hers, rather than his?

Janet brought herself up sharply. She could go on forever alternately finding reason to excuse him and reason to condemn him. But why should she deny herself the pure pleasure she felt each time she saw him anew?

She had decided to play a waiting game, but she had not reckoned with her own emotions. She was not just casually attracted to the man with whom she'd had a fleeting affair, a joyous carnal fling, five years earlier, she was strongly drawn to Berry Smith and not just physically. His presence not only stirred her, but made her feel secure, which was, to say the least, odd under the circumstances. He could become a habit – even an addiction.

Meanwhile, she enjoyed teasing him gently and making him plead with her to stay in Singapore. Mischievously, she repeated her earlier remark, 'No point in hanging around. I'll reserve a seat to New York tomorrow.'

'Just hold your horses, Jan,' he reiterated. 'Give it another week or so.'

'I've already given it nearly two weeks, Berry,' she replied. 'I can't keep feeding Alpha One bland features and warnings of impending doom. I need hard news.'

'Just a few more days. Tell your Kate the Great you'll end the vigil after four or five days. I'm sure it'll blow before then.'

'How can you be so sure, Berry?' She liked that pet name, which he no longer protested. 'Have you got a direct line to the mastermind?'

'I hear things. Johnnie Erbschlichter's office is a cave of the winds: whispers from all around the globe. Also my own sources.'

'What do they tell you? Armageddon tomorrow? Much as I enjoy dallying with you, my dear, I have a living to make … a career to tend.'

'Just trust me, Jan. You don't want to miss …'

'That old line again, Berry? Don't you know it went out with buggy whips and high-button shoes? *Just trust me, darling. You don't want to miss the greatest experience of your life, do you?* I've heard it a hundred times from men trying to hustle me into bed . . . Now, about this upcoming Armageddon . . . .'

Professional instinct kept her boring in, although she was virtually certain he would not tell her *how* he knew the assault on Singapore was coming very soon. Yet he was obviously certain. He was not pretending just to keep her in Singapore.

She probably would have lingered a few more days regardless. Sincere or not, Berry Smith was wildly attractive – to her, at least. In part it was his devil-may-care manner, so tantalizing that she sometimes totally forgot Alpha One when he was near. It was also his deceptively slim body. His shoulders were powerful, rather than overdeveloped, sloping like Michelangelo's *David*, and his forearms were knotted with muscle.

She had not asked Alpha One to look again into the disappearance of the Concordia Execujet he had been flying. Any new enquiry could set off a chain reaction – tearing off his mask, humiliating him, and condemning him to a court martial for desertion.

Yet she would not trust him professionally, much less emotionally, until he owned up to his true identity. He would have to explain both his disappearance and his present masquerade. No matter how much she wanted him, she would continue to fend him off until then. Going to bed with Salisbury Smith, alias George Fellows, would be like making love to a shop-window dummy. She would be sleeping with a myth, a fabrication, not a man.

Yet she had discovered qualities in this new man that the old Berry Smith did not possess. He now displayed a sensitivity that he had notably lacked in the past. He was now in tune with her emotionally, responsive to her feelings. He was also better attuned to the world in general, no longer so self-centred.

He had during their meetings over the past two weeks spoken with understanding about the Islamic fundamentalists, who, she believed, posed a mortal threat to the world order. You had to consider their past, he'd said, centuries of humiliation by the technologically and militarily superior West. Naturally, the fundamentalists thirsted for revenge. Yet, he'd said, common ground could be found on which the adversaries could compromise and make peace.

The old Berry Smith had given just as much thought to the threat of a new ice age as he had to the golden Mexican tree toad – that is, no thought at all. This new Berry Smith, alias George Fellows, was deeply concerned about the rape of Nature and was working hard to make jet aircraft less damaging to the ecological balance.

A little cynical about some of the environmental groups, he spoke with near awe of Amadeus Brinks. Such respect for anyone outside himself was also remarkable.

'Jan, about your new Armageddon,' he said slowly. 'The attack is sure to come soon. But it won't be any Armageddon; just a short, sharp lesson.'

Janet joined him at the railing, and slipped her hand into his. Dusk was almost upon Singapore, the brief, ardent dusk of the deep tropics. Lights were flickering all across the city, and floodlights glared on the stick figures playing tennis on the American Club's courts. In the distance, the skyscrapers that palisaded Raffles Place and Collier Quay along the waterfront were garlanded with brightness. Berry squeezed her hand and turned to kiss her.

When Janet pulled away, he looked hurt. She pointed and said, 'Look! Berry, over there!'

The horizon glowed red behind the skyscrapers, and their lights dimmed against that new radiance. An instant later, thunder rolled across the city, crashing again and again. Jan's eyelids trembled and her eardrums ached. The skyscrapers quivered in the shock waves, swaying perceptibly.

The red glow in the night sky gave way for an instant to utter darkness, for the skyscrapers' bright windows were no longer bright. The tropical night was, however, now lit by the yellow glare of fires below reflected by the clouds.

'Dear God!' Janet said softly. 'So they weren't just threatening. Dear merciful God!'

A second explosion dyed the sky over the waterfront a deeper red, almost scarlet. In that new radiance Janet glimpsed debris falling back to earth. A human shape pinwheeled downward, arms and legs outstretched. This was no fireworks display, no mock conflagration for the camera. Men and women were dying on the enormous pyre that was Singapore's financial district.

'Good God!' Salisbury Smith echoed her words. 'I never thought it would be ...'

Janet pounced on his exclamation and demanded, 'You never would've thought *what*? You knew this was coming, didn't you? Tell me, Berry! For God's sake, tell me who's behind this ... this hellfire!'

'I can't do that!' His denial was an admission. 'Not now!'

For a moment, he gazed silently at the flames leaping above the skyscrapers. When he spoke again, his tone was flat.

'Look, Jan, I have to go. They snatched me up for civil defence duty. What about you? Shouldn't you get in touch?'

'God, yes!' She took her minisat communicator from the capacious handbag that was always with her. 'So long, Berry. Let me know . . . .'

'New York flash!' Janet commanded the hairline microphone-slit in the black face of the three-inch cube of the minisat communicator. When the metallic voice of an inforobot answered, she voiced her bulletin.

'All net flash from Janet Seager in Singapore: at 6.17 p.m. local time Thursday, two massive explosions rocked downtown Singapore. They appeared to be forerunners of the threatened all-out attack. Muslim extremists have promised to punish the city-state they call a nest of vice, "a new Sodom and Gomorrah". Some buildings in the downtown financial and business district appear to have been shattered by the explosions. There is no information yet on how the explosions were triggered. This is Janet Seager of Alpha One in stricken Singapore. More soonest.'

That should hold them for a few minutes, she told herself, tucking the minisat communicator away. Before she could zip up her handbag, Mike Goldsworthy spoke to her.

'So you were right.' He might have been standing beside her. 'Now go get the story! We're giving you all nets clearance, audience of 1.2 billion . . . . By the way, you are all right, aren't you, Jan?'

'Yes,' she murmured, 'I'm fine, thanks. More very soon, Mike.'

Why, Janet wondered, were the men she attracted so matter of fact? Both took for granted her well-being amid danger, as if she were made of carbon-fibre or some other imperishable substance! I never said, she told herself, that I wanted to be treated as one of the boys.

Her eye was caught by the TV screen in the living-room, where her image shone, lifted from archive videotape. Loudspeakers boomed the report she had transmitted a minute earlier.

Next time, she told herself, I'll let the minisat send my picture as I say my piece, though the engineers in New York did not like using the minisat to transmit video as well as audio. They had to work too hard to bring the picture up to minimal broadcast standard, and it was still hazy and flat compared to the cameras' three-dimensional image. But a minisat picture was better for her than archive footage. Even a muzzy picture would convey the dramatic reality of her presence in embattled Singapore.

The minisat spoke peremptorily from the cluttered depths of her handbag: 'Juliet ... Ms Juliet Thompson, are you there? Oh, hell. Jan ... Janet Seager, please come in. This is Diminity Oei!'

Janet took the three-inch cube from her bag and keyed it to receive picture as well as sound.

'You're coming through clear, Diminity,' she said. 'What've you got for me?'

'Great confusion even at police headquarters!' The small pigtailed figure in white skirt and white blouse smiled ruefully. 'But some facts are beginning to emerge. I'm with the deputy commissioner in command of the Anti-Terrorism Unit.'

'What does he say? Quickly now. They're holding the network for me.'

'You will credit me, Jan?'

'Yes, of course, Diminity. Though the credit may get cut out. And they'll never use you on camera if they can get me.'

'But that's unfair,' Diminity protested. 'I get the facts ... the hard information. And you get the exposure ... the glory.'

'I'm sorry, Diminity,' Janet replied honestly. 'It's tough, but that's the way it works. Though I'll see what I can do for you. Now, what's the story?'

'Reports're still coming in. But it's clear that a big vessel, maybe two, blew up just off Collier Quay.'

On the tiny screen, Janet saw a tall, middle-aged Chinese with a raffish handlebar moustache and a cream safari jacket standing beside Diminity, who had struck a dramatic pose and was looking earnestly into a camera off to one side. The little bitch was trying to upstage her by getting a technically better image into New York and by showing herself feeding information to Janet.

Mike would be riding the inforobots, making sure they used Janet's image, rather than Diminity's. But the wrong impression might just slip through to management, as well as to viewers. Diminity was a damned fool to tangle with an old pro. She'd fix Diminity's wagon.

'Thank you, Diminity Oei, on scene. Now I'd like a word with the gentleman beside you.' Janet thumbed her minisat so that her next words would not go to New York. 'Sorry, Diminity dear, but your accent ... your British-Singaporean accent is foxing the audience. You're not coming through.'

Janet released her thumb's pressure, smiled into the lens, and said, 'Now, sir, can you tell the Alpha One audience more about this outrage? But, first, your job.'

'Deputy Commissioner, Singapore Police. In command of the

Office of Intelligence and Anti-Terrorism.' His wave indicated the desks, chairs, and telephones almost hidden by the mass of uniformed policemen and policewomen. 'The situation is now a little more clear. Centre of the explosion is *Haihuang* a hundred and ten-foot schooner which belongs to Marston Chua, the rubber and shoe tycoon. *Haihuang* seems to've blown up at her moorings. The second explosion I can't yet pinpoint. But, clearly, another yacht or small ship was involved.'

'Then you're treating this as an accident? One accidental explosion that triggered another?'

'Anything but! No yacht ever carried enough fuel to cause the damage this explosion's done. A thousand yachts wouldn't. It's got to be deliberate. My technical experts've given me a horseback estimate: twenty-five thousand pounds of Semtex went up in the *Haihuang*. That's equivalent to a quarter of a million tons of TNT or a tactical nuke.'

'Are you saying a nuclear explosion has occurred ... possibly occurred?'

'Certainly *not*, Ms Seager. I am saying that the two explosions together were *equivalent* to half a million tons of TNT or two battlefield nuclear shells.'

'And the effect?'

'Tentatively, a preliminary estimate is two office towers virtually wrecked and another dozen or so substantially damaged. They were probably mined as well. Of course, communications're a shambles. Telecoms House is out of operation, and there're no landlines to the satellite transmitting dishes. It's an unholy mess! You're lucky! Alpha One's lucky you transmit directly from your own dishes.'

'What does this mean for the future of Singapore, Commissioner?'

'That's not strictly my line of country. Besides, it's far too early. Anyway, you'd have to talk to the financial boys and girls. But it certainly means our commercial, shipping, and financial communities will be out of action for a while, maybe weeks. All those traders, insurance companies, steamship companies, and banks with shattered computers and incinerated disks! All their records and their accounts've vanished. Also the fear of another ...'

'So confidence in Singapore's security will be badly undermined and capital will cease to flow through the city?'

'Ms Seager, you must talk to others. But, yes, for a while it's going to be rough-going commercially.'

'I plan to talk to experts on commerce and finance later. Now just one more question . . . .' The deputy commissioner was growing restive, and his aides were whispering to him. 'As head of intelligence, you must have a good idea what this'll mean for the region: East Asia and South-east Asia.'

'Come now, Ms Seager,' he replied acerbically. 'As you well know, Singapore is the communications and transportation hub of the region, as well as one financial hub. So you can just imagine.'

'Thank you very much, Commissioner,' Janet said. 'We'll continue transmitting from police headquarters for a minute or so to show how Singapore is dealing with this emergency. Diminity Oei, can you tell us any more about this yacht the *Haihung* and Mr Marston Chua who owns it?'

Diminity cast a grateful glance at Janet. She would after all be seen on the satnet. Janet smiled in return, wondering about her own motives. The satnets conditioned you never to be generous for its own sake, only when it benefited you. Janet therefore found a cynical reason for her spontaneously generous gesture. Sure, the kid had earned the chance to get her face on a billion screens. But it was also good policy to keep your subordinates happy and co-operative. From here on in, Diminity Oei would all but die for her.

'Thank you, Janet,' Diminity said. 'Marston Chua is many times a billionaire ... one of those rare birds who made a lot of money in China and hung on to it. He owns no factories there, but used other people's factories to make his merchandise. So he lost nothing in the great China crash a couple of years ago. The Singapore authorities believe he's in China now.'

'Thanks, Diminity,' Jan said. 'Anything more on the yacht ... the uh ... *Huaihung*?'

'The *Haihuang*, Janet. It means *Empress of the Seas*. We've just had a report from the cook, who was ashore shopping. He says the crew were suspicious ... so much unexplained activity aboard. And the crew were evidently meant to die in the explosions. Dead men tell no tales, as we say in Chinese.

'Now the other vessel, the second explosion, it appears to have been on a small coaster, no more than a thousand tons. Registered in Liberia, it's been on the South China-Vietnam-Singapore run. No more is known about—'

Diminity Oei broke off abruptly, and the camera swung to the electronic map of Singapore on the glass wall behind her. The computer projected a black figure carrying a turbo assault rifle in the south-west corner of the island.

'We have reports of a landing in the wharf and shipyard section of Jurong!' Diminity's voice rising in excitement, she all but squeaked. 'No more just yet. I'll ...'

'This is Janet Seager in Singapore,' Janet cut in. 'I'll be back soon for further reports on this unfolding crisis . . . . Diminity Oei will keep you up to date until I can give you a first-hand account of the action at Jurong.'

As she signed off, Mike Goldsworthy's voice sounded in the glass-and-blond-wood living-room, 'Now, Jan, take it easy. Don't get your pretty head shot off.'

'Thanks for worrying, Mike. Just let me worry about my pretty head. Now I'll be out of touch for a while. They tell me I can't transmit from the chopper. Too much interference. But it won't be long.'

The rotor blades of the helicopter went *whop whop whop* when the pilot pushed the differential control forward. The little aircraft on charter to Alpha One edged cautiously towards a landing. The pilot, who had attained the rank of major flying helicopters for the Singapore Defence Force, was jittery – and his nervousness affected Janet, who sat beside him in the seat a co-pilot would occupy in combat. He swore steadily in the Hokkien dialect, and for once Janet was glad she did not understand another's language. He was evidently exploring the farthest shores of obscenity as he searched for a safe landing place.

It was reassuring to have an experienced former defence force officer at the controls. But he could not know where either enemy or friendly troops had taken up position.

No frontline divided the pool of darkness that was Jurong with the power cut off, and the cylindrical twin towers of the South Island Technical Centre reared black against the starry tropical night. Military helicopters flitted before the full moon like giant moths around a giant lamp. None showed a light. Normal red and green navigation lights would give the enemy's surface-to-air missiles an illuminated target.

'Goddamned mother of a fire fight!' The pilot spoke in English with an Alabama drawl, apparently reserving his harsh ancestral dialect for swearing. 'Just you look at that, lady! Ain't seen nothing like it since I trained with your 101st Airborne.'

The robust North Indian camerawoman leaned on Janet's shoulder to shoot through the helicopter's windshield. The even darker shadow of the Tech Centre's dark twin towers was split by intense light. Glowing orange streaks arced outward from the towers' base, and larger, bright blue streaks arced inward.

'Tracers!' The pilot's voice softened in relief at those deadly pyrotechnics. 'The enemy is Indonesian ... those orange tracers. Our boys' turbo-gas rifles fire blue tracers. Funny, the Israeli-Singapore design's not as reliable as the Indonesian one.'

Why, Janet wondered, was the pilot giving her a lecture on weapons while he searched for a place to put down? Still, it was all grist for her mill.

She realized with a start that the pilot was even more nervous than she. It was all new to her, but it was old hat to him. He obviously knew just what purgatory his fragile aircraft was entering.

The helicopter lurched, slid onto its side, and plummeted down, hurling Janet against the safety straps that crossed her shoulders. Above her, she saw a string of red, yellow, and blue balls make a flaming arc against the stars like a giant Roman candle.

'They're signalling?' she asked.

'Shit no, lady!' the pilot replied. 'That string of pretty lights is anti-chopper rockets ... automatic, magazine-loaded, multifiring, magnetic-guided turbo-rockets. Just get brushed by one of those babies and it's good night sweetheart. Gotta haul ass ... put *beaucoup* distance between us and that little popgun. I'm putting down over there. I see a command post.'

'How do you know,' Janet asked edgily, 'where the good guys are?'

'Simplest thing in the big wide world, lady. The enemy's holed up in the Tech Centre, trying to get out. The good guys are surrounding them. Remember when you hit terra firma: orange flashes are the bad guys; blue flashes're the good guys.'

When the helicopter's skids touched the ground, bumping and dragging for several seconds, Janet tumbled out. After her came Diminity Oei, who had turned up with the helicopter, having exchanged her tell-tale white skirt and blouse for a mottled camouflage suit. It struck Janet that her own white safari jacket with the big Alpha One silver microphone logo on the left breast pocket would stand out in the moonlight. Though that heightened visibility was dangerous, she would also stand out on tri-D screens all around the world.

Camerawoman, producer, sound technician, and two satcom specialists jumped after the correspondents. The helicopter buzzed along three feet from the ground before rising vertically. A stream of orange tracers arced lazily against the starry sky like a garden hose spraying distant rose bushes. The explosive bullets caressed the helicopter's dark flank for an instant – and fire erupted.

Heartsick and queasy, Janet heard the satcom specialists setting up their transmitting dish behind her. Amid the darkness of night and the uproar of combat, her own minisat could send only fuzzy pictures and mushy sound. Besides, the camerawoman would need the light intensifier of her big camera, which fed the dish.

The big dish was worth the risk of drawing fire, simply essential. This was, after all, show biz. Quality of image and sound was at least as important as actual content, maybe more important.

Janet slipped a tiny speaker behind her left ear and tucked a pinhead-microphone into the V of her bra. Feeding through the dish, they would give her a clear circuit.

'We're though to New York.' The camerawoman tapped Janet on the shoulder. 'Are you ready for a test transmission?'

'Hell no, lady.' Janet surprised herself with the dead pilot's style of speech. 'We'll go right to screen.'

'Good day, viewers all around the globe.' She slid smoothly into her customary introduction. 'It is night in Singapore, a fearful night. Within the past hour, I have seen close-up two outrages against the human spirit ... two vicious assaults on Singapore's peace and prosperity.

'The first you, also, have already seen. The two immense bombs that virtually wrecked Singapore's financial district started with the planned explosion of twenty-five-thousand pounds of Semtex. The bomb was hidden aboard the hundred and ten foot yacht of Marston Chua, the shoe billionaire, who has close ties with China. A second explosion of the same size followed on another vessel. The two bombs together had the power of a half-million tons of TNT.

'There is no reason, as yet, to believe that any government in China is responsible for the atrocity. The jury is out on that question. It may be out for a long time. Frankly, at this point no one knows who's behind the attack or what the objective may be.'

'Jan, baby, get to the meat.' Mike Goldsworthy's voice spoke through the speaker hidden behind her ear. 'You've got it exclusive and every satnet CEO in the world is watching you.'

Is Mike out to help me, Janet wondered, or to distract me? Nonetheless, she thumbed her hidden microphone off and spoke directly to the satcom specialists. 'Give them the ground-to-air footage at woof. Three ... two ... one ... woof.'

Janet continued, 'The second assault is a landing, in unknown strength, on the shore of the Jurong district, a centre of shipbuilding and other heavy industry. You can now see the deadly concentric circles of blue and orange tracers as the Singapore Defence Force closes in. As yet I have no information on the size of the assault force or its origin. For all we know, it could be a landing from the moon. Just as soon as I have solid information, I'll pass it on to you. Meanwhile ...'

She just controlled her involuntary start when Mike's voice sounded in her ear again. 'Enough of the painstaking fairness. Just tell 'em how you felt, babe. How you feel right now! It's all yours exclusive. Now run with it. Make me shiver! Make me weep!'

'The Alpha One team,' she resumed, 'has just landed behind the outer circle, the blue circle which . . . .'

'*I* ... *I* ... *I*,' Mike directed urgently. 'Make it an *I* piece. You're entitled.'

'And how does it feel to be in the middle of a fierce fire fight?' she shifted smoothly. 'Well, ladies and gentlemen, descending into the fiery pit, I felt my stomach clench and my heart race. Right now I'm plain scared. But not as scared as I thought I'd be. In fact, I forgot to be scared until we'd landed, even when anti-aircraft rockets reached for our chopper. Also I was too dumb to know what they were.

'Having a job to do keeps me from dwelling on my fear. And my job is to let you viewers know exactly what's going on. Some day, maybe tomorrow, your city could be under the same kind of assault.

'But I'm scared now, scared stiff. In a minute you'll see what became of our Alpha One helicopter a few seconds after your news team piled out.'

The alert producer signalled the satcom specialists to roll the disk of the helicopter going down. After a few seconds, he gave her the thumbs-up signal.

'That, ladies and gentlemen,' Janet said sombrely, 'is the Alpha One helicopter going down in a ball of flame. With his chopper died its pilot, a former major in the Singapore Defence Force, who was trained in the US. A soft-spoken, gentle man, the major is not the first casualty of this inexplicable, possibly insane action. Nor, I am very much afraid, will he be the last.

'This is Janet Seager of Alpha One in Singapore.'

'Lovely, babe, lovely,' Mike rhapsodized when she'd signed off. 'Not a dry eye in the house. I gather he was a rough son of a bitch. Now, go get the inside story.'

'Mike, that'll do!' She pushed two buttons on her minisat commanding it to double scramble her words so that only Mike

Goldsworthy's sister set could unscramble them. 'Stop pulling my strings. I appreciate your guidance, but I'm not an idiot who has to be *told* to go get the facts.'

'Sorry, Jan!' His tone was hurt. 'Do you want me to stop coaching?'

'Of course not, Mike. Only don't talk to me as if I were an idiot.'

Diminity Oei pulled gently on her sleeve, and said, 'Jan, this is Lieutenant Sharif, an old friend of mine. Your President Harry Truman once said the US Marines had a public relations officer in every squad. Singapore Defence Force does, too. They're always very helpful. Not maximum disclosure, though, just maximum publicity. Abdul?'

'Pay no attention to Dimmy, Ms Seager,' the slight Malay officer said. 'She's known me since kindergarten. No respect. We'll give you maximum disclosure ... what little we know. I've set up a briefing. First, let's get out of the line of fire.'

Janet was struck by the almost inhuman efficiency of the Singapore Defence Force when she entered the hastily dug trench behind a concrete public toilet. Despite the feeble light of the pallid moon and the flickering rainbow glare of computer screens, she saw that the headquarters detachment was functioning calmly and capably. They might have been in an air-conditioned concrete bunker, rather than a shallow trench with only a few sandbags protecting its vulnerable corrugated iron roof against the explosive mortar-rockets the enemy was firing.

XV

Amid the darkness, the stench of the public toilet, and the rain of fire, men and women in mottled jungle uniforms were working, receiving, relaying, and dispatching information through palm-top computers and boxy hand-transportable satcommunicators. The slight lieutenant colonel commanding the Alert Unit sat tensely in a tattered easychair with a bamboo frame, receiving his subordinates' reports and giving soft-voiced orders. Occasionally, he reached for a field telephone in a battered green-plastic case, which looked like a quaint antique beside the hi-tech gloss of the view-screens.

His white hair was a stiff brush above his youthful face with its unlined, old-ivory skin, high cheekbones, and narrow eyes. The crown and pip insignia of his rank was embroidered in black on his epaulets, as were Abdul Sharif's two pips.

The tumult of the battlefield reverberated in the relative safety of the bunker. Janet's heart was pounding, and her body was sweaty and gritty. Nonetheless, she realized abruptly, she had never felt more alive in all her thirty-two years. She now understood how men – more and more women, too, nowadays – could become addicted to combat. She had never felt more capable or more perceptive: every sight and every sound was preternaturally clear to her heightened senses. The same surge of adrenalin that made her gasp for breath also exhilarated her.

'The lieutenant colonel commanding.' The young Malay lieutenant saluted. 'Ms Janet Seager.'

'Can we wait a moment for the camera, Colonel?' Janet smiled. 'I'm a slave to the lens.'

'If the camera's running, Ms Seager, we won't talk,' the lieutenant colonel replied equably. 'My anonymity is ...'

'The colonel's job is super-secret,' Lieutenant Abdul Sharif explained. 'He's only seeing you because Dimmy pulled all kinds of strings. Just call him the colonel in your report. And no description, no direct quotes, and no shots in the bunker. If you want an officer on camera, I'm afraid you'll have to make do with me, a lowly lieutenant, instead of ...'

'You'll do, Lieutenant,' Janet broke in. 'You'll do fine.'

A burly Sikh captain tapped the strapping Indian camerawoman on the shoulder and held out his hand. Though normally feisty, the camerawoman docilely stripped the disk from her camera and handed it to him. With exaggerated courtesy, he passed the disk over a small magnetic eraser and handed it back.

'Now, Ms Seager, what can I do for you?' The colonel was coolly polite and businesslike. 'What can I tell you?'

'Everything, Colonel.' Charm might help, the straightforward approach having failed. 'I'm afraid I really know nothing about . . . .'

The colonel's thin lips relaxed into a smile, and he chuckled.

'That's not what I've heard, Ms Seager. I also know you charmed the pants off the staff. Anyway, I've got my orders.'

'Which are, Colonel?' She smiled tremulously, even considered batting her eyelashes. 'Can you tell me that?'

'My orders are to tell you everything – and to depend on your acuity to sort it out sensibly. So I shall. But no recording.'

The colonel glanced at Lieutenant Abdul Sharif, who was conferring with a sergeant seated at a circular monitor screen.

Abdul nodded and said, 'It's a go, sir. She's switched her minisat off.'

Janet flushed angrily perhaps unnoticed in the pallid light. She almost asked for a pencil and paper to dramatize the disadvantage under which she was working. But she had never learned to ask questions, listen, and take notes at the same time. She would have to depend on memory.

'Who are you fighting, Colonel?' she asked. 'Can you tell yet?'

'From the evidence of the two prisoners we've captured and the three corpses we've recovered, it's a strange unit. Three to four hundred strong – and lavishly equipped. Turbo-gas rifles, high velocity trench-mortar rockets, anti-aircraft turbo rockets, a-hundred-and-ten-millimetre, man-transportable artillery pieces – and a fantasy of electronic gear. It seems most are Americans, and almost all are black. They call themselves Saddamites.'

'Where did they come from? How did they get here?'

'From Indonesia, the Moluccan Islands, fifteen hundred miles away. They might have ridden a magic carpet for all the warning we had.'

The Sikh captain leaned over to murmur into Colonel Tan's ear, and he replied, 'On no account! I don't want them wiped out. I want them in the bag. I must know more about this peculiar unit. Capture me an officer or two . . . . I know we'll take more casualties that way. But it has to be.'

The flame of his lighter trembled minutely when the colonel lit the fat Burma cheroot he took from a leather cigar-case. He sighed, exhaled a cloudlet of pale-grey smoke, and shook his head slowly.

'I've just sentenced a dozen, maybe more, of my chaps to death, Ms Seager,' he confessed. 'I *must* know whom we're fighting.'

'I thought they were a myth, the Saddamites,' Janet observed. 'A myth made up by racists, bigots, and homophobes.'

'I promise you they're no myth, the Saddamites. And they're hand-in-glove with other Islamic extremists. My lads also came across a light-skinned corpse, a heavy-set fellow with a bashed-in nose and pomaded hair. He had the damnedest collection in his rucksack: two Korans with jewelled covers and several hundred copies of a leaflet promising "spiritual cleansing" throughout Central Asia and the Middle East. Signed by the Supreme Council of the Sacred Movement to Return to the Pure Teachings of the Prophet Mohammed. Also several kilos of Semtex, as well as assorted fuses and detonators.'

'Was he a bomb master?'

'I've no idea, except he obviously was *not* a black American Muslim. One of our prisoners mumbled about Comrade Sheikh Semtex. Otherwise, your guess is as good as mine.'

'Colonel, this is probably a naïve question considering what's already happened, but I'll ask anyway: you're obviously very worried. Why? Do you really fear there'll be more attacks, even though this assault force is being wiped out?'

'Soldiers aren't meant to have intuition, Ms Seager,' he replied slowly. 'Not until they're generals. But I've got a bad feeling about this shemozzle. Strikes me it's the beginning, not the end.'

'Why?' she pressed. 'Why exactly?'

'Because of their transport. We didn't see hide nor hair of the ships that carried this unit. Yet we've been clocking every movement of every vessel bigger than a sampan ever since the first alarm weeks ago. How could we have missed a ship big enough to carry a half battalion?'

'I don't see how unless ...'

'You're too polite to say it: *unless we were asleep at the switch*. I promise you, we weren't. The fact that we didn't get a sniff of that ship may well be the most important feature of this raid. Since we didn't pick them up on radar, they *must* be stealth vessels.'

'I've heard of stealth aircraft ... virtually unseeable on radar and very hard to eyeball, but stealth ships?'

'That's precisely the point, Ms Seager. They're not commonplace, stealth vessels. All big navies that tried to develop stealth surface ships soon gave up. Too expensive and too dicey. And wouldn't giant submarines do just as well?'

'Maybe that's what they were, giant submarines.'

'A minnow might've got through our underwater surveillance, but nothing much bigger. Not a mackerel and certainly not a tunny fish. Above all, not a whacking great submarine or two.

'Clearly, we're talking about new technology that can make an eighty thousand-ton aircraft carrier virtually invisible to electronic surveillance. Yet we have no evidence of anyone's actually developing a stealth surface vessel, not from any of the twenty-odd intelligence services we liaise with.'

'And that means?'

'There's a pile of money behind this assault – money, as well as great power and firm resolve. Imagine a private organization developing a stealth vessel in utter secrecy! We face a very strong and very determined enemy. But we have no idea who he is.'

'What's the trick, Colonel? How does it work?'

'Simple enough in theory, but the devil to apply. Are you really interested in the technical details, Ms Seager?'

'Vitally!' She smiled. 'Just try me!'

'First you place the engines above the water-line and set them on shock-absorbing mounts. So little or no vibration is transmitted through the water. No propellers to roil the water, but jet propulsion, that sucks in water and shoots it out. Sounds like whales courting far away. We haven't been monitoring every whale that pops up on our sonar. But we shall from now on. We'll track every last whale, even if we have to quadruple our electronic and human resources.'

'Just deadening engine and propeller sounds? What about radar?'

'The ideal stealth ship is all curves, no sharp angles. Rotundity jumbles radar wavelengths and prevents clear imaging. Also, fibreglass hulls virtually invisible to radar and paints loaded with iron filings to absorb radar waves. In theory, those techniques can make a half-million-ton, ultra-large crude oil carrier look no bigger than a rowboat.'

Mike Goldsworthy spoke from New York into Janet's ear, 'For Chris' sake, Jan, what're you up to? Goofing off? We haven't had a single word or picture from you for almost fifteen minutes. Kate says she didn't send you to Singapore for a vacation in the tropical sun.'

'Which, incidentally, is *not* shining just now.' Janet thumbed her minisat and answered just as sharply. 'I've been working hard, Mike, as you'll soon see. For God's sake, don't ride herd on me every minute. I know what I'm doing.'

The colonel was startled by her outburst, though it was obviously not directed at him. Realizing what was going on, he leaned back, relit his chewed cheroot, and smiled warmly at the big Sikh captain, who gaped in surprise.

'I know that, babe,' Mike retorted. 'But Her Imperial Majesty Catherine the Great doesn't. We've got nine hundred million sets ... an audience of more'n two billion ... all waiting for you to drop the other shoe. Nothing turns to shit faster than unfilled air time. You can't get it back, it's gone forever. Come on, Jan, get a move on. For my sake – for your *own* sake.'

The colonel touched Janet's shoulder and spoke urgently, his expression grave after hearing the Sikh captain's report.

'Something's up, Ms Seager. I'm going to see for myself. You're welcome to come along with your crew. But, do remember, no pictures of myself or the captain.'

An explosion roared just outside the command post: lights and view-screens flickered and failed for a few seconds. Shock waves vibrating in the intense darkness pounded Janet's eardrums. Clods of falling earth filled the command post with dust. Debris raining down on the corrugated-iron roof drummed a funeral march.

The night was darker when they emerged from the bunker, not quite so brightly lit by tracers and explosives as it had been twenty minutes earlier. The pale moon backlit the slim figure of Colonel Tan, who was distracted by the shrill summons of the boxy satcommunicator the Sikh captain carried. He spoke urgently into the funnel mouthpiece.

'Yes, sir! Yes, of course. Yes, I fully understand the importance. I know the park is crowded at this time of night with family parties, many children, as well as adults. I concur. It cannot be allowed to go on. I shall take action immediately. Yes, sir!'

'The prime minister,' he explained. 'We are . . . .'

An immense whirring reverberated above the thud of rocket-grenades and the popping of turbo-gas rifles. It was like the whirring of 10,000 wings, as if a gigantic flock of starlings were circling overhead, all cawing harshly.

A fountain of violet-and-orange fire rose from the base of the twin towers. Brilliant light soared meteor-like across the evening sky, obscuring the moon. The trajectory flattening abruptly, the trail of fire plummeted onto an unknown target – unknown to Janet Seager, but not to the two officers.

The Sikh captain said softly, 'As reported, sir. Their targets are the Ocean Amusement Park and the Jurong workers' housing estates. It's mass murder!'

Another fountain of flame rose from the towers' base to follow the same trajectory. Atop the pillar of fire, Janet saw the black dewdrop of the deadly warhead. An instant later, a third fountain of flame flared incandescent violet and orange. The arc of fire rose swiftly to its apogee to plunge down on a nearby target, so close that the crump of its impact reverberated above the din of the fire-fight. Janet saw a crimson-and-blue fireball swell among the tall apartment houses.

'Mortar rockets,' the colonel said. 'Captain, bring in the fighter-bombers and the gunships. They are to destroy the mortar tubes. The towers, too, if necessary. Also, Singh, all our artillery on the same target. I want the enemy obliterated.'

The Sikh captain spoke brusquely into the mouthpiece of his satcommunicator. An instant later, Janet heard the whine of jet engines overhead. The whine rose to an ear-blasting crescendo as the assault fighters swooped lower.

The *whop*, *whop*, *whop* of rotor-blades joined the tumult when the attack helicopters bored into the target. Their turbo-gas mini-Gatlings hosed the towers with blue tracers, and their rockets left a necklace of brilliant white flame around the base. The gunships then withdrew to give the infantry a clear field of fire.

Janet spoke into the mike that nestled between her breasts, hoping her voice would carry over the tumult. With hardly a pause, she spoke for more than fifteen minutes. She was never afterwards to be able to recall the words that underlined the fearful images beamed through to New York. Watching a replay later, she would hardly recognize the deceptively calm voice as her own. But she would vividly remember every individual image as she saw them again.

The assault fighters attacked in echelons of three, their sleek lines unmarred by protruding engines or control-surfaces. The dark trios were momentarily silhouetted against the pale moon like gigantic bats. They climbed straight up before abruptly flipping over to dive spear-straight towards the ground and merge again with the darkness.

Rockets ignited, spewing flame under the airplanes' bellies. Bombs tumbled free for half a second before plunging down. Powered by minute rocket-exhausts in their tail-fins, they were guided by on-board sensors. Their nose-cameras flashed images to the screens in the spotter plane circling overhead, which could command the bombs to alter course repeatedly.

Six three-plane echelons followed precisely the same trajectory, as if riding invisible rails in the sky. Drowning all other sound, the explosion buffeted the Singapore forces. They were for the moment only spectators of the devastation they had called down on their enemy.

Jan could not broadcast during the air assault. Her voice would have been fragmented by the reverberations the sat-dish was beaming to New York. An apologetic Mike Goldsworthy again spoke into her ear.

'They've taken the satnet back, released it to regular broadcasts,' he advised. 'Kate says: "No voice over, no story. It's dead monotonous, just swooping planes and shattering explosions". She wants another image. When you get one, call me and I'll grab the net back again. But don't wait too long.'

Janet's shoulders drooped in sudden exhaustion. The worst thing was that Kate the Great was right. Saturation coverage of a single event sapped viewers' interest and drove them to another channel.

An instant later, she stood erect and spoke into her mike. 'Alpha One, I have new material for you. Put me on.'

'It's all yours,' Mike replied after a few seconds. 'I hope you know what you're doing.'

Janet gestured roundly, directing the cameras to focus on the twin towers of the South Island Technical Centre. The enormous black cylinders still thrust their ninety-six storeys into the starry sky, although their base was submerged in a cauldron of fire. The tower on the left inclined slightly from the vertical. As the cameras watched, it inclined more sharply. Illuminated by the fires around its base, the tower slowly toppled. Gradually, so gradually it appeared to be unfolding in exaggerated slow motion, the entire 1,500-foot structure disintegrated in the air. The immense thunder of that immense collapse resounded over the din of the battlefield.

'You can see for yourself what's happening,' Janet said softly. 'One of the glories of Singapore is crashing to earth – destroyed by Singapore's own soldiers in order to crush the assault. The towers had to go to keep the enemy from murdering entire families in their homes and in the ever popular Ocean Park. Like a badger caught in a trap's steel jaws, Singapore has gnawed off one of its own legs to escape.

'I can see the towers no more. Billows of smoke and debris are rising high into the air.'

Janet lowered her voice for emphasis, and added, 'However, clouds of confusion still cover the purposes of this mass raid, as well as its consequences. I'll bring you the details just as soon as I can. Janet Seager in Singapore. Now back to Alpha One in New York.'

'Come and get us, mother fuckers.' An American voice spoke in raw anger from the sat-communicator in the Sikh captain's hand. 'We still got a shitload of bullets for you honky bastards.'

'Not long now,' the colonel said wearily. 'They'll all be dead within minutes unless they've burrowed into the ground like moles. What brave men!'

'Colonel, can you tell me *why*?' Janet demanded. 'What could drive men to such desperation, such fury?'

'Even if I'm an honorary honky now, Ms Seager, I'm afraid you'll have to answer that question for yourself. It's more an American question than a Singapore question. I can only surmise that the men may have known this was a suicide mission. Certainly their officers would know.

'I can only surmise further.' The colonel smiled wryly in the shifting light. 'I believe their purpose is to discredit Singapore in the eyes of East Asia and the world. They've forced us to inflict grave damage on ourselves. We could not stand by and let them commit mass murder on our citizens and our children. But their mission, their objective? I just can't say.'

'Did they want to die,' Janet mused, 'or were they betrayed?'

'Betrayed? Interesting thought! Perhaps so!'

XVI

Diminity Oei managed to keep her joy at the exposure she was getting on screen from colouring her voice when she delivered the doleful summing-up on the morning after the attack.

'...two high speed patrol boats of the Singapore Navy sunk. The airport disabled for at least another twenty-four hours. Sixty-eight service men and women killed, as well as at least a hundred and thirty civilians, children as well as adults. More dead and injured are being discovered constantly.

'Prisoner interrogation indicates at least four hundred raiders were killed. The grand total of Singapore casualties in this unexplained violence will certainly be over a thousand, including more than six hundred injured civilians. A disproportionate number are children. Yesterday was family night at Ocean Park.

'Alpha One will bring you further details just as soon as they are available. Meanwhile, highlights from the images recorded last night. The commentary is largely by Janet Seager, though you will from time to time hear me. Ladies and gentlemen, the voice of Alpha One's brilliant correspondent, Janet Seager.'

Diminity turned away from the camera and loosed the small smile she dared not show on screen. Singapore had suffered a devastating sneak attack, but Singapore had proved its mettle by rallying and crushing the raiders. Despite the tragic casualty list, she had reason to be proud of her city-state. She had even better reason to be pleased with herself. How often did a local correspondent, a part-time stringer, dominate coverage of the biggest story in the world for several hours?

That exposure was all due to Janet Seager, who had unselfishly allowed her to get on screen briefly even at the height of the attack. Janet had then won Diminity's heart completely by sending her back to police headquarters to broadcast updates while she herself pursued the story in the field. Diminity had thereafter virtually monopolized the reporting.

Diminity heard in her earphone the light, breathy voice that belonged to a woman introduced as Babs Berkeley, who had taken over the desk in New York to give Mike Goldsworthy a break.

'Where *is* Janet?' Babs Berkeley asked. 'You're doing all right – not at all bad for a local – but it's not the same. Kate is asking: *Where's Jan Seager? What've they done with my star?*'

'Well, you see ...' Diminity hardly hesitated, 'she had a hot lead to the *inside* story. What really happened and why. She said it might take a while . . . .'

'Five hours and we haven't heard a word, not a dicky bird!' The irate female voice spoke in the unmistakable quirky half-English, half-American accent of Catherine Loomis. 'Five hours! An eternity on a satnet. Five hours ... and not a single word from Janet. Where in hell's she got to?'

'I'm sorry, but I don't know, Miss ... Ms Loomis,' Diminity said. 'I'm sorry I can't help more. I'm trying my best to fill in.'

'No need to remind me you're pinch-hitting, Diminity. I can see you're doing a good job,' Catherine Loomis replied. 'Keep it up. And send out everyone on staff. No police, no official enquiries. Just get the staff to scour the city for Janet. Look in every single corner! I need her on screen. What a time to pick to disappear! She's the hottest item of the year.'

Diminity truly did not know where Janet had gone. But she had a shrewd idea. Janet had been chasing the aeronautical engineer called George Fellows, blatantly infatuated with him. Besides, she had hinted, George Fellows knew more about the raid than he said.

That was Janet to a T. She never forgot her calling. Even when infatuated, she remembered that he was a prime source.

Nor would Diminity Oei forget her calling. She was profoundly grateful to Janet Seager for getting her on screen so much and she would, of course, mount an intense search for the missing star, although Janet was sure to turn up when it suited her. A search would be mounted, but not too strenuously.

Meanwhile, Diminity Oei would ride the crest of the wave. Babs Berkeley, Mike Goldsworthy's temporary replacement, had told her that Alpha One was drawing record audiences from the other satnets because of its intensive and exclusive coverage of the raid on Jurong. And just *who* had tipped Janet to that action? No one but Diminity Oei herself!

Sorry though she was that Janet was not there to bask in the glory, Diminity Oei, a slight young woman from Singapore, was speaking to the largest audience ever to watch a satnet newscast. She admired Janet vastly. She all but revered Janet. Yet she was in no hurry to find Janet. No hurry at all!

Janet Seager had indeed set out to find the man called George Fellows, otherwise Berry Smith. When she found him, she would make him tell her all he knew about the origins and the purposes of the raid. He was susceptible to her charm, and he knew she could blow his cover.

She should, of course, be in touch with the Alpha One office in Singapore, but she could hardly ask Diminity to fill her in on developments without also speaking to New York. And she was not yet ready to talk to New York.

She had told Diminity she was going back to the Oriental Hotel for a catnap, a shower and some strong coffee, in that order. She would, she had said, then have a quick look around Singapore on the morning after.

Diminity had dutifully telephoned the Oriental when Babs Berkeley began harping on Janet's absence. The persona of Ms Juliette Thompson had been discarded sometime during the turbulent night when nine-tenths of Singapore was watching Alpha One to learn what was happening in their own city. Diminity had been told that Ms Seager had returned for an hour or so and had then set out again. No, she had said nothing about where she was bound.

Finding that Berry Smith was not at his apartment, Janet had then tried Singapore Civil Defence Headquarters in its bunker under Canning Rise. Berry had said he was posted to Civil Defence, and he might still be there. Since it was virtually impossible to get through on jammed telephone lines, she had gone to Canning Rise and gained admission with her press pass.

The big underground bunker was thick with cigarette smoke. Even the iron hand of the Singapore Government could not crush addiction to nicotine. Dozens of young men and young women appeared to be milling aimlessly around glowing computers while telephones shrilled. After a minute or so, it was evident that it was organized confusion. The staff knew exactly what they were doing at a frantic pace.

'Mr Fellows was here last night,' recalled the slender young Indian woman in the glowing scarlet sari who was deputy director of Civil Defence. 'He was a big help. He was also watching your reports, Ms

Seager. He winced every time anything exploded near you. Suddenly he said he was going to find you. He insisted I give him a curfew pass. I could hardly refuse.'

'Any idea where he might've ended up?'

'Perhaps not, Ms Seager, but perhaps yes.' The dark aquiline features smiled. 'Have you tried the Future Green Society? That big white building on the corner of North Bridge Road and Arab Street. It was stacked with big smelly bales of raw rubber until superbounce killed the market. All synthetic nowadays, isn't it? Better, they say, it is . . . .'

The tide of words rolled on, relentlessly didactic, but inspired by great goodwill. After listening for two long minutes, Janet pleaded that she had a deadline for her next 'cast. She did in truth have a deadline, not just one, but a multitude of deadlines, practically one every minute.

Yet she had still not yet run down the inside story: *who had launched this vicious assault and why?* Mike Goldsworthy always said you were only as good as your *next* broadcast and she wanted to make her next broadcast spectacular. But Kate the Great would undoubtedly be fuming at her disappearance, and Mike would be viciously sarcastic if she let any more time go by without checking in.

Janet resignedly pulled her minisat from her big pouch bag and touched the call button. Diminity Oei appeared on the screen, ostentatiously relieved by Janet's reappearance, yet clearly a little disappointed that she could no longer monopolize the 'cast.

Janet smiled ruefully. Her protégée was coming along fast, perhaps too fast.

Little had come in during the past few hours except sombre tallies of casualties and property damage. Still, damages totalling more than $75 billion would make a strong lead. And the casualty toll was still mounting after passing 2,000.

Fortunately perhaps, Kate was in the ladies' room when Janet raised New York on her minisat. Mike was not sarcastic, but vastly relieved.

'Where in God's name ...' he began, then caught himself and said, 'Never mind where! I can see you're all in one piece. I was worried about you, kid. And the net is screaming for you.

'You're the belle of the ball, the flavour of the decade. Kate says you can have as much time as you want for your report – within reason. Don't worry about the quality of your minisat 'cast. I'll make the engineers clean it up and enhance it – even if they have to do it one frame at a time. Anyway, we've got *beaucoup* unused Singapore footage.'

'How long a monologue,' Janet asked wryly, 'is within reason?'

'I'd say about ten to fifteen minutes,' Mike grinned. 'But don't push your luck.'

Her summing up of the Singapore outrage for Alpha One behind her, Janet finally ran Berry Smith down at the old rubber warehouse that was the East Asia headquarters of the militant Future Green Society. He was lounging in a cane longchair, immaculate in a crisply pressed, white linen suit.

'How are you, sweetheart?' He rose to embrace her perfunctorily and kiss her cheek fleetingly. 'What took you so long to find me?'

Hyper-casual Berry Smith, also known as George Fellows, was nothing like the worried lover the deputy director of Civil Defence had described. Still, Berry was most off-hand when concealing strong emotion. He casually raised in greeting a squat glass containing an acid-green mixture that was clearly a tropical gimlet: gin, lime juice, and shaved ice.

'I knew you'd come through without a scratch,' he said. 'Have a gimlet. The sun may not be over the yardarm, but it's time for a little refreshment.'

As always, Janet responded with irritation at his breezy manner, as well as with pleasure at seeing him again. As always, pleasure swiftly overcame irritation.

'Just *how*,' she nonetheless asked, 'did you expect me to find you, my easygoing friend?'

'You newshounds can sniff out anyone anywhere. You know, I tried to get to Jurong to see you, but the cops wouldn't let me through. Very dangerous, they said. Besides, I'd never have found you in the darkness and the confusion. I tried to bull my way through. When four cops grabbed me, I had to admit defeat.'

Well, Janet told herself, he's really working hard to convince me – and I mostly believe him. What a change from the past!

'So I left you notes, practically papered the town with notes. One with that cute little Diminity Oei, another at your hotel. Others too numerous to count all over town.'

Janet smiled at that typical exaggeration. She did not wholly believe him, but she did not challenge him. He might just be telling the truth. Both Diminity and the Oriental might well have failed to deliver his notes.

She had not come to this whitewashed old warehouse to fight with Berry: quite the contrary, she had come to seduce him.

She had only once slept with a man to get a story. She had assured herself that she felt no moral repugnance to doing so. She was, she had told herself, not so naïve as to believe she was committing a crass sin. Yet that once, when she was a raw cub reporter, she had failed to get the story, and she had been humiliated by the man.

Now she must try seduction again. Still, this was not some stranger, but Berry Smith. Not so long ago they had known each other's bodies very well indeed. Perhaps each other's spirits, too. Janet felt sheepish at speaking of their *spirits*, even if only to herself. She meant their souls, of course, but that word was totally passé among the satnet crowd.

'Have a chair, Jan,' Berry pressed. 'And have a drink.'

He pulled a wicker longchair from under a frieze of apoplectic posters warning of dire, indeed fatal consequences if all logging were not immediately halted in all remaining tropical rain forests. Janet heard the tread of feet and the buzz of conversation on the floor above. But he and she were alone in the reception room, which still smelled strongly of raw rubber. The plywood partitions bore even more portentous posters: *Only by supporting the Future Green Society* (advised one) *can you ensure that there is a future for mankind*.

Janet took a swig of her gimlet, shuddering at the bite of raw gin and the sickly sweetness of lime cordial. She lowered her glass into the hole in the arm of the longchair and spoke softly.

'Berry, you *must* know who's behind this barbarism. Last time I asked it was for my sake … for a story. But, after what's happened in the last eighteen hours, it's your duty to tell what you know. Your duty to … oh hell, I'll say it … your duty to humanity!'

'Strong words, Jan.' He paused, evidently pondering what to say, and resumed, 'Yes, I guess I do know who it is … in a general way.'

'He must be a monster!' Anger overcame her professional detachment. 'What kind of person could …'

'Jan, he's anything but a monster. He's the wisest man I've ever known. He's decisive, but very kind. He's a gentle man, an old-fashioned gentleman.'

'He's got an odd way of being gentle.'

'If only I could show you … let you talk with him.' Berry was inordinately earnest. 'He's a true idealist: concrete ideals, ideals in practice, not just in theory. But, sometimes, matters get out of hand. You know how it is.'

How, Janet wondered, could she possibly know how a gentle man with shining ideals could have inflicted such carnage on Singapore?

'I know,' Berry added, 'that he abhors bloodshed.'

'He's racked up a pretty high body count for a Mr Milquetoast,' Jan snorted. 'You're talking in contradictions, my friend.'

'If only I could show you.'

'Well why not?'

'Why not *what*, Jan?'

'Why not show me? Why not give me a chance to learn what's really going on? If I met your mysterious gentleman, I could make a better judgement. I need *all* the facts, full knowledge. Otherwise, I'm bound to go wrong – especially from your standpoint.'

She gazed into his eyes, which were still lit by the fire of a true believer, and asked softly, 'Could you, Berry? Could you really fix it for me to meet this man?'

'I could damned well give it the old college try. Though . . . .'

'Would you, Berry darling? Would you really? You know, everything I've seen up to now makes it look very bad. Not just grim, but outrageous ... atrocious. It's hard to keep an open mind.'

'I *do* know. Open mind and closed-knees policy, copyright Ms Janet Seager.'

'Not *always*,' she replied slowly, 'not always a closed-knees policy.'

He spoke softly, as if musing to himself. 'Well, that's true enough. I remember, Jan, one ...'

'That's enough of that. I'll be completely open with you, Berry. I do like ... I care for you very much. But you're an enigma. You're not real. You're like some half-sinister, half-delightful figure out of a spy story. So how can I? Sleeping together's not the most important part. But it's *not* the least important part, either.'

She let that provocative statement hang in mid-air, and he finally asked, 'What *is* the most important part?'

'Trust and understanding. Two people who want – believe in – the same things.' She hesitated, then blurted, 'If only I knew, truly knew, what you're really like! What you're really doing! Where it's all leading! I desperately *need* to know, Berry.'

'All right, Jan sweetheart. I'll show you. No cards up my sleeve. No fast shuffles. All the cards face up; everything on the table.'

Delighted, Janet leaned closer until her lips were brushing his. The kiss was longer and sweeter than any that had gone before.

'You'll have to swear to keep some things under your hat.' He made his terms clear. 'You'll see why.'

Janet nodded. She was instinctively averse to promising beforehand to leave out any part of a story. But that was the only way she could get near this story.

Berry Smith wondered just how much of Amadeus Brinks's crusade he could reveal to Janet. Hell, some things, a lot of things, he didn't know himself. The grand strategy was known only to the man who drafted it. Brinks played his cards very close to the chest.

Nonetheless, he had been forceful and clear when he declared: 'Publicity, Smith, publicity is of the essence. We'll need favourable publicity urgently, above all, favourable coverage on the satnets. We must awaken sympathy. Anything you can do, *anything at all*, to get us good publicity, do not hesitate. Do not ask. Just do it, even if it's risky.'

Janet Seager had thought Singapore could hold no more surprises for her. She had been surprised by Berry Smith's resurrection in the guise of George Fellows. She had then been astonished by the vicious, yet apparently purposeless assault. What more could happen?

She was, nonetheless, shocked when she saw the .60 calibre turbo-machine-guns standing at every window on the second floor of the Future Green headquarters. The loaded weapons were sited to repel an attack. Assault rifles and rocket-grenades were stacked among the battered grey-metal desks. Above them hung a twelve-foot-long banner exhorting: *It's your environment too! Save it or die!*

Were the well-meaning, peace-loving young men and women of Future Green planning an attack? Or were they expecting an attack? If so, why? What could possibly bring Singapore's security forces down on those innocent, if naïve, idealists?

She could not ask Berry. He had vanished through a door that snapped locked behind him. She had heard his footsteps climbing stairs and then no more.

How odd that crusaders for bio-diversity should have turned their offices into an arsenal. They were supposed to stand for life, not death. But it looked as if they were planning to start a small war.

Yet, Jan reflected, why not?

The ecological movement had expanded greatly during the past two decades, despite widely publicized scandals. It had survived embezzlement of very large sums; use of public influence for private ends; major errors in predicting climatic dangers; and blatantly faked publicity stunts. Membership had grown despite such negative reports, since favourable reports predominated.

Yet the movement was not appreciably closer to achieving its objectives than it had been two decades earlier. Why then should the Greens not resort to force, which their enemies already used with little restraint?

While Janet was rediscovering her enthusiasm for the green cause, Berry Smith was pacing the floor of the soundproof room on the third floor. He was arguing heatedly with the working group that had coordinated the attack on Singapore.

'Tse Hu,' he said, 'Mr Brinks's overriding priority right now is publicity, favourable publicity. You know that, don't you?'

'So you say, Commander.' The Maoist woman's serene features displayed none of the antagonism of her words. 'Yes, I've had indications that we should seek publicity. But would he sanction the revelation you propose?'

'Why not ask him!' Berry demanded. 'Right now!'

The Vixen smiled thinly and said, 'Commander Smith, I have decided. In the light of Amadeus's yearning for favourable publicity, you may let this Ms Seager look into this operation. No names, though. And for everyone's sake, don't tell her too much.'

'Of course I'll play it cosy.' Berry was relieved. 'Not give the whole show away.'

The Vixen continued, 'Ms Seager will argue that she must know all the facts before she can make a judgement. You may tell her everything you know about this operation. But no more. And, if you've misjudged Ms Seager, it will be your head!'

'It was a triple-pronged assault,' Berry Smith told Janet. 'Prong one: the explosions of Collier Quay. Prong two: the Jurong landing you saw. It was staged out of the Moluccas with the co-operation of friendly *ulamas*, Muslim clergy. And it was wiped out almost to a man. But it achieved its objective.'

'And that objective?' Jan looked up from the spiral notebook she was rapidly filling. 'What in God's name could justify ...?'

'Their objective was to sow maximum destruction and create maximum confusion.'

'Well, they certainly did that. But why?'

'If I knew, I couldn't tell you.'

'Berry, I just don't understand. You can't go all blank on me now.'

Meeting her direct gaze, Berry saw that her eyes were now indigo. It was dangerous mixing emotion and business. Yet if it were not for their personal relationship, they would not be sitting in the bare canteen of the Future Green Society sipping Oolong tea and anatomizing the Singapore operation.

'Well, I guess I can tell you just a little more. What do you know about stealth ships?'

'The colonel out in Jurong said any group that could build stealth ships in secret must be enormously wealthy and enormously influential.'

'That's true! But don't try to worm any names out of me.'

'Not yet, my friend. But later . . . .'

Janet's voice was light, though she was horrified by the atrocities they were so calmly discussing. She stole a quick glance at Berry Smith.

His normal exuberance had deserted him. His voice was flat, and his mobile features were set. He was clearly distressed by his role in the atrocities, clearly appalled by the consequences.

'About the explosions off Collier Quay.' His tone was dull. 'My colleague talked Marston Chua, the shoe tycoon, into lending us his schooner *Haihuang*. She's a beautiful lady, and Chua was smitten. The second explosion was a scabby tramp freighter we had on long charter for errands around the Indonesian archipelago. She won't be missed!'

'That's the first and second prongs. What about the third?'

Whatever she felt, Janet's manner was flatly matter-of-fact to avoid spooking him. They might have been discussing fish farming rather than the single greatest outrage in the outrageous history of terrorism.

'The third prong was air and naval action.' He was almost as matter-of-fact. 'We took out a couple of their fast patrol boats with Masadas.'

'Masadas?'

'The latest in ship-to-ship stealth missiles. A stand-off range of three hundred miles, no warning on radar, and a devastating TNT warhead.'

'Where, in the name of God, did you get hold of those missiles?'

'I can't tell you.'

'All right, Berry. And the air action?'

'I chose the targets ... chose very carefully to avoid casualties. But an Ataturk air-to-ground missile hit the aviary in the nature park. As you know, it killed all the birds ... also fifty-odd kids and parents. It was supposed to hole the reservoir.'

He rubbed his eyes with his knuckles and said softly, 'Jan, I don't know I'll ever get over that misfiring. Everything checked out, but the damned missile landed a mile off target. What could I do?'

Janet said nothing, only nodded. Part of her yearned to comfort him, for he was bitterly contrite. Yet so he should be! Part of her wanted to shout *Murderer*! – and walk out of the warehouse and out of his life. But her professional conscience commanded her to get the story, no matter what.

'We were supposed to take the airport ... hold it for a couple of hours,' he resumed. 'Surprise attack by a paratroop company dropped from supersonic stealth transports. We figured the Singapore Air Force couldn't keep a CAP over the island indefinitely . . . .'

'CAP being a combat air patrol?'

'Sure, Jan. And we were right. After several weeks on alert, the edge'd gone off Singapore's vigilance. We also used UN call signs and recognition codes to confuse them. But a new type of radar almost nabbed the stealth aircraft. We roughed up the Singapore Air Force, but our fighters had to turn back. Not enough fuel to dogfight. So we didn't take the airport. Just laid some bomblets along the runways. And it'll be back in operation tomorrow.'

'*You* planned the attack?'

'I also laid down the sensors and the beacons that created an electronic highway for our aircraft. I also co-ordinated the air action with a satbounce set. As you know, satbounce transmissions can't be jammed. Can hardly be detected.'

'Berry, don't you have any regrets?' Janet's indignation overcame her professional restraint. 'How do you *really* feel about all this?'

'Rotten, Jan, damn rotten.' He did not pause for reflection. 'I never wanted the killing. I planned the air action so there'd be *no* casualties. But that missile went astray. Not to speak of the unexpected fighter resistance. Too much bloodshed!'

'And the Saddamites, Berry?' Janet pressed him. 'They fired mortar-rockets at apartment houses all round the district, not to speak of the slaughter in the Ocean Park. Those weren't military targets.'

Berry Smith lifted his hand wearily, the gesture unaware, pleading with her to stop. He looked away, evading her gaze, and said slowly, 'That wasn't supposed to happen. Those boys, the Saddamites, they went crazy. Turned into rampaging, bloodthirsty lunatics.'

'And all this for what purpose?'

'I know it sounds nuts. But I can only tell you it was ... is ... ecological.'

He looked hurt when she snorted in disbelief. Yet, suddenly inspired, he asked, 'Jan, why don't you come with me? I'm leaving before they catch up with me, getting out of town just ahead of the sheriff. If you'll come ... can't tell you where ... could be I'll get you to meet the boss, the man I was talking about earlier.'

Janet forgot personal or professional caution and seized the opportunity. Although revolted by Berry's part in the carnage, she unhesitatingly put her professional reputation and her life into his hands. If she played it safe with no risk, she would miss the biggest story of the decade.

XVII

Prince Richard saw the slaughter in Singapore on the giant tri-D screen in the drawing-room of his suite in the Three Crowns Hotel in Stockholm. His first reaction was incredulity. Even watching Janet Seager report the carnage on Alpha One, he could not quite believe that mass terrorism initiated by Amadeus Brinks was slaughtering hundreds.

Richard was indignant at being deceived and furious at being used. He swore he would not lend his good name to camouflage such outrages. He resolved to quit the movement – and to reveal Brinks's perfidy – as well as Brinks's future targets.

But, he realized, he did not know what further action Brinks planned. Besides, he would simply not be believed if he befouled the generous, caring, jolly Santa Claus image of the world's most publicly concerned citizen.

He could get on the satnets without difficulty, since he never failed to put on a good show. Not air time but credibility was the problem. He had marched in the parades of too many outlandish gurus for too many years. He was too widely known as the 'zany prince' for such scandalous accusations to be taken seriously.

Prince Richard reluctantly concluded that he must remain a member of the working group that executed Amadeus Brinks's strategy. He told himself he could do more good within the movement than outside. He could restrain Amadeus's wilder plans as long as his mentor trusted him. That was the dilemma. He could not curb future atrocities except by standing up to Amadeus. Yet he must not alienate Amadeus.

When Janet Seager brought the outrage in Singapore to the world, Richard had been in Sweden pondering the next Nobel Peace Prize. The recipient was an Eskimo chieftain who had arranged a precarious armistice between his own clan of seventy-nine souls and a clan of ninety-two that lived nearby – only eighty-five miles across the frozen tundra. There was no more plausible candidate in a world roiled by ethnic, religious, economic, and random strife.

Having completed their deliberations three days early because there were so few likely candidates, the eminent members of the Peace Prize Committee had found themselves unable to get immediate reservations out of crowded Stockholm. Prince Richard had been wait-listed for a flight to Beijing, whence he would fly to Xian. For the first time in his life he had been forced to wait like a common mortal for a seat on an airliner.

Richard laughed harshly in the quasi-privacy of his first-class seat in the McDonnell-Taiwan Super 120 airliner of SAS-Austrian-Sabena Airlines. Monsignor Luigi Bernando, the maverick Jesuit, often observed, 'To say the end justifies the means also signifies that the means must justify the end!' How would Amadeus Brinks justify the gory means he employed?

Amadeus had told a press conference at his villa in the Pyrenees that he was contributing $500 million as seed money for a fund to repair the damages suffered by private individuals in Singapore. An additional $500 million he earmarked to redevelop the infrastructure and to encourage new enterprises. In addition, technical expertise and hi-tech equipment would be contributed by various Brightman/Schreiner enterprises, including the Everbright Corporation of Xian.

A reporter for Alpha One who believed that no charity was ever more than a self-glorifying stunt, had flatly demanded, 'Why such generosity?'

Smiling benignly, Amadeus had replied, 'Just to get a foot in the door. There's a big clean-up job to be done. We've got to be quick off the mark, or the competition'll jump in ahead of us!'

The reporter was satisfied with that disclaimer, although he marvelled at finally meeting a relatively honest billionaire. Seeing beyond the cynical twinkle in Amadeus's eye, other reporters had been convinced that he was truly a Good Samaritan who had no thought of self-aggrandizement.

A twenty-inch screen rose from the deck of the first-class compartment when Richard pushed a button on his armrest. He had no need of remote banking or long distance shopping, and he was not interested in fifty-eight channels of vapid or salacious satnet programming. He touched the stylized drawing of an old-fashioned telephone on the screen and instructed the compubrain to find Amadeus Brinks wherever he might be.

After forty seconds, Brinks was on the line from Xian. Richard murmured congratulations on the munificent gesture, adding as if in an afterthought, 'Amadeus, I want to see you as soon as I get in!'

Their meeting was tense despite Richard's resolve to remain in his guru's good graces. Amadeus not only smiled, but embraced Richard with almost Latin fervour. He was, however, irritated at being summoned as if by royal command. Richard could be as imperious as the kings who were his forefathers.

The two flamboyant figures met in the soundproofed privacy of the large backroom which had once been the women's quarters of the old *yamen*. The scarlet-and-gold wall-hangings embroidered with imperial five-clawed dragons, the hammered brass lamps, and the elegant 500-year-old Ming Dynasty rosewood furniture created an ambience at once imposing and serene.

That ambience helped calm the disciple who was one of Amadeus's most powerful weapons in the battle to save humanity and the earth. That weapon now required burnishing. Richard had undeniably hectored him in the call from the airliner. There would assuredly be a showdown between them. Nonetheless, when it came down to brass tacks, Richard was too dependent on him – emotionally as well as intellectually – to press a disagreement to a showdown.

Yet Prince Richard of Greece and Denmark was a true child of the age of the satcabnets, which he so often and so animatedly adorned. He thought in blacks and whites.

Broadcasts were today even more crudely adversarial than they had been in the old days. The simplistic mountebanks who presented the extinct *Panorama* of the BBC and that still living fossil, *60 Minutes* once of CBS, had pilloried the innocent and the guilty indiscriminately. Today, everyone was presented as either a pure saint or a black-hearted villain. Nuance or shading were not compatible with the need to hold an audience counted in billions.

Television could be stunning technically and breathtaking aesthetically. It could be many other things as well, but it could not be fair.

Amadeus Brinks had invited Marie-Jeanne Erlanger to be present in the hope of diverting Richard's literal mind. Marie-Jeanne, who had not so long ago confessed shyly that she ached to sleep with him, was now Amadeus's mistress. He had no idea that she was already somewhat disenchanted with him. The ruthlessness that had sacrificed Fatima and Khazhak could be brutally thrilling in bed; it could, however, be cruelly chilling by daylight.

Marie-Jeanne knew she was meant to serve as a lightning rod to divert Richard's indignation, in which he was not alone. The massacre in Singapore had shaken the working group, that small circle of Amadeus's closest collaborators. Most were nervous at being the objective of the biggest manhunt ever mounted. Moreover, the assault on Singapore had appalled all but the hard core, which was composed of political/religious fanatics, sadists, and homicidal maniacs.

Marie-Jeanne was meant to charm the prince. But she sat in silence, watching the two men who might well hold the fate of the world in their hands.

Neither was particularly tall. Neither had been cast in a conventional heroic mould, yet both the billionaire and the royal prince were commanding, each in his own way.

Although an unlikely looking hero in his light Chinese summer robe, Amadeus was imposing because of his overwhelming self-confidence and his intellect. Like Sir Winston Churchill, he was pudgy, no more than five foot nine, and his plump figure attested to his devotion to the table and the bottle. Yet Amadeus, at fifty-one, was charged with energy many half his age could not muster. His bald head shone like a beacon; his brigand's white moustache was jaunty; and his movements were vigorous. But his slate-grey eyes were always withdrawn and watchful.

Beside the vibrant Amadeus, Prince Richard was a pale shape of worn old gold. Two or three inches taller, he was neither as bulky nor as energetic. Despite the parching heat of the Shaanxi plain in early June, he wore a natural linen suit with a pale-blue rollneck, cotton jumper. His tarnished silver-blond goatee was newly trimmed. His gestures were graceful but emphatic. His unease was manifest in the shadows that haunted his slightly protuberant pale-blue eyes.

Marie-Jeanne Erlanger was herself for the first time in her twenty-seven years acutely conscious of her own appearance and its impact on others. A little disappointed she might already be with Amadeus, who was her first true lover, he had, nonetheless, aroused her awareness of her physical nature.

Her peacock-blue Chinese-silk robe was a shade darker than her eyes, which were now deprived of the shield of thick lenses in square frames. Amadeus's first gift to her had been soft contact lenses that could be worn for weeks without removal. His greatest gift, however, had been making her value her own body, which she now pampered with massages, sculptured coiffures, and artful make-up.

Her thick blonde hair, highlighted with silver, was drawn back to reveal the features previously hidden behind a thick fringe and gold-rimmed glasses. She no longer appeared bony and inquisitorial. Her face was as sharp and as clean as a sword's edge, yet feminine and open.

Marie-Jeanne was gingerly amused by this summit meeting. She was also apprehensive.

'My dear, Richard, how good to see you!' Amadeus took the offensive. 'You know of my gift to Singapore ...? Yes, of course. We discussed it on the telephone.'

'And I said, maestro, how impressed I was. How moved!'

'So you did. It's not all destruction you see, even if turbulent night must come before the radiant dawn.' Orotund even for Amadeus Brinks, that sentence was clearly rehearsed. 'I can also tell you that I ordered the execution of the three surviving officers of the Saddamite Legion. They grossly exceeded their orders.'

'I never thought you *wanted* slaughter,' Richard replied. 'But you ... we all ... are responsible for that slaughter. Shooting Saddamite officers won't wipe the slate clean. Besides, you'd promised to give Singapore advance warning to prevent loss of life.'

'I gave warning long in advance. After the Jakarta incident, you'll recall, Singapore was warned. There wouldn't have been so much killing if they hadn't resisted so strongly.'

Amadeus Brinks realized immediately that his last sentence was a tactical error. Determined to keep Richard on his side, he would humble himself to placate that vain and short-tempered sprig of royalty. But that argument, convincing to a more supple mind, might appear illogical, even stupid, to Richard's literal mind.

'A figure of speech, Richard.' Brinks hastened to repair the damage. 'Only a metaphor. Still, forewarning Singapore only stiffened its resistance. We miscalculated. Instead of reducing loss of life, the warning ratcheted the death toll higher.'

'But you knew,' Richard said hotly. 'You knew turning the Saddamites loose to avenge themselves was bound to bring slaughter. How you could possibly ...'

'I must husband my para-militaries ... I must save the best for the final action. For Singapore I had to use the force that was available, the American Muslims.'

Although Brinks loathed pleading with his disciple, he continued, 'I put safeguards in place: Salisbury Smith and the Vixen, the ex-CIA men, Smith and Jones. All were told to restrain the Saddamites. But the control group lost contact. And who was to know they would run amok?'

'Anyone could've warned you about the Saddamites!'

Brinks looked into the Prince's eyes and exclaimed, 'Why didn't you then? Why can't you see the action was a success? The goal is so much closer.'

Marie-Jeanne could no longer restrain herself. She might now be ornamental, but she was not prepared to play the dumb blonde.

'Amadeus, may I say a word?' she asked. 'Only to clarify ....'

'Of course, my dear. As you wish.'

He was all condescending gallantry. As if her cosmetic transformation, her physical upgrading as the computer nerds would say, had been accompanied by an intellectual downgrading. As if she could now say nothing that would interest serious men.

'Remember what Father Luigi says,' Marie-Jeanne urged. 'The means we use to attain our goals transform us, transform the goal as well. Each of us is the sum total of everything he has done.'

'Nonsense, my dear!' Amadeus replied, without an instant's reflection. 'Luigi's just another Jesuit getting old. Wondering if he hasn't spent too much time on worldly concerns and not enough on cultivating his soul.'

Prince Richard raised an eyebrow at that summary dismissal of the central moral issue. He looked enquiringly at Marie-Jeanne. She shrugged minutely, as if to say, *Look, I tried, but what can one do? I can only keep trying to rein him in. You must, too!*

During that mute interchange, Amadeus soared into rhetorical flight: 'Entropy, Richard, entropy! If we can convince the opinion-makers that civilization is suffering from acute entropy, further drastic action will not be necessary. *If* they were sufficiently frightened, they might take the decisions necessary to ensure human survival.'

'You know, Amadeus, I am not sure what entropy really means,' Marie-Jeanne said. 'Though we all talk about it.'

'Take the Singapore action,' Brinks replied. 'It proves *absolutely* that entropy has set in ... that the global system is breaking up spontaneously. How otherwise could such an apparently senseless action have occurred?'

Marie-Jeanne wrinkled her forehead, and asked in a small voice, 'Senseless? The action at Singapore, you mean?'

'Of course,' he replied. 'What else?'

Prince Richard stared at Amadeus Brinks as if seeing his mentor for the first time. He flushed red, but was so astonished and so angry he could not say a word. He finally spoke through clenched teeth.

'But *you* did it, Brinks!' Richard's voice rose despite himself. '*You* did it. *You* threw those murderers at Singapore. And you now say that what you yourself did is proof positive that entropy has set in! How in the name of all that's holy ...'

'I thought historical determinism'd gone out with Marxism-Leninism years ago,' Marie-Jeanne observed. 'Are you saying you're just a cog in a machine, my darling? That you can't help what you do?'

'You don't understand,' Brinks objected. 'Of course, I willed it, the action in Singapore. The very fact that I willed it *proves* it's entropy. How else do human institutions break down? Only by individuals taking extraordinary actions that may appear illogical, even irrational, to others. What do you expect, bands of winged angels parading with placards warning of imminent doom by entropy? Are you such a damned fool, Richard?'

'Enough of this nonsense!' His Royal Highness Prince Richard of Greece and Denmark was now forthrightly furious. 'I've had it! I'm getting out before I become a loony, too.'

'Bear with me, Richard, old friend!' Amadeus Brinks smiled, though the veins in his temples throbbed visibly. 'You must stay with me. I promise I'll go over all the issues with the working group. I must make all of you understand what I'm working for – and how. I must have your support, Richard, your ungrudging support. We are old allies, you and I, old campaigners and old comrades. Just a while longer. Then we'll thrash it out ... thrash everything out!'

His face still flushed, Richard conceded, 'All right, Amadeus. As long as it's understood we go over *all* the issues. Not just the Singapore atrocity, but the biggest issue: *exactly where we are going with you – and why!*'

'Agreed, my friend.'

Amadeus Brinks thrust out his hand, and Prince Richard took it after an instant. Their eyes moist with unshed tears, they shook hands ceremoniously.

Forgotten in her corner, Marie-Jeanne Erlanger shook her blonde head in astonishment. They were behaving just like Boy Scouts, these two powerful men. Having quarrelled, they were now ostentatiously burying the hatchet. She would never understand the male mind.

What exactly did he seek, her lover? What precisely did he foresee? How would his outlandish tactics keep mankind from extinction?

'Richard, my old friend, just one more thing,' Brinks said with transparent sincerity. 'Showing ... convincing the world that it is suffering from entropy is more than half the battle. Once mankind recognizes that it has come to a dead end, we can back out and try another road to the future.'

Mike Goldsworthy addressed his audience of two as if speaking to 200 million on Alpha One. 'If we don't fix 'em, the bridges're kaput. Also kaput is the great American way of life. No more driving a hundred miles for a ball game. No more Cokes, no more apple pie, maybe ... God forbid ... no more Alpha One. If you can imagine such a catastrophe!'

His derisive words drifted through the vast reception-room of the penthouse in the Alpha One Tower. Catherine Loomis, Babs Berkeley and he were seated around the twelve-foot long glass slab of a coffee table.

'Mike, we're trying to get a handle on what's really going on,' Catherine Loomis chided. 'Also, of course, to find out what's become of your offsider, Janet. This smart-ass talk isn't helping.'

'Come on, Mike, get serious!' urged Babs Berkeley, who was already in practice, if not yet in name, Janet Seager's replacement.

'I *am* serious,' he responded. 'Goddamned serious!'

Babs Berkeley, who had all her career been just a step or two behind Janet Seager, frowned intently to show Catherine Loomis how seriously she, for one, took the discussion. Babs shook her head emphatically, and her long black hair hissed back and forth on the shoulders of her mauve-and-green Thai-silk jacket. Her black eyes shone, but her interlaced fingers were white with tension.

'Mike, you're talking about bridges,' Babs insisted, 'when we must talk about poor dear Janet. Also, where they're all coming from ... these atrocities. I've been tapping my sources in Washington and ...'

'What do they say, Babs?' Mike interjected. 'Exactly what? Enlighten us!'

'Well, not very much just now,' Babs responded lamely. 'Just they're very worried, and they'll let me know the minute they get anything solid. What're your sources telling you, Mike?'

'Much the same, Babs,' he replied. 'They don't have the vaguest idea what's going down or where it's coming from.'

Babs realized that she had irritated Mike by trying to impress Catherine Loomis with her sources. Getting on the wrong side of Mike was no part of her plan. She would need his wholehearted support if she were to step into Janet Seager's shoes. Afterwards, she'd be working closely with him, as closely as Janet had, despite their constant clashes. She could not afford to have him turn against her.

'Very careless of Janet to disappear just now.' Babs made amends by playing on Mike's well-known animosity towards his co-star. 'Though there must be a perfectly logical explanation why we haven't heard from her in a week.'

'Nine days, now!' Catherine observed ominously. 'Practically a lifetime in our business.'

'She told me she'd be out of touch for four or five days,' Mike said defensively. 'A couple more days isn't such a big deal. Maybe she'll come up with the goods ... the answers everybody's looking for.'

'Anyway, Mike, it's not bridges,' Catherine said. 'Whatever else, Janet's not gone missing because of your collapsing bridges.'

'Don't bet on that,' he advised. 'Crazier things've happened.'

'Bridges?' Babs Berkeley asked. 'What's all this about bridges?'

'They're falling down all over these United States,' Mike replied. 'But don't get me on that right now. As for the atrocities ... the missing airplanes, Bangkok, Jakarta, and Singapore ... none of my sources thinks it was the Islamic fundamentalists alone. Sure they're powerful ... tens of millions of fanatical supporters, but they just don't have the organization.

'Right now, Washington, London, and Tokyo are madhouses. Everybody's scared, and everybody's speculating wildly. Even Beijing is all at sea. And for once the Chinese're admitting it, for once not hiding behind their usual sullen silence. At least everybody agrees on one thing: we're facing a major conspiracy, a deadly threat to civilization.'

'What do we do now?' Catherine asked. 'What's her name ... Janet ... did a wonderful job. But how do we cap it?'

'With a show on the fundamentalists,' Babs suggested breathily. 'We do know they have a hand in this terrible business.'

'Good idea, Babs,' Mike conceded after waiting for Catherine to speak. 'But not just the fundamentalists. A show on Islam, all Islam. We'd take a lot of flak if we do only the fundamentalists. So let's do the whole *megillah*. We've got plenty of usable footage, mostly shot for *The Next Thousand Years*. Jan's in a lot of the shots.'

Babs Berkeley incautiously glowered before pulling on a smile and enthusing: 'Wonderful, Mike. Alpha One can keep Jan on screen that way.'

'Yeah,' he replied shortly. 'That's what I figured.'

Despite the easychair his posture was taut, even pugnacious. His chin was thrust forward aggressively and his wiry copper hair glinted.

'We'll do it!' Catherine took her eyes from Mike's face and decided.

'Mike, take a break from *The Next Thousand Years* and do Islam ... with Babs as co-host. We can also keep Janet on air with archive footage. Do it *now*. I want it to air in two weeks' time.'

Babs Berkeley readjusted her triumphant smile to look serious and dedicated. Magnanimous in victory, she placated Mike Goldsworthy and asserted her new status as co-presenter by asking innocently, 'Your bridges, Mike dear? Can we fit them into Islam?'

'Yeah, the damned bridges. Only way they'd fit is if we say: *Inshallah*! It's the will of Allah, just fate! But don't you believe it, baby.

'Bridges are falling down all over the world. No warning, just kerplop – and one of our bridges is missing. Up to two hundred a year in the great United States alone.'

'Sabotage?' Babs asked.

'No! The bridges are just tired. Not enough maintenance and too many years of use. Also excessive strains from much higher loads than were planned on.

'Turns out bridges suffer from decay just like people. Water seeps into the structure. Elasticity's lost when expansion joints get stuffed full of muck – and so on and so on.'

'All right, Mike.' Catherine sounded resigned. 'You've got a new audience. Tell her about your blasted bridges.'

'Sure thing, Catherine.' He grinned. 'There are more than six hundred thousand vehicular bridges in the US, big ones. Weight restrictions have been placed on two hundred fifty thousand for safety's sake. And thirty thousand've had to be closed.'

Catherine was silent, giving him his head. Babs frowned in concentration, hanging on his every word.

'The whole infrastructure's creaky, starting to collapse. The gucky chlorine-saturated stuff which comes out of the faucet here,' he said, 'it's reused a hundred times. We're drinking somebody's bath water, or, worse, reprocessed industrial waste. Water is short in practically the whole world, except the Amazon Valley and Ireland. We've outstripped our resources, and nobody's making more. That's entropy, kid!'

'Entropy?' Babs echoed.

'A fancy word for an unfancy condition. Civilization's beginning to go down under its own weight. If we don't do something drastic pronto . . . .'

'Mike, remember you were moaning about our lack of objectivity the other day?' Catherine interposed. 'I've been thinking – and you're right, Alpha One's top investigative reporter's been brainwashed by the greenies.'

'Me?' he protested. 'Me brainwashed? Don't be ridiculous.'

'Then why parrot their line? We already give too much air time to their rubbishy warnings. That toffy-nosed bastard Amadeus Brinks is always sounding off. But the world hasn't ended yet. And it won't end tomorrow morning either.'

Catherine rose and walked slowly towards the double doors that led to her bedroom suite.

'Amadeus isn't all that worried about the ecological balance.' She turned and declared vehemently, 'He's a fraud ... only wants power for himself. And a glowing image that'll help him grab power.'

'That's hard to believe,' Mike objected. 'He's always on the right side.'

'Regardless, let's stay away from ecology for a while,' Catherine directed. 'Do me a hot show on Islam instead. Lots of colourful footage, the wilder the better. They're a bunch of savages in Cadillacs and Rollses, that's all. Just think, female circumcision, those poor little baby girls.'

Mike Goldsworthy concealed the grin he knew he should be ashamed of. Kate the Great never had her mind off sex for long. She was genuinely moved when she thought of other females deprived by crude surgery of the pleasures around which her scant leisure revolved.

'Give me lots of controversy,' she added over her shoulder. 'You're getting soft. Give me a hardnosed show on the Muslims. And forget about the environmentalists for a while.'

'And Jan?' he asked. 'What're we gonna do about Jan?'

'You can start making noises on screen: our brave war correspondent, our hard-hitting investigative reporter, her mysterious disappearance. Alpha One will turn over mountains to find her.'

Catherine opened the double doors of her bedroom.

'That's not enough, Catherine,' he rejoined. 'We need action, not more talk. We've got to look for her ourselves. Maybe I should go to Singapore.'

'Not now, chum,' Catherine commanded. 'Too much to do here. The show on Islam . . . .'

'Catherine,' he interposed, 'somebody's got to find her, and I'm the best one to ...'

'Just carry on, Mike. The usual bumph about our intrepid, brilliant correspondent. But don't overdo it. You two're a great team, but she's replaceable, you know. So're you. So's everyone.'

'Thanks a lot, Kate,' Mike muttered as she closed the bedroom doors behind her. 'There's times I'd like to replace you.'

Babs Berkeley smiled speculatively.

XVIII

The 2-D, mono-sound television set in the palm-leaf hut ran off an automobile battery. It was not only very small, just twenty-eight inches across, but very old, practically an antique. The brandname on the frame above the screen was GRUNDIG *happyboy*.

In the age of 3-D, wraparound-sound 'casts projected on 120-inch wall screens, the *happyboy* was a living fossil. Viewers would no more think of viewing 'casts on minisat communicators than on a console set. The big 3-D screen was impregnably established as the standard. Except for portables with unfurling screens, the once universal console was now restricted to scientific applications for which the message was all and presentation was secondary.

For the satcabnets the reverse was true. Picture quality was all important, while content hardly mattered. All that really mattered for billions of satnet addicts, it seemed, was a constantly moving image backed by unceasing sound. The ether was covered with electronic wallpaper.

Bemused by the ancient *happyboy* flickering in the half-darkness of the thatched hut, Janet Seager remembered Catherine Loomis's explosion against impractical technology a few years earlier.

'Tribespeople are our biggest market, not only for broadcasts but for hardware, too.' Catherine had exclaimed in exasperation at a sales conference for the latest products of Alpha One's factories. 'Can you imagine a tribe using a highly sophisticated, all-applications minisat communicator? Might as well expect an Orthodox rabbi to be a connoisseur of ham or a Mongol herdsman to judge Beluga caviar.

'You boffins are always coming up with spanking new toys. But we're lumbered with making those hi-tech toys commercially viable. Sometimes we just can't sell them. And we shouldn't try!'

That outburst, Janet recalled with a small smile, had cost Kate the Great dear. The hypersensitive Jewish and Mongol lobbies had spiritedly attacked her 'bigoted comments'. Other satcabnets had raged both on behalf of the supranational manufacturers they owned. For some months under a black cloud, Kate was slated as a racist, a reactionary, an enemy of growth, and a defeatist. If she had not early on bullied the Alpha One board of management into a resounding affirmation of confidence in her, she would have been finished.

You could say or do almost anything on the satcabnets – and someone was always pushing the limits further out. Everything except paedophiliac snuff films now regularly came on screen, right down to reconstructed rapes, unreconstructed snuffs, and close-ups of executions.

You could do almost anything on screen, but you could *not* cast doubt on the desirability, the sheer necessity, of technical progress and economic growth. An ever-expanding, totally integrated world economy was the Holy Grail of this era – as venerated, as elusive, and as amorphous as the original Holy Grail.

Abandoning her sceptical thoughts, Janet exclaimed in annoyance when the picture of the *happyboy* began cycling. Berry Smith rose from the bamboo stool beside hers to twirl the big knobs of the TV set. The obsolete cathode tube delivered faded and frayed colours even when working at its temperamental best.

An elongated image emerged from the surrealistic swirls on the screen, and Janet saw Mike Goldsworthy seated at the control-table ostensibly leafing through a sheaf of news dispatches.

'...we'll be bringing you that long look at present day Islam next week.' His voice was distorted by the ancient *happyboy*. 'Much of the footage features my co-presenter Janet Seager. Unfortunately ... tragically ... it could be the last time we'll see Jan on Alpha One, except for reruns.

'Tens of thousands have called to ask why Jan hasn't been with me on our regular shows for two weeks now. Of course, Babs Berkeley has very competently ... some would say brilliantly ... filled her shoes. But, somehow, it's not the same thing. Not at all!'

Janet smiled mirthlessly and tucked her hand into Berry's. Poor Babs must be having a rough time, even being run down on air. Having so often been subjected to Mike's low-key denigration herself, she knew how cutting it could be. She was, however, surprised at his earnest tone. He sounded as if he truly regretted her absence.

'Only now do we at Alpha One feel we can explain Janet's absence without imperilling her,' Mike Goldsworthy continued sombrely. 'Quite frankly, we do not know where she is. She vanished after her last spectacular broadcast from Singapore. We have heard nothing further.'

Mike glanced at the sheaf of papers in his hand and laid it aside. The gesture was dismissive.

'I can only tell you now what little we do know, what you may have guessed.' He was hesitant, almost diffident. 'Janet Seager set out to get to the heart of the enigma: *What were the forces that wreaked such havoc in Singapore, Jakarta and Bangkok?*

'She has now vanished.

'The connection is plain to see. We are dealing with a vast and ruthless conspiracy. That much is clear.

'How can we say that Janet Seager is not also its victim?

'We hope and pray that she will come back to us. If she does not . . . .' He paused for ten seconds of empty air. 'If she does not come back to us safe and sound, the conspirators will never rest easy again. We shall run them down with all the power of the mightiest network on earth: Alpha One!'

Berry Smith asked, 'Does he really think his bluster will frighten anyone?'

'You know, Berry darling, in some ways you're naïve,' Janet replied. 'Comes of living in the secure playpen of the US Navy, I suppose. Mike's not bluffing. Alpha One is more powerful than anything you can name. If Kate the Great demands it, the White House will reverse any policy. For her, your navy'll send out task forces. Ditto the air force, the army, and the UN.'

'Come on, Jan. Goldsworthy doesn't know what he's up against. It's all empty threats.'

'Mike can back up his words. Even your mysterious Good Samaritan who orders all this slaughter must want ... need ... Alpha One on his side.'

'Maybe so.'

'Berry, we've got to get out of here. If I'm off screen too long, they'll forget about me. First the audience, then management. Even Kate will and Mike, too.'

'Inside a couple of weeks? That's loony.'

'I'm afraid it's not. Babs Berkeley's a fool. That makes her even more dangerous.'

Janet walked her fingertips up his thigh under his khaki shorts. When he reached out she came into his arms, and he lowered her to the palm-leaf matting on the split-bamboo floor. She turned away when he caressed her nipple through the flimsy blouse she wore with her batik sarong. She grasped his hand and held it still.

'Just a second, friend,' she laughed. 'Let me finish first. Once we start that sort of thing, there'll be no more talk!'

'All right, ma'am.' He lifted his hand from her breast and gently stroked her hip while she spoke. 'But you started it.'

'We've got to get out of here, Berry. Otherwise, they're sure to find us – your bloodthirsty environmental playmates or the government. I told you our surest security would've been my broadcasting ...'

'And the anti-terrorism branch would've found us in a minute,' he objected. 'Even if you don't believe it, surveillance now covers the island like a mosquito net on an old fourposter.'

'I believe you. I haven't even touched my minisat communicator .... But we can't dodge both sides indefinitely. If the Future Green Society gets its hands on me, it'll be just as bad as the anti-terrorism branch grabbing you.'

'Curtains either way.' His old-fashioned slang amused her. 'The Future Green dragon lady is out for your head. And your government friends won't bother with a trial for a terrorist like me. Who's going to worry about a renegade, a deserter who took up terrorism as a sideline? You're right, Jan. We've gotta make our break .... Can't loll around this tropical love nest much longer.'

The Concordia Execujet would be secure in hiding where he'd left it. The ground crew, which was employed by the Brightman/Schreiner subsidiary, Everbright Corporation, would have serviced and fuelled the airplane for immediate takeoff. The jet was not the problem. Getting undetected to the small airfield twenty-eight miles north of Johore Bahru on the Malaysian peninsula was, however, a major problem.

Berry Smith lay awake in the darkness of the hut on stilts after Jan had fallen asleep. Her soft breathing, rather like a contented cat's, accompanied his roiled thoughts.

It would not be so bad if he were not at odds with his own allies of the Future Green Society. His colleagues from Xian had grudgingly approved his giving Janet the inside story of the massive raid on Singapore. The emaciated chairwoman of the Greenies had, however, been volubly unhappy at being forced to rubber-stamp the decision outsiders had made in her absence. She resented their usurping her prerogatives, and she was furious at their giving the world that story.

Secrecy was for the chairwoman not simply a safeguard: it was her passion. She saw herself as a new *la Pasionaria*, stealthily undermining the crass, exploiting, polluting capitalist tyranny that was the government of Singapore.

If she had her way, hardly a brick would be left standing on another brick anywhere on the island. She had been born too late to join Chairman Mao Zedong's great proletarian Cultural Revolution, that mass assault on all civilized values. She was, nonetheless, dedicated to the sacred mission for which the chairman had once rallied his Red Guards with the apocalyptic slogan: *Destroy all the old ways, smash every vestige of the old beliefs, crush the old learning, and wipe out the old morality!*

Though Amadeus Brinks valued the chairwoman highly, he had told Berry, 'She's monumentally confused. Doesn't know whether she's Joan of Arc, St Barbara of the Artillery, or a particularly determined termite gnawing away at the foundations of civilization!'

The chairwoman, Berry Smith reflected, had known exactly who she was and exactly what she was doing when she withdrew her previous grudging tolerance and decreed that Janet Seager must die for having revealed so many 'military secrets' of the ecological task force. He had not tarried to debate the issue, but had slipped away while she was still raving. Five minutes after the chairwoman had announced her decision 'to execute the capitalist spy woman', Jan and he were a mile away from the old rubber warehouse.

But his red Lamborghini was too conspicuous even in car-mad Singapore. He had found a solid family sedan in the parking lot of the Cold Storage Tower on Orchard Road, a Proton Saga made in Malaysia eight years earlier. While Berry bypassed the electronic lock, Jan was on her minisat to Diminity Oei.

Unless they were very unlucky, the government's electronic surveillance would not yet have reached down to prosaic short-range internal calls. Nor would official eavesdroppers yet connect Janet Seager, whom they had seen on the screen, with the fugitive George Fellows. Besides, he was still only a potential fugitive, although he would certainly be unmasked when twenty-one intelligence services pooled their information.

There was, however, as yet no indication that Singapore Intelligence had made the connection between Salisbury Smith and George Fellows or the further connection between the amiable aeronautical engineer and the assault. But he would certainly be smoked out if the police found him. No one would stand up to their brutal questioning. Anyway, his fingerprints were on file in the Pentagon.

Janet had only told Diminity that she needed a secluded hideaway for a few days. Diminity would not reveal their whereabouts, since reporting the hue and cry after the vanished Janet Seager would keep Diminity Oei on screen for a week or more. Moved as well by personal gratitude, as Janet liked to believe, Diminity had given terse directions over the scrambled minisat circuit to the palm-leaf hut in Singapore's last surviving kampong on the island's north-west shore.

The hut belonged to a great-uncle of Diminity's Malay admirer, Lieutenant Abdul Sharif. Many Malays had bemoaned the passing of the old life in rural kampongs. Given the choice of remaining in kampongs or moving to new apartments of the Singapore Housing Trust, the Malays had tearfully chosen to go. Preserved as a memento of an earlier, simpler and happier day, the last kampong was now deserted except for a flock of scrawny brown chickens with long, scaly, yellow legs.

An ideal place to hide, it had only one drawback: Diminity had warned Jan that the big hamadryads, king cobras, that grew to fifteen feet, liked to slither between the stilts of the huts to dine on the witless chickens. Fearless in the cockpit or the boudoir, Berry had a morbid fear of snakes.

Evading discovery was, however, easy. Wearing the simple Malay costume of a filmy blouse and a wraparound batik sarong cinched at the waist, Janet covered her head with a scarf like a devout Muslim woman whenever she left the hut. Although her crow-black hair would not single her out, the scarf hid her too-white skin and her too-familiar features. Camouflaged by baggy shorts and a grubby T-shirt, Berry hid his face beneath a tattered straw hat when foraging for food.

They'd had only one serious scare. Stealing eggs from the chickens by moonlight, Berry had been surprised by seven men dressed like himself in shorts, T-shirts, and rubber sandals. They were turning away to avoid him when he straightened up and saw them.

That eye contact could not be ignored. The wanderers in the night had stopped to talk, astonished at meeting a white *tuan* in a deserted kampong at one in the morning. Identifying himself simply as Ali, their leader happily acknowledged that he was a fisherman by day and a smuggler by night.

He said candidly in his creaky English that he was not afraid of Berry. Because many decades had passed since Europeans officered the Singapore Police Force, Berry could not be hunting the night-wanderers. The government, Ali complained, called them criminals, though they were only selling gold to rich and edgy Chinese as a movable nest egg.

Berry and Ali had parted with expressions of mutual esteem. Five minutes later, Berry had heard the rumble of powerful motors on the narrow straits that separated Singapore from peninsular Malaysia.

After that encounter in the night, Berry's caution denied them even a cooking fire. They were, however, not much worried about being discovered by chance. Diminity had told Jan that both Chinese and Malays believed the abandoned kampong was haunted by the spirits of ancestors left behind when the clan moved.

'If Abdul gets homesick for his kampong,' Diminity had added, 'I know just how to take his mind off that subject.'

Reassuring as was Diminity's salacious chuckle, the refuge was good for only a few days. Diminity was sure to crack in time, no matter how grateful she was to Jan. She had to live in Singapore after they were gone, and being a president's granddaughter imposed certain civil obligations. Besides, search helicopters would in time find the sturdy Proton Saga under the shallow water that lapped at the mangrove swamp behind the kampong.

Pressed by Jan, Berry had agreed to make their break within the next two days. He had no idea how they would get away, but characteristically trusted to inspiration to supply the answer. He had happily depended on fate all his feckless life. Fate had never failed him, though he'd had some very close shaves.

Yet a small harsh voice spoke to Berry Smith when he lay on the springy bamboo floor inviting sleep. The voice was not only harsh. It was insistent and abusive.

'Come on, Smith!' it grated. 'Charm and gall won't get you out of this pickle. You're not the same lucky scallywag any more. Whoever thought to see Berry Smith crusading for a better world? Whoever thought Berry Smith would risk his neck for a dame who wouldn't sleep with him till he proved he was a new and better man?'

XIX

In the distance, wood creaked on metal. Berry sat up, straining to identify the noise. The creaking grew louder, and he heard soft splashing, evidently oars dipping into the narrow channel that divides Singapore from Malaysia. The palm-leaf hut was no more than fifty feet from the water's edge. The splashing grew louder as the craft approached and then dwindled as it drew away.

'No woman's going to save you this time!' The grating voice resumed when Berry lay back again. 'You're stuck with this woman, *your* woman! No more playing the cavalier for admirals' wives! It's up to you to get her and yourself out safe and sound. Of course, there'll be some explaining to do when ... if ... you get back to Xian.'

The offensive voice first became familiar to Berry Smith, then monotonous and finally lulling. He had heard fellow pilots talk of being bored by prolonged exposure to danger, even though deathly scared at first. He had never experienced that paradoxical response himself, for his insouciant temperament made him virtually immune to fear.

He was now truly fearful – for the first time in his charmed life. His commitment to Janet, although still unspoken, had made him vulnerable. They had never discussed the future, much less a future together. Nonetheless, he felt responsible for her; for the first time in his thirty-four years committed to a woman.

Never before had he worried about the future, but her safety and her well-being now weighed on his shoulders. Astonished by that realization, he was exultant too. He was also frightened.

After a time, Berry slept. His deep regular breathing mingled with Jan's feline purring.

Alien sounds woke Berry: foliage rasping against cloth and whispers buzzing like awakening bees. He heard shoes creaking and metallic tinkling. Fully awake, he smelled burning cigarettes, the sweet Virginia tobacco the Chinese preferred and the pungent tobacco seeded with cloves the Malays smoked.

The interlopers were barely taking minimal precautions against being discovered. Everyone knew the kampong was deserted, everyone who roamed the north-west shore by night, which meant smugglers and police patrols.

Only a police patrol would be so careless. Besides, the smugglers were Malays almost to a man, and how many Malays smoked tailor-made cigarettes? No smuggler or fisherman wore creaky leather shoes. They favoured rubber sandals. Chinese and Malay constables, he concluded, were staking out a position in the deserted kampong, most likely hoping to ambush gold smugglers.

With the advent of nominal free trade throughout the world and the abolition of almost all tariffs and quotas, few goods were still worth smuggling. Why do it the hard way, the dangerous way, when the profits of legitimate trade were so high? But Singapore banned the importing of precious stones and precious metals. The official justification was protecting the rock-solid Singapore dollar. The true motivation was a puritanical determination not to leave such luxury goods untaxed.

The sensible Customs service did, however, attempt to halt the traffic in diamonds, rubies and emeralds, which were more valuable in Singapore, because banned, than anywhere else in East Asia. The stones could be hidden in clothing, books, cosmetics, and, of course, bodily orifices. Nor did the police enforce the ban on gems aside from following up an occasional tip or planting stones on a slippery criminal whom they could hold on no other charge.

Gold was another matter. An excess of gold in private hands could truly threaten the Singapore dollar by destabilizing monetary values. Besides, gold was bulky and heavy – and, therefore, difficult to conceal in bulk. Moreover, an efficient organization was required to market gold surreptitiously, and no large criminal organization could long evade police vigilance. The prohibition on gold was, therefore, rigorously enforced.

Berry clamped a hand over Jan's mouth and shook her gently. When she stirred, he cut off her confused protests with his palm and whispered into her ear, 'There's a police patrol practically underneath us. Get dressed and for God's sake don't make a sound!'

Were the police, Berry wondered, really after them? Had the car been sighted in its watery grave? Or were they only hunting smugglers?

He knew that his Lamborghini had been found. The news reader had been scathing about decadent foreign tastes when reporting that a flashy twenty-six-year-old scarlet sports car had been found abandoned. Only a millionaire several times over could run a vintage car in a city-state that imposed swingeing taxes on cars as they grew older, thus keeping aged and presumably unsafe vehicles off the road. George Fellows, who had rented the two-seater 12-cylinder Lamborghini, was 'requested to come forward'.

The authorities must have some kind of bead on him, Berry concluded, though they might not yet know of his role in the assault. The announcement was not friendly, but it was measured. It was not an urgent warning to report any sighting of a major criminal. It had not even described him.

Berry was distracted from his logic by the flash of a thigh and the glimpse of a breast in the moonlight. Janet was, somehow, even more erotic while dressing than when completely naked.

The entire thought process had taken no more than fifty-five seconds after his awakening. With Jan now ready for flight, Berry crept on hands and knees to the window, which was only a small square opening in the side of the hut.

Directly beneath him in the bright moonlight he saw twelve men wearing dark coveralls with POLICE emblazoned on their backs and heavy jungle boots with composite canvas-rubber-leather uppers. They were armed with high velocity Kuanyew turbo-submachine-guns. Having evidently halted for a smoke, they were now trudging down to the water's edge, inadvertently cutting him off from the mooring of the ramshackle sampan he used for fishing expeditions.

The noose was tightening around their necks, although the police were not aware of their presence. The knotted mangrove thicket might be their last chance to keep the patrol from finding them.

The ambush party settled into depressions strung along the bank, its right flank on a ramshackle jetty, its left flank on the edge of the mangrove thicket. Further to the left, the sampan swung on a frayed rope attached to a stone-filled jerrycan on the bottom of the straits. Not the most elegant anchor in the world, but neither was the sampan the most elegant craft in the world.

Cinching his baggy shorts, Berry motioned to Jan to kilt up her sarong so that it would not hobble her and she preceded him down the rickety ladder, watchful for the cobras he so feared, though he feared little else on earth. She knew that her sudden appearance would frighten away any snake that might be hunting chickens or rats in the darkness beneath the huts.

Berry picked up the stained canvas holdall that contained all their possessions except the passports they kept on their persons: a plastic zipbag holding Janet's remaining cosmetics and her minisat, a fresh skirt, a rumpled blouse, a small Malay-English dictionary, a pair of black pumps, and a basic change of underwear; his four-cell flashlight, a pair of chino trousers, a matching jacket, two pairs of boxer shorts, the .22 calibre pistol he had kept for target practice, and a small waterproof leather bag, which contained $25,000 in notes and gold coins. The clothing padded the metal articles so that they could not rattle, and the pistol was thrust into one of his well-worn suede Hush Puppies.

Unspeaking, they felt their way between the dark deserted huts towards the mangrove thickets, which stretched forty feet inland from the water's edge. A few weeks earlier he would have chortled at the suggestion that a woman's hand in his while he fled through the night would be an encouragement, rather than an impediment. Before Janet reappeared, he would not have been fleeing *with* a woman but *from* a jealous woman or an outraged husband.

A bare patch some fifteen feet across stretched from the last hut to the mangroves. Offering no cover, it was brightly lit by the full moon. Berry could see the twelve policemen as small dark humps along the bank, but he could not tell which way they faced.

Still, he had no choice. He had to act as if all were watching the moonlight on the wavelets where their natural prey, the smuggling boats, must appear.

Every field manual ever issued by any army anywhere directed an ambush party to guard its rear and its flanks against counter-ambush. Nonetheless, Berry Smith had to assume that this patrol, feeling itself totally secure in its island fortress, would flout that rule. Yet only one policeman need glance over his shoulder to spot them.

Berry motioned Jan to his left so that he stood between the police and her. It was only a gesture. Some shield he would be if the Kuanyew turbo-submachine-guns opened up with 1200 slugs a minute. Inconsequentially, he remembered the marine gunnery sergeant who gave naval officers refresher courses in small arms at San Diego.

'You gents ... ah ... *gentlemen.*' A lifetime of scorn and resentment loaded that word. 'You gotta remember only one goddamned thing: when the Kuanyews open up, it's goodnight sweetheart. Their titanium and carbon barrels never melt. They can keep firing all night.'

The temptation was almost irresistible. It seemed so much safer to crawl across the fifteen feet of open ground that divided them from the mangroves. Scanning the water, the police would not see them, and the cobras would have time to slither away. Even a dash across the clearing would leave them exposed for only seconds.

Berry decided against both obvious courses. Crawling would take too long, while running could be noisy – and rapid movement would attract police attention. They began to walk across the clearing, not tarrying but not rushing either.

Not his phobia about snakes, Berry reassured himself, had decided him against creeping, but reasoned judgement. He felt fifty feet wide and twice as tall, a gigantic, slow-moving target in the moonlight. But he was simply not much afraid of guns. Yet his hands were clenched so tight that his fingers were white. He could all but feel the rasp of the cobra's scales as it slithered over his feet, bare except for rubber sandals.

It was all nonsense, of course. Cobras were shy of men. Besides, a cornered cobra would strike before coming so close. If he could help it, he would not corner so much as a tiny cheechuk lizard, much less a fifteen-foot cobra. Berry forced one foot ahead of the other, exerting all his willpower to keep from running. Sweat dripped cold down his chest, and his breath rasped in his throat.

Janet was strolling along as coolly as if window shopping on Madison Avenue. Her composure made him proud of her and shamed his fear.

Berry glimpsed movement on the ground some five feet ahead. He forced himself not to dash back in panic. He forced himself to look at the slithering shape. He looked hard, shuddered, and moved his left leg forward against the resistance of its own muscles.

The enormous black serpent he had imagined was actually a slender sinuous shape only a foot or two long. Black, it was banded like a candy cane with brilliant yellow stripes. Limp with relief, he forgot to be afraid of the gaudy little snake.

It was almost pretty because it was not the feared black-scaled monster with its gaping mouth exposing two great poison fangs. It wasn't even venomous. Poisonous snakes had no need of the brilliant camouflage that protected this little fellow. He was, nonetheless, relieved when the creature disappeared into the darkness on the other side of the clearing.

In the cover of the close-growing mangroves, Jan laid her hand on his forearm in silent thanks for bringing them safe into the thicket. She was surprised to find his skin clammy cold and more surprised to feel him tremble.

'What's wrong, darling?' The whispered endearment was spontaneous. 'You're trembling.'

'I was scared to death!' He did not dissemble. 'I saw something moving. A snake! For a moment, I thought it was a cobra. But it was only a little fellow ... striped bright yellow. Then I remembered poisonous snakes don't need to camouflage themselves.'

'No shame in being afraid. You had good reason to be afraid. You know, I picked up some odd local lore reading myself into this assignment.' She did not add, since he already knew, that her memory was virtually indelible. 'You saw a banded krait. Its venom is just as deadly as a cobra's, and it strikes without warning. "Docile by day", the book said, "but active at night ... unpredictable and *very* dangerous". The gaudy colours're to warn off predators that might think it is only a tasty morsel.'

'You're some comforter!' His forced grin was just visible in the gloom of the thicket. 'A great little morale booster!'

'I'm sorry, Berry!'

She regretted having spoken without thinking. But his reaction was funny, as well as poignant, and she chuckled.

'What next?' Jan was demonstratively dependent to restore whatever confidence he might have lost by confessing to fear. 'Where do we go from here, Commander?'

'The sampan's our only hope, slim as it is,' he replied after a moment. 'We'll have to swim for it ... lie up till they leave. They checked it with field-glasses. Chances are they won't board it. But they're certain to search around the kampong.'

'And if they decide to search the sampan? I hate to be pessimistic, but . . . .'

'What else is there? Try to hide on land and they're sure to grab us.'

The council of war conducted in apprehensive whispers ended on that fatalistic note, but Berry added, 'Let me have your passport.'

'Whatever for?' Jan obediently fished the slim document from her bra. 'We're not going to meet an immigration officer, are we?'

'Just to keep it safe.' Berry's tone was again light and confident. 'I'll shove it into the waterproof cash-bag along with the pistol.'

'You're not planning to fight twelve cops, are you?' Janet asked. 'You're quite sure you're all right, Berry? Completely recovered?'

He almost snapped at her not to patronize him, but he caught himself. Wondering at his uncharacteristic irascibility, he answered easily, 'I'm fine now. Just don't tell me about poisonous white water-snakes.'

Warm and welcoming, the salt water washed away the glutinous black mud of the mangrove swamp. Swimming fifty feet to the sampan was easy, though they had to move very slowly. Abrupt movement could not only attract police notice, but stir up luminous algae to surround the swimmers with a glowing halo. Pulling themselves aboard on the side away from the ambush party, they hardly rocked the seventeen-foot craft. The pungent stench of fish and the film of iridescent scales on the deck welcomed them to their new refuge.

A refuge for how long? And would they be caught in crossfire between the patrol and the smugglers?

The stage was set, and all the actors were in place. Strung along the bank to their right, the police were unaware of their presence. Somewhere down channel to the left, driven by twin 350-horsepower inboard-outboard engines, the smugglers' long black 'serpent' boat was skimming at fifty knots towards an unknown rendezvous.

Since neither knew of Jan and Berry's presence, they had an edge. Exclusive information was always an advantage. But how to use it?

'My minisat,' Jan suggested. 'The smugglers're bound to have some kind of radio aboard. At the least, a telephone. I'll use the common channel.'

'Not now, Jan. If we tip them to the ambush, they'll turn around and leave us to rot here. *If* the cops don't pick up your message and grab us!'

'It's instinct,' Jan conceded. 'I always think: *only communicate*!'

'Not in this mess. But keep the minisat handy. Who knows when . . . .'

'Well, I ...' Janet acknowledged. 'It's not so easy, is it? But just sitting here? Maybe we could cut the sampan loose.'

'And drift towards the ambush! Even if we didn't use the little outboard, the cops'd wonder how the sampan just happened to tear loose from its mooring just now.'

'I see,' she said in a small voice. 'I'd like a hug, Berry.'

The muted rumble of the twin 350-horsepower engine drifted upstream half an hour later, when the first faint light began to touch the eastern sky. Jan and Berry saw the policemen stand and stretch before resuming their hidden positions.

It was still too soon to alert the smugglers even if it were Ali's band. Had they had been old friends or business partners, instead of the most casual of acquaintances, Ali would still not have risked his precious boat and his crew's lives for a pair of forlorn foreigners. Was there, Berry wondered, any point in alerting the smugglers at all?

Six minutes later, the serpent boat swept past the sampan. Its luminescent wake dwindled as it slowed to tie up at the ramshackle jetty 300 yards to the east. No lights showed; even the flare of the exhausts was suppressed. The black boat was only a more solid shadow on the moonlit water, a ghost vessel. It was slowing right in front of the patrol's Kuanyew submachine-guns, though still a little too far from shore for accurate ranging.

'Tell him now!' Berry directed. 'Tell him to turn around and pour on the gas. Tell him the cops've blocked the eastern straits with patrol boats.'

The twin 350s roared unmuffled into full power before Jan had finished her message. The serpent boat was swinging erratically, unable to turn its length at full power without yawing back and forth.

'He didn't even ask who I was,' Jan marvelled. 'Or why I was telling him. Just grunted!'

'He probably thinks you're a houri-angel from the Muslim heaven. Who'd ask at a time . . . .'

The Kuanyews opened up, blue fire arching across the moonlit straits. The serpent boat jinked as if it had hit an obstacle, and its bows swung towards its tormentors. Its diamond-bright searchlights raked the shore, making the night as bright as a floodlit stage. Dazzled by the glare, the police stopped firing.

The orange flare of Indonesian-made turbo-rifles rose from the boat, and blue fire arched again from the shore. The serpent boat was no longer moving forward, but inching backward as the helmsman strove to complete the sharp 180-degree turn.

The smugglers' searchlights raked the shore, again blinding the ambush party. Diminished blue flashes indicated that only six Kuanyews were still firing, as if the police had taken heavy casualties. But their accurate shooting knocked out both searchlights within seconds.

Berry levelled his long-barrelled target pistol. Loaded with .22 calibre long-rifle cartridges, it was extraordinarily accurate in the hands of an expert. Resting the barrel on his left forearm, he squeezed off ten shots. When the magazine was empty, he swept Jan to the deckboards and fell beside her.

A devil's carnival erupted. Cataracts of blue fire arched from the police position towards the sampan. Berry laughed, and his teeth flashed in the oncoming dawn. He laughed and lifted the oil-soaked rags that lay beside the fuel can of the Seagull outboard at the stern. He flicked the cigarette lighter he had in the past used to light the kerosene running lamps.

'Have you gone nuts?' Janet screamed. 'What *are* you doing?'

'Looks like they can't see us too well,' he replied. 'I'll give 'em something to shoot at.'

The flame touched the rags, which smouldered for a few seconds before little yellow tongues began to flicker in their midst. Berry tossed the rags towards the bow. A minute later, flames licked the deck's dry timbers. Within an instant the sampan was well ablaze.

Janet shrank towards the stern, which was still free of flame, though the timbers were already hot to the touch. A spark sailed through the air to land on her bare arm, then four or five, then a glowing fountain. To her surprise, they hardly hurt before they died.

Through the smoke she saw that the serpent boat had completed its turn and was bearing down on them. The Kuanyews' fire was now split between the two targets. The serpent boat was still accelerating.

The little Seagull outboard began popping beside her. When Berry cast off the mooring rope, the sampan chugged towards the serpent boat. Rising high above the luminous wave its bow raised, the black boat bore down on the frail sampan. An instant before a collision, it swerved. Slowing slightly, the black boat passed alongside the sampan. Many hands reached down to lift them to safety. The smuggler called Ali was paying his debt to the outsiders who had warned him of the ambush and fought his enemies.

XX

Mitchell Goldsworthy's mood was bleak when he was ushered to his suite by his old acquaintance, the portly general manager of the Oriental Hotel. Above all, he felt he should not have come to Singapore.

Only a bruising argument with Kate had finally won him her grudging permission to make the long journey after the *Report on Islam* was final-disked. He was also disturbed by Kate's personal distress at his insistence on dropping everything to go off and find the missing Janet Seager. Remarkably, Kate had allowed him to see that she was jealous of the bond that joined him to Jan, although he had patiently explained that it was professional, not personal.

No more than the US Marines would leave their dead on the battlefield, he had pointed out, should Alpha One allow one of its stars to simply disappear without making a damned serious effort to find her. Kate had finally accepted that argument, reinforced as it was by his indisputable assertion that Jan's disappearance was now a big story in itself.

'Who,' he had then asked, 'is better suited to cover that story than me?'

Nonetheless, Kate clearly believed that it was more than professional concern that drove him to Singapore. He had pointed out again that he did not particularly like Janet and had pointed out that they were constantly squabbling. Still, Kate insisted this search was an intensely personal matter.

With obvious bad grace, she had finally allowed him to go – but only after setting a strict timetable. He was to be back in New York to continue to work on *The Next Thousand Years* no more than four days after his departure.

He had just endured a rough twelve-hour flight on the Universal Global non-stop flight from New York, for the big 787 had been tossed about by clear air turbulence like a cork in a whirlpool. Yet there could be no question of his snatching even a catnap. His time in Singapore effectively reduced to a little more than two full days, he could not allow himself to rest until he was totally exhausted and could no longer function.

Diminity Oei, Alpha One's Singapore stringer, had met him at the airport and reported that all the efforts of the local staff had been in vain. He had not listened too carefully to her detailed account of visits to places and persons unknown to him in search of Janet Seager by staffers whose names were also unknown to him. Diminity had made a damned good case that she had mounted a thorough search by everyone she could muster except the police.

'Why no cops?' he had asked, marvelling that a major search for a major satnet star was being conducted without official assistance.

'Ms Loomis,' she had replied, 'told me to keep the police out of it.'

'For Chris' sake, Diminity, that was more than a week ago, when Catherine thought she could keep it quiet. The whole world and his imbecile brother now know Janet's missing . . . . Let's get the cops on it right now.'

She agreed immediately, and used her minisat to call the deputy commissioner for intelligence and counter-terrorism. Mike heard the policeman laugh and reply, 'Aren't you a little late, Dimmy? We've been looking for Janet Seager for six days now. So far nothing solid, but we'll keep at it.'

'I did wonder why you hadn't been around to give me the third degree,' she replied.

'No need. We're tracking her movements ... expect something very soon. Goodbye now.'

Even to Mike's ear, which was dulled by fatigue, that exchange sounded false, almost contrived. Somehow, he sensed, Diminity Oei was being less than candid with him. He made a mental note to grill her again just as soon as he felt half human. She was, after all, an employee of Alpha One and she must realize that he could destroy her if she did not co-operate fully.

As if she sensed his thoughts, Diminity murmured, half to herself, 'I wonder if it's anything to do with George Fellows. No, Jan wouldn't . . . .'

'Fellows?' Mike demanded. 'Who's he?'

'Oh, just an American who's something in aviation. Jan was seeing a lot of him. But it's absurd to think he had anything to do—'

Mike Goldsworthy was once again ambushed by his own emotions.

To his own surprise, he was annoyed at Jan's 'seeing a lot' of this unknown man. Why he should feel that way, he could not explain. As he had told Kate, his interest in Jan was solely professional. He didn't even like her particularly, but he couldn't desert her.

'Tell me more about this Fellows,' he asked.

'Very handsome,' Diminity replied slowly, 'if you like older men with silver hair and dark-green eyes. Looked like a demon to me, but Jan didn't seem to mind. I guess American demons don't have green eyes.'

'No, usually red,' Mike agreed absent-mindedly. 'Where can I find him?'

'I'm not sure, Mr Goldsworthy. You might try Universal Global's vice president, Johnnie Erbschlichter. George Fellows was working out of his office.'

Having thus salved her conscience, Diminity offered no more.

She had faithfully promised she would tell no one of the deserted kampong to which Jan Seager and George Fellows had fled. She did not even know whether they were still there. Anticipating questioning like Mike Goldsworthy's, she had made it her business *not* to know.

Yet she was an employee of Alpha One. She owed a certain professional loyalty to the satnet, though naturally not the intense personal loyalty she felt towards Janet. Still, she had to give Alpha One some assistance. Mike Goldsworthy's flurried arrival had brought that point home, and she had given him as much as she could without betraying Jan.

Finally alone in his suite, Mike shucked off his sweaty clothes and stepped under a cold shower. Sipping coffee afterwards and shivering in the icy air-conditioning, he felt he was beginning to come alive. He had already questioned the hotel manager, who could tell him no more than he had already told Diminity and the police: Janet Seager had left early on the morning of the day after the raid and had been seen no more in the Oriental Hotel.

Well, Mike concluded, there was one advantage of being known throughout the world: he could just call this airline vice president on the vue-phone. No need for a personal visit.

'I *am* honoured!' Johannes Erbaschlichter declared. 'First poor Janet and now the senior member of the team, Mitchell Goldsworthy himself. Sorry I couldn't meet you at the airport. I was totally tied up. And now? You've found her? You're calling to book passage back for both of you?'

'Unfortunately no, Mr Erbschlichter . . . .'

'Call me Johnnie. Everybody does. Easier than Erbschlichter.'

'No, Johnnie, we haven't found Jan. She's still very much missing. I suppose you have no idea ...?'

'Sadly, none whatsoever.'

'Well, then, can you tell me where to find George Fellows? Someone said he might . . . .'

'Oh, you don't know? I have seen not a trace of George since the attack. He also has disappeared.'

Promising himself he would give Diminity hell for withholding that vital information, Mike asked, 'At the same time as Jan?'

'Yes, you could say that. All I know is he went off to Civil Defence Headquarters, worked through the night there, and then vanished without a trace.'

'Could they be together?'

'All things are possible, Mr Goldsworthy. Yes, they were seeing much of each other.'

'You've tried his home ... wherever he was living?'

'Naturally. And not a trace.'

'I hate to go over the same ground again, but could you give me his address? Also, where do I find Civil Defence Headquarters? There's hardly a hope in hell of turning up anything new. But I've got to try.'

Despite the powerful air-conditioning in the chauffeur-driven Jaguar the hotel had provided, the stench of old fires and wet ashes blew through the car. The neat, all but polished, streets showed no sign of the vicious assault two weeks earlier, but clearing the damaged sites was releasing those unpleasant odours into the air. Although he was scanning the scene for material for his 'casts, part of Mike's mind was conducting a dialogue with itself.

Why, it asked, am I in Singapore anyway? Why don't I leave it to the cops?

Because she'd do the same for me, he answered himself. In our shitty business that kind of loyalty is rare. So, I guess, I've got to do as she would for me.

And then, apparently quite irrelevantly: God, sometimes I wish I could ditch the whole thing – cameras, notoriety, oversimplification to the point of imbecility, glamour, Kate the Great, and all!

And then, Buster, he asked, what would you do?

Damned if I know, he confessed to himself. I guess I'm hooked.

And the perks are great: first-class travel and hotels, lots of respect, and a licence to say what you please – as long as you don't make it too complicated or strike one of Kate the Great's taboos.

Inspection of George Fellows' penthouse had yielded only a question: what did the man do in aviation to afford a spread like that? A discarded minisat communicator disk and a half-used lipstick only confirmed what he already knew from Diminity and from Erbschlichter. Jan and this Fellows bozo had indeed seen a lot of each other.

The civil defence bunker on Canning Rise was manned by a skeleton staff. The receptionist directed him to the deputy director, who was seated at a battered grey-metal desk. Her sari was emerald green shot with gold thread, and her interest was wholly engaged the moment he approached her.

A flood of words threatened to overwhelm Mike. She expressed her admiration for his 'literate and fearless reporting, so unlike the others'. Although he enjoyed that praise, all the more welcome because it was not strictly true, he finally cut her off.

'Was George Fellows here with you the night of the attack?' he asked. 'Do you know where he went from here?'

'Yes he was,' she answered. 'But I don't know where he went.'

'No idea at all?'

'Only a guess. I can tell you what I told Ms Janet Seager.'

'She was here, too?' Mike was excited at picking up Jan's trail.

'Looking for Mr Fellows. I told her to try the Future Green Society on Northbridge Road. He was often there. And that was the last I saw of either of them. Oh, Mr Goldsworthy, I do hope you . . . .'

The smell of old rubber struck Mike when the chauffeur delivered him to the whitewashed former warehouse that now accommodated the Future Green Society. Once again, his fame won him instant access to the stick-lean, middle-aged Chinese lady in the ostentatiously plain blue sack of a dress who was the society's chairwoman for East Asia. She regarded him balefully, all but openly antagonistic. But, oddly enough, she was not loath to talk.

'Yes, they were both here,' she declared. 'And Janet Seager was alone ... no camera crew, no sat-dish. She was obviously not covering a story, just looking for George Fellows.'

'And then?' Mike prompted.

'Suddenly about noon they left. No farewell ... not a word to anyone. One minute they were here, and the next they'd vanished. You know, we're looking for them, too. George Fellows took some things that belong to us ... some very valuable things. But we've had no success.'

Finally overwhelmed by cumulative fatigue and the hot muggy atmosphere, Mike realized that it was past midnight. His travels across Singapore had consumed the day. He directed his driver to the hotel and collapsed into bed, confident that he would awaken automatically at his usual 7 a.m. despite the time change.

That was a miscalculation. He found, instead, that he could not sleep at all. Determined not to take a sedative, he checked with the desk in New York, which reported nothing new that would affect him. Then, just a little maliciously, he telephoned Diminity Oei at home.

Imperturbable, she displayed no resentment, but congratulated him, saying, 'How stupid of me. I never thought to follow up with civil defence. Too many other leads, all of which've come to nothing.'

'What else've you failed to do or say?' he demanded.

'Why, Mr Goldsworthy, how can you possibly think ...?'

'I know you're holding something back, Diminity. You'd better tell me now or—'

'But, Mr Goldsworthy, I know nothing more than—'

'Come on, Diminity, spit it out.'

Suddenly her resistance collapsed, and she confessed. 'I don't know whether Jan and George ever went there. But there is ... I told them ... a deserted kampong on the north-east shore. They might just . . .'

'Pick me up here in half an hour,' he directed. 'We're going out there.'

'At this time in the morning? Do you know what time it is?'

'Well past time to have a look at that kampong of yours.'

Diminity sulked during the half-hour drive north on the expressway, and Mike, lapped in wakeful fatigue, said little. Later would be time enough to raise hell with her for holding out so long. It was close to dawn when she turned down a narrow road that led to the kampong and the shore.

A police constable in khaki shorts stopped them with a peremptory wave. Recognizing Diminity, he nonetheless examined her press pass carefully before gesturing them to proceed.

They smelled the kampong before they saw it. The stench of kerosene fire permeated the damp air. When they stopped, Mike saw a burned-out sampan surrounded by a group of policemen. The acrid stench of cordite also hung heavy in the still, hot air. There had obviously been a clash with small arms.

'Got clean away,' the sergeant in command told Diminity. 'But this'll serve as a warning. We won't be troubled by smugglers for a while.'

'Smugglers?' Mike explained. 'That's all? No one else?'

'Not that I know of. Only the smugglers in the big serpent boat and two others in the sampan, who transferred to the big boat. I don't have a clue what they were up to. Funny, one looked like a woman. Hard to tell, but we got that impression.'

Mike Goldsworthy's quest ended at that moment on the charred edge of the mangrove swamp. He knew he could do no more. He could not grow wings and, if he hired a helicopter, where would he search? There were just too many places the fugitives could have fled, Jan among them.

Rather, Jan *possibly* among them. The police felt they had seen a woman. Even if they had, there was not the slightest evidence that she was Jan.

He would, Mike decided, take the full extra day allowed him. For one thing, he was stumbling about like a comic drunk, sodden with exhaustion. Since he could no longer keep awake, he would need the day to recuperate from the outward flight in order to make the return flight. Perhaps the police would have further news of the fugitives when he awoke.

XXI

It took three hours for the swift serpent boat to carry the fugitives to the inlet on the west coast of peninsular Malaysia. It was to take an additional hour and a half to walk to the improvised airstrip where the Concordia Execujet presumably awaited its pilot. Yet, Janet could afterwards remember little of the events that should have been vivid in her memory.

Two jet-engined helicopters of the Singapore armed forces had made a pass at the fleeing boat, which must have been sharply delineated on their multi-sensored viewing screens. The helicopters did not fire, and they veered away when the boat reached Malaysian waters. Still licking the wounds inflicted by the Islamic fundamentalists, Singapore was leery of arousing its prickly Muslim neighbour.

As the black boat slipped into the mouth of the inlet, a speedboat flying the emerald triangle of the Future Green Society approached. Ali, the smuggler captain, sent Janet and Berry below before the speedboat came alongside. Then he greeted the young Chinese men and women of Future Green in rapid Malay.

He later explained, laughing, 'They want me say where you be. If I seen you? I say I not see nobody ... have no idea. Only bastard p'licemen attack me. I never tell Chinese 'bout my friends who save my boat. Chinese dogs.'

Janet was later to recall vaguely Berry's half-carrying her when they went ashore and trekked to the improvised airstrip. She was lightheaded when the ground crew rolled out the Execujet and stripped off the palm-frond camouflage. She was only half awake during the steep takeoff, which was like riding a rocket.

'Detection's too good nowadays.' Berry smiled at her across the throttles that separated pilot's and co-pilot's seats. 'Make a gradual ascent and they'll nail you every time. Better straight up on afterburners and hydrogen drive with all electronic countermeasures operating.

Anyone who does catch a glimpse'll think it's a temporary malfunction of their own sensors.'

She slept after they levelled off above 70,000 feet. The rest of the flight she could never remember. No more could she remember demanding to broadcast a report to Alpha One.

'You were just a tad the worse for the booze,' Berry told her later. 'It would've been nuts for you to broadcast in that shape. But you took it very hard when I said no. Though how in hell you thought you could broadcast – and give our position away!'

The landing, too, was a blank. Only later did Berry tell her he had given her a sleeping pill among the codeine tablets he doled out for her pain. Only when he told her did she know she was in a city called Xian on the edge of Central Asia.

XXII

The immense bronze doors of the tomb of China's First Emperor had been hung on their immense hinges two millennia and two centuries earlier. Yet the enormous underground mausoleum near Xian was still hidden under a great hill. Few Chinese knew that the tomb of the monarch who created China had been unearthed during the frenzied archaeological exploration that followed the cataclysmic Cultural Revolution of the sixties and seventies.

A Brightman/Schreiner subsidiary, the Everbright Corporation, providing technical and financial support, the tomb had finally been penetrated by burrowing robots, which left the great bronze doors untouched. Technicians had then disarmed the scores of crossbows mounted so that their bolts would automatically impale any intruder who forced the doors open.

Amadeus Brinks was chiefly responsible for Chinese ignorance of the discovery of the burial place that would some day be a national shrine. The Everbright engineers who had assisted in the tomb's discovery would never reveal the secret, for they were bound to him by all but feudal loyalty. As for the handful of archaeologists involved, it was not difficult to stop their mouths with gold and honours.

Wishing his tomb to remain hidden from desecration, the First Emperor had sent the 50,000 prisoners-of-war and home-grown felons who constructed the vast tomb north to join 200,000 slave-labourers who were transforming earlier breastworks into a single massive fortification the Chinese were ever afterwards to call *Chang Cheng*, the Long Fortress, and foreigners, the Great Wall of China. None of the 50,000 had returned to civilization to reveal the emperor's greatest secret.

Upon breaching the tomb, the archaeologists found a treasure-house of gems, gold, silver and jade before the emperor's towering sarcophagus. Yet the library had excited the archaeologists most.

Preserved in the tomb were all the classic books of history, literature, and statecraft thought to have perished when the First Emperor burnt the libraries of the Confucianists, who opposed his stringent rule.

Some day, Amadeus Brinks promised himself, he would reveal that inestimable treasure of knowledge. Right now he was solely concerned with the campaign that would make his name either honoured or reviled. He was only momentarily distracted by the asthmatic wheezing of the improvised ventilation system, though he resented being compelled to convene this meeting of the working group in the underground chamber he had wished to keep secret. Secrecy was essential, and what could provide greater security than this unknown sepulchre?

Brinks sat in the cylinder of brightness the jury-rigged spotlights carved in the age-old darkness. The working group was just arriving. Some gave him their total confidence, as he had every right to expect after sheltering them and enlightening them. Others, however, objected to his tactics and virtually demanded that he reveal the final operation that would either crown all his endeavours with victory or crush all his hopes with defeat.

The next hour would determine his fate. Either the final operation would go ahead backed by a firm majority or the campaign would be abandoned just short of its culmination.

The dire crisis had sprung from a hypothetical discussion begun by Monsignor Luigi Bernando in the presence of most of the working group. The maverick Jesuit had posed a Jesuitical question while chatting in the courtyard of the old magistrate's *yamen*.

'Your crusade to save mankind begins to threaten the existence of mankind! Not to speak of its soul!' he had charged. 'Where do you stop, Amadeus?'

'Exactly what do you mean, Luigi?' Brinks had replied testily.

'I mean what moral or physical limits do you impose upon your campaign?'

'I'm not a visionary, Luigi, nor a saint, but a practical man. I shall do what is necessary ... *whatever* is necessary.'

'Will you use your neutron bombs to ensure your triumph?'

Without reflection, Brinks replied, 'Of course! To ensure our triumph and the survival of humanity.'

Shock blanched the Jesuit's ruddy face, but he still probed, 'Instant reaction, eh, Amadeus? No need for thought?'

'I've thought it through a hundred times,' Brinks retorted. 'It wouldn't be the worst way to attack acute over-population. A few small neutron bombs in selected places would wipe out all animals, humans included. But the explosions would leave buildings, machinery and roads intact for the survivors.'

Responding to the Jesuit's obvious horror, Brinks added, 'A hypothetical question deserves a hypothetical answer. I'm not planning to use nukes. But I never rule out use of any weapon when necessary.'

The men and women lounging in long chairs or perched on the courtyard's low dividing walls were listening intently. Brinks was pleased to have impressed upon them once again the mortal challenge that humanity faced and the absolute urgency of their mission, which was to ensure humanity's survival. They knew he would not entertain even a hypothetical discussion about using neutron bombs if the human predicament were not desperate.

Nonetheless, he grew uneasy at the protracted silence that greeted his last remark. Finally, the withered chairwoman of the Future Green Society spoke formally, almost coldly.

'Mr Brinks, do I learn from what you say that our movement holds nuclear weapons? Our goal is conserving bio-diversity. How can you even talk of wiping out so many species?'

'Madame Chairwoman,' Brinks replied as formally, 'extreme problems require extreme solutions. A short sharp shock is far more effective than piecemeal, dragged-out measures. We now face a full-blown—'

'Amadeus, no need explain!' the Mongol zealot called Temujin II expostulated. 'Why make water into your wine? Better drink it down hot and strong! Sometimes, often sometimes, is necessary kill many people. Is good for others to see.'

'Purification through blood and fire,' agreed the renegade Shinto high priest in his stilted English. 'Followed by rebirth for humanity. We Japanese are sunk in carnal and material pleasures. We urgently require purification.'

Marie-Jeanne Erlanger looked up from the *Elle* she was leafing through, having discovered the joys of occasional mindlessness. Not only was she wryly fascinated by the elaborate and expensive process of making herself conventionally attractive, she also refreshed herself with the bubbly, often gassy prose of glossy women's magazines after chewing the dry heavy prose of United Nations or environmentalist tracts.

She raised her eyebrows and asked gently, '*Okage-san*, Japan was already once purified by American firebombs. Do you want that again?'

'I pray it will not be necessary.' The high priest's eyes were fixed on the heron painted on his silk and sandalwood fan. 'But, if necessary, certainly.'

'Your Reverence.' Prince Richard was, as ever, punctilious with titles. 'Are you seriously saying—?'

'Your Royal Highness,' the high priest interjected, 'that is precisely what I am saying.'

'Good God, man!' Richard exploded. 'You can't really . . . .'

'Your Royal Highness, those firestorms were the will of Ameterasu Omikami, the Goddess of the Sun, who created the Japanese islands and the Japanese race. And what is an atomic bomb but judicious release of the essential power of the sun?'

'Your own people, Reverence?' Marie-Jeanne asked. 'Do you really want to immolate them?'

'Madam, it is necessary to burn out my people's obsession with material gewgaws and electronic toys. Just as the cleansing fire punished them for failing the emperor and losing the Pacific War. Other nations have not yet endured the fire. Above all, the Americans must feel the sun's lash on their fleshy backs.'

'*Okage-san*, we are all grateful for your view,' Brinks cut off his most extreme follower. 'Now we should hear others' views.'

No single person could take the place of Comrade Sheikh Semtex, the Islamic fundamentalist savant killed in Singapore. Nonetheless, forceful, younger spokesmen for the world's most dynamic religion were appearing. The most passionate, a Pakistani poet just twenty-five years old, now spoke.

'The fire, Master, the purging fire! However, I expect when you get damned good and ready you will damned well tell us what is our next operation. Also, as close as damnit, what is our final objective.'

'You Muslims!' a heavy-set Hindu woman said vehemently. 'You are always wanting to burn, to maim, and to kill. I am disgusted with this talk of bombs. Only peace is bringing—'

Tse Hu, the Maoist, rushed to her support. 'If we use our sunfire bombs, the warlords will use theirs. Chairman Mao Zedong never shared nuclear technology.'

Amadeus Brinks was initially pleased by the turmoil Luigi Bernando's hypothetical question aroused. He was, however, also disturbed by the reaction of many of his followers. The conflict within the working group now forced him to reveal not only the next operation and his final objective, but his war aims, as well.

*

Two days after that incident, Brinks summoned his war cabinet to meet in the tomb of the First Emperor. Assuredly no one would overhear their deliberations, above all neither Salisbury Smith nor the young satcabnet woman he had produced like a magician out of the carnage of Singapore. Brinks had ordered the guards at the entrance to the tunnel to shoot to kill.

His canvas camp-chair was set on the first broad tread leading to the alabaster, ivory, and silver sarcophagus that rose thirty feet over his head. His collaborators' chairs were set at the foot of those stairs. All around them the glories of the long dead monarch were graphically represented in clay, granite and marble, as well as gold, silver and mercury.

The terracotta figures of empresses and concubines, of musicians and dancers, of nobles, retainers and guards – all a shade over life-size – stared at the intruders with blank eyes. Above them the stone vault representing the heavens glinted with pinpoint stars. Beneath that vast dome spread a bas-relief representation of the world as it was known to the Chinese in the third century BC.

Most extraordinary were the rivers that meandered across the land till they flowed into seas that appeared to rise and ebb. A theatrical, though reverent impulse had inspired Brinks to refill the dry sea-basins and riverbeds with mercury, which the Chinese call water-silver. The liquid metal now tossed and sparkled like water in constant motion.

It was eerie to think of those streams in apparent flow amid utter darkness for so many centuries before they had finally evaporated. Awe of the past momentarily overcame Amadeus Brinks, who was normally awed by no human accomplishment, but bowed his head in homage only to the wonders of nature.

His grand design was to restore the original character of mankind, as well as the natural order in which mankind shared the fragile earth with diverse animals and plants. Sadly, most of the works of man were now depraved. Sadly, most men and women were now so corrupt and so intractable that persuasion alone was useless. Only violence could restore the proper order of Nature and, thus, preserve humanity from extinction.

He had to convince his followers: first, that he knew exactly where he was going; second, that his objective was attainable; and, finally, that attaining his objective would bring into existence a far better society in a restored environment. Then all the creatures of the earth would live harmoniously and happily.

Amadeus *knew* that God existed, and he *knew* he was doing the Lord's work. Regardless of the carping of some scientists and philosophers, he looked at the intricate handiwork that was the natural order and he knew it had been created by a supreme intelligence. He could not conceive that God should wish His handiwork to perish, particularly not His highest creation, humanity. He therefore *knew* that he was acting as God wished.

Amadeus he was called, One Who Loves God, and he was aptly named, for he was a believer in an unbelieving age. A number of his followers were, however, militantly atheistic or smugly agnostic. He would, therefore, not stress God's manifest command that all men and women, all His children, must live a joyous and blameless existence in a new world order. For the religious fundamentalists, who were the backbone of his military force, he would, however, ringingly affirm that he was doing God's will.

'I want to open my heart to you in this great subterranean chamber,' he began. 'Its splendour reflects the grandeur man can attain. Yet, however splendid, it is a tomb. However great any man's achievements, he must die. The human race, too, is mortal. But let us not rush to extinction!

'Continuing our ruthless exploitation of the natural world can have only one end: destruction of that world beyond hope of repair by our feeble hands. Then inevitably must follow the extinction of mankind, having destroyed its own habitat.

'Nature will when necessary control excessive human population with earthquakes and floods, famines and typhoons, droughts and epidemics. Mankind must alter radically, otherwise, Nature will surely destroy us.'

Amadeus laid his notes on his knee and surveyed his audience. He saw religious fanatics and simple devout believers. He also saw former KGB and CIA stalwarts, as well as Maoists like the Vixen, the last of the deputy ministers of public security who had orchestrated terror to keep China docile.

'I could not be wholly candid till this day,' he resumed. 'Word would inevitably have leaked out through secretaries, guards and servants – all those who learn something of our plans in the normal run of their duties.

'Had the world learned prematurely what we intend, our cause would have been lost. However, we are today on the point of action. Today I *must* outline my strategy for you so that we can triumph together.'

Brinks looked up from his notes to assess the impact of his words. Half his audience was nodding in agreement; the rest looked puzzled but impressed. That was the effect he wanted: agreement from the sophisticated and respect from the rest.

'The first and greatest of the evils that confront us,' he resumed, 'is the economic structure itself. The modified free enterprise system, whether called social capitalism or market socialism, is intent only on profits, regardless of the human cost or the havoc wreaked on nature.

'Here in Xian we are surrounded by its worst excesses. The tyranny of Chairman Mao Zedong was fanatical, harsh and cruel. But Maoism did not mortally threaten the natural world. Maoism's constant upheavals actually impeded industrial growth and thus reduced the pollution of air, water and food.

'In contrast, the market socialism practised throughout China's provinces will do anything, literally anything, for gain. The Maoists would not export atomic or missile technology. The market socialists have been selling such weapons to all-comers for decades.

'The Chinese are now so greedy they would dig up the sage Confucius, wire his bones together, and make the ancient skeleton dance in the streets if there were any money in it. They have sacrificed their heritage on the altar of the great god mammon.

'We must keep social capitalism and market socialism from spreading further havoc! We shall do so by crippling its circulatory system, that is, its financial flow.

'Our next operation, our last I hope, will strike at London, that capital of world finance. I shall drive the money-changers from the temples.

'We shall, however, not destroy London, not even inflict as much damage as Singapore suffered. We shall simply render London incapable of functioning as a financial centre for some time. Details of the operation will, as usual, be discussed with the combat leaders, but no others.'

Brinks stopped abruptly. He raised his eyes from his notes and glanced around the great tomb, whose utter darkness surrounded the well of light. Something bothered him, some sound that did not belong in the cavern. He frowned, then spoke again.

'So called free trade is ravaging our natural habitat. Competing ruthlessly, entrepreneurs totally disregard the environment. We are devouring the seed corn, burning our ploughs and our furniture to keep warm. Deprived of bread and bed by such reckless immediate gratification, we shall quite soon find life highly uncomfortable and in time unsupportable. We are in thrall to the monstrous international conglomerates whose sole purpose is growth, aimless mindless growth.'

Fundamentalists of various persuasions from terrorists and anarchists to militant Muslims and dinosaurian Marxist-Leninists nodded enthusiastically. They had been waiting for the second largest shareholder in Brightman/Schreiner to repudiate exploitative capitalism.

'The tyranny of growth,' he continued, 'oppresses us all: the universal conviction that we *must* progress and that progress means constant expansion. A child grows to maturity and growth halts. Unremitting economic growth is like cancer, an uncontrollable pathological proliferation that ends only with the death of the sufferer. So will the unremitting expansion of production and consumption, with its alternating boom and bust, kill humanity.

'Cut back savagely in the US and later Europe, nuclear power is rampant elsewhere. Yet no one knows how to dispose of radioactive waste safely. Our legacy to our grandchildren is cancer, blindness, genetic maiming and infertility!'

This audience was already convinced that man's assault on the natural world must be stopped – by force, where necessary. Nonetheless, all were intent on his words. Brinks was himself, however, marginally puzzled by the alien noise, which was softer when he paused.

'Perhaps – a large perhaps – our resources and our ingenuity will prove capable of feeding and clothing and housing the population of eleven billion that will, if unchecked, inhabit the globe by 2050. Regardless of material sufficiency, mankind will not be happy, not even marginally content.

'Rats normally live in peace with each other, even co-operate, but they savage each other when a colony grows beyond a critical number. How will humans react to their excessive numbers? Humans armed with weapons of total destruction!'

Brinks heard the alien sound again. Like the whispering of water over pebbles, it was assuredly the soughing of the wind through the entry tunnel.

His mild anxiety relieved, Amadeus Brinks spoke again. His lieutenants were eager to learn his ultimate objective, the Final Solution, as Hassan the Poet macabrely equated his guru's aims to the Nazi attempt to exterminate the Jews.

'Perhaps humanity could somehow live in the new wasteland we are creating,' Brinks suggested. 'Survive we might, but we would not be truly human.

'We are already dehumanized by the satcabnets and their pernicious spawn, virtual reality. Who today reads for edification or pleasure when we see novels dancing and singing on the screen? Who seeks actual experience when he can enjoy the same sensations in an easy chair – passively, safely?

'Virtual sex is now all but universal, making a once shared physical and psychic experience a solitary activity, negating the emotional and intellectual nuances that once coloured and deepened the physical frictions. Essentially electronic masturbation, virtual sex, alienates the individual from other individuals and from reality.

'Yet virtusex is now practised far more often than mutual sex, which is scorned as no more than a reproductive technique that is, besides, by no means as varied as virtusex. Normal reproduction is spurned for *in vitro* conception with its gene-spliced, pre-fixed traits ranging from gender to hair colour.

'No longer is it necessary – or even desirable – to have a human partner. The best babies are available *in vitro*. The best sexual experience is available from "experts" who perform remotely on disks or chips.

'Almost all experience is now vicarious – not through physical contact and the five primary senses, but through fibreoptic filaments. Who now seeks actual experience?'

Brinks poured mineral water and grimaced at the taste of bicarbonate of soda. But he had the audience. They were all his at the instant, and a quick wind-up was in order.

'Meaningful face-to-face contact between human beings is vanishing.' His voice dropped. 'They do their journeying and their work remotely ... electronically. Such is the generation that is at the peak of its powers and its power today.

'And future generations? Parents and teachers have abdicated their responsibilities. The next generation is being brought up by the satcabnets. Squalid commercial enterprises are shaping the future of the human race by shaping future adults.'

Amadeus Brinks paused for effect, though the audience was galvanized by his pungent summary of their greatest fears. And the monitor camera was functioning without a hitch, as he knew from its muted hissing.

Brinks was taken aback. The intrusive alien sound was, of course, an automatic camera, which switched angles on its own and zoomed in for a close-up when the speaker raised or lowered his voice. He had ordered total security, but had failed to specifically exclude the monitor camera that normally recorded all his public moments.

No help for it now. He had to go on. He had to strike while his audience was malleable. Besides, a record of this address could some later day be released to historians.

'You have sometimes wondered at my tactics, my friends, have you not?' he asked. 'Some of you have even protested against "eco-terrorism".

'Yet terror was ... is ... the sole possible course. Only thus can a small group demoralize the established order. Since the juggernaut will not alter its course, we must stop it by overturning it.

'I welcome terror! I embrace terror as my sister and my brother! Terror has served us well!'

Applause rattled from the audience, amid a few audible sighs of dismay.

'To the fainthearted I can, however, say, *terror is almost at an end*!

'I shall accompany the action against London with other blows to the establishment's circulation, its cardio-vascular system, which is the movement of funds. Deprived of that life blood, the establishment will weaken and soon die. Again, the specifics of the action will be discussed only with the combat leaders.'

Brinks leisurely sipped his mineral water. He had them in the palm of his hand now.

'It will not be long now.' He spoke softly to ensure their attention and heard the automatic camera zoom into a close-up. 'We will make a frontal attack. We will not shrink from violence. We will raze present society and on its rubble build a simpler way of life. Great nation-states and great commercial entities must pass away. We must live as our ancestors lived – at one with the greater non-human world around us.

'I do not yearn for some mythical Golden Age. I am not a utopian, nor do I imagine that all strife will cease. Nothing can alter the fundamental impulse of humanity to compete. Quarrels will occur, but at a far lower pitch. Nor do I believe for an instant that mechanical ingenuity will not find new toys for adults. Nonetheless, we shall win a breathing spell by smashing the present system and its deadly toys. We shall also rid ourselves of the Devil's grip of the satcabnets.

'We shall enter not the post-industrial, but the post-information age. We shall find it far more comfortable and far less stressful than our present age of electronic anxiety.

'I cannot predict how mankind will develop thereafter. I am not a prophet. I am a practical man acting to avert an immediate practical danger.

'However, I hope that future leaders and thinkers, seeing what we have done, will make their own choices intelligently. I hope they will choose a path into the future utterly divergent from the path we are presently treading towards oblivion. No matter what happens, at the very least humanity will have had several additional centuries.'

Applause cascaded through the small audience, and Amadeus Brinks raised his voice to ensure that his final words were heard.

'We can do no more than give mankind another chance! We can do no less!'

XXIII

Mike Goldsworthy had put his quest in Singapore firmly behind him, telling himself that he was no longer concerned about the fate of Jan Seager. He had, he further assured himself, finally grown up.

He reflected idly that the stage-setting was just about perfect for the hackneyed little drama he was playing in the Silver Microphone with Babs Berkeley, his new co-presenter. That restaurant, known to all as the Iron Mike, was the hangout of senior staffers who were jaded with the deep-carpeted lounge and dining-room reserved for them in the Alpha One Tower.

Their hands were just touching on the time-burnished mahogany bar. Their heads close together, he was speaking softly into her ear. Her long black hair shone with the ruddy mahogany patina bestowed by henna. His copper bristles were lightly frosted with white.

Since the last late lunchers had staggered back to their desks and the afternoon boozers had still to arrive, Mike and Babs were alone in the perpetual half-light. The ostentatiously bored bartender was studying the ceiling while they re-enacted the ritual seduction he had so often seen.

Mike's cues and Babs's responses were all rote, almost mechanical. The outcome was inevitable. After another hour or so, they would end up in the tiger-striped bedroom of his penthouse a few blocks away.

Babs was not coy. Making no secret of her intentions, she had done everything but lift her skirt to reveal a sign reading: *Enter Here*!'

The outcome was also inevitable, Mike reflected, because of his own damned Pygmalion complex. No sooner did he start to work closely with a woman, than he was driven to make her over into the perfect satnet partner. Invariably, the first step in that transformation was to take her to bed and establish his dominance.

Only with Jan Seager had that not happened. Nobody could dominate Jan. Besides, she would not sleep with a man unless he met her own mysterious criteria. Neither wealth nor fame could persuade her, not even the aphrodisiac of high office. Five years earlier, she had spurned the advances of US President Townsend de Witt and had then fallen into the arms of an obscure navy lieutenant.

Babs Berkeley didn't possess a quarter of the talent of Jan Seager. But the audience loved Babs's winsome, dark-eyed *naïveté*. With her knowing smile and her come-hither-right-now air, that was all Babs needed. Kate the Great had decided she was audience friendly, which *almost* made up for all she lacked compared to Jan.

Despite himself, Mike realized how much he missed Jan – professionally of course. Her edged comments had often infuriated him, but had almost as often led to new insights. He missed her barbed wit, even missed their volcanic quarrels. No nonsense about a romantic attachment, of course, but he also missed her presence. Life had somehow been flat, lacking sparkle since she left. If she had not curtly rejected all his advances, emotional as well as sexual, he could almost have imagined that he was a little in love with her.

Despite himself, he was also deeply worried about her. She had not been heard from since her last brilliant report on the origins of the Singapore assault closed with a promise of a follow-up very soon. Her whereabouts were totally unknown. She had simply dropped out of all circuits, probably prevented from appearing by illness or by constraint. The alternative he would not even think about.

Mike had been babbling nonsense into Babs's ear while his thoughts ranged elsewhere. Babs would unquestionably be malleable, even eager, in bed. But she was unlikely to show either the enthusiasm or the ingenuity that made Catherine Loomis so exciting and so formidable.

What, Mike wondered again, made him do it? Why move in on Babs Berkeley? Why go through the elaborate ritual of seduction that was now such a bore?

Anyway, it was a damned fool thing to do. Kate was unabashedly jealous, despite her own roving eye. What was sauce for the goose was definitely not sauce for the gander, especially when the goose had virtual life-or-death power over the poor gander.

That he supposed was the answer: her power over him. He had to prove that she had not hogtied and put her brand on him. He had to prove to himself that he was still his own man. He had to prove it to himself, but definitely *not* provoke Kate herself. She was a generous mistress, but she was also a jealous mistress. He was living very dangerously.

Catherine Loomis was fuming in a booth at the back of the Silver Microphone, where she could see the well-lit bar, but could not be seen. Although distracted, she treated her three guests with astringent self-confidence. She had not wanted to meet them in her office or her penthouse apartment. If she had, her two personal assistants and her three secretaries would have known of their visit.

She used her staff to leak information, some true, some doctored. Right now she wanted their silence, which was best ensured by keeping them in ignorance. She had, therefore, met the auditors in the rearmost booth of the Iron Mike.

Lunch was long over, and Catherine was sipping her third cup of coffee. By an act of will she focused on her intensely important and intensely boring conversation with the young man and the young woman, who were in their early thirties. She did not remember their names, for they were not important. They were not the first lawyers and accountants with whom she had discussed her plans for expansion. Nor, sadly, would they be the last.

She held a substantial block of shares in Alpha One, but, naturally, nowhere near a majority. Nonetheless, she had always won her wrestling matches with the majority stockholders in the past and she would win this one too.

At stake was Alpha One's continuing dominance of the six satcabnets that vied for ever greater audiences and ever more advertising throughout the world. The immediate issue was her determination to build fibreoptic networks in South America and sub-Saharan Africa, which were now served by expensive and erratic line-of-sight microwave and satellite transmissions rebroadcast conventionally.

'May I remind you,' she asked, 'that it will actually be cheaper in the long run?'

'Maybe so, but not in the short run,' responded the young man. 'An investment of fifteen billion isn't exactly cheap.'

'Compared to what we'll lose if we don't, it's very cheap,' Catherine retorted. 'First the revenues: one and a half billion dollars a year in rental fees and advertising. Besides, do you have any idea what it's worth in cold, hard cash to be the number one net? Do you know how much revenue we'd lose if we lost that?'

'Of course, we do, Ms Loomis,' interjected the pinstriped young woman. 'We factor in goodwill as—'

'Goodwill be damned. We're either up or we're down. Nothing in the middle.'

'Ms Loomis,' the pinstriped young man asked, 'how will the State Department react to your plans? Or the World Trading Organization?'

'Bugger the State Department,' Catherine snapped. 'They'll do as I say ... as we say. As for the WTO, it's supposed to stand for free trade, isn't it?'

Sometimes Catherine Loomis, who secretly rather liked being known as Kate the Great, felt like tossing in her hand in disgust. But she knew she would win in the end, after haggling with more senior lawyers and accountants. She wondered why she was wasting her gunpowder on these striplings.

She crossed her legs tightly under the ankle-length blue-wool skirt she had worn with a severe white silk blouse, presumably to show her serious approach to these negotiations. Her bladder was bursting after the cocktails and the wine she had hoped would lighten the interrogators. Then came three cups of coffee and a large brandy. She crossed her legs the other way and pressed them tight together.

A grizzled test-pilot with whom she'd had a brief fling used to growl aloud, 'My back teeth are floating!' He would then stomp off to relieve himself. But she could not do so, not even more delicately. She simply had to control her overburdened bladder.

To reach the ladies' room, she would have to pass through the bar and she did not want Mike to discover that his two-timing had been observed. She would coolly let him know in her own good time, rather than rushing hot blooded to a confrontation now.

Unaware that he had been marked out, Mike Goldsworthy pressed his casual pursuit of Babs Berkeley. The glances were more meaningful and the silences more ardent.

'Would you mind stopping by my place?' Mike finally asked. 'Some papers I need for tonight's 'cast.'

'Finally got around to it, did you?' she answered. 'Let's go, boss!'

Mike told the bartender to add the drinks to his tab, and they rose. Unseen in the high-sided booth in the rear, Catherine watched their departure balefully. She was, however, delighted at the prospect of reaching the ladies' room within the next half-minute.

Mike's hand was on the brass knob of the mahogany door when the room shivered. It shivered again, then rocked. A second shock, much stronger, doused the lights and showered debris from the ceiling. A third shock followed a rumble like distant thunder.

Coughing out dust, Mike and Babs pushed into the street. Five doors down the long avenue, smoke was rolling through the copper-and-gilt doors of the Alpha One Tower. Alarm bells hammered inside and sirens shrilled around the corner.

'The bloody bombs almost scared the piss out of me – literally. (So Kate declared later.) But I made it to the loo just before another disaster happened. I didn't care if those two nerds saw me waddle like a knock-kneed duck to the potty. I didn't even care about the explosions. First things first, you know. Then I got myself out onto the street and into the tower.'

When Babs and Mike burst into the smoke-filled lobby a few minutes before Kate, they were virtually blinded. Dark fumes wreathed the enormous chrome microphone that bestrode a gigantic spun-silver globe in the middle of the lobby. On that model, every Alpha One station, every antenna, and every relay point was depicted in miniature, as were the net's seven satellites. That arrogant display was now veiled by smoke.

The smoke was rolling out of the auditorium on the mezzanine, a short flight of copper-and-gilt stairs above the marble lobby. Firemen wearing ion-scrubbing masks and night-vision goggles were just entering the auditorium.

As they watched, the volume of smoke began to diminish. When most of the smoke had eddied into the street or had been sucked up by the air-conditioning, the chaos in the big lobby was apparent. Building staff who should have been at their emergency stations were milling back and forth. They rushed importantly to their posts and found nothing to do except answer telephones that were shrilling continuously.

A murmur of many voices now underlay the sirens and the alarms. All the voices were saying into telephones: 'Too soon to tell!' 'Yes, a bomb, but no details yet.' 'True, but no major damage.' 'Call back later when we'll know better.'

Normally a fountainhead of global news, Alpha One was itself news. Catherine Loomis was imperiously indignant at that reversal of the proper order of things. Astonished that anyone had dared to attack her mighty satcabnet, she stormed across the jam-packed lobby. Sweating firemen, manoeuvring their foam generators, gave her a wide berth. Even the tall, totally bald deputy commissioner of police whose presence testified to the importance of this incident kept out of her way. He could not tell her flatly, as he ached to, that her conflicting and purposeless orders were a damn nuisance.

Mike Goldsworthy was flabbergasted at Kate the Great's showing herself less than wholly self-controlled in public. This was the first time he had seen her in an honest rage, rather than raging for effect. He shooed Babs Berkeley upstairs to warn the studio that he would be going on air from the lobby to the entire satcabnet, all 156 stations and subsidiaries. The emergency elevators were operating now that it was clear that only the auditorium had been attacked by the three separate bombs.

'Tell them I'll use the surveillance cameras,' he had directed Babs. 'If the image is a little fuzzy, all the more dramatic.'

Mike now took Catherine's arm and led her to a relatively quiet corner.

'No use crying over spilled champagne,' he advised. 'Anyway, we've lost only a few drops.'

'But they dared ...' Catherine said fiercely. 'Who would have the sheer bottle to ... the gall ... the effrontery.'

'That's not the point right now, Catherine. We've got to get a statement on air. It'd be hell to be beaten on our own story.'

'All right, Mike. As you wish. Only make sure you say we'll hunt down those responsible for this outrage, no matter how much money and time it takes.'

'Let's just find out first if anybody's got any idea how it happened ... who did it.'

Damage, Mike learned in the next few moments, was minimal. A sitcom had been rehearsing before a small audience, but only nine among nearly 400 in the auditorium were affected. Two actors had been injured, and seven members of the audience, three seriously.

The injured were borne on gantries to the ambulances waiting outside. There would be no bumps or jars, although the streets of Manhattan were rutted and potholed. In motion, the ambulances did not touch the ground. They rode on a cushion of air blown downward like hovercraft.

A blubbering messenger-girl told Mike that the two actors who had been swelling a crowd at the rear of the stage had been killed outright, not just injured, when a bomb exploded beneath their feet. Mike comforted himself sardonically with the old show biz saying that extras were the lowest form of life. But he flinched, and his professional bravado briefly deserted him when he saw the frilly petticoat of a scarlet evening gown trailing from the zipper of a black plastic body bag.

Shaking off his horror, he made sure that a surveillance camera was trained on him and lifted a microphone.

'... summing up, very little damage done,' he concluded two minutes later. 'And minimal loss of life, though that loss is deplorable. I'll bring you more just as soon as we have further details. Meanwhile, stay tuned to Alpha One. They think they can knock us off the air! Fat chance!'

Mike signed off, standing dramatically amid the snakelike tangle of hoses wielded by yellow-slickered firemen as the last stretcher-gantries carried the lightly wounded away. He was wondering what to say on his next 'cast when he felt a tug on his sleeve.

'Take a gander at this, Mike,' the deputy commissioner directed. 'Left at the information desk, God knows how. We'll send it for forensic examination. Right now, it's a hot potato for you and your boss lady. Though she seems to've simmered down.'

A laser-printed message was sandwiched by the plastic evidence bag. It read:

> The Future Green Society proudly claims credit for placing the admonitory explosives in the auditorium of the Alpha One Satellite-Cable-Network. We deeply regret any loss of human life or injury the bombs may cause.
>
> But it was the only way. You have ignored our repeated pleas that Alpha One present more forcefully and more frequently the story of our deteriorating environment and the danger humankind faces. The imminent ecological crisis, though by far the most critical issue of our times, has virtually been ignored by the biggest satcabnet.
>
> We are not bloodthirsty. Quite the reverse! We seek to save mankind – to ensure humanity's survival. Left alone to follow its present disastrous course, mankind will destroy itself in no more than a century – if that long.
>
> Now that we have gained your attention, we shall expect far more frequent and more extensive, as well as more intelligent and emphatic coverage of the environmental movement.
>
> We shall be watching you!

Kate laughed when she read that awkward statement, and she remarked with the callousness of near hysteria, 'Well, if they had to kill somebody, bit actors are two a penny, easiest thing in the world to replace.'

'Get a grip on yourself, Catherine.' Mike grasped her arms. 'Pull yourself together, or, by God, I'll slap you. Right here, with hundreds watching ... and on camera!'

'My God, what've I said?' Catherine wiped her eyes with the back of her hand, shuddered, and drew herself erect. 'You mustn't slap me. That would never do ... not for the iron woman, not for Kate the Great. Of course, I know you all call me that .... Mike, I hate to lose my people, even two extras I never met. But I'm ready now. And, Mike, much thanks!'

Outwardly quite calm, although her hand trembled, whether in anger or in sorrow Mike could not tell, Catherine Loomis read the threat again. She pondered for no more than twenty seconds before making her decision.

Regardless of her misgivings about the exploitation of the public's conscience and its pocketbook by the aggressive ecological movement, regardless of her acid disdain for Amadeus Brinks, she declared, 'I've got no choice. I've got to wrap myself in the green flag. Mike, I want Babs to read my statement, not you, and if I went on air, it would look like a public surrender. It would give the whole miserable affair too much weight.'

Given the climate of world opinion, Catherine told herself, her decision was only prudent. Besides, what better public reason for expanding in Africa and Latin America than eagerness to broadcast the ecological message to their billions? The environment was most immediately imperilled in those two regions, and the opportunities for Alpha One there were greatest.

She would have to let that eager beaver, that sexy Girl Guide Janet Seager, have her way. She would encourage Mike and Janet to stress the environmental crisis in *The Next Thousand Years*. If, of course, Janet ever reappeared.

Trying to make the decision appear a little less hasty and opportunistic, Mike waited half an hour before going on air again. That time was filled with the normal soap operas, interrupted by fragmentary bulletins aired by others.

From the impressive studio he finally introduced Babs Berkeley, who read without further comment Catherine Loomis's statement as president, chief executive officer and chief programmer of Satcabnet Alpha One.

'Perhaps this terrible incident was needed to show us how we must face up to the future, although I feel we have been too harshly judged. I pride myself on having already broadcast the brilliant reports of our own Janet Seager on environmental issues. We shall in the future, as we are duty bound to do, show you much more in much greater depth on this vital issue. I have high hopes that Janet Seager, now absent on an assignment I cannot yet reveal, will play a leading role in that greatly expanded coverage.'

Babs Berkeley muttered when the hidden mikes went dead, 'She's sure hyping our Jan's few little squibs on ecology. Also, didn't you tell two billion viewers that Jan was missing?'

'Kate's the boss!' Mike answered shortly. 'Maybe she knows something we don't.'

Babs said not another word until they were walking to Mike's nearby duplex at one in the morning. The Manhattan night was sultry, almost tropical. But it was scented with stale gasoline fumes, rancid cooking oil, and stuffy subway exhausts, not the fragrance of frangipani and pepper or the salt sea breaking on coral reefs.

'Well,' Babs finally said, 'this is going to be interesting. When ... *if* ... Jan turns up, she's gonna have her hands full with the Greenies, isn't she? So I'll ...'

'Looks that way,' Mike replied negligently. 'Look, babe, I'm fed to the teeth with Alpha One. Can't we forget it for tonight?'

When the door closed behind them, Babs and Mike hurled themselves at each other with reckless urgency. They had just heard the wings of the Angel of Death rustle overhead.

XXIV

If it weren't for the spice of danger, his fear that Kate would learn of the affair, Mike Goldsworthy told himself he'd dump Babs Berkeley tomorrow. She was not only soggily uninventive in the act – any act – but her inane chatter was maddening. And he had to listen to her half-baked ideas and her frivolous enthusiasms in bed, as well as in the studio.

Kate's own demands on him had ceased for the past week and a half. She appeared to be involved in a major deal, which she would not discuss with him. But she could never hide any strong feeling from him and he had sensed nothing untoward in her manner, no suspicion of his playing around with Babs.

'Mr Goldsworthy ... ah ... Mike,' the inforobot called Jason, always diffident, broke into his thoughts. 'I have a transmission for you.'

'Put it through, Jason, please.' Mike had learned that a little courtesy got him far better co-operation from the inforobots. 'Why wait?'

'Well, Mike, it's a little odd,' Jason replied. 'High intensity signal ... definitely broadcast quality, though it's only a logo so far. Some twisty writing, maybe Japanese or Chinese. Sorry, I can't track it to source. It's bounced around twenty-odd ground stations and six or seven satellites. For sure, though, it's a personal call to you.'

'Just put it through, Jason. Let's not sit around gossiping like old men.'

Tapping his fingers impatiently on the control console, Mike did not hear the faint note of reproach in the inforobot's tinny voice. Unlike Inforobot Inez, Jason was not only shy, but was also hypersensitive. So much for the technologists' assertion that robots would always behave identically and would never feel emotion.

Mike was annoyed at the interruption, but he could not ignore it. Just say 'No calls!' to an inforobot, and you were totally out of the circuit. Anything could happen to the world while you were cut off. Anything could happen to you, too, none of it good.

Yet he really needed every moment for *The Next Thousand Years*. Without Jan, putting the series together was like hanging wallpaper with one hand tied behind you. It could be done, but the result would not be totally professional. One go-around with Birdbrain Babs had proved conclusively that she could never fill Jan's shoes, not when it came to serious programming, unlike the chatty *His & Hers Show*.

He couldn't confess to Catherine that he couldn't hack it alone – certainly not now. In time – not such a long time, he feared – they would have to discuss the problem seriously. *The Next Thousand Years* had already eaten up $66 million. Unless she was ready to junk the series, Catherine would have to find him another partner. Yet who could be as polished and as incisive as Janet?

'Caller's ready ... ah ... Mike,' Jason announced. 'A beautiful image.'

Wondering when inforobots had been programmed to kibitz about callers, Mike barked, 'Goldsworthy. I'm listening!'

'My dear, I'm very glad of that.'

The pleasantly husky contralto voice reached his eardrums an instant before the swirling image on the screen resolved itself into intelligibility. So clear, however, was the three-dimensional image that he almost reached out his hand in wonder to stroke the sunburnt cheek.

'God, Janet!' he said. 'I've missed the hell out of you. Where in God's name are you?'

Janet Seager smiled joyously. She was obviously pleased with her surprise and delighted at being once again in touch with Alpha One. But she did not look well to Mike Goldsworthy.

She was Jan, the old Jan, no doubt about that. But she was poignantly altered. It was not just the gauze bandages on her forearms or the small scab on her forehead that were worrying. She was subdued: she seemed pensive, almost abstracted, even when she smiled.

She was terribly thin in the wash-bleached jacket that had been spanking new a few weeks ago. Her collarbone protruded sharp and fragile between the threadbare lapels. Her oval face was drawn, almost haggard, her cheeks hollowed, and her cheekbones too prominent. Her matte-white skin was roughened, as if by wind and exposure as well as the sun. A horizontal line was incised above the bridge of her nose, and the colour of her extraordinary eyes, which normally ranged from aquamarine to indigo, was a faded pale blue.

Her hands were in constant nervous motion, her nails, evidently just manicured, glistening with vermilion polish. Her long black hair was drawn into an intricate swirl, which Mike had heard described as a double French knot.

'Where in hell are you, kid?' he repeated. 'How are you really? You're not looking so hot, you know. When are you coming home?'

She smiled again, unmistakably the old Jan: spunky, tough, and humorous. She smiled and replied, 'I'm not looking so hot? Always the gallant cavalier, aren't you, Mike? Yes, I've had a touch of fever, but I'm fine now … and not so fast with the questions, buster. I can't tell you where I am. I gave my word.'

'What kind of dumb game is this, Janet? Are they holding you prisoner? Why the mystery, the hocus-pocus?'

'I'll explain all when I see you.'

'Then you *are* coming home. Soon?'

'That depends on you … also on Kate and Alpha One. Mike, I've got the damnedest story you could ever imagine. And it's all ours, completely exclusive.'

'*If* …' he anticipated. 'I can hear the big *if* rolling down the road towards me.'

'Two *ifs*, Mike. The first is a personal *if*, something I want … need … you to do for me.'

'Anything I can do, you know we will, Jan.'

'Lieutenant Commander Salisbury Smith. You remember he disappeared in a Concordia Execujet the day all the airplanes fell out of the sky?'

'Sure I remember. What about him?'

'He's here beside me and he, too, wants to come home. I want him reinstated and promoted to full commander. Also, no questions asked about where he's been or what he's been doing.'

'So your old flame Berry Smith's alive! I'd be happy to help, kid, but I don't have that kind of clout. Of course, Kate could swing it with the navy if she wants to.'

'Oh, she'll want to after all her blather about my new career as an eco-presenter. She'd *better* want to or I'll take the biggest story of the decade to Southern Cross Satnet. They'd jump at it and give me a fat long-term contract to boot.'

'Well, Kate *can* be blackmailed.' Mike remembered his boss's abrupt reversal on environmental coverage a few days earlier. 'You're really talking tough, kid. You're certain you've got the stuff, the real stuff?'

'I do, Mike. Within forty-eight hours I can give you the full story behind everything that's been going on. All the mysterious events that've buffaloed everybody these past few months.'

'Well, that's not such bad trading material,' he drawled. 'So let's have it. What's it all about?'

'Not before my second *if*, Mike. Though it's not *my* if, but theirs. I'll give you an hour show in two segments so you can sell commercial time in the break as well as at the beginning and the end. The show will be complete. Not a word is to be removed or added, not a frame left out. Incidentally, the pictures are great.'

'I don't know, Jan. I can hardly promise without talking to Kate and she's off somewhere in Colorado with the money boys and girls. Just give me a couple of hours and ...'

'Mike, it has to be *now*. I *must* have an answer right now. That's part of my deal with my source. Otherwise, I go to Southern Cross.'

He snorted at that renewed threat, and she continued urgently, 'Mike, remember, *I* am making this show. I have the final cut. They just don't want anyone tinkering with it in New York. Trust me, Mike. Trust my news judgement and my presentation. Believe me, it's a humdinger, the blockbuster of the decade.'

'All right, kid, I'll buy it.' He made a decision, though he should have stalled. 'You know our heads'll roll if Kate doesn't like it. Anyway, she's sure to be pissed at surrendering editorial control, even to you. But we'll ride it out.'

'With your agreement,' Jan persisted, 'I've got a teaser I want to air right now. Just words ... no background pix. You can show me on screen if you want.'

'Nailing it right down, aren't you, kid? Making sure Kate can't duck out of the commitment you've wormed out of me.'

'That's the idea, partner. Yes or no? Right now!'

'Yes, damn it. I'll clear the net for you.'

Two minutes later, Mike Goldsworthy broke into the 232 different programmes on Alpha One's stations and subsidiaries to announce, 'I am now deeply privileged and very happy to bring you Janet Seager, who's been missing for three weeks now. Even I didn't know where she was. I still don't. I don't even know where her broadcast's coming from. Janet has a brief report for you. Brief, but very exciting. Sensational!'

Realizing that he was perched on the edge of his chair like a harried housewife with a stew on the stove, Mike settled back to watch and listen. He was profoundly relieved to learn that she was neither ill nor buried in some unmarked grave. He was also elated at Alpha One's getting the biggest story of the decade, the biggest story of the young century.

In honesty, total honesty, he would have been even happier if he had the story, rather than Jan. But he would be introducing the show, as well as commenting afterwards. And look at the interest she was whipping up for *The Next Thousand Years.*

No, it was not professional jealousy that clouded his elation. It was that damned flyboy, Berry Smith, whom she'd been hooked up with once before.

Jan was no dewy-eyed teenager, no naïve lass infatuated after her first roll in the hay. Yet she was risking her biggest story ever for Berry Smith by making his pardon and his promotion preconditions for her broadcasting. She had to be serious about him, dead serious.

'Well, it's nothing to me who she screws,' Mike said under his breath. 'But I'd better get rid of Babs anyway.'

On the big screen Jan was just beginning to speak. Without professional make-up she was wan, yet still attractive. Poignantly frail in her tight-belted jacket, she looked vulnerable, but gallant – a combination just about impossible to beat on camera.

'Ladies and gentlemen, all my old friends of the airwaves,' Jan said slowly. 'I want to tell you that I am alive and well and working hard to bring you the story of the decade. I heard that many of you were worried about me ... about my absence. As you can see, rumours of my being deathly ill or worse where all vastly exaggerated.'

She glanced at the clipboard in her left hand, disdaining to pretend that she was not using notes.

'Most important, however, is the report in depth I shall bring you in exactly two weeks' time on all these stations. I can only say now that it will explain and illuminate the strange events, the apparently pointless upheavals, the world has been experiencing for the past few months. Not only will I bring you face to face with the men and women who are working for a tomorrow that might never come without their efforts, I shall also introduce you to the great man who leads the fight for humanity's survival. Nothing less is at stake. And I shall . . . .

'But that's enough for now,' she concluded briskly. 'Good night, ladies and gentlemen, all my old friends and all my new friends of the airwaves. Good night, Mike.'

The three-dimensional image on the screens in 1.2 billion homes faded with those last words. Forgetting his resolution to be polite to inforobots, Mike Goldsworthy swore at Jason, who was working frantically with the central compubrain itself to determine where the transmission had originated. That effort failed, as did the even more sophisticated search by the National Security Agency, which was virtually a branch of Alpha One nowadays. No one could get a fix on Janet Seager's transmission, which had lasted just six minutes from her initial appearance until her fadeout.

Still, an eager Mike Goldsworthy, a peeved Babs Berkeley, and a suspicious Catherine Loomis wondered why Janet Seager was not coming home to Alpha One with her tapes. Why should she not savour her triumph at the satcabnet that was the centre of world power?

Because *they* wouldn't let her, Mike realized. *They*, whoever they were, wanted Jan and her disks under their thumb, presumably to make sure the hour-long report was not altered in any way.

Much of the lengthy preparatory work for the report Janet Seager called *Old World Going! New World Coming?* was routine. At once demanding and mechanical, it was, in a word, wearing.

She had initially resolved to look over every frame of every image on the voluminous tapes and disks herself. But she had to leave the gross sorting and the first weeding to the five technicians from the Everbright Corporation Amadeus Brinks had assigned to her. All were top notch, and two of the shy Chinese women were geniuses at scanning, selecting, and cutting the tapes to Janet's needs. Nonetheless, she had to be present in the splendidly equipped studio throughout the process to ensure that she did not miss a sequence that was either particularly moving or particularly pertinent.

Consciously attempting to relax, Janet reviewed again the events that had led to this show, which was the peak of her career. Those events would give the show the framework it needed, like the wire armature on which a sculptor models clay. This show would be intensely personal, for she was herself the armature.

She remembered awakening in a steel-framed hospital bed in a spick and span room that smelled of whitewash, disinfectant, and jasmine. Her first thought was for the audio-video disks she had made on her minisat during their escape; her second thought was for Berry. She needed him badly – and not just to tell her where she was.

She did not have to look far. Even before she turned her head, Jan felt a hard palm in her own. She realized that she was clutching Berry's hand like a lifeline when she heard his deep baritone.

'The doctors thought it was about time you came to, darling.

You've goofed off long enough.'

'Where?' she asked weakly. 'What? How?'

'What's this, a textbook for journalism students? *Where? What? How? Where* is Xian, the old capital of imperial China, now the nerve-centre of our movement. And *what*? You've been zonked out for eight days now. Sleep therapy they call it. You were suffering from exhaustion and, believe it or not, malnutrition. Also pretty bad burns. That's *why* the bandages on your arms and ... ah ... your beautiful butt. They had to do some grafting.'

'Grafting? There'll be scars then. How bad is it?'

'No scars at all. We've got the best plastic surgeon in the world on call. Only he doesn't know where he is – or who he's treating.'

'Berry, you're sure? No scars?'

'I'm absolutely certain. *How*, I guess, is that I landed in Xian, rather than going on to the desert. I figured you needed medical attention fast.'

'The desert?'

'Yeah, near Lopnor, our big base. Now Mr Brinks has cleared you, I can tell you the whole story, the way it looks where I'm sitting. And then, he'll talk with you. Could be he'll talk on camera, too.'

'Berry, let me get this absolutely straight,' she commanded. 'You mean Amadeus Brinks? He's running this horrible campaign? To keep humanity from becoming extinct, as you say? That's one hell of a screwy note, a massive contradiction: *kill to save life ... to save the human race*! It simply doesn't make sense to me. I just don't see ... and how *you* can ...'

'You trust me, don't you, Jan? You know I wouldn't lie to you.'

'Only about other women, Berry.' She laughed. 'Otherwise, you're as straight as a die. So far, at least, you haven't loaded the dice.'

'So just be patient for a while,' he advised. 'Don't make any judgements till I fill you in. Afterwards, you get a couple of hours with Mr Brinks. More if you really need it and you're beginning to understand what he's working for, and why.

'Now look at it this way ....'

After two days, Janet had regained much of her strength. The physiotherapists were already twisting her into knots to restore the muscle tone she had lost during more than a week in bed. Another tonic: she saw as much of Berry Smith as she wished. As he told her candidly, she was now his chief assignment; the aircraft could look after themselves for a while.

Janet finally admitted to herself that she was in love with the new Berry Smith. He was, as always, relaxed and amiable; as always, his easy charm was half his attraction. Evidently free of all worry and all responsibilities, he was almost a different man. In his new character, he was far more sensitive to her feelings and more receptive to her ideas, as she was to his.

His only thought seemed to be to please her as they strolled hand in hand through the new pine groves on the outskirts of Xian. He was spontaneously attentive, as he had not always been during their earlier intense but brief affair. Nor did she see any sign of the calculating, manipulative, small-minded self-concern that had broken up that affair five years ago. Quite clearly, Berry Smith was as strongly attracted as she was.

As they strolled through the new museum of the Tang Dynasty one sunlit afternoon, Jan said softly, 'You know, Berry, this could be real romance.'

'What did we have last time, Jan? It wasn't exactly a prize fight, was it?'

'No, Berry, it wasn't. But last time we had a relationship, not a romance. It was convenient, not love.'

A watchful Amadeus Brinks may have feared that Berry was shirking his assignment, which was, of course, to win Janet to the environmental cause. Berry would not press her, and he could not dissemble. He, who had made a career of charming women, could not dissemble with this woman.

In truth, Jan required little persuading, while a strong pitch might put her off. She was, however, easily persuaded by his drawled comments that the ecological crusade led by Amadeus Brinks was virtually the sole hope for embattled humanity. She believed Berry in good part because she *wanted* to believe him. Beyond that, she had for some time been convinced that more forceful measures were required to preserve the environment and all life, human, animal, or vegetable.

Berry would not – could not – bring her completely up to date. Excluded from the meeting in the tomb, he knew only the general outline of Amadeus Brinks's campaign to make the bull-headed, monkey-mischievous human race stop sawing off the limb on which it perched. Brinks saw no need to entrust him with the details and many reasons not to do so.

Although sympathetic to Amadeus Brinks's cause, Janet Seager challenged him directly after he had delivered a virtual monologue to the camera for half an hour, as would any self-respecting interviewer.

'Commander Smith tells me you're very distrustful of many new inventions,' she said bluntly. 'Do you really believe progress scourges the environment? Menaces human survival? And what do you plan to do about it?'

'Not quite, Ms Seager.' Brinks was beaming, avuncular, but, her professional scepticism told her, not wholly sincere. 'Some new things we need. Some we can manage without. And some are an abomination!'

'Abomination? That's strong language, Mr Brinks! What're you thinking of?'

'For one, the feelies, as I believe your profession calls them. Manufacturing false sensations that are all but indistinguishable from real sensations.'

'Why, Mr Brinks? Do you so dislike its sensual ... sexual ... nature?'

'It's not the sexual aspect that disturbs me. Men and women have used ingenious devices to enhance their mutual pleasure since the dawn of time.'

'Then what *is* biting you?'

'Nothing's biting me, Ms Seager. That's the point. I don't want to feel something's biting me when it's not. I don't want to substitute false sensation ... verisimilitude ... for reality. If I do so habitually, I shall soon be unable to distinguish between reality and virtuality.'

'What do you plan to do about the things you call abominations?' Though Jan herself was intrigued by Brinks's argument, the exchange was becoming too abstruse for the general viewer. 'What *can* you possibly do about them?'

'We'll destroy some and bypass most.'

'I don't follow. How can you destroy inventions that're already widespread?'

Janet had retorted strongly, hoping to draw Amadeus Brinks out by angering him. She would cut her own questions later, as she would his replies, since she had only an hour for her entire programme. She would certainly crop all words and all concepts that were too difficult for a mass audience. What viewers would see and hear would, as always, be quite different from the actual interchange.

'Ms Seager, you really must not ask me to confide all to you. There are limits of decency to self-disclosure, limits beyond which lies indecency.'

Dressed for dramatic effect in her weathered old jacket and faded cotton slacks, Jan wore on her right wrist the barbarically chunky gold bracelet set with cabochon emeralds Berry had given her. 'A pledge,' he'd said, without saying just what he was pledging. But that would do for the moment.

Comfortably filling his austere Ming Dynasty rosewood armchair, Amadeus Brinks might have been a creation of Joseph Conrad or Somerset Maugham. His big round face was flushed with the heat of the mid-morning in the inner courtyard of the *yamen*, but he refused to loosen his sartorial standards. His white linen jacket was tightly buttoned over his slight paunch, and a red paisley cravat filled the open collar of his powder-blue silk shirt. He wiped his sweat-shiny bald head with a red bandanna when the lens was looking the other way.

His manner and his clothes, Janet realized, were all part of his studied persona. He played to the hilt the role of a bluff old relic of the Victorian era. Yet his slate-grey eyes watched her unblinking, except when he deliberately made them twinkle like a kindly old gentleman who was beyond all human ambition. His eyes were, however, disconcertingly opaque, uncommunicative even when they twinkled.

Amadeus Brinks gave very little away: no involuntary grimaces, no fidgeting, no chagrin or triumph. Jan saw without resentment, indeed with some admiration, that he was a seasoned performer, as professional as herself. She would get nothing from him except what he had already decided to give her – or, at a long shot, what she could provoke him into giving her.

Amadeus Brinks knew that she was all but convinced that his crusade was the chief hope for a viable future and he would certainly not reveal any aspect of his doctrine or his strategy that would give her any reason for doubt.

It was not his obligation to cry stinking fish, he had told Marie-Jeanne Erlanger, who was sitting just outside the lens's reach. Besides, he had further observed, he was not peddling over-ripe fish, but the freshest and most delectable seafood. Her logical French brain irritated by that extended and not wholly fitting metaphor, Marie-Jeanne had laughed and placed her finger on his lips.

Jan decided to change her tactics, no longer trying to anger him, but hoping to draw him out by such innocuous questions as: 'How far has the destruction of the world environment gone? And how much can be reclaimed?'

'Nature, Ms Seager, is almost infinitely adaptable,' he replied. 'I say *infinitely*, since there are no limits to her capacity to heal herself – at least no limits our finite human minds can comprehend. How much damage have we already done? Who knows precisely? But the damage is immense. Yet we need only stop destroying the environment like a wrecking crew and Nature will heal herself.'

'But so many species have already been destroyed.'

'Multitudes, Ms Seager, many millions. I love the stern beauty of a great redwood and, just as much, the fragile beauty of an evanescent butterfly. But both are passing. In the Philippines ninety-five per cent of indigenous butterfly species have already vanished. But I digress.'

'Please digress as you wish.'

'I cannot afford to indulge my sentimentality. I must be very hard-headed. What can I do to make Filipino entrepreneurs stop dynamiting their few remaining coral reefs? Their private armies would run me off. What can I threaten to keep them from eroding the topsoil, which then flows into the sea and silts up the reefs? At one fell swoop, these island people have virtually destroyed both their agriculture and their fisheries.

'What can I do, except to shriek my warnings? Only an aroused global public opinion can stop this lunatic self-destruction.'

'There's nothing more you can do?' Janet still probed for something more concrete, although she was by now convinced that he had no master plan, no grand strategy.

'I'm afraid not, Ms Seager.'

'Just one other thing.' Janet tried a last frontal assault. 'The incidents in Bangkok and Jakarta, the massacre in Singapore . . . .'

'What of them?'

'There've been reports that you were behind them ... intimately involved.'

'Behind them? Hardly! Intimately involved? Balderdash! At most, tangentially involved. Glancingly!'

Janet had expected an elaborate justification, rather than this feeble evasion. Why else had Brinks allowed Berry to confide to her his movement's connection with the outrages?

'That's not the way I heard it, Mr Brinks,' she retorted. 'A *much* closer connection. I've been told your forces made those attacks.'

Amadeus Brinks's lips drew back in a wintry smile, and he said with ostentatious patience, 'Ms Seager, I possess no armed forces. What would I do with a private army? Shoot everyone who didn't get behind the green movement?

'True, some of my associates command minor paramilitary units. Particularly the Muslims, who are struggling to assert their dignity in a hostile and condescending world. Yet, so alien were those actions, above all the atrocities at Singapore, that we here could hardly believe they were happening. My misguided associates simply got out of hand. Commanders on the scene became ...'

'Then you're in *no* way responsible?'

'Of course I am responsible. You see . . . .'

Brinks paused, and Janet waited silent. Finally it was coming, the revelation she needed.

'I am responsible because I am the titular head of the movement,' he continued. 'Just as the captain is ultimately to blame if his ship is run aground by a junior third officer's stupidity. I suppose that bright young spark Berry Smith told you of my distant involvement.'

Janet put on a poker face and did not speak. After a long pause, Brinks went on, 'You know, Berry was himself manipulated by an ill-advised, misguided, yet very small, group among my followers. Actually two groups: the Moluccan Liberation Army and the Future Green Society of East Asia. Future Green is in part a cover for malignant malcontents, rapacious multinationals, and megalomaniacal multibillionaires. How else was the tycoon Marston Chua's yacht involved in the Singapore incident?

'I have now cut them off, all except idealistic dupes like Berry Smith who deserve a second chance to participate in our movement.'

'And that's all you have to say?'

'What more do you expect, a false confession of guilt? I have, of course, ensured that such things never happen again.'

'And that is all?'

'Except for my deep regrets at being involved, however tangentially, in those outrages.'

'Thank you very much, Mr Brinks. You've enlightened me. I'm sure Alpha One's viewers will appreciate what you're doing and understand how acute is the crisis of the natural world and how urgent the need for radical action. I'm sure they'll want to help.'

Janet surprised herself by closing the interview, although she still had a few more secondary questions. Yet there was nothing to be gained by prolonging the filming. She could always go back to him if she needed a specific remark to knit together the images on tape, film, and disk she was now editing. Otherwise, she told herself, the well was dry.

Amadeus Brinks had already said everything significant he would say. Sadly enough, he had no master strategy to reveal, no magic formula to save the natural world and the human race.

XXV

You could take Janet Seager's epochal broadcast from Xian any way you liked.

You could simply see it and hear it. You could sniff it and sing along with its signature tune, optionally syncopated or jazzed or bee-bopped or heavy plutoniumed, but *always* loud. You could read it in silence or with virtual sound effects. You could play it on your arthritic old computer: desktop, laptop, or palmtop.

You could feel it with your naked hands or virtu-really enter it. In forty-nine languages and fifty-seven dialects you could do everything except interact and change it. Also you could not avoid it.

In an imperial mood, Catherine Loomis had decreed that Janet Seager's worldwide exclusive on the outrages that had shaken humanity would have the best launch ever given any show that was not about virtual sexology or share-trading.

Though Mike Goldsworthy cautioned against endorsing a production she would not see before it was aired, Kate had decided that she herself would introduce Jan. Kate had further disdained to distance herself from whatever Jan had to say by declaring that she had not seen the broadcast before its transmission. Evidently frightened by the green bombs, Kate had apparently forgotten her own warnings about Amadeus Brinks's duplicity, as well as her habitual caution in public statements.

Mike yawned his way through Kate the Great's introduction, which preceded Jan's full hour. Though drama was inherent in the empress of the satcabnets herself introducing the scoop, her words were flat. She controlled the ears and eyes, the hearts and minds of three billion viewers; she made and broke the most articulate and highest-paid performers on earth; but she could not put on a credible performance herself.

'Alpha One stands behind *everything* Janet Seager will tell you and show you tonight,' Kate concluded woodenly, yet dangerously. 'We are uniquely proud of her enterprise, her daring, and her persistence. Together they have empowered the most important, as well as the most shocking report of this entire decade.'

No electronic stuttering marred the smooth transition to Jan Seager. The link between herself and Alpha One had been humming companionably, though blankly, for half an hour before the scheduled time of transmission. Inforobots Jason and Inez, both on duty this vital night, had already reported, with elation at their success somehow colouring their tinny voices: 'Point of origin is Valparaiso, Chile. We have established beyond doubt that Ms Janet Seager is sending from Valparaiso.'

The legend filled the screen: *Alpha One Proudly Presents A Special Report From Correspondent Janet Seager At The Working Group's Base.*

Janet stood before a vast emptiness hardly touched by light, which strongly suggested the eternal, illimitable vastnesses of space. She wore her habitual safari jacket, and her black hair was caught in a simple yellow Alice band. She had omitted her screen make-up, omitted in fact any make-up, except lipstick and eyeliner.

She nonetheless appeared to Mike to be as beautiful as she was unattainable. An instant later, he saw that Janet Seager bestrode the world like a new colossus of Rhodes.

Her long legs, encased in worn slacks, straddled a globe that revolved slowly without visible support. The lens did not appear to zoom in; rather did the globe appear to fill the screen. Even comparatively close up, at a range a subtitle noted as '80 kilometres (50 miles) above the surface', it was not merely a faultless replica of the planet Earth, it was, somehow, the Earth itself.

'I am here tonight to give you what may well be the most important report presented in this decade.'

Jan's tone was grave, and her indigo eyes were fixed on the lens. Every viewer felt she was talking directly to him.

'I shall share with you a terrifying vision of the immediate future, a vision based on the horrific realities of today. I shall also reveal what lay behind the killings in Bangkok, Jakarta and Singapore, as well as the recent scattered bomb explosions elsewhere.

'One man is responsible. He himself declares that he is responsible.

'Amadeus Brinks is famous for his philanthropy and for his vision. He is now waging a campaign to preserve the human race. Our own survival, yours and mine, is at stake. If we continue destroying our environment at the present rate, the human race will perish. That is a simple fact.'

Jan glanced briefly at the clipboard in her left hand. She was, however, speaking almost spontaneously following the briefest notes. She was telling them what lay in her heart.

'Gimmicks like sorting refuse into paper, brown glass, clear glass, and green glass will not do. Reusing bottles only makes us feel better. It actually takes more energy to transport bottles for recycling and back again than is consumed by far lighter plastic bottles, biodegradable or not.'

Jan stared hard at her invisible audience as if daring them to disagree.

'But you are, naturally, interested in the outrages above all. I repeat: Amadeus Brinks takes full responsibility. It does not excuse him, he says, that demonstrations planned to be peaceful became so gory. Some of his sub-commanders got out of hand, especially the radical Islamic fundamentalists, who of course, must not be confused with our peaceful, productive and law-abiding Muslim fellow citizens.

'Nonetheless, Amadeus Brinks takes full responsibility. He will, if asked, submit an accounting to any duly constituted international entity, even to the quarrelsome United Nations or the pettifogging Court of International Appeals. He will, if duly summoned, submit himself for trial before any truly objective international court, if such a court can be constituted.

'And he will tell his judges the patent truth: he had to mount his crusade because the powerful men and women of the world are concerned above all, perhaps solely, with their own advancement, their own pleasure, their own fame, and their own wealth.

'I hope, however, to persuade you that Amadeus Brinks is more worthy of our gratitude, the gratitude of all humanity, than he is of censure and punishment.'

Mike listened critically. Surprised at Jan's scoring this mega-scoop, he was amazed at her going out on a limb for a man who was, by his own testimony, a mass murderer. Appalled, Mike gazed at the big screen.

He could see the great sphere of the Earth move, turning on its tilted axis while revolving around an unseen distant sun. So overwhelming was the illusion that he, who had dealt with illusions all his working life, was all but deluded. For a moment or two he believed he was seeing the Earth itself. It was fruitful and serene, the ellipsoid sphere with the ice glittering diamond white and blue on the slightly flattened poles and the gleaming aquamarine seas lapping at the green-and-brown landmasses.

This Earth, Mike realized abruptly, was too serene and too fruitful. The Earth had not looked like its twin here for many centuries.

'This is your Earth,' Janet said conversationally, 'as it was a million years ago.'

The Earth rose into the picture to display a primeval forest with clear rivers in which swam many-finned fish, knobbly alligators and sportive dolphins. In the rainforest that reached down to the banks, brilliant parrots flitted from branch to branch, and monkeys howled a welcome to the rising sun in treetops 200 feet above the underbrush. Easily visible, though distant, a chain of jagged mountains was clothed from its foothills almost to its summits with foliage only broken here and there by a gigantic rockface or a crystalline waterfall.

'As it *was*!' Janet repeated off screen. 'Only one thing is missing: *we* are missing, *we*, the human race.'

A vast hand reached down and tore a great swathe in the rainforest, peeling away trees, hurling silt into the rivers, and gouging paths among the mountains. The destruction took no more than ten seconds. But the shock was palpable, a blow to the eye, as if the hand of some infinitely large Creator had defiled His own handiwork. The illusion was so perfect it surpassed illusion and became a momentary reality. If that were so for Mike, the professional, how much more convincing to the ordinary viewer!

'This is your Earth as it *is* today!' Still unseen, Janet spoke with incandescent fervour. 'The force that wrecked – utterly despoiled – the idyllic past, was – still is – you and me: the mindlessly destructive human race!'

The lens shifted to Janet. She held a crude digging stick and a flint-tipped spear in her left hand and in her right a hammer and a screw-driver. She regarded her billions of viewers sternly.

'We humans,' she said softly, 'have wreaked destruction all across the globe in a historical instant, a moment no longer in the eternal annals of time than the ten seconds in brief human time it took the great hand to level the rainforest on our electronic model of the Earth.'

She flourished the digging stick and said, 'This, this crude implement began the destruction, the alteration of the Earth. But Nature could repair the damage it did, even reforest the relatively small areas where our remote ancestors practised slash-and-burn agriculture. Anyway, humans had to break the ground and to spear game if they were to survive as Nature intended.'

Mike virtually heard the capital N of the word Nature, which Jan pronounced with profound reverence. She spoke with the God-given conviction of Moses descending from Mount Sinai with the Tablets of the Law, all truth having been revealed to him. Mike wondered if his hitherto happily agnostic partner had experienced a spiritual revelation.

'But these,' Janet said, 'these are another matter entirely.'

She thrust the screwdriver forward – and billions of viewers shrank from the three-dimensional image rammed into their eyes. She slammed the hammer down on the globe, and her immense audience flinched.

'Then man began to use tools, simple tools like these, which are the ancestors of all other tools,' she declared. 'That was a different story. Once equipped with sophisticated mechanical tools, man's irrepressible greed and his incessant monkey-like curiosity devoured much of the vegetation of planet Earth and destroyed hordes of its diverse animal beings. It all happened in no more than a century or two.

'Please remember, all of you! Remember that the Earth is the *only* home for you and your children and their children. And look at your Earth now!'

The globe filled the screen again. Distance and viewpoint altered rapidly, as if the audience were riding a supersonic helicopter that jumped in seconds from one continent to another, hovering over one spot only briefly. The more susceptible among some five billion viewers grew a little dizzy.

The brown, rust, tan, and black blotches of deserts, cities, mass farms, and vast clearings covered most of the landmass, which was fringed here and there by faded green vegetation. Smoke boiled from millions of chimneys, obscuring the sunlight, and the rivers ran *café au lait* with silt, also stained blue, orange and red by industry's chemical wastes. Angular and ugly cities deposited millions of tons of refuse around them, until they were encircled on land and on water by bands of stinking putrid garbage. Nuclear explosions threw up towering mushrooms of smoke and debris. Under those grim canopies armies and navies hurled high explosives at each other, while above them flew warplanes and rockets. Trains and automobiles, above all automobiles, scurried to and fro on ribbons of greasy concrete, filling the air with toxic fumes, as well as mangling pedestrians and each other.

Few creatures swam in seas that were crisscrossed by thousands of ships, which dragged behind them oily wakes that stretched over thousands of miles, covering the oceans with iridescent film.

Submarines lurked under the murky water. Three of the submarines ejected rockets whose fiery trails ended in nuclear explosions capped by new mushroom clouds.

Jan appeared on screen again. She waved away the living Earth, which dwindled into a dingy sphere no larger than a marble as it moved further and further into the distance.

'That is *not* our Earth as it is today,' Jan reassured her viewers. 'It *is* our Earth as it will be within a decade if we continue as we are now. Even then, you could not see the welling up of radioactivity that maims the genes that shape our bodies and our minds thus deforming future generations. *If* there are any generations after our own! Total destruction cannot be ruled out.'

Mike reflected that a brilliant director had been lost when Janet Seager decided to make her career in front of the camera, rather than behind it. The show, so far, was extraordinary, adroitly shaped for maximum dramatic effect, as well as for easy comprehension. Images and words intertwined gracefully, each emphasizing the other, none redundant or irrelevant. No scene had lasted more than forty-five seconds, which was daringly close to the limit of viewers' sustainable interest.

Mike's only remaining fear was that Jan – star, director, and editor in one – would make the fatal error of hogging the lens. He saw an instant later that he need not have worried.

'Yes, I said the *total* destruction, the end of the human race, cannot be ruled out,' she reiterated. 'Nuclear destruction ... nuclear *extinction* ... is an ever present danger in an age when twenty-eight so-called nations, most no more than marauding tribes under rapacious warlords, are nuclear-armed. Twenty-eight nation-tribes possess fission/fusion weapons and the means to deliver them almost anywhere on earth.

'My friends and fellow victims, at least twelve of those groups also possess neutron bombs, which could simply destroy all mammalian life. That means *us*. The "neuts" they're endearingly called, as if they were some cute species of lizard. Those neuts could kill all humans, but leave unscathed all wealth: buildings and bridges, factories and mines, gold and gems ... if anyone still existed to care about gold and gems.'

She stopped abruptly on that bitter note, having retreated to a corner of the image as she spoke. She spoke again as a figure in a white linen suit filled the screen.

'Amadeus Brinks, the philanthropist and Green crusader, has devoted much study to the nuclear issue.'

'We are closer to nuclear extinction than we think.' Amadeus's tone was light; his mid-Atlantic accent was pleasant; his manner was affable. 'The proliferation we face today was inevitable after the collapse of the Communist world and, with it, the dismantling of MAD, the balance of nuclear terror ensured by the reality of *mutually assured destruction*. Lunatic as it sounds, MAD worked.

'The remaining major powers – the chastened bewildered United States, divided China, and bloated erratic Russia – do not *know* whether they are truly secure behind their anti-ballistic missile defences, the pie-in-the-sky system once called Star Wars. But the midi-powers, Britain, France, could test Star Wars at any time. Besides, any of the twenty-eight nation-tribes, as well as dozens of warlords could at any time put a bomb anywhere on Earth, and a remote detonator thousands of miles away could trigger the explosion.'

Brinks hauled out a red bandanna and mopped his bald pate, and resumed in the insinuating tone of one confiding critical intelligence.

'My friends, we have been fortunate – so far. Proliferation has been extensive. Former Soviet experts turned up everywhere in the '90s, eager to earn their keep by building N-bombs and rockets.

'Also, Beijing sold everything nuclear anyone wanted and could pay for. The Chinese were ... are ... desperate to make money, even risking self-destruction. They still believe, with their secular demigod, Mao Zedong, that China could survive a nuclear world war and emerge as the dominant power because of its vast population. That is nonsense! But the rump government in Beijing, which controls a thousand-odd warheads, implicitly believes such nonsense.'

Amadeus Brinks cocked his head attentively as Janet Seager's voice asked, 'And the answer?'

'There is *no* solution short of drawing a noose of armed men around every nuclear site and lancing those pustules one by one.'

Jan asked, 'And the future?'

'We'll be lucky if the nukes don't get us in the end. More likely the collapse, the implosion of the natural environment will get us first.'

'Your solution, Mr Brinks?'

'We must return to an earlier time, a happier time. No one lived under the nuclear shadow, and human work was then valued above primitive machines.'

'You sound as if you want to go back to the Dark Ages. Do you?'

Brinks laughed easily and replied, 'Of course not. I certainly don't want to give up my library of compact disks. But we must find a *modus vivendi* that does not depend on ever greater destruction of the world around us. Our present approach is rather like that of the Chinese lady who was delighted by her husband's love making. For his own good – and her own, of course – she cut off his penis while he slept, as if pruning a rosebush. She was confident that he would grow a new and larger penis, thus providing her with even more delights.'

Once more on screen, Jan smiled tolerantly at that phallocentric analogy as Amadeus Brinks faded into the pastel pink, and blue image of a smiling baby disappearing down a drain. That gruesome image had been the television commercial of a French manufacturer of bidets.

'Pretty bizarre, isn't it?' Jan tested her viewers' vocabularies – and set off near panic in the soundproof boxes where teams of interpreters were simultaneously putting her words into forty-six languages.

'The problem in much of the world is still overpopulation,' she said. 'The number of human beings is inching inexorably towards the eight billion who will live on planet Earth at the end of the next decade. In the still undeveloped world of Africa and Latin America most will be quite young. But in the so-called fully developed world the problem is the opposite.'

As Jan spoke, a cartoon was projected onto viewers' screens. A strapping young man and young woman stood side by side, both smiling confidently and both clad in green jeans and work tunics. The perspective lengthened, and two grey figures appeared astride the shoulders of the pair. Assertively strong and hale as both young people were, they began to bend at the knees, and their smiles faded into grimaces. The indistinct figures on their shoulders came into sharp focus: a bent man with a long white beard and a crone with an accordion-pleated face. The aged couple grew larger and larger until they dwarfed the young pair, who were now forced to their knees by their human burdens.

'Quite different!' Jan repeated. 'Look just three decades ahead. Persons over sixty will be almost half ... forty-two per cent to be exact ... of the population of the world. The elderly will, of course, work much longer and their seasoned wisdom will make for greater productivity. Nonetheless, ultimately they will be a burden to the young. More medical care will be directed to the elderly, overburdening health-care facilities. And millions more will require custodial care.

'The only immediate solution is as immoral in our terms as it was moral to the Quinacot Eskimos. They abandoned every person who reached the age of forty. Left those individuals on the ice to die or to live by their own efforts.'

Images reinforcing words and words illuminating images, Jan's show captivated Mike Goldsworthy, Catherine Loomis beside him, and billions of viewers. She touched on a variety of problems, immediate and future, all linked somehow to the destruction, the despoiling, the corrupting, and the degrading of Nature. Her report was a passionate affirmation of Amadeus Brinks's motivations and purposes – a tide of adulatory publicity that would make it impossible to try him for his apparent crimes.

The dramatic images and the impassioned words spilled into billions of homes. They depicted men dying in the torment of AIDS, and also men, women, and children suffering the new scourge, the cophagus virus that devours muscles, leaving the skin unmarred.

'Comes of tinkering with genetic systems and the natural environment.' Amadeus Brinks flashed on the screen for a moment to comment. 'We of the developed world are almost all city-dwellers now. Hygienic conditions are so good that our immune systems virtually turn off, wither from disuse. At the same time, new versions of old microbes and viruses are developed by geneticists – in theory to learn how to fight existing pests.'

Graphic electron-microscope pictures showed some of the thousands of varieties of natural and man-made viruses. Projected off the screen in 3-D, they appeared to be as large as dinosaurs and as fierce as sabre-toothed tigers.

As her allotted hour drew to its close, Jan stood before a vast automobile graveyard, wrecks piled high and rusting parts scattered helter-skelter and said, 'Just one more thing before I tell you what I think.'

Beside Mike, Catherine Loomis snorted in disgust and muttered, 'What the hell else've you been doing for an hour!' Mike smiled wryly in the dimness, but did not reply.

'It may be too late,' Jan said. 'We are already in the throes of entropy – the breakdown and collapse of systems too old and/or too complicated, like these old wrecks – yet we can still save ourselves.

'Funds are not a problem. Nonetheless, send money, even if you can spare only a single dollar. A contribution will publicly ally you with Amadeus Brinks's crusade. Send your contributions to me, Janet Seager, Alpha One Tower, New York.'

Kate the Great snorted again and asked hotly, 'Who the hell does this cunt think she is? Joan of Arc?'

'I'll be reporting regularly on the fight for survival on these same stations,' Janet closed. 'But for now, good night.'

In the hushed studio, another woman raised her voice. Kate the Great exploded in wrath, punching Mike Goldsworthy's arm for emphasis with every other word.

'That cunning little bitch!' she cried. 'What a whitewash! And she's committed *my* satcabnet! I'll *have* to give her air time for follow-ups. Worse, we'll have to let her collect funds and followers for that whited sepulchre, Amady Brinks.'

Stopping abruptly, she asked, 'Mike, have you ever heard me admit I made a mistake?'

'Just once, Catherine,' he replied. 'And that was so long ago I can't remember what it was all about.'

'Well, this'll be the second time. I've made a humdinger of a mistake. Letting that simpering little tart take editorial control. I'll bet she's sleeping with that great white whale, Amady Brinks. And I've got to go along with her to show Alpha One is true green!'

Mike did not speak. Just before she paused in emotional exhaustion, Kate the Great swore flatly, 'But I'll fix her! And him, too!'

XXVI

It was a very strange conspiracy, if it were a conspiracy at all. Neither common interests nor common antipathies bound the conspirators, if conspirators they were indeed. Each had independently arrived at the conviction that Amadeus Brinks's campaign would maim, rather than save, humanity. All believed that the great environmental crusade had gone fearfully astray and must be stopped before it did irreparable damage.

Marie-Jeanne Erlanger, who loved Amadeus Brinks, was repelled, as well as surprised, at finding herself plotting with Tse Hu, who now spoke of Marie-Jeanne's lover with contempt. Marie-Jeanne was further surprised that it was Prince Richard who had invited the conspirators to meet in the back room of the obscure and odorous Old China Restaurant at the unsavoury heart of old Xian. He had until yesterday been Amadeus's most slavish disciple. Marie-Jeanne was not surprised by the presence of Monsignor Luigi Bernando. The Jesuit roundly condemned the despoilers of Nature, but he could no longer stomach Amadeus's tactics.

Marie-Jeanne reassured herself that she still loved Amadeus, although she, too, was sickened by his tactics. Still, she recognized wryly, her feminine pride might be deceiving her. She could not acknowledge that she had been misled by his power and his inherent authority into believing she loved him, when she was only dazzled by him.

Regardless, Amadeus had already done much harm – and would do far greater harm if he were not checked. Continuing to support him would have been treason to humanity. She had therefore reluctantly accepted Prince Richard's invitation to the covert meeting at the Old China Restaurant, which was far too slovenly to attract Amadeus's other followers.

Richard was moved as much by wounded self-esteem, Marie-

Jeanne felt, as by concern for his fellow man. He had been grossly deceived by Amadeus's promise to halt the bloodshed. Monsignor Luigi Bernando she considered the most logical, the most intelligent and the most steadfast of Amadeus's followers. Yet the fierce conscience that had brought the Jesuit into the crusade now recoiled from Amadeus's excesses.

Marie-Jeanne was in no doubt about the motivation of the Maoist Tse Hu, whom she despised. She was revolted by the Vixen's delight in others' suffering, whether it was a rat trapped by a terrier, a blind child beggar, or a thousand innocents slaughtered in Singapore. Pure self-interest moved the Vixen, above all and always self-interest.

Marie-Jeanne knew from the spies' reports Amadeus had shown her that the Vixen was Beijing's agent. Her mission was to report his intentions and his strength so that the enfeebled central Government of China could assist or hinder him for its own advantage as it saw fit. Beijing was determined to reunite a splintering China under its sway and to reassert Chinese hegemony over enormously wealthy East Asia.

Mindful of her masters' ambitions, Tse Hu had opposed using nuclear weapons when Luigi Bernando posed his presumably hypothetical question. Little point in reasserting sovereignty over all China and the overlordship of East Asia if factories, housing, roads and fibre-optic nets had been destroyed by nuclear explosions that, further, sowed the land with deadly radioactivity. Beijing had briefly been attracted by the surgical precision of neutron bombs, which would destroy life, but spare property. But the men of Beijing then asked themselves: *what good is controlling all the means of production if there is no one to work them?*

Marie-Jeanne's reverie was broken by Prince Richard's mellifluous baritone. 'I won't waste time. I won't bore you with slogans or speeches or ...'

'We've had a bellyful of both,' Luigi Bernando rumbled. 'Let's cut the cackle and get down to cases.'

'Thank you, Monsignor.' Richard smiled at the Italian's old-fashioned English. 'Now, we all agree this monstrous campaign's got to be stopped? I'll go round the room. Marie-Jeanne, you're closest to our friend Amadeus, closest to his heart and his spirit.'

Marie-Jeanne was startled. She had unthinkingly assumed that she was still an onlooker, rather than a participant. After all, she had for years been a reasonably objective reporter, always uncommitted or, at least, non-committal. Besides, her assumption of neutrality salved but did not wipe out the guilt she felt at turning against her lover.

'It was the bears you see,' she said. 'You all know how it started with the big brown bears of the Pyrenees. And it's ending with the bears. The highway is building again after all our struggles! And the bears are doomed! So Amadeus Brinks must be stopped.'

'Quite a jump,' Luigi Bernando observed. 'From the poor bears to repudiating all Amadeus says he fights for.'

'He *says*,' she echoed bitterly. 'But he has already slain so many and he will soon do untold harm to the environment as well. He has failed the bears. And he will fail us all. For me it began with the bears and it must now end with the bears.'

The others saw only Marie-Jeanne's immaculate façade, the fashionable blonde beauty that she had made herself to please her lover's conventional tastes. She would not allow them to see the agony at betraying her lover behind that façade.

No longer Mao-suited, Tse Hu, the Vixen, was attired in a fashionable Shanghai *cheongsam* of red silk embroidered with many-coloured butterflies. The high-slit skirt showed off her sleek legs, and the collar framed her serene face. Her lacquered black hair was tied in an intricate knot, and her make-up was minutely excessive, as if Kuan Yin, the Goddess of Mercy, had been done over in a beauty parlour on the Shanghai Bund.

She spoke at length, rehearsing the justification for her abrupt shift she would offer Beijing. Amadeus Brinks was out of control, she declared, a missile-launcher firing at will, its own robotic will. He was, she said, extremely dangerous, a demon plunging mankind again into *luan*, primeval chaos. By whatever means, assassination if necessary, he must be restrained, disarmed and disabled.

Marie-Jeanne savoured the silence when Tse Hu finally stopped talking. Clearly Amadeus Brinks's implicit threat of worldwide devastation had dimmed Beijing's enthusiasm for him. The chaos he could invoke would deprive China of customers for its ships, its automobiles, its machine tools, its warplanes and its rockets.

Monsignor Luigi Bernando smiled wryly when Prince Richard shot an enquiring glance at him. He placed his big hands on the threadbare tablecloth, which was littered with duck bones, shrimp shells, spilled sauces, and other debris of their meal. He was quite at home in the squalor. Even in a light-blue sport shirt with only a tiny silver cross on the collar, Luigi Bernando's authority was unmistakable.

'Each of us possesses free will,' he said. 'And each of us must answer to his own conscience. It is said, "Man proposes, and God disposes!" That is true. We, nonetheless, have much leeway.'

Marie-Jeanne wondered how long it would take the Jesuit to get to the point. Clearly, he, too, was appalled at turning against Amadeus, though his conscience told him it was inescapable duty.

'So, my friends, where do I stand?' Luigi Bernando lifted his hands from the table and spread them palms up in a gesture of perplexity. 'My old friend Amadeus has gone too far. In another age I would have said unhesitatingly that he was possessed by devils. Regardless of the roots of his madness, I know he will go much further if unchecked. In him free will has become criminal irresponsibility. No matter how we grieve at deserting our leader . . . .'

Prince Richard stared at Luigi Bernando, evidently expecting counsel that was more concrete, above all, more practical. But the Jesuit looked down at his hands and volunteered no more.

Marie-Jeanne saw as if for the first time that Richard's forehead was wrinkled with worry, and his neat beard was now more silver than gilt. For the first time in his life, Richard of Greece and Denmark was required to lead, rather than simply follow a guru.

'Then it's agreed,' he said. 'We're unanimous. Brinks *must* be stopped. For a start we must sabotage him in every way we can.'

'How?' Tse Hu demanded. 'Brinks keeps us all in the dark. Only combat leaders are given details and then only the details they must know. All *we* know is London is next. We do not know what is next for London. We must recruit. If we can recruit enough workers here and at the Takla Makan base, we can paralyse Brinks's efforts.'

'It is already too far along for such tactics,' Marie-Jeanne interjected. 'Amadeus would be tipped off immediately. And we would be very lucky if we only ended in the jail.'

'A frontal attack is out,' Richard concluded gloomily. 'He's clamped on total security, hasn't he?'

'So he has,' Marie-Jeanne replied forthrightly, although heartsick at playing the spy on her lover. 'Any attempt at direct action will only doom us. Last night the curtain came down. He says that not even a very small mouse can leave Xian without his knowing and stopping it if he wishes.'

'But he lets us wander freely inside the city,' the Jesuit observed.

'Roughly so,' Marie-Jeanne responded. 'He does not wish any confrontation. Though I fear he suspects ...'

'Not only suspects,' the Jesuit broke in. 'He is certain some of us are ... how do I say it? ... disaffected. And he has his spies everywhere.'

Suspicion rippled around the circular table like a sudden wind flattening the rushes that ring a lake. Marie-Jeanne smiled sturdily. She was the obvious suspect, the most likely *agent provocateur* because she was closest to Amadeus.

'He knows us all too well,' she said. 'You, of course, Richard. He knows your unhappiness. You have told him often enough. And what, Monsignor Luigi, keeps one who makes confession from using what he thus learns about his priest? Amadeus does not know that we are meeting here now but it is for sure he will soon learn of it.'

'The city is shut tight, you say?' The Vixen returned to the fray. 'That's hard to believe. We have our own channels, and we can ...'

'Closed down,' Marie-Jeanne countered. 'All extra and back channels were closed last night.'

'So, we are cut off,' Richard observed. 'And the London scenario is already beginning to roll. What is left for us? Only that I must now try to do what it was impossible to even think about only a week ago. Assassinate Amadeus! What a monstrous thought!'

'There *is* another weapon,' Luigi Bernando interjected. 'A tape was made of his speech in the tomb of the First Emperor. Please do not ask how I obtained a duplicate.' Nonetheless he rubbed his thumb and forefinger together in the universal gesture meaning bribery. 'If we could get that out, the world would be alert. Amadeus might well be deterred by that foreknowledge.'

'What good is your tape?' the Vixen asked. 'If all channels are truly closed.'

Richard grimaced and declared, 'Since there is no other way, I shall . . . .'

'Less haste, my son,' Luigi Bernando cautioned. 'Murder is a mortal sin, even under these circumstances.'

He paused in thought, then sighed finally and said, 'It's no good. Even if we could get the tape out, who would believe it? Defaming Amadeus Brinks, the good angel of the environment, would appear as heinous as trampling on the cross.'

Richard added gloomily, 'You could spread the entire story across every screen in the world, and the tube-boobs would think it was only another terrifying episode of the *War of the Galaxies*.'

'There *is* one way,' Marie-Jeanne pondered aloud. 'It is possible, just. You must not ask me how, but I believe I can ...'

The Vixen snapped, 'Come now, you can't expect us to trust ...'

'Only one person could now stop Amadeus in his tracks,' the Jesuit pointed out. 'His sister Theodora has the weight and the power. But how even get close to her?'

'We've left it all too late,' Richard said. 'All my fault. I should have moved much sooner. Only one thing's left, assassination. I must ...'

Marie-Jeanne cut into that grim pledge. 'Let me try, Richard. Just give me the chance to try. No, I can't tell you how or what. There are around here already too many leaks.'

XXVII

Janet Seager luxuriated in the familiar comfort of her duplex on Sutton Place. Her hands, now unpacking the few belongings salvaged from her turbulent journey, as well as her forearms, had been darkened by the Asian sun. Fine scars, which were still angry red, showed where the surgeon had grafted new skin 'from your beautiful butt', as Berry Smith had laughed.

Smiling reminiscently, Janet pushed her hair away from her forehead. Meditatively rubbing the sore spot on her left buttock, she drifted into the large kitchen. She needed a strong espresso with a twist of lemon peel that left its iridescent, aromatic, oily residue on the tar-black surface.

Then she could get down to sorting the tapes she had brought back with her, more than 200. Amadeus Brinks had pressed them on her as a farewell gift, promising that she would find in them colourful and authoritative footage to backdrop her environmental reports.

She had better know roughly what she had in hand before obeying Kate the Great's summons. Kate had summarily ordered her to come home the day after her triumphant broadcast. She had argued that another week in Xian would pay dividends, but, she had to admit to herself, her professional judgement was clouded by the nearness of Berry Smith. Kate had peremptorily replied, 'No more delay! Come back to New York right now!'

Well, Berry himself would be coming back shortly, in a few days at most. Since he was posted missing in action, not as a deserter, the navy had been happy to replace his lieutenant commander's gold oak leaf with a full commander's silver oak leaf. It was not every day a mid-level politician like the Secretary of the Navy had a chance to speak with the president of Satcabnet Alpha One, much less do her a favour.

The admirals had bridled when the secretary, eager to ingratiate himself with Alpha One, suggested that newly minted Commander Salisbury Smith be decorated with the Navy Cross for heroism. The

Bureau of Personnel had, however, happily agreed that Commander Smith should be assigned to temporary duty as technical expert to Alpha One. Advising on environmental and military matters, he would work on the flagship series, *The Next Thousand Years*. How many young officers had an in with such powerful personalities as Janet Seager and Catherine Loomis?

Catherine had told Jan to come to the penthouse of the Alpha One Tower at six, which was still two hours away. Reviewing at leisure her big show from Xian, Janet felt she might have gone too far in pledging Alpha One's support for Amadeus's crusade. Nonetheless, it was a riveting and exclusive show. '*The* report of the decade', as Mike said.

On the balance, Janet told herself, she should be greeted with praise, perhaps lightly seasoned with reproof. Yet Kate hated Amadeus Brinks, Amady as she called him.

You never knew with Kate. You could be sipping coffee and amicably discussing your next show when she could say without apparent emotion: 'Oh, I almost forgot. The board wants you out of here. Desk cleaned out ... all ID turned in before five tonight. Sorry, but that's the way it is!'

Since Kate *was* the board as far as hiring and firing went, it was always advisable to have an ace in the hole when Kate summoned you. Jan's ace in the hole was the vast potential of the tapes Amadeus had over several decades spend hundreds of millions to assemble. Kate would not throw away that electronic treasure out of personal pique, even though Janet knew from Mike Goldsworthy that Kate was still angry at Janet's seizing editorial control of the spectacular report from Xian. Kate was also infuriated by Janet's declaring that Alpha One supported the crusade of Amadeus Brinks, whom the report had made a folk-hero.

Besides, Kate had flip-flopped by scheduling much environmental programming after the bombs in the Alpha One building. She needed her new super-star Janet Seager to give ecology a big ride, even if Janet Seager was too independent for her taste.

Sipping her espresso, Jan wondered about changing to something more demure than the high-necked but form-hugging scarlet sheath she planned to wear in a mood of defiance. But she was a seasoned correspondent, not a twenty-year-old applying for an internship. The matching jacket would, moreover, hide the scars on her arms.

Besides, she had no time to change. She had to look over the tapes and see just what ammunition she had in her locker.

The tapes were jumbled in the woven-straw suitcase Berry had given her as a going away present. Most were labelled in heavy black penstrokes by area and by topic. *Africa: Last Hundred Elephants* and *Java: Mercury Poisoning* were typical. A dozen or so were, however, either unlabelled or confusingly labelled.

One impromptu label bordered with Christmas bells and holly leaves read in hasty scrawl: *AB: prlim. interv.*, presumably for *Amadeus Brinks: preliminary interview*. Jan had no idea what she might find on that tape, and she had no player in the duplex that could handle the extra-width professional cassette.

Satisfied that she did indeed possess a treasure trove, Jan bundled the tapes back into the suitcase, which she placed in the safe under the floorboards. It opened only to her left thumbprint *after* the combination was inputted. No one else could gain access.

As she pushed the tape on Africa's all but extinct elephants into the crammed suitcase, her thumbnail caught on a slip of paper. It clung to the underside of the plastic cover, evidently fixed by static electricity.

See this in a private place (it read in Berry's unmistakable handwriting) *when you are alone. All my love, B.*

Jan smiled fondly. He must have slipped the tape into the suitcase while he was lounging about watching her pack. Irritatingly, she could not play it immediately. She could not even tell to which of the dozen-odd unlabelled tapes that note had been attached. Nonetheless, she smiled confidently. Not only was Berry Smith in her corner for her encounter with Kate the Great, but her own track record of the past three months as well.

Catherine Loomis received Janet Seager in her small private sitting-room off the vast reception hall of the penthouse, which was flooded with golden light by the setting sun. When Jan paused in the doorway, the bright twilight clothed her in a brilliant aura, and she appeared utterly self-assured.

Kate was startled. So this, reflected the woman who had created so many stars, is what superstardom does for a once diffident correspondent. Whatever star quality meant, Janet now had it.

Kate recalibrated her strategy. She could no more overlook Janet Seager's great potential for Alpha One than she could forget that Janet Seager had, however unavoidably, defied her own authority.

Kate's blonde hair was swept back. Her pale-brown eyes were set off by her tawny-orange kaftan and the gold-linked chain of rough-cut emeralds round her neck.

'Sit down, my dear,' she invited. 'You must be weary after all your adventures. Though I must say you don't look it.'

When Janet settled into an easy chair, Kate filled a Bohemian crystal flute from the bottle of Krug Vintage 1986 in the silver cooler at her elbow.

Jan was enjoying the prickling of the bubbles on her palate, when Kate spoke regally, 'Great job of work,' she said. 'Better than the lounge lizard males around here. Alpha One is proud of you. I'm proud of you – as a professional and as a woman.'

Janet relaxed. You never could tell with Kate, but an encounter that began on such a high note was not likely to end in disaster. She was leaning back in her chair, sipping champagne in relief and in celebration, when Kate's voice cracked like a whiplash.

'Now tell me why, you witless little slag! Why did you let Amady Brinks manoeuvre you into taking the final cut into your own hands? You know bloody well we never release the final cut to the field, never! Don't tell me it was the only choice: your editorial control or no broadcast. Amady is slavering for publicity we alone can give him. He even tried to bomb us into giving him more exposure.'

Shaken by the abrupt change of tone, Janet made no reply. She only put down her flute of champagne and mentally girded herself for battle.

'You must have been brainless, freaked out of your mind,' Kate stormed. 'Not only the final cut, outrageous as that is, but also shilling for him. You've practically made Alpha One Amady's partner in whatever swindle he's up to.'

'Catherine, you weren't there!' Jan retorted. 'Maybe I was wrong. Maybe I should've held out. Maybe he would've cracked. That's easy to say now. But I couldn't risk it then. Remember, he's practically an absolute monarch in Xian. If I hadn't agreed, God knows what he could've done.

'How in heaven's name could you make that judgement sitting in New York? You can't run a satnet like a battleship, everything decided by the captain.'

'The hell I can't. That's why I'm sitting where I am and you're where you are.'

'Where I'd rather be. If you want to run Alpha One without ...'

Kate cut in before Jan could complete her threat to resign. As a matter of unswerving policy, she never yielded to such a threat. She always allowed the angry employee to leave – though she might hire him/her back a few weeks later at a much increased salary. But she had no time now to play job roulette with Jan, not if *The Next Thousand Years* were to be finished in time.

Besides, she rather liked Jan's defiance. At the very least, it proved that Alpha One was *not* an absolute despotism whose cowering subjects were totally manipulated by cash and by fear.

'All right, it's over,' Kate decreed. 'But I want you to remember for next time: you can give away anything you please for a good story, including your fair white body. I've sometimes suspected you did. Not just with Mike . . . . But you can*not* give away the final cut. It's not negotiable! And don't forget that next time around!'

'Then there is to be a next time? I wondered. I certainly don't want you to keep me on for pity's sake.' Jan's spirited response surprised even herself. 'You're quite sure now?'

'Why ever not?' Kate was genuinely puzzled, since she could not conceive of any sane individual's rejecting Alpha One. 'Have I said anything to the contrary?'

'Fine, Catherine. But let's lay down some guidelines. First, I will *not* be talked to ever again the way you ...'

'What did I say, Janet? I can't recall anything nasty.'

'You called me a slag. That's much the same as a tart – a whore in plain American. Also, I do *not* trade my body for a story. I never have. Not ever! Though sometimes I wonder: *is satnet work a hell of a lot more than sophisticated whoring? And who's the madam?*'

Kate chortled at that direct insult. She leaned back in her yellow-plush chair and gave herself to laughter. Janet was almost taken in by that hearty display, but the wariness she had learned in Asia warned her not to let her guard down. Kate could either lash back or Kate could laugh – and Kate had chosen to laugh.

'All right,' Kate abruptly directed. 'Now let's get down to work.'

'What work?'

Kate chuckled and said, 'I want you on the environment beat. Your own show. But you'll have to double in brass. Mike still needs you on *The Next Thousand Years*. We'll hike up your pay in a new contract. Satisfactory?'

'Sounds good. But what about *His & Hers*?'

'Oh, Babs Berkeley can handle that with Mike for a while. Until we re-examine the show.'

'You're not thinking of . . . ? You can't mean to dump *His & Hers*?'

'I've had the feeling a while now that *His & Hers* was *passé*. It's had its chips. Besides, it'll do them both good being on a sinking ship.'

'Do them good?' Janet felt no pleasure at learning of the temporary difficulties of her partner, who was also her antagonist. 'What do you mean?'

'Mike's been misbehaving rather badly. It'll sober him up standing on the burning deck for a while. Anyway, without you, *His & Hers* is just another chatty breakfast show. And not necessarily the best one.'

'And I thought Babs was doing so well.'

'Couldn't let that one go by, could you, my girl? Had to get your knife into little Babs.'

'What about Babs?'

'I wouldn't be at all surprised if she was on her way to Southern Cross sometime in the next few months. If Southern Cross'll have her.'

The images on the six-inch screen moved in response to the controls manipulated by Cyril Ladberger, Alpha One's best technical engineer. In theory, an inforobot could do the job he was doing and do it much faster. In practice, no inforobot could match the judgement of an experienced engineer.

Plump and short, his yellow hair cascading to his shoulders to merge with his beard, Cyril Ladberger looked like a particularly shaggy teddy bear and was normally just as amiable.

He was gleaning fifteen unlabelled tapes Janet had dropped on his desk before hurrying to a meeting with Mike Goldsworthy and Catherine Loomis regarding *The Next Thousand Years*. Kate was watching over that developing series with the mixed pride and anxiety with which another woman might watch the progress of a beloved daughter.

'Laddy, be an angel and check these tapes for me,' Janet had said. 'I got them in Xian but they're not labelled. Can you give them a quick once over? And, Laddy, you may strike one that's personal. Could you just let me have it back? The rest can go into the archives for my new environmental show.'

Cyril Ladberger was an inveterate gossip. Did that matter? What could Berry have said that the whole world would not soon know? She almost hoped Cyril would tell everyone that the aloof Jan Seager had finally fallen – and fallen hard.

The engineer was now checking the beginning and end of each segment on each two-hour tape and dipping into what lay between. He treated the work as a game, allowing himself only three hours to complete the task. He had already found two tapes that contained only unrelated fragments on diverse subjects, none longer than four minutes. They, too, opened with the stylized green Earth logo that was Amadeus Brinks's trademark.

Cyril still had twelve tapes to go, but lifted his eyes from the screen when he caught a whiff of 'Sacrifice', the newest perfume. Swivelling, he saw Babs Berkeley. An unworthy thought intruded: *Take me, I'm yours!* was the slogan of 'Sacrifice', and Babs Berkeley embodied that post-feminist sentiment. She had even had a brief affair with a lowly engineer, himself, breaking it off when he could no longer help her career.

'Can I watch? Do you mind?'

Cyril inserted a new tape and shrugged. 'Go right ahead. You will anyway, whatever I say.'

Unfazed by that gruff permission, Babs leaned on his shoulder as he spooled a new tape through the viewer. Distracted by her nearness and her musky scent, Cyril spooled rapidly through the new tape. It was a comprehensive essay on the disappearance of the forests that had once clothed Borneo and the catastrophic floods and erosion that now threatened.

The tape's second half delineated the creeping menace of desertification, the drying up of enormous areas. Vegetation-denuded land was rapidly eroded by winds and floods, which, however paradoxically, left immense sandy areas. Since no crops could grow on those deserts, even more in Africa starved. The essay ended with a sonorous voice repeating the first tenet of the creed of Amadeus Brinks: *unless the human race does something radical about the despoiling of Nature very soon, the human race will destroy itself by destroying its habitat.*

Babs yawned and delicately patted her crimson lips with her crimson-tipped fingers.

'This is getting boring,' she said. 'I'll just run along.'

'The next one could be a humdinger. It's like a grab-bag,' Cyril cajoled to his own surprise. 'Why not stick around for one more.'

'Well, if you really want me . . . .'

Babs could charge an order for a ham sandwich with sexual innuendo, and Cyril was highly susceptible. With automatic haste, he spooled the next tape to its beginning. If he did not get moving, he would lose his bet with himself that he could glean all fifteen tapes inside three hours.

This tape opened not with the customary green Earth logo, but with a striking blonde with sharp intelligent features.

'Jan, I must hurry,' she said, with a trilled French accent. 'You must see the sequence that follows and decide what to do. We think Amady's sister Theodora must be told without any delay whatsoever. Who else can cope? You will next see Amady speaking to his confidantes in the secret tomb of the First Emperor.

'I shall get Salisbury to slip this into your bag. He does not know what it holds. He does not know, and you do not know. So Amady will let you both go, to make more propaganda for him.'

The blonde young woman looked intently into the eye of the camera and declared, 'Our lives are in your hands. Be very careful, I beg you.'

'Jan said one might be personal,' Cyril observed. 'I'll just slip it out and label it.'

'How could it be personal?' asked Babs, as ever getting down to essentials. 'It's from a female.'

'Well, if you think . . . .'

'Let's see some more, Laddy.'

Obligingly, Cyril let the tape run, though he commented, 'Very poor quality. Must be one of those automatic cameras.'

Normally Cyril Ladberger was painstakingly scrupulous in manipulating electronic impulses. Today, however, his mind was on other matters. He automatically spooled through the tape that had been smuggled out of Xian in Janet's baggage.

'By dismantling the existing order we shall restore the natural order, in which mankind will thrive,' Amadeus Brinks declared towards the end. 'We shall make a frontal attack. We shall use whatever force and whatever guile are necessary. We shall not shrink from any violence . . . .

'I welcome terror! I embrace terror as my sister and my brother! Terror has served us well!'

Cyril was diverted by Babs Berkeley, but her attention was fixed on the screen. Perhaps she didn't have Janet Seager's abrasive cleverness, Babs reflected, but she was not the empty-headed chit Mike Goldsworthy thought her. She was not so dense that she could not see that Amadeus Brinks's remarks were dynamite. She knew just where to plant that dynamite so that the inevitable explosion would do the most damage.

'Jan hasn't seen this?' she asked. 'You're sure?'

'She wouldn't've given it to me to label if she'd seen it, would she?' Cyril replied. 'Anyway, it's only a sci-fi send up, Babs. Not worth worrying about.'

'Sure, that's it, Laddy. Just a send up! Could you make me a copy, please? Then give the original back to Jan labelled sci-fi. No rush. Whenever you see her next.'

'A copy? Sure. And she didn't say there was any urgency.'

'All right, then.' Babs pursed her lips in a mock kiss. 'See you soon. I'd like to see much more of you.'

XXVIII

'Chris' sake, woman, you've won!' Mike Goldsworthy exploded at Jan Seager. 'What more do you want? She's handed you your own programme, environmental no less. She's agreed to a big environmental input for *TNTY*, and she's approved our rough disks. On top of that you get a big jump in pay. It beats the hell out of me why you're always whining. What more do you want?'

Having seen the emotional clouds building up, Mike had hustled Jan into a rear booth at that favourite Alpha One restaurant, the Iron Mike, where they could talk in private. The goldfish bowl of the newsroom was no place for a conversation that could become stormy, if past example was any guide. Even from their individual offices a raised voice would be heard clearly in the newsroom.

'You don't understand, Mike. It's all so phoney. I don't believe for a minute that Kate really gives a tinker's damn for the environment. It's just an act – and she could cut me down just as fast as she's raised me up.'

'What's it to you how Kate really feels? You're not the keeper of her conscience. Anyway, I know she's changed her mind about environmental issues. She suddenly saw the light ... saw Alpha One would be up shit creek if it didn't get on the bandwagon.'

'Hardly a very sincere conversion, Mike.'

'What more do you want?' he repeated. 'Everything's coming up roses – and you're not satisfied.'

'I'm afraid she'll jump off the bandwagon just as fast as she climbed on. And where would that leave us? If she truly believed, it would be different. She wouldn't be so quick to take another tack and maybe dump us.'

Jan wondered for a moment why she was confiding her fears to the man with whom she was forced to collaborate despite their distaste for each other. Yet, Mike was the only one to whom she could talk freely, the only one whose problems were virtually the same as her own. Besides, wholly committed as she was to Berry Smith now, Mike Goldsworthy somehow no longer appeared quite so detestable.

She had, she supposed, always been wary of Mike's unsubtle passes, his frontal attacks attempting to get her into bed with him. He had always been after her to try again despite the miserable failure of their encounter in Kashmir. Not out of love, not even out of some kind of affection or even a modicum of tenderness, only because she was unconquered, a challenge to his male swaggering.

Well, she was now fireproof, impregnable you might even say. As long as she had Berry, and she certainly did, Mike was no longer a threat. In fact, he had never been a threat that way, she realized, just a nuisance. Of course, he was a professional rival, as well as a collaborator. But that was another problem.

Above all, Berry would be with her soon, very soon. The Navy Department had confirmed that he was *en route* to Washington, where he would be detained for only a day or two.

A pity that his taped message had somehow gotten lost. Babs Berkeley had told her that Cyril Ladberger, that teddy-bear of a satnet engineer, found no personal note on the tapes given him. If there had been a loving message from Berry, Laddy would surely have found it. She dismissed that minor puzzle from her mind; sometimes even major segments of a story inexplicably disappeared from a tape. Anyway, she knew that Berry loved her deeply, and she needed no further demonstration. Why else would he have risked his own life to thwart the Future Green assassins and get her out of Singapore safely?

'Look, Jan.' Mike was elaborately patient. 'Kate's not going to dump us. Not now or in the foreseeable future. She's got too much riding on us.'

'She didn't seem so worried about losing me as a big asset when I was in Singapore ... when I had to disappear. Neither did you. What were you two plotting? Replacing me with Babs Berkeley?'

'That's just paranoia, Jan. Babs is a nothing . . . .'

'Even in bed?' she interjected. 'It's pretty obvious that ...'

'That's my business, not yours, Jan. It's nothing to do with our professional relationship or our professional future.'

'It could, you damn fool, if Kate got to know about your little romance on the side.'

'Again, that's my risk and ...'

'And you could drag me down with you. Kate's mad about us as a team ... not otherwise. Maybe that's why she's giving me the environmental show, so I can fall on my face.'

'You're really getting paranoid, kid,' he rejoined. 'Kate's not wasting her money or her time on you just to pull a doublecross. That's not the way she operates.'

'Maybe so, but you did leave me to twist in the wind in Singapore. You only came out to do my obituary on scene.'

'What in hell do you want me to tell you, Jan?' Mike stormed. 'I broke my ass looking for you, even had a dust up with Kate to get out there. What in hell more could I do after you and that aviator took off in a cloud of smoke? Also, I've been holding the fort here. While you traipsed around the world, I was doing the dirty work, the hard spade work for *TNTY*.'

Mike wondered why he was trying so hard to mollify her. Sure, it was easier to work with Jan when she wasn't in an emotional tizzy, full of fears and anxieties. How many of their squabbles had arisen because he paid little attention to her occasional attacks of insecurity. Only a while ago, he would have said 'To hell with it. Let her work out her own problems'. He never would have spent so much time and energy calming her down. Their relationship was professional, unavoidably. It was not personal, not in any way. In that respect nothing had changed, whatever his new insights into her feelings.

'Some traipsing,' she said bitterly. 'You're welcome to it, my friend. Next time *you* get shot at, half-incinerated, almost assassinated. It's all yours.'

'What else is bothering you, Jan?' He ignored her last outburst. 'What're you really worried about?'

She looked at him dubiously. This new, concerned Mike Goldsworthy would make anyone suspicious. Nonetheless, Jan felt she could confide in him. There was an unfamiliar warmth about him, a patent sincerity that was different and reassuring. Somehow, their entire relationship seemed to have changed. Why, they had just had a fairly acrimonious conversation with neither's voice really raised.

'You're right, Mike,' she confessed. 'Something is bothering me. Amadeus Brinks rings true, sounds like solid gold, but I still wonder if I questioned him hard enough. Could be I was taken into camp a little ... so committed to the story I was beginning to lose my judgement.'

'What more could you've got out of him? He's a pro, as much a satnet pro as you or me. You couldn't get him to say what he didn't want to say. Brinks is no dumb politician with his foot stuck in his mouth. You couldn't trick him. Anyway, what's to hide?'

'Even so, Mike, there's just that trace of suspicion left in my mind. He's a little too good to be wholly true.'

'Lots of people are, Jan,' he consoled her. 'But you can let your doubts colour your voice, even your words, on either show. Both shows if you want.'

'Thanks, Mike,' she said slowly. 'I'm ... I'm sorry if I've been bitchy. I'll try not to let it happen again.'

'Of course it'll happen again, Jan. That's what they call creative anger, striking sparks off each other, and getting more light. Anyway, I wasn't exactly the soul of courtesy myself. I'm sorry I bullied you.'

'That's all right, Mike,' she replied to her own surprise. 'I deserved it.'

'Enough of this politeness, this competing for the blame.' He smiled broadly. 'We've never made up like this before. We're beginning to sound like a couple of Japanese struggling to outdo each other in self-abasement.'

When Berry Smith appeared at the Alpha One Tower two days later, Jan was almost too preoccupied with her first programme on the environment, as well as with *The Next Thousand Years*, to give him the welcome he deserved. Almost, but not quite.

Although it was silly, almost adolescent, she was proud of everything about him, even his appearance. Trim and dashing, he was dazzling in crisp summer whites with gold wings and medal ribbons. She admired the insignia of his new rank: the three broad gold stripes on his black epaulettes and, on the brim of his peaked cap, the gold laurel leaves he deprecatingly called scrambled eggs.

But, Alpha One was, as ever, demanding, keeping her busy well into the night. She could hardly expect Kate the Great to make Berry her assignment, as Amadeus Brinks had made her Berry's assignment. Why, it almost looked as if Kate wanted to monopolize Berry.

Calling on Kate to thrash out the start up problems of her ecological series, Jan several times found her employer deep in conference with her lover. She would have been jealous if she had not known in her bones that Berry was now a reformed character, no longer a gigolo for powerful older women. Besides, his eloquence would inevitably inspire Kate to even stronger support for her new programme and the series. Berry was fervidly devoted to Amadeus Brinks's crusade.

Their brief encounters in Jan's duplex were, besides, as charged with feeling and with pleasure as those in Singapore and Xian. He would not move in with her, but kept the suite provided by Alpha One in the

Sutton Fairfield Hotel. Nonetheless, they were once again in perfect harmony: emotionally, physically and intellectually.

Still, two things were mildly worrying. Berry could not understand why Jan had so little time to give him, while her boss, Catherine Loomis, seemed to have all the leisure in the world. Nor could Berry adjust completely to the fact that Jan had so much more money to spend, while he relied on his navy pay and the cost-of-living allowance the satnet paid him. He hated letting her pick up the tab in the very expensive restaurants she frequented as a matter of course. He even complained, though lightly, that it was more humiliating for her to slip him her computer-readable account under the table than for her to pay outright.

Yet both irritants had silver linings. Not seeing enough of her, Berry was even more eager to please her. Even more important, his mild grumbling about the disparity between their incomes demonstrated conclusively that he had broken his habit of living off women.

XXIX

'I wondered how long it would take you!'

Catherine Loomis's brusque greeting was an accusation. She had agreed to meet Jan and Mike in the big corner office on the 124th floor of the Alpha One Tower she normally used for those administrative chores she could neither delegate nor evade. The room was unmarked by her own strong personality. Mahogany, smoked glass, and aluminium dominated its opulent but characterless decor.

Kate firmly closed the door to the anteroom where her personal staff of five worked. Both the satnet's star presenters were ill-at-ease, almost sheepish, despite the self-assurance nurtured by their popularity and their astronomical salaries.

'I've been waiting,' Kate added. 'Waiting for you two to give me the word.'

'Well, we could hardly ...' Jan automatically riposted as Mike asked, 'You know why we've come?'

'It hardly takes a mind reader,' Kate replied. 'It's about Amady Brinks's latest stunt, isn't it?'

'It is,' Jan replied. 'And it sounds like you know all about it.'

'Not *all*. Nobody knows all the ins and outs of Amady's loony intrigues. But I know enough to be frightened. And I know, courtesy of raven-haired Babs Berkeley, with no help from raven-haired Janet Seager.'

'We only learned this morning, hardly an hour ago.' Jan was defensive. 'We only saw the tape then. Also courtesy of raven-haired Babs Berkeley. She lied to me and got her stooge Cyril Ladberger to lose it for a while.'

'How long've you known?' Mike asked.

'Three days now,' Kate replied. 'Little Miss Goody Two Shoes couldn't wait to tell me about her exclusive.'

'And you haven't broken the story?' He was unabashedly

surprised. 'What're you waiting for, a spectacular exposé? Babs queening it over her big scoop?'

'Babs isn't doing much queening at the moment, Mike. She's ... let me see, it's coming up to one o'clock. She's either packing or on her way to the airport.'

'You're not sending her to cover the story, *my* story, are you Catherine?' Jan demanded. 'I can see it now: *Alpha One's new star.*'

'She's not Alpha One's new star. Not anybody's. If she's very lucky, Babs'll be hosting a once-a-week fashion show for Southern Cross.'

'You fired her?'

'Of course. If she'd pull that trick on you what would she've done to me when she got the chance? Of course I fired her, but I'm not vindictive. So I handed her on. She's just the type for Southern Cross! She *belongs* with those second-raters .... Now, I've been wondering how to handle this hot potato.'

'They don't come much hotter,' Mike agreed. 'Imminent destruction of modern civilization threatened by a very powerful maverick who's already taken big bites out of East Asia! What's so hard about handling it? We only need to spread Brinks's threats all across the world. A terrific exclusive – and the best way to stymie him!'

'Maybe the best way to enrage him and make him twice as stubborn,' Catherine objected. 'Also make him look like the victim of a satnet smear.'

'There's no choice,' Jan asserted. 'We *have* to break the story.'

'Janet, my girl, it's too damned hot to break right now.' Kate the Great was magisterial. 'Besides, he's threatening to put satcabnets out of business. That's a threat I've got to take seriously.'

'Just talk,' Jan scoffed. 'He's puffing himself up like a bullfrog. He talks big, your Amadeus Brinks.'

'He also thinks big and acts big,' Kate answered. 'Are you sore because he fooled you, Janet? He's fooled people who're a hell of a lot more suspicious than you are. Even some who're smarter. He fooled me for a while. Remember: Amady does *not* make empty threats. Whatever he's up to is sure to prove damned serious.'

'So what do we do now?' Mike asked. 'You've got an answer?'

'Actually, yes!' Kate was uncharacteristically tentative. 'Well, sort of ... almost!'

She smiled fleetingly and added, 'Really, it wasn't my idea how to stymie Amady's mischief-making. It was Berry's. Shall we have him in?'

She pressed a button on her console and cooed, 'Berry dear, could you come to my office, please?'

They waited for Berry Smith to brush back his hair, clip on the high collar of his summer whites, and traverse the corridors from the other end of the 124th floor. Jan made notes for her next environmental show, and Mike stared at the familiar but nonetheless breathtaking cityscape framed by the high windows, while Kate abstractedly buffed her nails. Berry Smith knocked perfunctorily and opened the door as easily as if he had done so a hundred times before.

'Hi, Berry, good to see you.' Though Mike's words were warm, his tone was cold. 'I hear you're going to solve all our problems for us.'

'Do me a favour, Mike. Lay off!' Berry responded. 'I don't even know if I can solve one problem, much less the whole shooting match.'

He smiled at Jan, inviting her support for the humble role in which he had cast himself. Her pulse jumped, and she reflexively returned his smile. Berry turned to Kate and flashed a megawatt smile.

Nothing that had happened so far today was remotely funny, Jan reflected. There was absolutely nothing to laugh at. It was, nonetheless, wryly amusing to watch Mike out of the corner of her eye. He was bristling like a watchdog that sees his master playing with a new puppy. Jan adjusted her own expression lest she give away her feelings as Mike was giving his away.

Berry Smith addressed them all, but saved his most intense glances for Catherine.

'Of course,' he said, 'I only heard the day before yesterday about Amadeus's crazy plans. I'm still reeling. I don't really know what to say.'

'Just try! Try real hard!' Mike advised. 'I figure you can get it out if you try hard enough. What's this big, top-secret plan you and Catherine're hatching?'

'It's not a plan, Mike. Only a suggestion. Let me bird-dog it for you!'

Berry took his stand before the picture-windows of the corner office. Far below, the crazy-quilt of New York City spread almost to the horizon. Twin rivers were a muddy, green-brown moat around Manhattan Island. The Statue of Liberty leaned wearily into the wind that whipped up white froth on the *café au lait* water.

'So?' Mike interjected.

'Amadeus *could* do it!' Berry replied. 'Easily, I'm afraid. He could throw even New York into chaos. Mind you, I'm not saying that's what he intends. We only know that London is high in his strategy. But he'd only have to throw a big rock into this muddy pond and ...'

'A big rock, Berry?' Jan asked. 'I thought we were talking about weapons. Not big rocks, but nukes and lasers and turbo-cannon.'

Berry smiled condescendingly, and Jan bit back her angry response to being patronized. If Mike had remarked on the weapons that Brinks could use, Berry would have treated the question seriously. But he obviously put her remark down to female light-mindedness.

Yet, why make a fuss about that assumption of male superiority? She was a little fed up with Berry today, although he looked good. Really, he looked too good.

'Jan and Mike want to break the story. So do I ...way down deep,' Kate observed. 'Before we decide, Berry, who don't you run through your reasoning again?'

'Brinks always thinks big,' Berry began. 'That's why he hit Bangkok, Jakarta and Singapore in quick succession – and upped the ante each time. Those metropolises capsulize the big basic problems of humanity. They're very rich. But, except for antiseptic Singapore, they're so swollen by mass migration of ex-farmers and refugees they're no longer fit to live in.

'Add the megalopolises of Shanghai-Pudong, Tokyo-Yokohama, Delhi-Agra and Saigon-Cholon, and you see the unbearable shape of the future. Not one of those cities has less than twenty million inhabitants!

'Not another lecture, for Chris' sake!' Mike protested. 'I can't take more of Brinks's vainglorious rhetoric, not even at second hand .... Jan and I want to blast the story: *loony philanthropist wants to destroy our way of life, in fact, our entire civilization and hurl us all back to the Stone Age!*'

'Can you think of a better way to halt Brinks in his tracks?' Jan demanded.

Indignant at Brinks's deceit and humiliated by the ease with which he had deceived her, Jan was also resentful of her lover's duplicity. He had known for two days what the smuggled tape contained, but he had said not a word to her. In fairness, they'd not had more than a minute or two alone together over the last few days. Still, he should have made her sit down and listen.

'It won't work, Jan,' Berry responded. 'Broadcasting the story will only make him strike earlier.'

'So we just clam up?' Jan objected. 'And wait for Brinks to make his play? We always raise Cain with Catherine about pussy-footing, but we know she has to be careful. Comes of being top management. But you, Berry! Whose side are you really on, anyway?'

'Lord knows,' he replied slowly, 'I'm not defending Brinks.'

Berry was shaken, but not entirely surprised by Jan's ferocity. Her greatest strength and her gravest fault were one: intellectual integrity so severe that she often placed principle above human beings.

'All I'm saying, is you won't ... you can't ... frighten him into backing off,' Berry explained. 'It's plumb impossible when he's gone this far.

'It was all chewed over in Xian just before I left: *how to stop Amadeus now that he's gone off the rails*? At first they pretended it was only hypothetical, but they didn't pretend for long. Marie-Jeanne, Prince Richard, and Monsignor Luigi, they went at it hammer and tongs. Marie-Jeanne and Richard told me on the runway just before I boarded the Concordia. Hell of a shock!'

'Come on, Berry,' Kate interjected. 'Not all that analysis again. Just your conclusions.'

'All right, Catherine. Of course I will.'

Berry beamed on Kate and Jan seethed. For a moment, sheer fury at her lover's inconstancy overcame her concern over the crisis that humanity faced. Berry was *still* that way. She had thought him purged of his instinctive attraction to powerful older women, as well as his automatic subservience to such women. But she had been wrong.

Mike was glowering, his coppery hair bristling. Jan suddenly felt hollow, one great empty ache from head to toe. Mike had warned her that Kate the Great was never loath to amuse herself with a new man – when Kate made her play, Berry might lack the strength to pull away.

'... push Amadeus and he'll only dig in his heels,' Berry was saying. 'And order the attack all the sooner.'

'Come on, Berry!' Jan prodded him. 'What's *your* answer? Play it straight this time!'

'Jan, please don't push me!' He flared, but instantly resumed his accustomed air of ironic good humour.

'Who can stop him?' Kate demanded. 'Lay it on the line, Berry. Janet's not the only one wondering whose side you're on.'

'Hold on now, Catherine!' Berry's smile was at once hurt and wistful. 'I'm still getting my bearings ... can't get used to thinking of Amadeus as a bad guy. He only talked me onto his side half a year ago. And now you all come along and tell me ...'

'Berry!' Kate exclaimed, and Jan advised, 'Just say your piece!'

'Sure thing, ma'am. I reckon only one person's got the clout to hold Amadeus back. Marie-Jeanne, Prince Richard, and Father Luigi agree, *only* Theodora Brightman can make him listen. Maybe pull the plug on him if he won't back off. He still relies on Brightman/Schreiner assets, especially top technicians.'

'So all we have to do,' Janet summed up wryly, 'is convince Theodora Brightman that her twin brother's decided to blow up the world and that she has to stop him.'

Janet still did not take for granted the automatic adulation and helpfulness she received when she identified herself on a telephonic link-up. She had, therefore, decided to put her face on screen for Theodora Brightman with Mike beside her. No one who had ever seen an Alpha One transmission could fail to react with pleasure to their call.

Emma Hope-Basse, senior executive assistant to Theodora Brightman, was no exception. She appeared all but worshipful on the small screen after four breathless junior executive assistants had told Jan Seager how much they loved her programmes before admitting her to the next rung of the ladder that led so slowly to the innermost sanctum. Yet the conversation went steadily downhill after Jan asked to be put through to Theodora Brightman.

'I'm afraid that's impossible, Ms Seager,' Emma Hope-Basse responded. 'Mrs Brightman is on her annual retreat. Every year she goes off somewhere for a couple of weeks entirely alone ... totally removed from Brightman/Schreiner. To get her head back together she says. Even if I knew exactly where she is, I wouldn't *dare* disturb her.'

'It's important,' Jan insisted, 'desperately important. You absolutely have no way of reaching her?'

'No way, Ms Seager, would I trouble her if I could get in touch. Can't I be of assistance? Or the corporate and public affairs office? If you'll just tell me what it's about, I'm sure . . . .'

'I'm sorry, Ms Hope-Basse, but it has to be Mrs Brightman herself. It's urgent, desperate, a matter of life and death for millions . . . . You're *absolutely* sure you can't reach her?'

'I didn't say that, Ms Seager. I said I wouldn't dare. Not even for you.'

'Could you send something to her then? Say a short tape?'

'That would be the same thing: disturbing her retreat, breaking off her recharging. I'm sorry, but not even for you.'

Mike underlined Jan's pleading. 'Ms Hope-Basse, do you think Jan Seager and I have nothing better to do than beg you to put us in touch with Theodora Brightman? The fact that we're begging you shows how absolutely vital it is. Not only life or death for millions, maybe tens of millions, even life and death for civilization. Surely . . . .'

Emma Hope-Basse reluctantly descended from the pink clouds to which Mike's plea had lifted her. It was bliss to hear that familiar resonant voice pleading for her favours and to see those wonderfully craggy features smile in supplication. How heavenly it would have been to be able to grant his request!

Nonetheless, she had to face one of the most unpleasant tasks she had ever undertaken. She had to refuse not only charming Janet Seager but magnetic Mitchell Goldsworthy. She simply did not dare put them in touch with her employer. Theodora Brightman would not only fire her for disobeying rigid instructions, but would see that she never got another job anywhere.

'Mr Goldsworthy, this morning I had the President of the United States on screen pleading to talk to Mrs Brightman and I had to tell him he couldn't. No, I'm not confusing things: I know you're more important than any president. I'm very sorry. But I can't do it!'

'Well, thanks for listening to us, Ms Hope-Basse.' Janet's thumb was on the cut-off sensor. 'Just remember in a few weeks what you've done. You won't need any telling. It'll be all around you – if you're still alive.'

'Oh, Ms Seager you didn't say so before. It's that urgent, is it? Maybe . . . .' Emma Hope-Basse paused, evidently struck by a new thought. 'You know, I couldn't refuse Catherine Loomis. Mrs Brightman would be annoyed if I did.'

Kate made her call five minutes later and found herself talking to her old acquaintance and almost friend Theodora Brightman a minute after that. It was a true summit conference, a meeting of two of the world's six most powerful individuals. Theodora Brightman herself was charming and not unreceptive.

Kate was nonetheless glad that Amadeus Brinks's self-incriminating tape was ready to spool down the fibreoptic channels that linked her to Theodora Brightman, wherever she was. Kate was also glad she had kept Janet and Mike beside her, for Theodora Brightman wanted hard facts before she watched the tape.

Theodora questioned the two exhaustively. After a half-hour, she conceded that the emergency was overwhelming.

'It's cosmic all right,' the throaty voice acknowledged quite calmly. 'I'm sorry, Catherine, but I had to make sure this wasn't a put up job. Otherwise, between Amady and myself it would be worse than unwarranted interference: it would be betrayal.'

'You're convinced now, Mrs Brightman?' Mike asked urgently. 'You do see it's got to be dealt with immediately?'

Once again, Mike Goldsworthy found that neither his charm nor his prestige was quite strong enough.

'I only see that it's worth looking into,' Theodora Brightman said. 'I'll do so.'

XXX

At half past two in the morning of August 15, 2009, Amadeus Brinks sat alone in his darkened operations centre in the lowermost cavern of his underground base 125 miles south-west of Lopnor in the Takla Makhan, the Great Desert, sometimes called the Gobi Desert. He had just summoned his thirteen troop commanders for a final briefing. Since they were already at their posts in the field, it would be an electronic conference.

Besides Brinks himself, only Tsao Liwong, his confidential assistant and bodyguard, held the keys to the three deadlocks and also knew the combinations of the three armoured padlocks that secured the bolts on the hardened titanium-steel door. Only his own thumbprint or Liwong's would release the four additional locks, disarm the system that enveloped intruders in noxious gas, and engage the motor that lifted the steel grille behind the door.

Tonight, however, Liwong stood guard outside the locked door, while Brinks himself operated the simple controls of the complex equipment that put him into instant touch with his field generals. The multiple circuit was untappable with less than ten hours of intense computer calculation.

Amadeus Brinks knew he had to contend with a traitor among his intimates. Since he did not yet know who that traitor was, he had locked out everyone who could possibly leak information on his grand strategy or the immediate operation.

Even Tsao Liwong was excluded, although Brinks trusted Liwong totally. Well *almost* totally. Not only the young man himself, but his entire family were alive only by the grace of Amadeus Brinks. That family-centred debt made the twenty-eight-year-old Chinese even more obedient to Brinks than to his own father.

Best of all, Liwong was not a zealot. He was not a demi-lunatic like so many of the cause-intoxicated soldiers of the motley Green forces.

Liwong was, rather, bound by an obligation that was for a Chinese unbreakable.

He and his parents had been snatched from flood-water by Brinks twenty years earlier, and Liwong himself had been educated by Brinks's generosity. He would otherwise have died of starvation or would, at best, have served as a miserable foot-soldier for one of the quasi-viceroys who dominated the regions of old China. He now held a doctorate in electronics from MIT and an eighth degree qualification in *gungfu*, the Chinese martial arts. Short, broad, and powerful, he was nominally employed by the Everbright Corporation.

Alarmed by evidence of gross disloyalty, Brinks had no choice but to assume that the working group had been penetrated. Perhaps by the highly accurate private intelligence service that helped make Alpha One so powerful; perhaps by the CIA; perhaps by the intelligence service of Brightman/Schreiner.

Probably not Brightman/Schreiner, for he would already have heard from his confidential agents in the conglomerate if it were spying on him. Yet he had learned of the leakage of his most secret plans in a sat-conversation with his sister Theodora.

Amadeus had naturally been courteous, even gently playful, with Theodora. He loved his only sister, and he still needed some support from the ubiquitous Brightman/Schreiner organization. Just the sight of her on the screen had moved him deeply. She was, at fifty-three, still as splendidly Titian-haired and as Rubenesquely voluptuous as she had been at seventeen.

Theodora aroused not only his fraternal devotion, but great tenderness. He vividly remembered his early manhood, when she virtually worshipped him. But she had refused to tell him *how* she knew that his next target was London. He had, therefore, not been totally candid with her.

Yes, he had promised, I'll think about calling a halt! Yes, he had agreed, it would be a shame to see more deaths and more destruction! Yes, he had finally said, he would think only of the best interests of all men and women!

He was in truth always thinking of the best interests of all men, women and children. Why else had he subjected himself to harsh self-discipline and the enormous strain of his campaign to save humanity.

Thirteen lights were now blinking green on his console, signalling that all the leaders of the assault were waiting for him to speak on Liwong's interception-proof circuits. Their deeds this day would determine his own fate – and the fate of humanity.

He plunged to the heart of the matter. His field commanders were so entangled in Liwong's electronic snares that none could now pass secrets to his enemies. Besides, Theodora's information smelled of a high-level headquarters' source.

'I have good news for you!' he began. 'You will *not* be expected! Our deception is functioning perfectly. Any outsider who has an inkling believes we will strike in force at London. As you know, our chief target is Zurich, while London is a secondary target, as are Tokyo, Hong Kong, Johannesburg and Frankfurt.

'We go in just seven and a half hours, at midnight in Zurich. No one is prepared, though London is beginning to shift a battalion or two, a few warplanes, and scattered naval units, the few the Brits have left. They will be far too late, as well as far too few.'

Brinks glanced at his notepad and resumed, 'Thus did George Washington address his troops at Valley Forge and Caesar at the Rubicon. I am no great generalissimo. Nonetheless, your deeds this day will be even more epoch-making than the birth of the United States or the fall of the Roman Republic.

'You will determine whether the human race continues on the path towards the sunlit uplands it began to tread some fifty thousand years ago – or becomes just another evolutionary dead end.'

Amadeus Brinks stared hard at the thirteen faces on the big screen before him.

'Is this world one you wish to preserve?' he asked. 'The society you wish your children and grandchildren to inherit? Or is this society so rotten it cannot be saved, but must be razed to the ground?'

Stirred by vicarious memories of the Cultural Revolution, the Vixen shouted, 'Destroy all vestiges of the old civilization! Clear the ground for a totally new civilization!'

Just refraining from lifting a fastidious eyebrow at that primitive screaming, Brinks held up the rough, green-tinted pad bearing his perfunctory notes and said, 'This paper is recycled, ostensibly to save energy and trees. Recycling makes for large profits. After all, the raw material is provided virtually free of charge . . . .'

'We already hear too much these things, Amadeus!' The full lips of the Mongol called Temujin II twisted in derision on the screen. 'Now is time to torch all bad things. Not time to talk!'

'There'll be plenty of action, my bellicose Mongol friend, when your units descent from the hills ranging Zurich,' Brinks exclaimed. 'Moreover, I have already taken decisive action. I have ordered the de Vries-Fermi Laboratory outside Magdeburg taken out with low-yield battlefield nukes. Fallout will be minimal.'

At that point, Brinks reflected, Marie-Jeanne would have exclaimed that he was the destroyer of mankind, rather than its saviour. Nuclear weapons, no matter how small or how clean, were her sticking point. He would also have faced the concerted opposition of Prince Richard and Monsignor Luigi Bernando if he had not made certain of their silence. Like Marie-Jeanne, they were under house arrest.

'Why, Amadeus?' exploded the Vixen. 'Why go nuclear?'

'To sterilize the site, comrade,' Brinks replied. 'Ensure that nothing lives on, not insects or birds, voles, ferrets or mice. Because it is one of the most dangerous places on earth.'

'A simple genetics laboratory critically dangerous?' scoffed the Shinto high priest, who was to lead the action in Tokyo. 'How, master?'

'Because it breeds rogue genes, Reverence,' Brinks answered. 'Not only humans, but all life is endangered by the rogue genes escaping from the Magdeburg Laboratory.'

'How come, Brinks?' demanded the former CIA operative variously called Jones.

'For twenty-odd years foolhardy experiments have been unloosing stray genes into the world. Also viruses that go from pigs to chickens to farmers. The viruses pick up DNA, raw genetic material, and transfer it to the host. Presto, a new mutation ... often highly damaging. Besides, certain cancers arise from viruses that transfer to normal cells genes that trigger unlimited growth.'

Jones replied, 'A great little lecture. But nukes're heavy stuff.'

'Listen, Mr Jones, and you shall learn. Normal human cells die after some fifty divisions. But cancer cells apparently live and divide for ever.'

Jones insisted from his underground post in Kowloon, where the small Hong Kong force was staging, 'Why's this scientific horseshit got your bowels in an uproar?'

'You've heard,' Amadeus murmured, hiding his irritation, 'how rogue genes penetrate human, animal and plant hosts. Around Magdeburg in the lovely lower Elbe Valley, they're now accustomed to trees with five trunks and rats with six legs or only two.

'The de Vries-Fermi Laboratory has for two decades been combining normal cells with cancerous genes for eternal growth. Starting with apparently immortal cancer cells, men and women in white coats have been looking for an elixir of immortality.'

Brinks sipped mineral water, grimaced at the alkaline taste, and resumed, 'Accidents will happen. During the past year, the incident of unnatural life forms in the Magdeburg region has doubled, redoubled, and redoubled again. We do not know what new genes are abroad. We only know that an immediate, unparalleled threat to the human race now stalks the Elbe Valley.

'I have, therefore, commanded the valley be reduced to glassy rubble by low radioactivity battlefield nukes. The inhabitants have been warned to move within the next six hours or perish.'

The multiplex circuits rattled with many voices. The operations room under the desert reverberated with their cheers and with their protests.

'We are meant to be preserving life, not destroying,' declared the plump Hindu lady with the classical Greek features. 'The *Ramayana* epic is teaching us that Indians possessed nuclear weapons all of four thousand years ago. But we are giving them up ... destroying all ... for the general good of humanity. Why cannot ...'

'Then why are you bloody Indians stockpiling nukes today?' demanded the Muslim poet who had been educated in Pakistan. 'You must be giving them up again. That is one big reason I am together with Brinks-sahib in . . . .'

Amadeus Brinks extended his hands palm down and drew them apart like a conductor signalling an orchestra to silence. His followers gradually subsided.

'There is little more to say,' he promised. 'Except that, as you know, mankind's complex economic and financial machinery is highly vulnerable. Very little intervention is required to make it freeze up!

'We shall strike hardest not at London, but Zurich, that other great centre of financial manipulation. More than a third of the ten trillion US dollars traded every day moves through Zurich. Well over half the world's gold reserves are held in the underground vaults at Kloten Airport. We shall take Zurich and keep its financial machinery from functioning for three days.

'Simultaneously we shall disable the communications of other financial centres. By many means: low-yield nuclear explosions that harm neither animals nor plants, but utterly destroy the chips that govern humanity's present way of life. Also brilliant pebbles to take out satellites. And specialized devices to disrupt the fibreoptic nerve-net of the present world order. One of the first casualties will be Brightman/Schreiner, which I have already gutted of hundreds of billions. Then the general collapse.

'I shall join you in the field, fighting beside my lion-hearted friend

Temujin II, the new Genghis Khan.'

Amadeus Brinks halted. He surveyed the screen images of his field generals, and each individual felt that Amadeus stared into his soul.

'We shall within the next seventy-two hours save humanity or we shall perish,' he finally resumed. 'If we perish, we shall have lit for ourselves a funeral pyre such as mankind has never before seen!

'But we shall *not* perish,' he declared. 'We shall prevail. We shall destroy the present corrupt and vicious order of human society! We shall ensure a great and glorious future for all humanity!'

XXXI

The Concordia Execujet called Dove raced across the pine-dark mountains, invisible to the radar, metal, and heat sensors of the Swiss Air Alert Brigade. The Concordia deployed every stealth measure known, some not yet on the market. Nonetheless, Air Alert would normally have picked up some trace, if only a faint gamma-ray trail. The aircraft was invisible because it flew so low and so fast that no sensor could distinguish its image from the ground.

At 1,800 miles an hour, the Dove was the centre of an intangible spiderweb of radar-sonar-magnetic-and-heat counter emanations. Precisely guided by its terrain-mapping sensors, it maintained an altitude of exactly forty-six feet above the ground. Swallowing its own shadow, the aircraft had raced the sun westward over oceans and deserts until it skimmed the placid Alpine lakes and the high pastures of late summer. Six hours after leaving its secret base south-west of Lopnor, the Dove was closing on its destination.

In the left-hand seat of the spacious cockpit, Group Captain Kelvin Sykes of the Royal Air Force rotated his neck to relieve a cramp. Although flying the Execujet was effortless physically, intense concentration was required to monitor all systems at virtually nil altitude and stand ready to take manual control in an instant.

Kelvin Sykes did not wholly trust the onboard computer to cope with an emergency. He flatly distrusted the co-pilot who had been foisted upon him. In the right-hand seat, his face lit by a broad smile, Tsao Liwong was talking about the current Test Match, which pitted England's best cricketers against the West Indies'. During his years at Cambridge, Liwong had found cricket as subtle and as slow moving as *Wu Chi*, the ancient Chinese game of strategic encirclement and counter-encirclement the Japanese call *Go*. But Kelvin Sykes was no longer interested in the Test Match.

The group captain was irritated by the constant offers of coffee and mineral water from Chief Petty Officer Betty Yang, US Navy, who had betrayed him. He was irritated and intimidated by the pistol in the hand of Flight Sergeant Adam Livonsky, once of the Royal Air Force.

Amadeus Brinks had given Adam Livonsky his instructions in Kelvin Sykes's presence: *Shoot if he twitches an eyebrow the wrong way. He is a convenience, no more. He is* not *indispensable. Liwong can fly the Concordia alone if he must.*

A ghost crew was flying a ghost aeroplane, the group captain reflected sourly. No one on earth except Brinks's gang would miss them if the multiple guidance systems broke down and the Dove plastered itself against a mountain. Betty Yang and Adam Livonsky were also posted *Missing, Believed Dead*. The Dove itself had been written off after vanishing inexplicably.

In the passenger-cabin Amadeus Brinks was alone. Although strapped in tight, he had been tossed up and down, back and forth, and side to side by the Dove's gyrations.

Yet his mood was beatific, as festive as the white linen suit he wore with a blue Oxford shirt and a red-and-blue striped tie. Very soon everything would come together, everything he had so arduously planned, and his destiny would be fulfilled.

The Dove soared, thrusting Brinks back in his seat. Through the oblong porthole he saw the ground dwindle behind them. Flying a loose spiral, the aircraft rose to a thousand feet by altimeter on the forward bulkhead. It then began to descend in tight circles.

Group Captain Sykes was bleeding off speed while confusing any possible surveillance by an approach perfected during the Vietnam War. Any fleeting trace on the screens of the Air Alert Brigade would be judged a ghost image when the Dove vanished again among the mountains to land on the grass-overgrown strip abandoned years earlier by the Pilatus Aircraft Company.

The ground force commanded by Temujin II had been airlifted by six-engined Atlas transports, which were also shielded by active and passive counter-measures. The troops had deplaned during a forty-eight-hour window in time. Any longer and the surveillance counter-measures that camouflaged the shuttle service would themselves have attracted attention and led to discovery.

Without that strip, the surprise strike at Zurich would be impossible. Not even the vast resources of the unwitting Brightman/Schreiner organization could enable Brinks to land his troops inside the mountain bowl that surrounded the city. And where could the Concordia come to earth?

*

Wearing a banker's dark suit, a white shirt, and a modest foulard tie, Temujin II had assumed a new manner with his new clothes. His English was still mangled, but his voice was low as he briefed Amadeus Brinks in the cave which was their headquarters beside the airstrip.

'Zurich, metropolis of about million along Limmat River.' The Mongol flourished a telescopic pointer at the big wall map. 'To north, Lake Zurich, mile and a half widest point, crossed by causeway and hover-ferries. Four to five trillion US dollars in securities, currencies, bonds, and gold are traded every day by little men of Zurich.'

'Gnomes, Temujin, gnomes,' Brinks interjected with a smile. 'Like mountain dwarves.'

'Also like three Chinee monkeys. See no evil, hear no evil, say no evil . . . .'

'They *will* do *anything* to make a few million dollars,' Brinks agreed.

'Little men buried second biggest gold pile in entire world,' Temujin said. 'Every country in Africa keeps gold in deep storage at Kloten Airport. Also private stocks from dictators, Mafia, and drug barons. Maybe twenty trillion together. All in nuclear-proof caverns, behind self-firing minefields, super-cannon, and regiment of Swiss Army. So we take airport. What then, Amadeus?'

'As far as the world knows, all that gold has disappeared. Think of the shock to the financial community . . . as severe as if we'd seized the gold. Two of our battalions will seal off the airport and its guard regiment and also cut all its communications. Precisely where do we stand now?'

'Everything moving by your plan, Amadeus,' Temujin said. 'Not so?'

The young American icthyologist who was Temujin's staff officer looked enquiringly at the radioman seated before the communications console's two keyboards and five screens. He simply nodded.

'All advance parties already in place or moving into final position,' he reported. 'All undetected.'

Temujin's pointer darted like a hummingbird over the wall map. A semicircular motion indicated the city's six television antennae, eight satellite receiving stations, and ten microwave towers, all in the foothills. Assault parties were to seize those vital points at 2 a.m.

'Hopefully no killing because not much defended,' Temujin

affirmed. 'Our troops moved out night before. All in leather with big helmets over heads and faces. So many Swissies always riding motorcycles in herds. So no one takes notice.'

The Islamic Fundamentalist Brigade moving to cut all roads out of Zurich wore workmen's clothing. Escorted by police motorcycles manned by local Greens, they filled the brightly coloured vans seized from the contractors who maintained the expressways. One in ten of the assault troops was also a local volunteer. Whenever talking was necessary, they would speak the local dialect of Swiss German, which was quite unintelligible to outsiders.

Other Green troops, wearing the drab combat uniform of the Swiss Army, waited near police stations, army posts, and signal centres. All communications, even landlines, were to be blanketed by a manmade electronic storm. No word of the action would go out until Amadeus Brinks chose.

In all, 15,000 Green soldiers were committed to the operation against Zurich. Orange garbage trucks had transported troops and *matériel* to resupply points. Ponderous buses had brought hundreds of men and women in the frivolous garb of tourists. Four times the usual number of slovenly figures lounged about Needle Park, where addicts received free marijuana, heroin and cocaine, as well as sterile hypodermics and condoms from the paternalistic and frightened municipal government.

Brinks had decided on no more than a token air arm. The risk of premature exposure was too high, as was the massive infrastructure required for even a single fighter-bomber squadron. He would deploy just two vertical-take-off-and-landing, fourth generation Harriers for reconnaissance and to intimidate any stubborn resistance.

In the centre of the city, three white Telecom-PTT vans were parked. Red-and-white barriers isolated the manholes where crews were working against the clock to penetrate the man-size tunnel that ran for twenty blocks under the wide Bahnhofstrasse from the National Bank to the main railway station. The skeins of fibreoptic cables slung on its sides carried the lifeblood of financial information to the heart of Zurich.

The five bridges across the Limmat River, as well as the Lady Church and the Great Church, which faced each other across the river moat, were being seeded with mines by Green troops in workmen's coveralls. If resistance persisted or the Swiss Air Force intervened, Brinks would destroy those monuments, which were the soul of Zurich in stone. He reckoned that the Swiss might sacrifice some historic monuments to salvage their self-respect, but would not sacrifice the entire old city, which brought in billions from investors, as well as tourists.

A recorded message would soon inform the world that the Provisional Green Force now holding Zurich would leave after seventy-two hours if it were not molested. But the old city would be razed if all opposition did not halt immediately. The 500 banks in those buildings would be dynamited and Zurich's reason for being would vanish.

A massive black Mercedes limousine rolled down the hills, convoyed by smaller cars carrying armed men in the blue-grey uniform of the Zurich Police. A staff on the bumper flew the flag of the Principality of Mongolia. The distinctive white-and-black diplomatic licence plate read CD-132-01.

How could any Swiss guard know that Temujin was not truly the Mongolian Ambassador to Switzerland, Germany, and Austria?

The Zurich volunteer in the front seat, who wore the uniform and the single star of a lieutenant in the Zurich Police, would do the talking if they were stopped. Tsao Liwong was perched on a jump-seat opposite Amadeus Brinks and Temujin. The stocky Chinese wore the uniform of a captain of the Mongolian Army with three small stars on his shoulder straps. A submachine-gun lay ready on his lap. The pistol's bullets tumbled in flight to inflict maximum damage on entry; their tips were split to fragment inside a living target.

Yet Liwong's Oriental features would occasion no surprise. The xenophobic Swiss police had been forced to recruit Vietnamese, Thais, and Filipinos to deal with compatriots who had poured across the borders in thousands when turmoil shook their native lands.

The big Mercedes halted at the junction of Tal Strasse and Bleicherweg, respecting the prohibition on motor vehicles in the inner city. Its passengers alighted and strolled towards the broad Bahnhofstrasse, which is at once the Fifth Avenue, Bond Street and the Ginza of Zurich. Communicators linked them to the limousine, which was in turn linked to Green headquarters at the mountain airstrip by the powerful radios and computers in its cavernous boot.

Amadeus Brinks entered the deserted Bahnhofstrasse at four in the morning. First light was creeping pink and gold over the massive fortresses that were the banks. He stood at the heart of Zurich.

Fifty men were advancing towards him at a measured pace. Their garb was curiously archaic: narrow fedoras adorned with the beards of wild goats, and grey suede knickerbockers held up by richly embroidered suspenders over even more richly embroidered shirts. All carried shotguns, which they aimed at the grey pigeons gleaning the sidewalks for food.

Twenty shotguns spat lead shot and killed fifteen pigeons. Wings whirring, the rest fled into the sky. A second volley brought down a dozen more. Blood ran red among the torn feathers and the limp little carcasses that littered the pavement.

It was an old Zurich custom. Every morning gamekeepers in traditional garb ensured that neither financiers nor tourists would be bothered by importunate pigeons. The pigeons not only left deposits on pavements, statues, and window sills, but constantly got underfoot. As ever, Zurich's solution was efficient – if a little bloody.

The pigeon patrol this morning was all Brinks's men. Two million dollars had persuaded the gamekeepers that the strangers were eager to win a bet.

The bogus gamekeepers provided protection for the technicians working down the manholes behind the red-and-white barriers of Telecom-PTT. Their volleys covered the explosions that were breaking into the reinforced tunnel through which ran the fibreoptic nervous system of Zurich.

The ten men and three women waiting to enter the tunnel were computer wizards. Their task was to scramble the city's nervous system so thoroughly that international finance could not be restored to normal functioning in less than a year. Virulent viruses and corrupt algorithms fed into those circuits would infect every computer linked to Zurich, which meant every finance-tied computer in the world.

The last hacker's respirator-masked face, like nothing so much as a black-snouted pig, vanished into the manhole. No one knew what toxic gases might be released when the tunnel was breached. In that respect, Green Force intelligence had fallen down, defeated by the ingrained – virtually congenital – secretiveness of the Swiss.

Brinks's strategy was quick in and quick out. The nimble Green Force would occupy and evacuate the city before the Swiss could fully assess the threat, much less launch effective counter-attacks. The Green Force would, in effect, briefly hold Zurich to ransom. Not for the first time was an entire city to be a hostage.

Temujin II consulted his wristwatch and clucked unhappily. 'Six . . . seven minutes after schedule.'

'You'll make it up.' Brinks's euphoria was unassailable. 'Anyway, I built in an hour's leeway.'

The rising sun glinted on thousands of windows of the financial fortresses that palisaded the Bahnhofstrasse. The oncoming dawn also threw over the old town a blanket of sodden heat as stifling as the featherbeds beloved of Swiss housewives. Although the full heat of the mid-August day was yet to break, Brinks was already sweating heavily. His bald head was bedewed; his white moustache drooped; his shirt and suit were so crumpled he might have spent the night in a Turkish bath.

His high spirits were, however, unimpaired. The Mongol, no stranger to wild elation himself, glanced warily at his commander. He was reassured by the level gaze of Amadeus Brinks's slate-grey eyes.

A stream of reports from the cave in the mountains poured through the pinhead earphone each man wore. Brinks nodded happily. The financial markets of Tokyo, Singapore, Karachi, and Jerusalem had been interdicted. Half the global village's trading facilities were already inactive. Computers and communications had gone down mysteriously. They would remain down far longer than anyone could imagine.

Temujin the Mongol smiled expansively, and his small eyes all but vanished into the creases of his broad face. He was, nonetheless, worried. The situation was *too* favourable. The delays and frustrations that normally dog all military actions had not occurred.

All the units assigned to shut down communications reported their objectives attained. Only the satellite station in the old City Hall was still unsecured and intact. Brinks wanted that single link with the outside kept open so that he could broadcast his apocalyptic message to the world when all Zurich was secured.

The airport was already interdicted. No aircraft would land or take off for the next three days. The gold reserves in their underground cavern were thus isolated. No one could touch that treasure, not one of the self-avowed nations or the legitimized gangsters who were its legal owners.

The Green Force had also flung an iron noose around the metropolis. Short of a major attack, the perimeter was secure. And the world was now being continuously informed by the mountain transmitter that any attack, however minor, could precipitate the destruction of the old city.

Temujin was cheered by the five small fire fights that had broken out. His field commander's reflexes, sharpened by the continual battles of Central Asia, warned that his troops were only a trained rabble until they had been shot at and had returned fire. Yet casualties had been light: six Green soldiers killed and twenty wounded, perhaps twice that number among the doughty but surprised Swiss.

Incongruous in his dark banker's suit, Temujin anxiously scanned the pale-blue sky. Brinks had overruled his warning that the occupying force would be naked without air cover, declaring, 'Our missiles'll take care of anything that flies, manned or unmanned.'

Temujin barely noticed the bogus gamekeepers firing another volley. Tsao Liwong had passed on the report received on his low wattage link. The burrowers under the Bahnhofstrasse were setting off further explosions to breach the armoured tunnel. Nonetheless, Temujin looked up in annoyance when a second volley broke the muggy dawn.

The reprimand died on his lips. He saw, spilling into the Bahnhofstrasse from Paradeplatz, a company of paramilitary Instant Action Police, all in black, all wearing long flak jackets as well as globular steel helmets, and all armed with submachine-pistols.

The Mongol pushed Amadeus Brinks to the ground, drawing his pistol as he threw himself down. The riot police fired short bursts in response to the gamekeepers' salvo. Twelve of the hundred-odd policemen lay bleeding on the pavement. The gamekeepers suffered twenty killed and wounded in the first exchange.

Firing his pistol at the massed police, Temujin saw that his own men were sheltering in doorways and behind kiosks. The riot police, however, closed up the holes in their ranks and advanced in formation, as if crushing a student demonstration.

Crawling on his belly across the newly swept pavement, Temujin joined Brinks, who had retreated behind a padlocked news-stand with Tsao Liwong. The Chinese was alternately firing his submachine-gun at the police and speaking into the microphone clipped to the collar of his uniform.

The outcome was all but certain. The riot police were skilled in suppressing riots, but had no idea how to deal with a modern infantry unit.

The stuttering of a heavy turbo-machine-gun underlined the foolhardiness of the police. When the big man-portable weapons began firing explosive shells, no police on earth could stand against them – certainly no police too stubborn to take cover, whose officers were too stupid to order them to take cover.

Firing intermittently, the Instant Action Police withdrew in formation around the corner of the golden-glass and crimson-steel Etna Fire

Insurance Corporation. As the last man in the last rank turned the corner towards safety, exploding tracers struck him. No neat holes appeared in his black flak jacket, no macabre pattern at all: the flak jacket simply vanished with his torso.

One instant the straggler was scurrying to safety; the next his helmeted head hung in midair three feet above his untouched legs, which strode on for a millisecond before collapsing into a small crimson heap. Quite untouched, the head in the unmarked helmet tumbled down upright to crown that grisly mound.

Temujin grinned mirthlessly when he saw that Amadeus Brinks was pale with nausea at the scattered limbs and the tangled intestines that marked the police line of retreat. Tsao Liwong appeared unmoved, although his right knee twitched slightly. He was clipping another magazine into his submachine-gun while coolly describing the action into his collar microphone for the audio-and-video battle diary Brinks wanted for later historians.

'The Stadthaus . . . City Hall . . . is still holding out,' Liwong reported. 'Cadets from the Infantry School have reinforced the normal guards. Our units await orders. They're coming under small arms, grenade, and rocket fire. The battalion commander asks urgently: "Is the order retracted yet? Not to use overwhelming force? Request permission to attack in force".'

Amadeus Brinks saw the Mongol and the Chinese looking at him quizzically, almost sceptically. For the first time in decades he had to make an immediate tactical decision that could cost many lives.

'The battalion commander craves an answer right now,' Liwong repeated. 'Attack or hold? He respectfully points out that delay will result in higher casualties.'

'He's to hold his fire ten minutes longer,' Brinks directed. '*Minimal force for minimal loss of life!* remains our basic principle.'

Temujin observed wryly, 'Could also be *minimal force, maximum delay – and maximum casualties*!'

Amadeus Brinks smiled defensively, mopped his sweaty scalp, and said, 'We'll take the Stadthaus all right. I don't want the Swiss massacred. And I don't want the Stadthaus gutted. It's a symbol of old Zurich ... before this lunatic age. Also, I *must* broadcast in person from the Stadthaus.'

'Only decide, Amadeus,' Temujin urged. 'More better ...'

Liwong's shout cut in, '*Condition Red!* Kloten Airport is calling *Condition Red!* Three fully armed Cougar choppers've taken off. Hostiles. They're heading for the city.'

'How in the name of ...?' Brinks demanded hotly.

'Momentary lapse of vigilance, says our airport commander,' Liwong answered. 'No excuses.'

'Get the Harriers in the air, Liwong,' Brinks directed. 'Temujin, surface-to-air teams in position?'

The Mongol nodded, and Brinks further directed, 'Liwong, tell the battalion CO to secure the area around the Stadthaus. Use whatever force is necessary. Then take cover and hold. *No* attack on the Stadthaus itself until I give the order.'

'Harriers getting airborne,' Liwong reported. 'Vectored towards Banhofstrasse. Estimated time of arrival seven and a half minutes. Kloten's tracking the choppers. Cougars' ETA three minutes.'

Temujin observed unnecessarily, 'Many bad things can happen in four and one-half minutes, Amadeus.'

'I know that, my friend.' Brinks was now quite calm. 'But your SAM teams are ready.'

'Surface to air missiles not always ... how you say? Can screw up, even best.'

The *whop whop whop* of rotors and the whine of turbine engines heralded the helicopters' arrival. Though painted in mottled browns and greens, the three boxlike machines boldly displayed the white cross of Switzerland on a red field. Rockets alternated under their stubby winglets with pods of anti-personnel flechettes and air-to-air missiles. Gunners still in gaudy civilian sports shirts glared from the glasshouse noses, their scowls as menacing as their 60-millimetre rapid-firing cannon. The Cougars swooped on the Bahnhofstrasse, and the nervous gunners opened fire.

No target was visible, except the white vans of Telecom-PTT and the red-and-white barriers around the open manholes. Sheltering in the marble lobby of the Etna Fire Insurance Building, Brinks, Liwong and Temujin watched the gunships hose the deserted street with exploding shells. Anti-personnel flechettes and air-to-ground rockets remained in their pods. A heavy turbo-machine-gun chattered on the ground when the gunships turned for another pass.

'They're beating up their own town,' Liwong laughed. 'What a joke!'

A single gunship made a lower pass while its mates held back. Machine-gun bullets ricocheted through the lobby of the Etna Building, forcing Brinks, Temujin and Liwong to the floor. A hail of three-inch anti-personnel flechettes rattled on the black-marble floor and gouged the green-marble walls.

The lead helicopter dipped lower and wheeled on its rotors so that its cannon pointed into the lobby. Brinks saw the gunner squinting into his sights an instant before the gunship exploded.

One moment the menacing machine had filled the entire world; the next moment incandescent orange-and-blue light filled the lobby, and heat waves broke against the marble walls.

'Finally, but too long!' Temujin ran his hands over his body checking for wounds. 'Our missiles too damned long reaction time.'

'*Fangsin, Meng'gu!*' Liwong spoke in Chinese, unaware that blood was welling from his right forearm where a splinter had slashed it. 'Relax, Mongol! If they'd hit you, you'd know it.'

Venturing from the lobby into the partial cover of the granite portico, Brinks saw that the remaining two gunships had drawn away, clearly chastened by the instantaneous cremation of their partner. An instant later the pilots gathered all their courage, and swooped low again.

The two gunships were on their final run, drab boxy predators. Temujin tugged at Brinks's arm, anxious to get him under better cover. The implacable gunships swooped lower, filling the world with their clatter and their menace.

Both gunships abruptly jinked in midair, checked as if they had run into an invisible wall in the sky. They jinked, recoiled, and exploded into orange-and-blue fireballs. The furnace heat filled the lobby, and falling debris pattered on the marble floor.

'My Excalibur missiles very great,' Temujin grinned in triumph. 'Even if so slow into action.'

Overhead the tardy Harriers performed victory rolls, tumbling and twirling against the cloud-flecked, pale-blue sky. The broad Vs of their flat bodies were like the wedge-shaped paper airplanes made by bored schoolchildren.

'Now for the Stadthaus.' Amadeus Brinks was palpably relieved. 'Temujin, pass my order to use brilliant pebbles against satellites now. But hold off the nukes in space.'

'If we take one of Temujin's jeeps, we can drive along the quays.' Liwong was tying a field dressing around his injured arm. 'No snipers reported there.'

The jeep was weirdly futuristic: a sphere of toughened plastic transparent above and dark-green below. Its twelve small wheels gave it remarkable manoeuvrability on difficult terrain. Sections of the upper hemisphere could be rolled aside to provide further firing ports for its devastating array of weapons.

Liwong slid into the driver's seat and briskly programmed the single-chip onboard guidance system. Brinks gingerly eased himself into the gunner's seat.

Noiselessly, the jeep rolled along Boesen Strasse towards Stadthaus Quai. In the pink-streaked dawn, the Limmat River sparkled dark blue behind its screen of trees. The crystal morning was not contaminated by the exhalations of the automobiles that would normally be jostling for access to the five bridges that spanned the river like the rungs of a ladder.

'A new world, isn't it?' Brinks exclaimed. 'As the entire world will soon be.'

Liwong's head was swivelling continually to scan the streets, pausing only to check the heads-up sensor array projected before the windshield. A minor explosion flared red on their right. Even before he heard the warning horn, Liwong seized the tiller, taking control away from the guidance chip. The jeep darted into an alley as shells scarred the stately eighteenth-century buildings on either side.

'Good God!' Brinks squinted at the warning array. 'Sensors report two Leopard 2 tanks on the Quai Bridge.'

'Might as well be a couple of Mastodons,' Liwong said. 'Leopard 2s have been obsolescent for years. But they've still got sharp teeth.'

Liwong was unlimbering the hand-held Thor missile-launchers when the on-board speaker announced in the clear voice of the female staff officer, 'Radio intercept establishes: Leopards manned by scratch crews from cadet honour guard at National Museum exhibit of historic weapons. They're amateurs, but dangerous. Leopard's main battery is a five-inch smoothbore, firing eight shells a minute.'

'Thanks for nothing,' Liwong muttered, and handed the compact anti-tank weapon to Brinks. The jeep was still sheltered from the shells rattling on the stone quay, but one was bound to find the mouth of the alley soon.

'Move out now,' Brinks commanded. 'Just give me a clear shot.'

Totally exposed, the two Mastodons on the broad Quai Bridge were inadequately protected by two-inch armour. Their battered bogey-wheels screeched, and their steel tracks yammered, tearing up the road surface. The five-inch cannon in their flat turrets firing repeatedly, they rolled on broadside to the jeep.

With the plastic armour rolled back, Brinks and Liwong were naked even to machine-pistol fire. They tumbled out, Brinks a few seconds after his agile aide.

'Lock! Lock!' The synthesized voice of the control system commanded. 'Fire! Fire!'

Neither had waited for the command. The laser-guided steel-and-plutonium arrows were already in the air. Liwong's pierced the thin turret armour of the first Leopard. An instant later, Brinks's struck the second. Both tanks were enveloped by a single ball of fire which was pale yellow in the sunlight. Thirty seconds after the jeep poked its bulbous nose out of the alley, the battle was over. But the jeep itself was a twisted mass of charred and melted plastic.

A replacement arrived within a minute, a gunner perched on the rear seat. Temujin at the controls now wore a mottled green and tan combat suit. The Mongol fussed over Brinks like a shepherd with an ailing lamb until satisfied that his commander-in-chief was uninjured. While Brinks obediently pulled a combat suit over his stained but conspicuous whites, Liwong clambered into the rear seat beside the gunner. His submachine-gun clattered on the pie-wedge ammunition storage lockers along the curved sides.

'This time we go fast.' Temujin overrode the dynamic chip and accelerated. 'No more stopping for shoot Leopards.'

The slender spire of Zurich's much loved Lady Church cast a narrow shadow across the Limmat River. The church's ochre walls were pocked by bullets, grenades, and rockets fired from its neighbour, the Stadthaus, Zurich's dusty-yellow City Hall.

The attacking Green Force battalion had withdrawn to whatever cover the soldiers could find. Five melted jeeps, a dozen burnt-out automobiles, and two commandeered armoured personnel carriers, now twisted by explosions, demonstrated Swiss determination. A dozen of the small pleasure boats moored to long poles in the river were sunk or sinking, their gay red-and-blue cockpit covers holed and charred.

'Suggest you walk the last hundred yards.' The voice of the battalion commander was faint in Brinks's earphones. 'It's not just snipers here, but heavy MGs, rockets, and rapid-firing cannon.'

Groaning in mock protest, Brinks slid out of the jeep and strode along the quay towards the Stadthaus. Alight with satisfaction and hope, he approached the improvised fortress that was the last obstacle to his grand design for the human race.

It did not occur to Brinks to bypass the four-storey Stadthaus, on whose green-verdigrised cupolas poked stubby spires into the pale-blue sky. It had become a personal affront to him, the obstinate Swiss resistance. He had sworn that he would speak to the peoples of the world from the Stadthaus – and it was unthinkable to compromise that pledge.

Brinks advanced on the Stadthaus as if to force its scratch garrison to surrender by an act of will. The satellite dish on the red-tiled roof drew him on. Forgetting the hundreds of channels already at his command, he strode forward, hardly hearing his soldiers' warning shouts. As he drew close to the doublegates overlooking the river, only Tsao Liwong followed him.

Automatic cameras disked the action.

A sniper with an old AK-47 assault rifle leaned out of a narrow window on the third floor of the Stadthaus, careless of the shots aimed at him. Amadeus Brinks was to him a tempting target in a mottled combat uniform, no more. The sniper took aim and loosed a short burst.

Tsao Liwong took a single step forward, swivelled on his heel, and emptied the boomerang magazine of his submachine-gun at the sniper. As Amadeus Brinks dropped to the ground, the sniper tumbled from the window and plunged downwards.

Heavy Green Force fire raked the Stadthaus, and four men joined Liwong to bundle Brinks to safety. Temujin kneeled beside his stricken commander-in-chief, hoping to stanch his wounds. Finally Temujin looked up and shook his head. Tsao Liwong closed his fallen leader's eyelids.

The swashbuckling Mongol's eyes were wet, and the stolid Chinese wept openly.

The Green Force battalion did not wait for orders. Its heavy weapons all but levelled the Stadthaus. Entering, the soldiers shot eight cadets who had somehow survived that explosive demolition.

Deaf to the tumult around them, Temujin and Liwong looked at each other, but did not speak. At last, Temujin nodded heavily and said in Chinese, '*Mei yu*. No use is it? You tell them. You can tell them better in English.'

Liwong triggered the microphone clipped to the collar of his stained uniform and said, 'Amadeus Brinks is dead, slain like a hero in battle. Tell all the commanders. It is the judgement of Field Commander Temujin that we must withdraw from Zurich. He advises the other task forces to withdraw as well, though he cannot command them to do so.'

The Mongol spoke again in Chinese, and Liwong interpreted again into English. 'Without Amadeus Brinks what else can we do? Without his vision, without his direction, we are hardly better than mercenar-

ies. Who knows what our next step forward should be without him? We can only retreat. The cause is lost, though perhaps not entirely lost. But for now we must withdraw.'

Liwong conferred again with Temujin before speaking again into the microphone. 'We further recommend the immediate release of those leaders under house arrest in the desert base. Tell them what has happened. Perhaps they can salvage something from the disaster.'

It was late afternoon at the desert base near Lopnor when Marie-Jeanne Erlanger, Prince Richard, and Monsignor Luigi Bernando met. Once set free, all had been drawn to Amadeus's quarters as if by a single will.

Marie-Jeanne was still weeping, though unaware that she was weeping, tears trickling unchecked down her cheeks. Luigi Bernando's eyes were red, and Prince Richard, despite the self-discipline to which he had been reared, touched his eyes with a linen handkerchief.

'So he is gone!' Marie-Jeanne said softly. 'Thank God he was given to me ... to us all ... for a time.'

'I opposed this final operation.' The Jesuit crossed himself. 'We all three did. But, after a few decades, Amadeus Brinks may well be known as another Cassandra, a prophet who was always right, but was never heeded.'

'I've never felt so desolate, so crushed,' Richard confessed. 'He was a great man with great vision, the greatest man I ever met. But I cannot deny that he was mad – stark, gibbering mad!'

'Was he really?' the Jesuit asked meditatively. 'I wonder if he was not the only sane one among us.'

EPILOGUE

Despite some highly imaginative later reports, the death of Amadeus Brinks was not heroic. He did not die, as so many were to believe, leading the Green Force against Swiss armoured infantry. Yet his death was not trivial, as it may appear from the bare account of his being shot at random by a sniper. In truth, he was assassinated, cut down by deliberate political murder.

The autopsy report was long suppressed by Theodora Brightman, his sister. It revealed that he had indeed been struck by the sniper's bullets. Wounds in his shoulders showed the penetration path expected of a Kalashnikov assault rifle fired from above. The bullet that shattered his right shoulder-blade also shattered itself. But a bullet found intact was unmistakably identified as having been fired from an AK-47 recovered from the wreckage of the Stadthaus.

Neither of those bullets was, however, the cause of death. Given competent medical attention, Amadeus Brinks would have survived those wounds.

He was killed by the bullets that stitched a diagonal pattern across his chest. Those five slugs displayed the characteristic fragmentation pattern of X-scored plastic bullets. Tsao Liwong, Brinks's confidential aide and bodyguard, of course, carried a submachine-gun that fired plastic slugs.

Tsao Liwong it was who slew Amadeus Brinks, who was his benefactor and his leader.

Why?

Liwong was devoted to Amadeus Brinks, but he owed his primary loyalty to Theodora Brightman, who had protected his family when her brother was preoccupied with other matters. Theodora not only saw that the Tsao family prospered, but had watched over his own education and his subsequent career as an electronic specialist with the Everbright Corporation. Being singularly tough-minded as well as generous, Theodora also held as virtual hostages Liwong's youngest brother and sister, who were students in Cambridge, Massachusetts.

Liwong himself feared above all else *luan*, the ancient Chinese scourge that translates roughly as primeval chaos. Anarchy and disorder were to him, as to most Chinese, even more fearful than oppression. He therefore accepted Theodora Brightman's instructions: 'If you must, *absolutely* must, you are authorized to use that degree of force necessary to keep this lunatic assault from destroying our civilization.' Liwong acted at the last possible moment before Amadeus Brinks could throw the entire world into turmoil.

Tsao Liwong was to live with his own expanding family, as well as his brothers' and sisters' families, in a village not far from sacred Mount Omei in Sichuan Province. The Tsaos supported themselves by scientific organic farming and by contracting to perform advanced electronic functions. Liwong was also to become the senior judge of the province's highest court. He would never discuss the assassination of Amadeus Brinks.

And what became of the other chief players in this drama?

First, the bears, without whom events would have taken an utterly different course. Happily, close to 200 big brown bears now range over their sanctuary, which has been left virtually undisturbed.

The Trans-Pyrenees Super Highway was, of course, unstoppable in the long run. It was, however, routed far to the west, making a big semicircle around the bears' habitat. Children of the High Pyrenees are once again told tales of the good bears who rescue the snowbound and the injured.

Marie-Jeanne Erlanger was to become the senior commentator and deputy chief executive officer of the Southern Cross Satcabnet, which soon acquired a reputation for a high level of programming without losing its advertising revenues. Indeed, advertising actually increased, as did advertising rates, because canny sales executives wished to reach the élite and, therefore, more wealthy audience Southern Cross attracted.

In Sydney, Marie-Jeanne met and married a multimillionaire grazier who was, she joked, 'notable for his enterprise, his big biceps, and his classic profile, but not for his brains'. She invariably added: 'Bruce has, thank God, no urge to change the world!' She was to give him three children gladly and to live happily with him for decades.

Monsignor Luigi Bernando was to become chaplain to the Father General of the Society of Jesus before withdrawing to work as a simple parish priest in Uganda.

Catherine Loomis, otherwise Kate the Great, did not release her hold on Mike Goldsworthy lightly. It was several months after the Zurich Incident before she let Mike go and took as her primary lover Commander Salisbury Smith. He was, as always, incapable of resisting an older woman who possessed great power. Kate was all the more irresistible because she possessed that power in her own right, rather than through a husband.

They had met their match, Kate and Berry, each in the other. Their tumultuous relationship, stormy with melodrama, was the closest to love either was capable of sustaining.

Nonetheless, Kate made a pass at Prince Richard. But she could never quite get him into bed. She declared philosophically, 'Hell's bells! I would've needed a crash course of hormone treatment before he could put me in the family way. What other reason to go to bed with him except to make a beautiful baby?'

Richard of Greece and Denmark, however, returned after the great adventure to the slender blonde heiress who was his wife. Always available for an interview, he was called upon far less frequently than he had been during the glory days when Amadeus Brinks and he were on the verge of remaking the world.

What of Janet Seager and Mitchell Goldsworthy?

Both were abandoned when Salisbury Smith and Catherine Loomis became, as they say, an item. Yet the link between them was stronger than either's link to anyone else, male or female. *His & Hers* was on the air again, forcing them into each other's company. Linked inextricably in the minds of billions of viewers, they nonetheless resisted that linkage in their private lives.

The Next Thousand Years, all sixteen hours of it, raised a tremendous – if not always laudatory – furor. The series was launched with enormous ballyhoo. The razzmatazz included virtureality stars who thought they could actually think; academics who were paid small sums, which they thought large sums, to engage in criticism and expansion, as if *TNTY* were the Dead Sea Scrolls; weeks of pre-airing and post-airing television drum-beating and paper-mag coverage; debates in legislatures throughout the world; and frenzied attacks by both humanist and religious groups.

Jan and Mike were further transformed by the overwhelming success of *TNTY*. Already all but venerated because of their prominence on Alpha One, they were practically canonized after *TNTY* claimed the greatest audience ever attracted to other than major sporting events. They were, however, hailed as a pair, not as individuals.

Being public figures, they in time accepted the public's valuation and acknowledged to each other that they were truly bound together.

From that time onward, they slept with each other, truly slept together as well as making love, not just making love and scurrying away.

One night in the big tiger-striped bed of his penthouse, Mike suggested breezily, 'What about getting married?'

Jan replied with gentle sarcasm, 'Married? What a quaint idea! Whatever for?'

Nonplussed, Mike answered, 'Well, we seem to be together a lot nowadays. Why not make it legal?'

'You mean institutionalize our famous spats?'

'Why not?' he asked. 'Anyway, you might like a baby. Me, too. And a very bourgeois lady like you wouldn't want a baby without the conventional trappings of marriage.'

'Maybe yes! Maybe no!' Jan answered. 'And maybe it's worth a try. But marriage isn't just a contract, not just an agreement about rights and obligations and property; marriage is a sacrament. So no more playing around for you or for me! OK?'

'Agreed,' Mike said. 'If you can be chaste after your lurid past, I certainly can stay out of other beds.'

Jan smiled at that broad jest and said no more.

Intelligently, they were to leave Alpha One at the height of their fame. And they were to acquire a small paper-mag even before they produced their first baby, a girl with coppery hair. That paper-mag was transformed into a semi-weekly info-mag when the print media made a partial comeback. Jan and Mike never outgrew their fascination with print, not even when Jan produced twin boys at the age of thirty-eight.

And the overall effect of the failed great crusade?

Amadeus Brinks had done no more than undermine a few hundred of the thousands of props that support the maze that is our world-wide civilization. Like beavers, his followers gnawed away at those massive timbers, inflicting great damage, but only on a few.

Yet the effect of that damage was epoch-making. A new world-view began to shape itself, a process that should now continue for centuries.

The leaders of opinion are today not anti-technological, but they do not worship technology. Above all, their perspective has changed. There are certain things, men and women of intelligence now understand, that we need not necessarily know. Also, certain discoveries we need not make and certain places in the solar system we need not venture.

We have begun to learn that we need not live on a constantly rising spiral of increasing consumption of goods and services. As a corollary, we are learning that we need not vandalize the natural environment for our own gratification. Restraint, rather than trendy active measures, appears to be the key to keeping physical and mental pollution from destroying all other creatures and, eventually, ourselves.

We have also begun to learn how to control the insatiable curiosity and the hubris aroused by our discoveries and inventions that all but brought the old world down. We recognize today that limits are set upon human knowledge by the force some call Nature and others call God and His higher creatures, which are to the religious saints and angels, *lohans* and *boddhisatvas*. You may, of course, call it what you will, the supranatural, all cognizant, all powerful, supernally conscientious force that has shaped our world – and, somewhat tragically, allowed us humans free will.